Also by Nick Stone

Mr Clarinet
King of Swords

NICK STONE

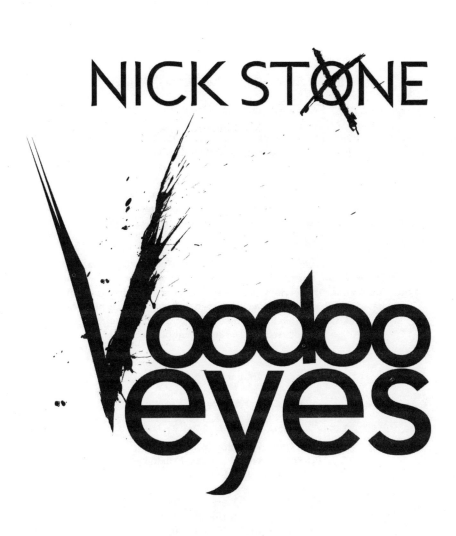

Voodoo eyes

sphere

SPHERE

First published in Great Britain in 2011 by Sphere

Copyright © Nick Stone 2011

The right of Nick Stone to be identified as the author of this
work has been asserted by him in accordance with the
Copyright, Designs and Patents Act 1988.

A CIP catalogue record for this book
is available from the British Library.

ISBN HB 978-1-84744-324-3
ISBN CF 978-1-84744-325-0

Typeset in Plantin by M Rules
Printed and bound in Great Britain by
Clays Ltd, St Ives plc

Sphere
An imprint of
Little, Brown Book Group
100 Victoria Embankment
London EC4Y 0DY

An Hachette UK Company
www.hachette.co.uk

www.littlebrown.co.uk

For ...

My wife, Hyacinth

My agent, Lesley Thorne

My first editor, Beverley Cousins

My good friends, The Count and The Prince

And also in loving memory of Elaine Flinn,
Cal de Grammont, Dick Gallagher,
Birdie Lena Bent and
John Weller

Acknowledgements

With very special thanks to Sally Riley, for showing me that the way back was the way forward; Aurelien Masson, for ze tuff (gong) luv; Joe Finder, for his wise and timely counsel; *Mister Burns*, for the smelling salts and cornertalk.

Thanks also to David Shelley and all at Little, Brown; Clare Alexander and all at Aitken Alexander Associates; Seb and Rupert Stone, Nick Guyatt, Jan and Michael, Frankie, Mark and Tom, Big T, The Mighty Bromfields, The Bents, The Mabes, Ana-Maria Rivera, The Kanners, Mitch Kaplan, Roger Smith, Nic Joss, Stav Sherez, Darrell and Lynette Davis, Iain Munn – Honorary Councillor, Rory Gilmartin, Richard Thomas, Lloyd Strickland, Tim Heath and Clare Oxborrow.

'Ah-ha-ha! Ever get the feeling you've been cheated?'

Johnny Rotten

EMPTY RING

October 28, 2008

Every morning, without fail, Eldon Burns took a cab from his home in Coconut Grove to the boxing gym he owned on 7th Avenue in Liberty City – Miami's roughest and most rundown neighbourhood, and no place for a sane man his age. Although the gym hadn't functioned as such in over eight years, Eldon had refused to sell or rent out the building, because it was there, within its four walls, that he still felt a little like his old self, communing with his memories, smiling at the ghosts of past triumphs, remembering the time when, as Deputy Chief of Police, he'd as good as run the city.

Inside, the gym was an ongoing ruin. Every day it fell apart a little more. The concrete floor, once painted with intricate diagrams of numbered feet, lay buried under a coating of dust so thick it looked like rancid manna. And it just kept on coming. The air was cut with a steady snow of fine filth, sullying the thick slants of sunlight that poured through the windows. The heavy bags hung rigid from rust-stiffened chains and brackets. The gym's huge ring – once the biggest of its kind in Florida – stood in the centre, an ungainly heap of rotted oak and mildewed fabric. It had collapsed after an unattended leak in the roof opened up into a waterfall during a storm. Rain had soaked through the canvas and got into the wood. With time, heat and neglect, the structure had subsided as would an overwhelmed fighter, one leg at a time. It was now home to a colony of large brown rats, whose squeals and scuttlings had replaced the sounds of the gym; as had the distinct drone of the thousands of airborne insects that had found their way in through the ever-widening hole in the roof. Sometimes parrots, gulls and even pelicans got in too, but rarely found their way out; what the rats left of them added to the smell of militant decay about the place.

The rats weren't scared of Eldon. They were used to his daily visits, this eighty-four-year-old man literally retracing his steps across the dirt, walking slowly, his head bowed because he could no longer hold it as high as he used to. They'd peer out at him from under the canvas, eyes glinting in the darkness, as if wondering whether today was the day he too would become like those stray birds.

Eldon paid them no more mind than he did what was left of his gym. He went into his office, on the right, its door in the middle of a wall of mirrors. The mirrors were two-way, just like in police interrogation rooms.

He sat down behind the desk and looked out at the gym. He didn't see it the way it was, but the way it used to be, back in the day, back in *his* day: a dozen fighters of all ages, skipping, sparring, speedbagging, shadowboxing in front of the mirror, as oblivious to his presence now as they had been then. He heard the sounds of fists slamming into bags, the steady patter of feet jumping rope; then he heard the three-minute buzzer and Abe Watson – the gym's head trainer, manager and co-owner – calling time on the two prospects sparring in the ring. He saw his old friend, very much alive, in his red Kangol cap, giving advice to the greenhorns he'd just supervised.

Eldon Burns was so enraptured by the sounds and visions in his head that he didn't hear the quiet creak of the gym door opening, and neither did he see the person who walked in.

Eldon's fall from grace had been quick and hard.

First, on the eve of their fiftieth wedding anniversary, his wife Lexi had asked for a divorce. She'd beaten the alcoholism Eldon had driven her to with his inattention and his affairs, and she'd wanted rid of the other bad thing in her life. Or so she claimed.

In reality, things hadn't been right between them since their youngest daughter, Leanne, and their adopted son, Frankie Lafayette-Burns – a Haitian boxing prodigy he'd trained – had died in a boat accident in Mexico in 1990. It later turned out they'd just got married and Leanne was pregnant. That had devastated Eldon more than the news of the accident – the kid he'd taken in and raised as his own had been fucking his youngest daughter.

Eldon was glad to be rid of Lexi though, so the divorce didn't hurt much, even if the parting price did: $10 million and their house in Hialeah. He'd loved that house.

Then he lost Abe. His best friend and former partner in the Miami PD had been diagnosed with lung cancer in the summer of 1999. Abe had smoked two packs of untipped Chesterfields every day for forty-three years. Eldon watched him waste away on a hospital bed until he was little more than a wheezing head on a stick, breathing, feeding, pissing and shitting through tubes. He died a few minutes before midnight on Millennium Eve.

Abe had been buried according to his wishes – in dress blues, with his pearl-handled 1911 Colt on his hip and, on his feet, the boots his dead son had worn in Vietnam. His hand held a bottle of the Wray & Nephew rum he'd liked to drink and in his trouser pockets were two packs of smokes, his Zippo lighter and a bag of silver dollars. Abe had explained his burial requirements to Eldon thus: 'I'm'a have ta buy or shoot my way outsa hell fo' the shit I done. If I cain't, then I'm'a have me a drink with the Devil.'

Over the next two months, the gym gradually emptied. Eldon had neither the time nor the desire to train the fighters himself and he wouldn't hire a replacement for Abe. His stable drifted away, to other gyms, other sports or back to the streets they'd stepped in from.

Then came the rest.

Eldon started the new millennium as Special Consultant to

the Chief of Police, but anyone familiar with the way things really worked in the city knew that the title was nominal, a way of legitimising his ongoing presence in the ranks after he'd officially retired from the Miami PD.

Then Internal Affairs began investigating Eldon's links with Victor Marko, a political fixer who'd been indicted for murder. Eldon was suspended from duty while they looked into the association, which had spanned more than thirty years.

Three months later they brought him in for questioning. Eldon was ready for them. He'd always been ready. He went without a lawyer. He didn't need one. Over his many years in the police, he'd amassed a mountain of dirt on just about anyone who'd ever taken the oath.

The investigators kept him in the interrogation room for all of twenty minutes. He spoke frankly and very plainly to them, revealing the tip of the shitberg he had on their superiors – all of whom were watching him on a videoscreen in the adjoining office.

He was offered a deal. He could keep everything – his fortune, his houses, his pension, his reputation and his freedom – but he had to resign immediately and go quickly and *very* quietly into obscurity.

So he retreated to the 7th Avenue gym, where, in many ways, it had all really begun for him.

It took Eldon a while to separate the man standing in front of his office window from the ghosts he'd conjured up in the gym. When he realised that the nigra wasn't a figment of his imagination, the gym returned to its ruinous empty present, and it was just the two of them there.

The man seemed to be looking right at Eldon through the mirror, his steady and unwavering eyes two dark beams piercing his own reflection.

He was tall and thin, going on malnourished. His clothes – a short-sleeved black shirt and chinos the same shade of deep brown as his skin – billowed about him in the gentle breeze from the broken windows and ruptured roof. The shirt had gold birds on it.

Eldon didn't know him. What the fuck did he want? In the last eight years Burns hadn't had a single visitor here.

Not one.

The kid didn't look like a bum. The clothes were too good for that, and his hair was too short.

Perhaps he'd come to learn to fight.

How about that?

Eldon thought about it. How long had it been since he'd tested a greenhorn? Could he still – even at his age?

The impulse went through him in a pleasant, invigorating surge and he chuckled to himself.

Eldon scoped the kid out. He looked all of fourteen. And *soft*. His features were still puppy-fat smooth, no edges, little character. Except for his *mouth*. Jesus – what a fucked-up kisser! How the fuck had *that* happened? But he couldn't see him as a fighter, not really, not at all. A boxer's punch would cut him in half. In fact, the more Eldon looked at him, the more he failed to see any athletic potential in him whatsoever. He had the height of a basketballer, but none of the robustness. Too wan, too wasted, too fucken' feeble.

Then, as if he'd read Eldon's thoughts, the kid walked away and headed for the front door.

He was leaving.

He couldn't.

Not yet.

Eldon got up from his chair as quickly as he could. He had to catch the nigra before he left.

He opened his office door and stepped out.

'Wait!'

The kid turned around and looked at Eldon, who started towards him across the filthy floor.

'Elton Booorns?' He had a strong Hispanic accent. An off-the-

7

boat immigrant, Eldon guessed, possibly Cuban, even though the dry-footers were way down now.

Eldon nodded and approached him, noticing how the kid's eyes were moving around the gym while keeping him in view. He was sharp and very quick. Eldon bet his reflexes were on point.

Eldon decided to have himself a little fun, treat the nigra like every newcomer who stepped through the gym doors wanting to be a fighter. Back then Eldon had had his own particular – and legendary – way of sorting out the serious from the seriously deluded.

'What do you want?' Eldon stopped and stood in front of him. Nothing but a kid – a kid who was a good foot taller, with a head a couple of sizes too big for his emaciated body. And Eldon couldn't help but stare at his mouth, at that heap of natural, arbitrary carnage piled up under his nose.

'You wanna be a fighter? *Usted desea ser boxeador?*'

The kid nodded.

'What's your name?'

'Osso.'

'*Osso?* You what, *Cubano?*'

Osso didn't respond. Probably an illegal, thought Eldon. Like Frankie'd been.

'Good fighters come out of your country, you know that? Best amateur boxers in the world. *Los mejores boxeadores son Cubanos.*'

The kid smiled at that, and his smile was a horrible sight, like a strip of fresh roadkill splattered across a freeway. No discernible teeth. In a way, thought Eldon, it was a good start. Up close he saw that he'd been wrong. The kid was young but far from fresh. He didn't have much of a face to lose. His nose was already flat and there were two deep parallel scars across his right cheek. Maybe Eldon could do something for him, send him to one of two gyms he knew, run by ex-fighters he'd trained.

But first he needed to see how much Osso wanted to fight, just how determined he was. The kid needed to pass the test.

'OK, Osso. Here's what I want you to do,' said Eldon. 'I want you to hit me in the face.'

Osso looked at him with complete bewilderment.

That was always the greenhorn's first reaction, and it meant nothing. But their next one did.

'Hit me in the face. I mean it,' Eldon said. Osso didn't budge. He looked confused.

Then Burns realised that maybe the nigra hadn't fully understood him, so he made a fist and said it in Spanish.

'*Golpée me en la cara. Da me to mejor golpe. Vamos cabron!*'

That got through. He saw it in the eyes. Something passed behind them, like a shadow had crossed his brain.

Osso drew back his right arm and Eldon got ready to duck a wild haymaker.

But the kid didn't throw a punch.

He pulled a gun instead.

Not just any gun.

Abe's gun – his .45 Colt, his pride and joy – the gun he'd been *buried* with.

Eldon recognised the pearl grips, the chip at the mouth of the barrel and, lastly, Abe's initials – 'A.J.W.' – scratched up the trigger guard.

Eldon had lived half his life expecting this moment, but now that it had finally come, he wasn't even scared. Only people who believed in God or had something to live for feared death. He wasn't one of those people. And at this range it would be as painless as dying in a coma. He'd be dead before his body knew it.

The only thing he felt was curiosity.

'*Quién le envió?*' he asked his future killer.

'Vanetta Brown.'

'What?'

The door opened behind the gunman. And the very last thing Eldon Burns saw was a person walking back into his life.

PART I

CITY OF WORMS

1

Miami was bad for marriages. That's what Max Mingus concluded as he sat in Room 29 of the Zurich Hotel on the corner
of 8th and Collins waiting for the adulterers next door to get
down to business so he could get along with his.

Of all the people he knew, only his best friend, Joe Liston, was
still with his first wife. The rest were either on second or third
marriages, divorce-stunted loners, or – like him – widowers who
lived with ghosts.

This city wasn't a place for long-term commitments. Its nature
was transient, its spirit restless. It was ever evolving; shedding one
glitzy layer of skin after another, like a rhinestone snake on speed.
Miami was the midpoint between somewhere else and somewhere better, so hardly anyone was from here and hardly anyone
ever stayed. People passed through, moved on and made way for
more of the same. That was Max's theory, how he understood
things. Miami was a river rushing over quicksand: you couldn't
stand up in it and you sure as hell couldn't build on it.

He wiped the sweat from his brow. He hadn't been in the
room long, but his handkerchief was already soaked to the corners. The air con was broken. The heat was damn near stifling
and the place smelled of puke and food fights. He didn't want to
open the window because the noise from the street would drown
out the goings-on next door. Right now the two of them were
talking. That's what they liked to do first. Talk. And laugh a little.
Her mostly.

*

13

He'd been watching the couple for six weeks. Fabiana Prescott and Will Cortland. They were both married to other people. Cortland, thirty-one, worked for a chauffeured-car company called Island Limos. He was tall, blond, gym-built and had the sort of safe, wholesome, all-American good looks you'd see in TV ads for banks or holiday resorts. Fabiana, twenty-five, was the fourth trophy wife of Emerson Prescott, Max's client. She was a Latin firecracker: long black hair, olive skin and big dark eyes set atop the kind of body whose curves were too perfect and generous to be real. She turned every straight man's head wherever she went.

Max really didn't blame either of them. Especially not Fabiana.

Emerson Prescott was a wealthy dentist who catered to an upscale clientele from three practices in LA, New York and Miami. Max had met him at his office Downtown. He'd hated him on sight. Prescott was a small, sixty-something remnant of a man, trying to cheat time with hairplugs, facelifts, botox and buy-a-brides like Fabiana. So, naturally, Max had taken the job. He really had no choice, financially; and, anyway, one look at Prescott and he'd figured it'd be quick and easy. Of course his wife was cheating on him.

They lived in Los Angeles. Their marriage had been rocky for the last couple of years, Emerson had explained, ever since his business started doing well in New York, where he was spending more and more of his time.

Each Thursday morning Fabiana would fly in to Miami from LA and Will Cortland would meet her at the airport with a blank expression and a sign with her name on it. They'd act like strangers. He'd drive her to the Shore Club, where she kept a suite. In the evening he'd collect her and drive her to the Zurich Hotel. Cortland would follow her in after a few minutes. When they were done, he'd drive her back to the Shore Club. He'd return his car to the Island Limos garage and go home to a rented condo in Hallandale.

The next morning, he'd return to the Shore Club at around

10 a.m., collect Fabiana and drive her around town. She visited a doctor, an accountant and then met a friend for lunch. Afterwards Cortland drove her to the airport, stopping off along the way for a back-seat farewell. By 6 p.m. she was on a plane back. When they met up the following week they started the charade from scratch. Max guessed the role play was part of the whole thrill, the way they made it work.

Max had spent the regulation two weeks following Fabiana Prescott, photographing everything from a distance with a zoom lens. He kept a record of the times of each assignation, as well as a description of what he saw. He was struck by how Fabiana and Will had kept a professional distance, allowing for only the slightest thaw on the second day, totally in keeping with surface appearances. He decided to omit this last observation from the report he took to Emerson Prescott. It was none of the creep's business – even if he was paying for it to be.

Max was good at delivering bad news. It was all about expression and timing, something he'd learned and perfected in ten years as a Miami cop. He had a routine, an act. He let his clients know what was coming by wearing sombre clothes and a matching look – profound disappointment with a strong hint of crushed optimism, as if he'd somehow been expecting a different result. He didn't have to try too hard either. He wasn't one of life's smilers. His lined and craggy fifty-eight-year-old mien was well suited to the dour, seen-it-all, done-it-all, so-*please*-go-fuck-yourself expression he wore like a uniform. It stopped people looking too hard, kept them moving on. That way they missed the sadness about him, the trail littered with regret.

Once he'd set the scene, he got straight to the point. He didn't soften the blow. 'Mr/Mrs Cheated-On, you were right. Your husband/wife *is* having an affair.' He talked for a minute to a minute and a half, covering the basic details. He handed them his report, complete with photographs. Then he let the client register and absorb. Once they had, he went into customer-support mode. He apologised. Then he empathised or comforted, or listened to

15

the poisonous and pained rant – or all three. When they were done, he told them they could call him whenever they wanted, and said his goodbyes. A week later he mailed his invoice.

That's the way it had always gone.

Until Emerson Prescott.

When Max had walked into Prescott's offices with his game-face on, his client's reaction threw him completely. Prescott read Max's look and smiled. And the smile had just gotten broader – or as broad as his surgically stretched and botoxed skin would allow – his lips thinning out to near-translucent pink slivers, like elastic bands pulled close to snapping, displaying tens of thousands of dollars' worth of perfect white teeth. They made Max think of rows of toilet bowls in a showroom.

Before Max could finish running down the details, Prescott asked him if he had any pictures of the couple actually fucking. When he told Prescott no, the client was unmistakably crest-fallen.

Max didn't know what else to do but stay in character and finish off his routine. He got within a breath of cueing up the apology when Prescott waved him silent.

'This is a good start. A very good start,' the dentist said.

'A good start?'

'You're to get me more.'

'More?'

'Proof.'

'Proof?'

'Yes, proof, Mr Mingus. Proof of actual penetration. You know – gonzo shit,' Prescott said. When Max looked at him non-plussed, he'd made it perfectly clear. 'Fuck pics. Lots 'n' lotsa fuck pics. No hidden cameras either. I want the hand-held touch. That herky-jerky feel. And I want them by the end of next month, right in time for Halloween.'

And that was how Max Mingus found himself in a room at the Zurich Hotel.

*

16

First he'd come to an arrangement with Teddy, the night manager, a red-haired guy with rimless glasses who looked all of eighteen. He and a security guard were the only visible people on duty.

For $400 Teddy told him the couple stayed in Room 30 every Thursday night, between 7 p.m. and 9 p.m., and that Fabiana had booked the place until the end of the year. Max took the room next door for a month.

Rooms 29 and 30 were separated by an adjoining door. Teddy explained that the rooms used to be let out as suites, back when the Zurich catered to families and an older clientele. Max had Teddy give him the key to the adjoining door for another $400. Teddy oiled the squeaks and stiffness out of the hinges for free. Another $400 – with the promise of more later – bought Teddy's silence, discretion and vigilance.

Max checked out the love nest. It was identical to his room in almost every way – a double bed with a framed vintage Miami tourist board poster above it, next to the window a round table with two bucket chairs and a lamp, by the main door three small flying geese-shaped mirrors going up the wall, a TV and DVD player in the corner. Teddy had explained that the pictures were the hotel's only remarkable feature – each room had a unique historical poster. In Max's it was 1950 – the year of his birth. Room 30's was 1961. The only noticeable difference was that the air conditioning worked in here – it smelled much fresher.

The following Thursday night he timed them.

7.07 p.m.–7.23 p.m.: talking. Cortland mostly, but Max couldn't hear what he was saying because he spoke quietly, in a deep murmur. It must have been funny, or Fabiana was in love, because she laughed a lot.

7.24 p.m.–7.41 p.m.: quiet mostly, then random moans.

7.43 p.m.–8.17 p.m.: fucking. They were loud. She moaned, cried and yelped. He grunted and gasped. Then she started screaming and shouting. In Spanish. *'Más profuuuundo! Másss pro!-fuuuundo! Sí! Sí! Mi amor! Si mi amor! Allí! Allí! Sí! Síííí! Mi amor! Mi ángel.'*

By then Max was sitting by the door with his fingers vainly stuck in his ears to block out the worst. He felt deeply embarrassed to be there, ashamed to be making money this way.

8.18 p.m.–9.04 p.m.: deep, exhausted breathing – his and hers. Fabiana said, '*Su pene es una varita mágica,*' which made Cortland laugh and reply, 'Call me Harry Focker, baby.'

Max heard the shower.

9.38 p.m.: the door closed.

Max looked out of the window and saw Fabiana come out of the hotel and head for Collins Avenue.

9.52 p.m.: the door closed again.

Cortland left the hotel and headed in the same direction Fabiana had.

Max listened in on them for the next three weeks. It was more time than he needed, but he had no new work coming in, and he didn't like his client, so he stretched things out to their reasonable limit.

The couple started slightly later than before, but the timings were near identical.

All the while he'd been pondering how best to sneak into the room and take pictures without being noticed. He came up with two options. The first was hiding in the wardrobe opposite the couple's bed. But when he tried it out for size, he couldn't quite fit. The entrance was too narrow for his shoulders, and the only way he could get on board was by squeezing in from the side. He just about managed this, yet once inside he discovered he could barely turn his head, let alone use a camera. And then his foot had gone through the floor. So he'd had to default to his least preferred method – creeping into the room while they were fucking. This was a high-risk strategy. His job was as good as defined by his invisibility. If he blew that, he'd expose his client.

18

Thankfully, he found a way around the problem. The room's connecting door opened right to left. If he slid it ajar a mere four inches, he had a clear view of the bed and could take as many pictures as he wanted without being seen. He wouldn't even have to step into Room 30.

Problem solved. He was all set.

7.56 p.m. Max turned on his camera – a Canon SLR with a top-grade Leica lens, ten frames a second – and stood by the adjoining door. Fabiana hadn't quite started screaming yet, but her moans were becoming louder. He heard Cortland's grunts and snorts too.

It was time.

He put his hand to the door handle, but withdrew it suddenly as a great greasy coil of nausea slithered across the pit of his stomach, making him gag.

He'd always sworn he'd never work divorces, right from when he first thought of leaving the Miami PD to go private. Not for him that sleazy paparazzi shit. Sure, the money was good, the work plentiful, and, outside the corporate sector, it was the safest part of the profession to get into – the most you risked was a black eye or a split lip, if the adulterers managed to put their pants on quick enough to catch you. But he hadn't wanted to make a living that way. He'd wanted to help people, not destroy marriages and make divorce lawyers rich.

Life had a way of poisoning your principles.

He let the feeling ebb and then opened the door a fraction. They'd left the lights on. Fabiana was screaming '*Mi angel!*' Cortland was alternately snorting and gasping. Max felt sure everyone in the damn hotel could hear them.

He pushed the door a little more and the image of the bed came into the camera's viewfinder. He could see white. Just white. He zoomed in. Nothing. He zoomed out. Now he had a clear view of the whole bed – sheets, pillows, bluey shadows playing at the edge.

19

There was no one on it.

The sounds coming from the room were getting even louder, the couple screaming in chorus. Maybe they were on the floor.

He lowered the camera and peered through the gap in the door. He could see most of the room. And what he couldn't see was too small an area for two people to be in. He was deeply confused. He could still hear them. They were deafening. But the room appeared empty.

He opened the door all the way and took a few tentative steps forward. Now he was standing in Room 30. He looked around. The bed hadn't been disturbed at all. It was freshly made up.

He looked in the bathroom – but it was empty too.

He was baffled, asking himself a hundred questions.

Then he saw the TV.

On the screen a dark-haired woman on all fours was getting boned by a tall blond man, both his arms sleeved in tattoos. The man was Will Cortland. And the woman was Fabiana Prescott. She was also tattooed – two overlapping hearts on her lower back, a devil with a pitchfork on the side of her abdomen, a swirl of stars on a thigh.

The film was coming off the DVD player, the sounds those he'd memorised over the last three weeks.

He stood there, numbly watching but not seeing the TV screen, trying to work out what had just happened, what had been happening.

Something on the screen caught his eye. The poster on the wall above the bed was identical to the one in Room 30. He kept watching. The film had been shot here, in the very room he was standing in.

He opened the front door and looked out down the corridor. Empty and totally quiet. Weird for a Thursday night, he thought. That's when the out-of-town clubbers usually arrived.

He went back into the room and looked out the window onto the street, but he knew he wouldn't see them.

He turned off the TV and ejected the DVD.

No title on the disc.

Teddy wasn't at reception when Max went downstairs. It was some Asian guy he hadn't seen before, with a name tag that said 'George'.

'Where's the manager?' he asked.

'I'm the manager. How can I help you?'

'The *other* manager, where is he?'

Max thought back to when he'd walked into the hotel. Had he seen Teddy at reception? He hadn't looked for him. He'd just gone straight up to the room.

'You mean Ted? He quit Sunday,' said the manager.

'Sunday? Why?'

'I don't know. I didn't ask. I just got the job.'

'What day did you start?' Max asked, feeling anger creep into him.

'Is there a problem with your room, sir?'

'Have you got an address for Teddy? Or a number?'

'We can't give out that information, sir.'

'How much?' Max sighed.

'Sir?'

'How much for his details? What's this going to cost?'

'Sir, I'm going to have to ask you to leave.'

'What?'

'I'm not giving you his details,' the man insisted self-righteously, underlining it by puffing out his small chest and squaring his coathanger-frame shoulders.

'Who put you up to this?'

The manager raised a hand and beckoned to someone over Max's shoulder.

'Sir, I'm going to have to ask you to leave the hotel with immediate effect. Security will escort you back to your room to pack.'

In the mirror behind the reception Max could see the fat, bald black security guard standing ready, thumbs hooked in the huge

21

leather gunbelt slung around his bulging stomach like a lethal rubber tyre. A thin moustache crested the edge of his upper lip like dirty foam.

Max caught a look at himself. Bald too. Snow-white-dome stubble mingling with small beads of sweat. Tired-looking. Face flushed with anger and humiliation, eyes icy blue pinpricks. He still just about had his powerful build, but flab was starting to gain on muscle. The manager was thirty years younger. Back in the day he'd have hauled the little prick over the desk and threatened the information out of him. Back in the day he'd been a cop.

He glowered at the little man. Was he in on it? Maybe not. He was just a guy working the shitty end of a shitty job in a shitty hotel. There were a lot of them around here.

He walked past the security guard and out into the street. The hot blast of nocturnal Miami air hit him in the face. The breeze carried smells of food, perfume and the sea. As he walked, music came from everywhere – cars, restaurants, clubs, stores. He didn't recognise any of it. They were alien sounds, no more than bleeps to his ears. Hip hop, R & B, robotic salsa and something that sounded like an elephant's coronary. People passed him by, brushed against him, bumped him. Summer clothes, all young, smiling, talking excitedly. Heading down to Ocean Drive for dinner and pussy or to Washington Avenue for clubs and pussy. Not a care in the world. Problems parked at the door. He envied each and every one of them.

He thought about what to do next. Go to the Shore Club, to see if Fabiana was there? He wouldn't get much information that way. Deluxe hotels guarded their customers well. He was curious about what had just happened, but another part of him really didn't want to know, just wanted to walk away, forget it.

In the middle of his confusion and indecision, he saw a tall black man across the street looking right at him. He couldn't make out the man's face too clearly; it blended in with the night and blurred with the neon. But he sensed the stare, its probing insistence, its magnetism. The man had specifically picked Max out in the milling crowd, focused on him, targeted him. There were a lot of homeless crazies in Miami. They migrated here for the climate and the guilty generosity of tourists. Max might have dismissed him as one of those, but his old cop instincts kicked in, the sense of a person not being right.

Just then his phone rang, Bruce Springsteen's irritatingly chirpy 'Waitin' on a Sunny Day' playing out of the pouch on his hip. It was a ringtone he'd assigned to Joe Liston – his ex-partner and the only black Springsteen fan he'd yet encountered.

Joe never called Max at night. He was usually home with his family.

This had to be urgent, had to be bad.

Joe was a Captain in Homicide.

Max braced for the worst.

It came.

'It's about Eldon,' said Joe. 'They found him in the 7th Avenue gym two nights ago. He's been murdered.'

It should have been a shock, but it wasn't. At the very moment he heard the news, Max's mind was abruptly distracted. The man across the street had disappeared, vanished without trace, as if he'd never been there.

'Two *nights* ago?' Max asked. 'Why didn't you call me as soon as you heard?'

'Couldn't. There's some stuff going on we need to talk about. I'm at the gym right now. Can you get over here?'

'I'm on my way.'

2

Joe Liston was waiting outside the gym, dressed to the nines, as usual. Beige linen suit, white shirt, brown tie and gleaming brown leather shoes. He'd always taken great pride in his appearance, considering it a reflection of how seriously he took his job and the responsibilities that went with it. The Miami PD had long before dispensed with its jacket-and-tie dress code for detectives, after complaints that tropical heat and formal attire weren't conducive to efficient policing. Most plainclothes cops now turned up to work as they would to a barbecue – in loud beach shirts, faded jeans and worn sneakers. Joe had reacted to this sartorial liberalisation by wearing three-piece suits instead of two.

He was imposingly tall and thickset. His short-cropped hair was grey, where he still had it. His wife's great cooking and ten years spent delegating from behind a desk showed on his round face and rounder belly. That didn't bother him. He didn't try to hide it or lose it. He'd turned sixty the previous year. At that age, he reasoned, a man was entitled to let himself go a little.

Max parked his car close by and walked over.

7th Avenue was absolutely quiet.

'I'm sorry,' said Joe. He held out his hand in condolence.

'Thanks.' Max had tried to focus on Eldon's murder on the way over, but his mind kept returning to what had just happened in the hotel. And to the man in the street.

Joe cut through the seal on the door and they went inside.

Max hadn't been to the gym in close to ten years, the last time he'd seen Eldon. He was shocked by the state of the place, its abject ruin – the collapsed ring, the hole in the roof, the debris, the rust, the stacked-up filth. The spot where so many young lives had been turned around was now a scrapheap.

He'd heard about the gym closing down after Abe Watson died, and how Eldon had still been going there day after day, staying from dawn to dusk. Looking around and taking it all in, trying and failing to rebuild it from memory, Max understood just how broken up the old man must have felt. The gym had been his pride and joy, the cornerstone of everything he'd built; and he'd sat by and watched it all fall apart around him. For the very first time since Joe's call, Max felt a needle of ragged grief pierce him. It took him by surprise.

March 8, 1964. That's when Eldon Burns had come into his life. It was here, by the door, where he was now standing, that they'd first spoken.

Max had gone to the gym with his friend, Manny Gomez. He hadn't wanted to be a fighter that day, or any other day before. The closest he'd come to boxing was seeing Muhammad Ali on the corner of 5th Street, signing autographs for a gaggle of black kids. He'd never seen a live fight, let alone watched one the whole way through on TV. He simply wasn't interested. He'd just gone along to the gym for something to do.

Yet once he'd followed Manny inside, a whole other world had opened up and swallowed him whole. Blacks, Latinos and a few whites of all ages and sizes. Industrious, busy, concentrated, intense, focused. Do-or-die ambitions. Dreams of glory and wealth. Broken noses, sliced-up brows, cauliflower ears. Hard faces, dripping wet. Trapped heat. The smell of sweat, blood, leather, rubbing alcohol. Choreographed violence. Punches thrown so fast hands blurred into a haze. The muffled poly-rhythm of fists on bags, rattling speedballs, the whirl and whip of a dozen jump ropes, the pit-a-pat of bouncing feet.

Eldon Burns had stepped out of the middle of it all, its embodiment, its soul. A big guy in track pants and a short-sleeved shirt. Big freckled arms, big square hands, scarred scowling face, steady but impatient eyes, a round reddish wart at the edge of his forehead. 'Hit me in the face,' he'd said to Max. And Max had knocked Eldon on his ass with a short fast right hook. First time a newcomer had ever touched him, let alone put him down. Eldon had looked up at Max from the floor, smiling. Everything in the gym had stopped and fallen absolutely silent.

Just like it was now.

The outline of Eldon's body was marked out on the floor in bright white chalk, the contours rendered in crude geometry, everything straight. If it hadn't been for the crescent of blackened blood that clung around the head in a hellish halo, the image would have been primitive in its simplicity. But then, wasn't murder the most primitive of acts, the deed that linked man to his dumb cave-dwelling forebears?

Joe handed Max a set of photographs.

The first showed Eldon's body. Arms thrown back, fists clenched, legs slightly apart in a wretched parody of a victorious boxer at the end of a bout. A rat sat on his chest, bearing two long front teeth, its black eyes looking into the camera.

'Had to get pest control in here. Rats everywhere,' said Joe. 'Couldn't wait to get at him, huh? Some would find that fitting.' Max looked across at his friend, met his eyes, watched them dip.

Joe had hated Eldon and Eldon had hated Joe. Behind his back Eldon had referred to him as 'that nigra'. Joe had dubbed Eldon 'Sixdeep' – 'Sixth Degree Burns' – the worst.

Eldon had been their boss when they were partners in the Miami Task Force, an elite unit within the Miami PD, active during the 1970s and most of the 1980s, when the city was a cocaine delta and its population collateral damage in an escalating war between rival drug gangs. Eldon ran MTF like a paramilitary outfit, another armed gang, only with badges and a licence to kill. He had a mandate from state politicians to solve all high-profile crimes by any and all means necessary – or at least to be *seen* to solve them. An illusion of safety was better than no illusion at all.

26

'Make it fit and make it stick' was his motto. It didn't matter who MTF took down for the crimes, as long as they had criminal records and were guilty of something. MTF broke every point of procedure and every damn law. For every single crime they genuinely solved, they framed and sometimes killed people for dozens more. It didn't make the slightest bit of difference. The innocent continued to die in droves and Miami turned into a billion-dollar sewer.

Eventually Joe found it all too hard to stomach and got himself transferred out. A year after, Max, damaged by his last major case and sickened by many of the things he'd done in and out of MTF, quit the force altogether. Eldon begged him to stay, made all manner of promises. When Max refused, Burns called him every obscenity ever invented. He'd intended for Max to follow in his footsteps, run MTF as before, while he climbed the last few rungs of the career ladder. Max had fucked up his carefully laid daydream, for ever ruining the order of succession.

They didn't speak for close to sixteen years after that.

Yet the bond between them remained curiously strong. Eldon had been a father figure to Max when he'd most needed one. Max had been the son Eldon never had. Eldon never stopped watching over him. When Max went to prison for manslaughter in 1989, Eldon paid off the gangs in Attica to ensure nothing happened to him. His reach was long and occasionally benevolent.

The next pictures Max looked at were close-ups of Eldon's head. He'd been shot clean through each eye, making the sockets look like they were covered with black pennies.

'Shooter got real close here,' said Max, pointing to the powder burns above and under Eldon's right eye, far more on the top than the bottom.

'They're saying this was a gang initiation,' said Joe.

Max went back to the photograph of the body on the floor. He shook his head.

'Killer shot him through the right eye at close range. Eldon went down. Killer stood over him, put another bullet in the left eye,' he said. 'This was no initiation. This was an execution.'

'What I thought too. When they moved the body, the casings fell out of his hands. The killer put them there, closed the fingers around them. Rigor mortis sealed them in,' said Joe.

Max gave him a quizzical look.

'Yeah, beats me too.' Joe shrugged.

'What was it? A forty-five?'

'Haven't seen the ballistics report, but the mess says yes.'

Max looked around the gym and tried to picture the murder. Had Eldon been on his way out when he'd met his killer? Had the killer come to the gym before? The powder above the brow meant the killer had fired the first shot at a downward angle, which meant he was taller than Eldon. The old man was around five foot eleven. That made the shooter at least six-two.

Why shoot him through the eyes? Was that a message? Something Eldon had seen that he wasn't supposed to? Or was it the killer's MO, the way he liked to do things?

Max stopped right there. He hadn't thought this way in years. He hadn't had to. He was amazed at how quickly it came back.

He'd last worked a crime scene with Joe twenty-seven years before, when they'd been after Solomon Boukman, the Haitian who'd ruled over the Miami underworld in the bad *bad* old days of cocaine and chainsaws.

They still collaborated on cases now, occasionally and strictly off the books. If Joe needed information he couldn't get through normal channels, he asked Max to look into it. And if Max needed to do a background check on someone, he called Joe. But that was as far as it went, favours asked and rendered in private. Nothing more. No facts, no details.

'Why d'you bring me here, Joe?' Max asked, although he already knew the answer and was preparing his response. 'We

28

both know I'm not meant to be here. And you'd cut your head off before you'd violate procedure.'

'*Plus ça change, plus c'est la même chose.*'

'Could you be a little more cryptic?'

'You know who's heading-up this investigation? That inspiration to morons everywhere: Deputy Commissioner Alex Ricon,' Joe said.

'He couldn't catch air in a bag. Eldon hated him as much as he hated you. And the feeling was mutual.'

'What's that tell you?'

'They're not serious about catching the shooter.'

'Exactly.'

'But you know how it goes with hits,' said Max. 'You never go after the triggerman. You go after the person who paid him. Takes time and perseverance. The bigger the victim, the longer it takes. A lot of digging in dark corners. And with Eldon, you can be sure there's going to be a major excavation.'

'That's just it,' said Joe. 'The only digging that's gonna get done around Eldon is his grave. Tomorrow morning, they're gonna tell the press it was some local teenage gangbanger popping his cherry.'

'You're kidding, right?'

'Wish I was.' Joe frowned and his brow creased into deep, broken grooves. 'They don't want to dig in case they don't like what they find. And they know some of what's down there. MTF put a lot of innocent people away. Most of 'em are doing life without. Imagine what would happen if an investigation led to just one of those guys being sprung? We'd have one overturned conviction after another. And then the multi-million-dollar lawsuits. The city can't afford that.

'Rumour is the Commissioner wants to run for Mayor soon. The Commissioner was tight with Eldon. That would squash his campaign dead on the drawing board.'

'So they've put Ricon on it because he really won't give two fucks if Eldon's killer goes free,' said Max.

They were quiet for a moment. Max looked back through the photographs, and again at the dried blood on the ground, all that remained of Eldon Burns.

'Eldon was one of those people I couldn't imagine dying,' he said. 'And not like this. No way. I thought he'd live to be a hundred and ten and go in his sleep.'

'I hear you,' said Joe. 'Someone close to you dying never makes sense, does it? Why them, why now? Questions no one can really answer, except to say it's God's way.'

'Or it's just the way it is.'

'Some people grow more religious the older they get.'

'I doubt Eldon did,' said Max.

'How about you? You used to go to church when you had problems.'

'Problems with a *case*,' Max corrected him. That had been his thing as a cop, a little habit whenever a case dead-ended. He'd go to the nearest, quietest, emptiest church. Get away from the incessant noise of the office – the ringing phones, the typewriter chatter, the arguments, the joshing – and its stink of overworked cops sweating bad diets and booze binges into the tobacco-fugged air. He'd sit in a pew and sift through the piles of information in his head, jotting things down in a notebook, hoping a vital piece of information would shake loose, help explain why people did the nasty, repugnant, depraved shit they did to each other. Sometimes it worked: the lead he'd forgotten to chase up, the dull clue he'd overlooked in favour of a shinier one, the throwaway witness remark he'd dismissed. Other times he'd drawn a blank; a solitary guy sitting in an empty church, looking at the stained glass and stone saints, getting nowhere.

'You ever think about what's next – after this?' Joe asked.

'No.'

'Never?'

'No.'

Joe looked around the gym and then at his friend.

'Well, I do. And I've got something to ask you. It may sound strange.'

'I'll be the judge of that. Ask away.'

'If you . . . go – as in, die, before me, can you do me a favour?'

'What? I'll be busy being dead.'

'I mean, if this is just the first stop on some big old ride we're all on, if there's something after this – this life – can you let me know? Send me a sign. Let me know you're OK and there's nothing to worry about.'

Liston was being serious. And Max didn't find the request at all strange. In 1997 Joe had lost both his parents within months of each other. The following year, his younger brother dropped dead of a heart attack. Since then Joe had been given to ruminating on mortality, mostly his own. Max had always indulged him. He knew Joe was scared of dying in a way he wasn't. In fact, he didn't even think about death, because he didn't have to. Max was essentially alone. His parents were gone. He had no wife, no girlfriend, no kids, no siblings, no nephews and nieces. In short: no responsibilities, no one to leave behind, no one to worry about, no reason to hold on. Joe, on the other hand, had a family of five and a loving wife. He wanted to stay with them for ever.

'If there is a heaven, you think they're gonna let me in?' Max asked doubtfully. 'You think God's going to forgive me for the things I've done?'

'Guess we'll just have to wait and see.'

'What kind of "sign" do you want me to send?'

'Oh, I dunno,' Joe shrugged. 'Something – anything – so I'll know it's you.'

'And you'll do the same for me, right?' Max smiled.

'You can count on it. I've got one already picked out.'

'Can you do something for me now – as in right now?'

'Sure,' Liston said.

And Max lanced the uncomfortable feeling that had been growing in the back of his mind ever since he'd stepped into the gym.

'Tell me the real reason you brought me here.'

'I didn't like Eldon Burns. I'm sorry to say it now and here, but it's the truth. Eldon was the worst thing ever happened to Miami – worse than any hurricane, race riot or drug epidemic. Those things peak 'n' pass. People like Eldon they peak but they do not pass. What they do gets followed, handed down, refined, repeated. Ricon's doing to Eldon what Eldon did to hundreds. You can call it "divine justice", but it isn't. It's the same old, same old "make it fit, make it stick". And I can't be a party to that. I wasn't then. I'm not now.

'To me, this isn't Eldon Burns getting killed. This is an old man being gunned down in cold blood and nobody wanting to know. And I'm seeing *all* the consequences coming down. The media spin – an old, defenceless white man killed in a black area – an area I grew up in, an area you did some growing up in too. Liberty City's gonna be officially fucked and scorched. All the grassroots progress that's been going on here, that nobody ever talks about? It'll count for nothing. It'll go back in the dirt. They'll blame those dumbass rappers for all the guns and drugs here, and Ricon's freshly minted goon squad'll roll in and start knocking heads, until eventually there's another race riot.'

Joe was out of breath and sweating. Max waited until he'd regained his composure a little before speaking.

'This isn't your fight, Joe.'

'I'm making it my fight.'

'You're seven months away from retirement.'

'Means I got seven months to do this.'

'But it's not like before,' said Max. 'When we were chasing down Solomon Boukman, we had options. We could afford to get shitcanned by Eldon, because we were young enough to start over. You've got nowhere to go after this. You can't start over. They find out, they'll take your pension.'

'By the time they find out, it's their pensions that'll be getting took.'

'What about Jet? Think of him at least.' Jethro – Jet – Liston was Joe's eldest son, and Max's godson. He'd been a promising ball player until a bad tackle put an end to his career. He was now a Patrol cop, like his father had been.

'It ain't gonna come down to that, Max. I've got a plan.'

Max knew what Joe was about to ask of him.

'I can't help you on this, Joe,' he said. 'I'm not a cop any more. I'm little people.'

'We'd be working this thing together.'

'How? No way am I getting inside headquarters. Not even with a visitor's pass. My name's mud there.'

'I'd do all the database stuff. Look at the forensics reports, the ballistics. You'd canvass the street.'

Max choked back a laugh.

'Canvass the street – *me*? Here? Doing the door to door? What kind of plan is *that*? People don't talk to cops here. And they sure as hell ain't gonna talk to some white guy *used* to be a cop in the bad old days.'

'It'd just be for a week. Maybe two. At the most. See what you find out,' said Joe. 'If you turn up any information, better still an eye-wit, let me know, and I'll handle it from there.'

'What are you going to do?'

'I'm trying to stop a murder being pinned on someone who didn't do it. Because that's what Ricon's working on right now – getting himself a yo in the frame. If I can get information that contradicts his, well, I'll find a way of using it and stopping this. What you say, Max? Look into it. One more time. You and me. Born to Run.'

'Bruce *fucken'* Springsteen!' Eldon had christened the pair of them 'Born to Run' after the poster of the album cover he'd seen on his daughter's bedroom wall.

Joe stood a little closer to the spot where Eldon had fallen. Just then he looked old, tired and completely out of his depth. Max knew that Joe wouldn't let this one go, as long as he could do something about it. His friend was tilting at one windmill too far now. He didn't have the heart to tell him.

'Can I think about it?' said Max.

'What's there to think about?' Joe turned around, looking plain pissed off. 'A couple of weeks is all I'm asking. Two *weeks*, Max. What are you doing now? Chasing after more bedhoppers?'

'As a matter of fact, yeah. This case I'm on has gone weirdsville.'

'A case? You call this crap you're doing a *case*? This – what we've got here – Eldon Burns. *Dead. Murdered.* That's a *case*, Max. Some guy banging some chick young enough to be his daughter ain't no case. That's just some horny middle-aged asshole should know better. A *case*. Damn! Listen to yourself. You were one of the great ones. Now you're just living on your knees.'

Joe stared at Max. Liston had contempt in his eyes. A lot of anger. He used to scare the living shit out of suspects by giving them that very look. Max finally had an idea how they must have felt. Joe had never before passed judgement on the way he made his money. The hint of disapproval had been there though, whenever their conversation turned to work.

They'd been friends for close to forty years. Twelve years together as cops. They'd been something then, the two of them, Max thought. A great team. And Joe was *still* something. He had every ounce of his integrity. He'd never compromised, never looked the other way, never cut corners, never taken money. Max had no integrity. It hadn't been prison that had broken him. It hadn't even been his wife's death. It was what had come afterwards – the mess he'd made of his life. Fate had thrown him a line and he'd made of it a noose.

That was why he didn't want to look into Eldon's murder. He felt so defiled, so removed from everything he'd once been good at and taken pride in, that he didn't think he could do it any more.

Joe turned away from him and went over to the door of the gym. He opened it wide and stepped aside, as though asking Max to leave for good. Outside, it was pitch black. They heard crickets in the air.

Max walked through the open door and turned to look back at the gym, as if in valediction.

The last time he'd seen Eldon alive was here, almost ten years ago, on December 18, 1998. There'd been a function, a reunion of the old MTF crew, and everyone who was still alive or healthy enough had turned up. Max had had a lot to overcome before deciding to go. Sure, he was grateful to Eldon for protecting him in prison, but his old boss reminded him of the past – a past he spent a small part of every day wishing he could change, and the rest of those same days trying to live down. Max and Eldon had never spoken about the things they'd done. Max had never bothered even trying to bring it up, because Eldon would have thought he was wearing a wire and clammed up; and after he'd patted him down and found he was clean, he would have chewed out his former protégé for being a born-again pussy and clammed up even harder. That was Eldon through and through, always had been – a brick wall; his way or no way.

Max had walked into the gym that day in December, but he hadn't gotten much further than the doorway. He'd looked around and spotted the familiar faces, some withered and soured with age and bad living, others bloated with success, a few looking pretty much the way he remembered them, give or take thinner hair and a few extra wrinkles. Every single one of them had blood on their hands. Every single one of them had gotten away with murder. And him? He was just the newest arrival, the baddest of them all, the tip of the MTF spear.

His former colleagues gradually noticed him and, one by one, they fell quiet, until the gym was silent. Then someone started clapping. And soon everyone joined in. More than that – they stamped their feet and called out his name and whistled and cheered. He was the returning hero, the prodigal son, the last of the Miami gunfighters taking a final bow. He'd felt sick. They weren't just celebrating him, they were revelling in everything they'd once been and everything they'd done – the planted evidence, the coerced confessions, the perjury, the hundreds of wrongful convictions, the killings – the eternal 'make it stick, make it fit' credo. No guilt, no conscience, no accountability.

Then Eldon had stepped out of the crowd and come over to him, smiling, arms open in expectant embrace. Max had suddenly thought of Sandra and how she'd hated Burns. It was in part because of her that he'd left the force. She would never have married him otherwise. He'd seen her face again then, right in front of him, clear as day. He'd frozen up and stepped back. Eldon had dropped his smile and his arms.

They'd managed a polite but awkward conversation, Eldon trying to make inroads, trying to draw Max back, Max retreating, all short sentences, monosyllables, grunts. Finally Eldon had given up on formality and held out his hand to say goodbye.

'You were one of the great ones,' he'd said.

Those were the last words he spoke to Max. Same thing Joe had said to him just now, almost in the same damn spot too.

Max headed for his car. He thought about what he'd be doing tomorrow, next week, and for as long as he could hang on. It was all about that now, hanging on – hanging on to a job he hated, hanging on until he'd put enough money away so he wouldn't wind up a homeless bum on the beach.

He thought of Joe about to go off on a crusade, getting justice for someone he'd despised, because it was the right thing to do, because that was what he did, what he felt he was here for.

What did he think he was doing, walking away?

Joe was his friend.

Eldon had been his friend.

He owed Eldon.

He owed Joe.

He closed his eyes and looked for his wife, Sandra. She wasn't there.

It was on him.

His decision.

It was OK.

He could do this.

One more time.

Born to Run.

He turned around.

Joe was standing outside the gym, looking at him. He'd either been watching him disappear or waiting around in case he changed his mind – probably knowing that he would, that this was something he couldn't pass up.

3

Max went home to his beachfront penthouse on Collins Avenue. He'd paid half a million bucks for it in 1997. It was the only smart investment he'd made – or so he'd thought at the time. Shortly after he moved in, Miami had become a magnet for the hip and the beautiful and property value rocketed to the sort of ridiculous levels not seen since the cocaine boom. Now, as then, things had changed.

The economy was in freefall, banks were failing, businesses were going to the wall and house prices were crashing. The country was being sucked feet first into a new Depression and Miami was hopscotching around the plughole.

The penthouse was on the fourteenth floor, and in the evenings he liked to sit outside on the balcony, facing the ocean. When he listened in on the waves and felt the fresh, salty air on his face, he could empty his head and find something close to peace.

Inside, behind the thick floor-to-ceiling windows, it was dark, quiet and practically empty. In the daytime, the sun would pour in, its beams warming the dark mahogany floors, drawn to them like feathers to an oil slick, blunting and dulling the light in the penthouse. It gave the room a graphite tinge. A few pieces of furniture stood off to the far right, almost hidden in shadow, as if abandoned or moved to maximise the vast remaining space.

Max hadn't done any entertaining nor had any visitors here in quite a while – not since going on the eighteen-month-long bender that had put him in hospital and cost him the bulk of his fortune and his self-respect.

In December 1996 he came back from Haiti with $20 million in drug money. It was payment for finding a missing child. He should have been all right then, set for life, but things hadn't worked out that way.

He didn't know what to do with the money. The only time he'd ever been near that much was as a cop on drug raids. By the time he'd left the Miami PD, traffickers were making so much cash they were literally buying up fields to bury it in. The cops built mini-mountain ranges out of the seized cash and had their pictures taken next to them. Some made the pictures into personalised greetings cards.

He knew he couldn't put the money in a bank because questions would be asked and he'd be investigated – by the police, the FBI and the IRS. They'd confiscate the money and put him on a shitlist. He didn't need the hassle.

He bought a safe, which he installed in the house on Key Biscayne he'd shared with Sandra. He planned on staying there the rest of his life, close to the physical memories of his wife. While he was in prison, she had kept the place looking exactly the same, probably so that when he came out he'd have something familiar to return to and build upon. She'd died of a brain haemorrhage a year before his release. He'd found her clothes still in the wardrobe and chest of drawers, a faint trace of perfume weaving through the fabric. In dreams he'd be lying next to her, holding her, listening to her breathing. In the mornings he woke up with his arms folded over empty space. He went to her graveside every Sunday with fresh flowers; he sat on a hunting stool and read one of her many books to her. Rain or shine. Life was simple. No one would replace Sandra, so he hadn't bothered looking, hadn't given it any thought.

He placed $6 million in trust funds for Joe Liston's kids: $2 million for Jet, $1 million apiece for the others. They couldn't access it until they were thirty. He reasoned that they'd be mature enough by then to handle the money responsibly.

In 1997 he met Yolande Pétion, a Haitian-American ex-cop, at Joe's house. She talked about opening a private detective agency in Miami's Little Haiti devoted to handling local cases. They went into business together. Max put up the capital for an office. They called it Pétion-Mingus Investigations.

The agency was Max's way of giving something back to Haiti, the country and the people who'd made him rich – and of turning bad money to good. After a slow start, the clientele started coming in. They handled everything from insurance jobs to missing persons. They cleared every case. Then, in August 1999, Yolande was shot and killed after surprising burglars at her home. Jewellery, credit cards and cash were missing from her house.

Max closed down the agency.

He turned fifty in March the following year. Joe threw him a surprise party. They went to a stripclub. He felt uncomfortable being there, all that gyrating bare flesh. He thought of the five years he'd been grieving. He started drinking some of the over-priced cheap champagne. It went straight to his head. He loosened up and a smile came to his face. By evening's end he was wasted and smoking cigarettes, a girl grinding her bare ass on his crotch, him getting aroused as hell, her asking him how bad he wanted her, him saying bad as hell, baby, bad as hell. They negotiated a fee.

The big five-o hit him hard. He knew he'd never be young again, and that he only had a limited amount of time left to enjoy life before his body started falling apart. Winter was tuning up. He didn't want to add on more regrets and let potential good times pass him by. He had a lot of money, and he still had his health and some of his looks.

All those things he supposedly couldn't do any more he did as much as possible. He carried on smoking, sparingly at first, no more than five or six a day. But he soon rediscovered that bygone comfort in nicotine and the routine of addiction: it was something to organise his aimless life around. He started drinking again too. And chasing after women.

Then he fell in love.

Tameka Barber.

Or Hurricane Tameka, as Joe later called her.

They met in May 2000. She was a trainer at his gym. A six-foot-tall ebony goddess, fit, muscular, lean, beautiful. He deliberately took her abs class to have a pretext to talk to her, noticing the red rose tattoo on her ankle, the other on her right breast, when she bent over. He liked her wicked smile and the laugh that went with it, a knowing, earthy cackle, three parts sex, one part danger. Eventually he asked her out and they got together. On paper it didn't look too bad – she was thirty-seven (although she looked ten years younger, thanks to a healthy lifestyle). In public, however, they looked like the typical Miami Beach couple – the rich, bald old white man with his young, statuesque exotic trophy squeeze. It couldn't be helped. It was what it was.

They had some great times. The sex was wild – intense, gymnastic and inventive. He found it went even better with coke – which he'd only ever tried once before. He fell in love and told her so. She said she loved him too. He contemplated marrying her. She told him he'd make a good dad.

Over the next year he and Tameka got through most of the Haiti millions. They moved into the penthouse. She had it redecorated. He gave her half a million dollars to start up her own gym. He took her to the Bahamas. First class, five star, everywhere. He took her to Vegas, and lost a fortune at the tables, to Mexico and Rio. He bought her a Mercedes and himself a Porsche. After totalling the Porsche, he bought a Mercedes to go with hers.

Joe saw what was happening and where it was all going. He didn't like Tameka, felt there was something not quite right about her. He ran her prints. Nothing whatsoever on record, not even a parking ticket to her name. But he trusted his instincts and dug deeper. First there was the teenage daughter she'd left behind in Tucson, Arizona. Then the boyfriend in Miami Springs, the one she visited every other day, the one she was giving Max's money to. His name was Hector Givens. He'd done time in Arizona for an insurance scam.

When Joe told Max, he didn't believe him and got seriously pissed. Then he went round to Givens's condo and Tameka opened the door, wearing one of the Chanel towels he'd bought her. She didn't even bother denying it. He was the biggest dumbass of all, she told him, if he hadn't so much as suspected what was going on: the only reason her fine ass was with him was money, honey. He told her she was a great actress and a complete bitch. She gave him a weird smile – a smirking grimace he interpreted as sadistic glee – and then slammed the door. Hector came after him with a tyre iron, yelling something about how he couldn't be calling his woman a gold-digging bitch, or whatever it was he'd said to her. Max busted Hector's front teeth with one punch and his jaw with another. He thought of going back and doing the same to Tameka, but he didn't hit women. Instead he went to a bar on Ocean Drive, got too wasted to walk and tripped down some stairs on the way to the bathroom.

He came to in hospital. Broken collar bone, broken left arm, broken leg, Joe standing there with a bowl of grapes and two sets of news: Tameka and Givens had split town for places unknown, and the Twin Towers had just come down in New York. It was September 11, 2001.

When he got out of hospital, Max vowed never to drink, smoke or take drugs again, and if a woman that hot ever so much as smiled at him, he'd make sure he vetted her before he smiled back.

He moved back into the Key Biscayne house. He had trouble sleeping and his healing bones were causing him pain. He took pills for both. On December 19, he woke up on the sidewalk,

42

being slapped awake by a paramedic. His house and the house next door had gone up in flames. How he'd gotten out – or who'd gotten him out – he didn't know. Investigators later said the next-door neighbour had doused himself and his house in gasoline and set himself ablaze.

They told Max he was lucky to be alive. He wasn't so sure. The fire had taken almost everything from him. His money was gone, as were every single one of his physical memories of Sandra, which hurt the most. Police later gave him back the only things they'd been able to salvage from the ruins – two photographs: one of him and Sandra on their wedding day in 1985, and the other of Solomon Boukman holding a gun to his head in Haiti in 1996.

There was a kind of sick symmetry to that, he had to admit, the way the fire had taken everything but those two pictures. He'd met Sandra around the time he'd been drawn into Solomon Boukman's orbit. She died the year Boukman had been released from prison and deported to Haiti.

Solomon Boukman . . . *Christ.*

Thinking about him sent fresh chills down long-distance wires. Max had been as good as broken by that case, the career-maker turned career-ender – the proverbial abyss he'd stared into and seen his true reflection winking back at him. He'd always thought that was some smartass bullshit made up to dodge the burden of personal responsibility, but the truth of it hit him right between the eyes in the shape of Boukman.

Boukman was into everything big and illegal in Miami in his heyday: drugs, prostitution, gambling, extortion, gun-running, money laundering – the works. Yet he was more than the sum of his crimes and the multi-million-dollar organisation that he ran. He used voodoo, black magic and extreme violence to control his people and to keep anyone who ever heard his name in a state of fear. He practised human sacrifice. He zombified his enemies with potions and hypnosis and used them as weapons –

his very own suicide killers. And he turned himself into a myth, an urban legend in his own lifetime, a spook story parents told their kids at night to terrify them into goodness. Newly arrived Haitians swore Boukman was the earthly incarnation of Baron Samedi, the voodoo god of death. Others said he was the Devil incarnate because he'd been seen in multiple places at the same time. Most agreed that he was a shapeshifter – he could transform his appearance at will, from a young Californian blonde woman to an old black man, and everything in between. No one knew what he really looked like. Or so went the whispers on the street.

In reality, he was just a man – albeit a clever, manipulative, evil man who dressed himself up as a superstition and played on fear.

Max and Joe caught Boukman in 1981. They'd chased him through Little Haiti, Boukman bleeding from a cut femoral artery. Boukman had collapsed inside a disused building. Max had tied off the wound and given him mouth-to-mouth. Then they'd taken him in.

A year later, Boukman was tried, found guilty of first-degree murder and sentenced to death. In court he refused to take the stand and said absolutely nothing throughout his trial, until Max had finished giving his testimony. Then Boukman had locked eyes with Max and broke his silence for the one and only time: 'You give me reason to live,' he said.

Those words had haunted Max for a good long while. Boukman's quiet, hissy murmur lodged in some corner of his mind, echoing back at him. He hadn't understood what the Haitian meant then. Was it a threat, a promise or the desperate bluster of a sinking man? He'd tried to let it go, tried reasoning with himself. But the case had gotten to him, fucked him up good. When Max and Joe were closing in and Boukman's grip had started weakening, the Haitian had kidnapped Max, tortured him, zombified him and then put a gun in his hand and turned him loose on Eldon and Joe.

In his dreams, Max had relived those memories and woken up screaming, reaching for his cigarettes, his booze, his tranqs. One by one, Sandra got rid of the pacifiers until the only thing he could reach out for when he woke in terror was her. She held him and soothed him back to sleep, telling him it was just a bad dream, that Boukman was long gone, that dreams always passed. And she was right.

Over time the nightmares faded.

Then Max went to prison.

And Sandra died a year before he was released.

Which was why he'd taken the job in Haiti – where he'd last encountered Boukman, unwittingly, unknowingly.

Although he'd been on death row, awaiting the outcome of his penultimate appeal, Boukman had been deported back to Haiti in 1995. The year before, the US had invaded the country to restore its deposed president in the name of democracy. Someone somewhere in Washington had decided to take the opportunity to free up the prisons, by very quietly deporting all Haitian criminals taking up valuable cell space. As Boukman was not an American citizen, he got a plane ride home, the argument being that it was cheaper to ship him than to kill him. At the time, Haiti had no prisons, no courts and no police, just the occupying US Army, and it was too busy stopping the country from sliding into anarchy to play cop. So when they arrived back home, the expelled criminals were set free, unleashed on their vulnerable, near destitute countrymen like starving wolves in a sheep pen. No checks, no balances, no one in authority even crossing their fingers.

Max had been at a club outside Port-au-Prince, when Boukman had crept up behind him, taken his gun out of his holster and held it to his head, smiling. Someone had snapped the picture.

The photograph later turned up in one of the two bags he carried that $20 million reward home in. Boukman had written him a message on the back: 'You give me reason to live.'

45

Max *still* didn't get what he meant, but he knew one thing for sure: Boukman didn't want to kill him. He'd had ample opportunity to get to him in Haiti and he hadn't.

So as far as Max was concerned, it was over.

He'd put the partially burned photograph in a safety deposit box and tossed the key into the ocean.

In 2002 Max went back to work as a private detective. He put an ad in the *Herald* and set up a website. He got his first call within a week, a woman who wanted to know if he handled divorce cases. He figured he was well qualified, so said, yes, how could he help.

Insurance paid out $350,000 on the house. It was all the money he had left.

4

Max made himself a four-shot espresso with Bustelo coffee and took the brew into his office. He sat down, turned on his computer and waited for it to power up. His desk was otherwise bare, save a phone and a framed photograph of him with the Liston family taken the previous Christmas. Since splitting with Tameka, he'd spent almost every public holiday and birthday with them. Joe's kids called him 'Uncle Max'.

The penthouse's workspace looked out on the city – a spray of multi-coloured lights caught in the burnt-ochre wash of thousands of street lamps. He could see all the way to the illuminated towers that formed the Downtown skyline. In a few hours the same view would become a dull, flat sweep of hard greys and beiges, concrete, glass and extinguished neon. For somewhere so famous and popular, Miami was short on memorable landmarks. It had nothing that instantly defined it, no cultural shorthand symbol – no Statue of Liberty, no White House, no Hollywood sign. It was just beaches, hotels and palm trees – any ocean resort anywhere hot and affluent. Maybe that was the point. Maybe that was all there really was. A blank canvas. Miami was what you made of it.

Max called Emerson Prescott's cell. He left a message asking his client to call him, and followed it up with an email. It was the way he operated, confirming everything in writing just in case he got sued.

When he was done, he checked his inbox.

Nothing.

*

The following morning Max stood on the gym steps and looked up and down 7th Avenue. Boarded-up stores on either side, a row of burned-out or boarded-up houses opposite. Beyond them a long stretch of open ground, all dirt, wild untended grass and piled trash.

Eldon had been shot around midday on Tuesday October 28. Broad daylight. Someone must have seen or heard something.

Or had they?

In a place like Liberty City, where a wrong look could land you in a sea of shit, people tended to mind their own business, which meant they saw and heard only what they wanted to and nothing else.

Then there was the triggerman. With his skills, he'd be nothing less than a consummate pro. He would have calculated his ins and outs, checked for regular passers-by, gone in when it was quietest. He wouldn't have drawn attention to himself. People might have noticed him but no one would remember him.

So, Max guessed, that made the hitman black and – from the crime-scene photos of Eldon's face – slightly over six foot tall.

It wasn't much, but it was a start.

He crossed the road to look at the gym. A faded mural covered the outside, the faces of all the fighters who'd won titles, most of them local kids. It had been a point of pride for them to come by, years later, and see themselves still up there, a reminder of their achievements. Something to show their kids or impress their girlfriends with. The press said this was why the gym had remained unscathed in the riots of the 1980s, but that wasn't altogether true. Rage wasn't big on nostalgia. The main reason it hadn't been looted and torched was that a lot of people in Liberty City had been scared of Eldon and what he could do. Simple as that. Max searched for his own face on the wall. He found it again quite easily, the only white face there. Not a bad likeness of how he'd once been.

He headed left, determined to talk to the first person he found.

He met no one. Midday, Friday, Halloween, and it was completely deserted. Not the natural stillness of a Sunday or a public holiday, where people stayed home to relax or left town to visit their relatives, but an abiding desolation that had settled on the area, as if it had been hastily abandoned in the face of a plague or other calamity. He passed more rows of empty houses with clusters of boarded-up stores in-between. Nothing was open, nothing was working. He half-expected to see tumbleweed bouncing across the road.

After ten minutes he came across two little girls standing on the sidewalk, identical twins in matching clothes – black T-shirts emblazoned with a picture of a smiling man cradling two babies in his arms. Max noted the family resemblance before noticing what was written around the photograph:

Pookie Brown. 1985–2008. We Will Always Luv U.

The girls stared up at him with the kind of look locals always gave cops, white ones in particular. The cops even had a name for it: the Liberty Clock. The look was one part suspicion, one part hostility, two parts fear, undercut with a resigned weariness. The girls already resembled little adults. He smiled at them and said, 'Hi', but they backed away, looks intensifying. It made him sad – for them and for their future – to see in their faces that long history of hatred and resentment, handed down in the DNA and whispered in the wind that blew through these wretched streets. It was said that the sound of gunfire was so common in Liberty City, kids could tell calibre by ear and knew to hit the deck before they could walk and talk.

He continued up the road. He noticed how grass and weeds were growing tall and wild through cracks in the sidewalk, how nature was exploding with abandon around the vacant buildings. It felt like the neighbourhood was gradually being dismantled from below, to be sucked back into the earth.

A little further on he heard the sweet sound of Al Green singing 'Belle', and he followed it all the way to the open entrance of a bookstore called Swopes.

He walked in to the smell of cooking and a man in a crisp white shirt sitting at a table by the door eating a plate of country-fried steak, collard greens, grits, yam and white gravy. The man had coppery brown skin, a salt-and-pepper moustache that complimented his greying 'fro, and steady hazel eyes. Max guessed he was the owner or manager because he was trying hard not to give Max the Liberty Clock, in case Max turned out to be a customer.

Max smiled and nodded and the man nodded back.

Inside, the store was a lot bigger than it appeared from the street. And it sold more than books.

Through an arch at the very back was what looked like a photography gallery. The black walls were covered with Polaroids. When Max got closer he saw that these were nearly all of young black men, none older than their mid-twenties. There were a few exceptions – some women, a couple of children, a baby. A banner above the display read 'Liberty City (1997–present)'.

On a high round table draped with a black cloth, a bundle of purple incense sticks burned. A soothing smell of lavender filled the gallery space. A big board shaped like a T-shirt stood to the right with details of designs, sizes and prices. Costs ranged from $10 for children to $25 for supersize. He thought of the twins he'd seen up the road.

The adjoining bookstore's shelves ran four high and covered three walls. They were subdivided into autobiography, fiction, history, race relations, self-help guides, diet and exercise, and conspiracy theories – the last, by far the biggest section. There were framed photographs on the walls – Malcolm X, Marcus Garvey, Martin Luther King, Booker T. Washington, Rosa Parks, Maya Angelou, Angela Davis, Muhammad Ali, Jesse Owens, Barack Obama.

He pulled out a book from the conspiracy theory section called *The Melanin Thieves* by Alvin Sheen. It claimed that white scientists were harvesting melanin from the bodies of black people, for use in everyday consumer goods – everything from

50

car tyres to sunglasses. There was even a picture of the top-secret laboratory in Africa where the harvesting was supposedly taking place.

Max laughed out loud as he leafed through the book. Then he saw the man who'd been eating standing in the archway.

'One of my biggest sellers,' he said.

'You believe this crap?' Max held up the book.

'There's something in it, for sure.' The man smiled. 'But you're not here to buy books, right?'

The man had a quiet voice and spoke fairly slowly, someone who thought carefully before he opened his mouth.

'You're right. Sorry.' Max put the book back. 'I'm here about the shooting at the 7th Avenue gym. You hear anything about that?'

'You a cop?'

'Not any more. Private detective. I'm helping out a friend.'

'Must be a good friend, got you coming out here asking questions 'bout a shooting.'

'He is,' said Max.

'All I know is what I saw on TV. They're saying it's some kinda gang initiation. That's bullshit. This ain't LA. Gangs round here don't kill old white men on purpose. They're too busy wipin' each other out.'

'You ever meet the victim – man called Eldon Burns?'

'No. But I heard 'bout him from time to time. I knew a few of the fighters he trained. They all respected him. Some of them became cops 'cause of him.'

'Sure they did.' Max smiled wryly.

'He was killed Tuesday, right? You know what time?'

'Around midday, I think. Why?'

'Someone was shot right outside-a-here at 12.30. Out back in the alley,' the man said. 'I was in here. Heard a car brake. Then some shouting. Then a shot. Car pulls off quick. I went outside and saw White Flight lying there.'

'Who?'

51

'White Flight. Guy lives in the alley. He was lying there on the ground. Been shot in the neck. He was still alive. I called an ambulance. They took him to Jackson Memorial.'

'Did he make it?'

'Yeah. He's out of intensive care.'

'Did you see any of it?'

'No. Just heard it. You know the cops never came to see me? I even told 'em it might be the same guy killed Eldon Burns – given the time.' The man shook his head. 'Were you selective like that, when you were a cop?'

'I followed every lead.'

Max went outside into the alley behind the store. A few feet in he saw a large comma of dried blood. There were two sets of tyre streaks on the ground nearby – short before the blood, long after it.

He searched around the area adjacent to the patch of blood. Spray pattern on the ground, some spatter on the walls. A broken wine bottle close to the wall, sand all around it, blood in the sand and on the glass. The cap screwed on the bottle.

The bottle, filled with sand, had served as a weapon, a club.

Max walked a little further down the alley. A stench hit him like a clear glass wall. He found where White Flight lived – a makeshift tent of blue plastic sheeting, poles and bricks, a patched-up sleeping bag inside and, nearby, a supermarket cart spilling over with filthy rags and bric-a-brac. A bum's ideal home.

He went back to the tyre tracks and blood. Roughly working out the angles, he guessed the driver had turned into the alley suddenly and almost hit White Flight. The hobo had tried to swing his bottle at the car. The driver had shot him once.

Back in the store, Max gave the man one of his cards.

'Did you see the car or anything?'

'No. A few people I talked to say they saw a brown Sierra come out of the alley. Didn't get the plate.'

'You know what White Flight's real name is?'

'No. Sometimes I'm not sure he does.' The man looked at the card and frowned. 'Max Mingus?'

'Yeah. I know what you're going to say. And I'm not related to Charles Mingus. My dad was a jazz musician. Played double bass too. He was such a fan he changed his name to Mingus.'

'My name's Lamar Swope.'

They shook hands. Max noticed the Obama-Biden button on his shirt: 'Vote for Change'.

'You know, I thought I recognised you from some place, when you walked in,' Lamar said.

Whenever people told Max they recognised him these days, he either got evasive or defensive, depending on the situation. They were usually one of two kinds – internet-prowling creeps who'd read up about the murders that had landed him in prison or journalists looking to write books or make documentaries. He'd been offered plenty of money to tell his story, but he'd never been tempted. Two reasons: he didn't want to make money that way and he didn't want anyone digging too hard into his past.

'You're still called Pétion-Mingus Investigations.' Swope tapped his card. 'I knew Yolande.'

'Yeah? How?'

'I helped her out on a couple of community events at the Miami Book Fair. They ever find the guy who killed her?'

'No.'

No, they never had.

'I've got something for you. Stay there.' Lamar Swope went back inside and came back with a small glassine bag containing a single .45 casing. 'I found this right by where I found White Flight. I didn't touch it at all. Used a pen to pick it up, like they do on TV.'

'Thanks.' Max took the bag and slipped it into his shirt pocket. 'If you think of anything else give me a call or drop me an email.'

'Sure will. Think you'll get the guy killed Eldon Burns?'

'I doubt it.'

'Then why are you doing this? It's dangerous work, looking for killers. And – no offence – but at your age, man . . .'

Max chuckled at that. 'This isn't really about getting the shooter, Lamar. This is about putting a stop to something Eldon started way back when. Kind of shit that made Liberty City burn in 1980.'

'I remember that time. I remember the riots,' Swope said. 'My grandparents lost their house then. It burned down. My grandpa liked to read. He was always reading. Read in his sleep. Had books everywhere. Someone threw a petrol bomb through their window. Why, I don't know. I hope it was an accident. Their house went up real quick, all those books, you know.

'This store? It's my tribute to him. He taught me to read and to love books. Hardly anyone comes in here to buy books. I make most of my money on those memorial T-shirts – and the restaurant. But I'm keeping the bookstore open here, in memory of my grandpa.'

'That's a noble thing to do,' said Max.

'Even if I'm just pissing in the wind, right?'

'Maybe. But at least you're pissing with a purpose. Unlike most people.'

5

For someone who'd been shot in the throat, lost half his jaw, part of his tongue and would never speak again, the man people in Liberty City knew as White Flight looked vaguely happy, a smile playing on the small part of his face not covered by bandages. He was on some good painkiller dope, propped up on pillows, plugged into saline and blood drips and hooked into a monitor.

'He may fall to sleep when you talk to him. Don't worry. It's nothing personal. It's the painkillers,' the nurse said. Twentysomething Latina called Zulay Garcia. Petite, dark hair, dark eyes. Married or engaged, judging from the tan line around her ring finger.

Max was merely noticing, not lining up. She was way too young for him – like almost every great-looking woman in Miami.

'Mr Flight? This is a policeman. He wants to talk about what happen to you. I give you paper and pencil. You just write what you can, OK?'

White Flight nodded slowly, his good eye on Max, twinkling.

Max hadn't identified himself as a cop. He'd just acted the part from the moment he turned up at Jackson Memorial and asked to see the victim. It hadn't exactly been a stretch. He still had the bearing, the imperious swagger, the stare that overstayed, the procedural, box-ticking diction and the officious, inflexible tone. He was so good at being his old self he didn't need a badge or a gun to gain leverage.

Nurse Garcia sat next to White Flight holding the pencil in his hand and resting it on the pad.

'Did you see the person who shot you?'

White Flight gurgled and gasped, his eye straining in its socket, the smile, though, still eerily plastered there.

'Don't try to talk,' the nurse implored him gently but firmly. 'Write down.'

Max watched as White Flight slowly scratched a single, shaky letter on the page, each element of the letter taking an eternity to form.

A big capital *Y*.

'Male or female?'

The heart monitor began beeping a little faster as the patient started gurgling again and thrashed his legs.

'Please.' Nurse Garcia laid a hand on White Flight's chest. 'No get angry. Help this man so he help you.'

White Flight snorted derisively before he resumed his slow, scraping writing.

M.

'Was he black or white?'

B, written like half a figure 8, the back missing.

'Anything else you can tell me about him? Did you see his face?'

White Flight wrote *N.*

'What about the car he was driving? Do you remember the colour?'

B R.

'Brown?'

He circled the *Y.*

'Do you know the make of the car?'

The *N* was circled this time.

'Did the man who shot you get out of the car?'

N ringed again.

'How many people in the car?'

The patient wrote *2.*

'Two? Are you sure?'

He looped the *Y*.

The shooter had an accomplice.

'Was the man who shot you driving the car?'

N.

'Did you see the driver?'

Y.

'Male or female?'

?

'You don't know?'

White Flight circled the question mark, then wrote *Y*.

'Was the driver black or white?'

W.

'Anything else you remember about the man who shot you? Did you see his face?'

White Flight wrote two words.

HAREMOUTH.

'He had a moustache?'

A third ring around *N*, and another around *HARE*.

'He had a hare *lip*?'

Y.

A solid lead.

But White Flight hadn't finished writing.

Max waited.

The heart monitor's beeping quickened again as the pencil scraped across the paper.

Two more words.

BIRDSHIRT.

'The gunman had birds on his shirt?'

White Flight nodded.

'Thank you very much, sir. You've been very helpful. I wish you a speedy recovery.'

White Flight snorted again.

Nurse Garcia walked Max out of the room and down the corridor.

'What's going to happen to him when he gets out?' Max asked her.

'No insurance. No family. No social security number. What you think?' she said. 'When he can walk, they put him back out on the street. That's the way it is in this country. You no interested in people who fall through the cracks.'

'Where are you from, originally?'

'Cuba.'

'I see,' said Max. 'And people don't fall through the cracks there?'

'They all have free healthcare.'

'So I heard. I also heard it's a brutal, repressive dictatorship. Which is probably why you're here, right?'

He immediately regretted being such a sarcastic prick. It was a cheap shot and a deeply insensitive one. But it was too late for apologies.

'This is a great country, detective,' Nurse Garcia said. 'You just don't know how to make it better.'

Max called Joe as soon as he was out of the hospital.

Before he could say much of anything, Liston cut him off.

'You can stop what you're doing, Max.'

'What do you mean?'

'There's been a breakthrough – if you can call it that.' Joe sounded worried.

'They get the shooter?'

'Not exactly, but they think they know who did it.'

'Who?'

'Let's meet tonight. Usual place, usual time,' said Joe. 'I'll tell you all about it.'

6

The usual place was the Mariposa on Lincoln Road – a Cuban restaurant run by the same people who ran the famous Versailles restaurant on Calle Ocho, Little Havana. The menu was identical, and the food tasted just as good, but because it was located in the heart of South Beach's shopping district, it cost five times more. That didn't stop people coming. Today it was busier than usual. Halloween night and a Friday – they'd got the last free table.

'There's things I can tell you and a lot I can't,' Joe said after the waitress had brought the menus.

Liston was leaning in, keeping his voice to a murmur. Max could tell he'd had a long and difficult day. There was the extra set of luggage under his eyes, the cauliflower pattern of his screwed-up forehead, the anxiety unbalancing his usually calm stare.

'You know whose gun the shooter used?' said Joe. 'Abe Watson's. We got his ballistics on file. They matched his forty-five.'

'How'd the shooter get hold of it?'

'Abe was *buried* with his gun. 1911 Colt. His grave was robbed a week before Eldon was killed. You know he made history with that gun, right? He was the first cop in Miami with an automatic. Back then, everyone had thirty-eights. Peashooters. Even Eldon.'

'Who knew he was buried with the gun? Outside of his family and friends?'

'People at the funeral parlour. They're on the list for questioning.'

'So Abe Watson's connected to all of this too?' Max started tying up the leads. 'Eldon was shot with his gun. They were partners and close friends. The shooter dug up the gun. What do you exhume? Things that've been buried, hidden away. The past. So this could be related to something Eldon and Abe did when they were cops. And Eldon was shot through both eyes. What's that telling us? Something – or someone – he saw that he wasn't supposed to? Or something we – *you're* – not seeing?'

'Eldon was shot with Black Talons,' said Joe. 'Aka "the bullets that kill you better": cop-killer rounds, on account of their being able to pierce Kevlar vests – or so interested parties thought.'

'Weren't those discontinued ten, fifteen years ago?'

'From public sale, yeah. Law enforcement and the military used them for a while. Then Winchester modified the bullet and rebranded it the Ranger SXT. The new bullets aren't black 'cause they stopped spraying them with Lubalox. But the ones Eldon got shot with? Vintage lead.'

'Can you track the batch?'

'They're working on it,' Joe said. 'It won't be easy. A lot of discontinued weaponry gets sold to the Third World via back-door deals. Between us, the killer might be a foreigner.'

'Tell me more.'

'I can't,' said Joe. 'I shouldn't even have told you that much.'

'Why not?'

'I just can't. I'd like to. There's all kinds of things I'd like to tell you.'

'Like what?'

'Like stuff I can't talk about.'

Max had never known Joe to be like this. He'd seen him down and close to defeat, he'd seen him angry and capable of murder, he'd seen him heartbroken and on the verge of tears, he'd seen him at the edge, but never going over. Joe's innate restraint and stolidity had always seen him through, enabled him to weather

60

the worst without losing his head. Life may sometimes have confused him, but it had never overwhelmed him, never got the
better of him. Until now.

'What kind of trouble are you in, Joe?'

'I don't know yet,' said Liston.

'Anything I can do?'

'No.'

'Sure?'

'Yeah.'

But Max sensed Joe wanted to talk. He just wasn't there yet;
he was still finding the right way to present the information,
release it in a way he could live with.

Give him time. Change the subject.

Max looked out over Lincoln Road. It had become lush and
prosperous, with restaurants, cafés, bars, cigar stores, art galleries
and boutiques all doing a roaring trade under its natural canopy
of spotlight-strewn, parrot-laden trees. Not that long before, the
road had been two miles of arid sewer, connecting Collins
Avenue to a group of dilapidated condos by the marina. Mounds
of stinking trash everywhere, buildings either boarded up or
colonised by bums. The only people who went down there were
lost tourists, crazy old folk who'd come off their meds and the
cops and medics rescuing them. Hard to believe it was the same
place now. They'd even renovated the theatre. Max remembered
chasing a purse-snatcher in there, only to discover a whole boatload of newly washed-ashore Haitians hiding under the stage,
terrified and starving.

It was always busy on Lincoln at night, although it wasn't
uncommon to see the same people three or four times. In the
early evening it was couples and families, many with children
and pets, looking for a place to eat, checking out the blown-up
menus and plates of artfully arranged, cellophane-covered
seafood in front of the restaurants. Later on it was the turn of the
hustlers and exhibitionists – the cheap guitar slingers hustling
you for a song, the freaks carrying parakeets and snakes, the ugly

transvestite who mimed arias, the failed circus acts. And then, later still, when the clubs opened, out came the true Miami freaks, the kind of beautiful but utterly vacant starfucking types who wound up on reality TV shows – an endless parade of the tattooed, pumped-up, pierced, depilated, liposucked, collagened, botoxed, implanted and plugged. Narcissistic vulgarity taking the long walk to absolutely nowhere.

Tonight that crew had to compete with the Halloween crowd. It was mostly adult. People were dressed as witches, wizards, vampires, ghouls, goblins. There was a Michael Myers with a plastic butcher's knife, a few Jasons in hockey masks, assorted Leatherfaces, Pinheads, Freddie Kruegers. Max saw a Robocop, a Boris Karloff, a Lion, a Tin Man and a male Dorothy skipping down the street, hand in hand. Here came a Pinball Wizard in towering platforms and a woolly hat, next a seventies pimp trailing a gaggle of chained women wearing glitter, gold thongs and Bin Laden masks. There were plenty of presidents around – a Washington in a powdered wig, lipstick and rouge; a pregnant woman as Benjamin Franklin; a handful of Lincolns, one of them on stilts; a couple of Reagans; and a lot of Nixons and Dubyas, the latter outnumbering the former.

Then, cutting right through the cartoon freakery, running and bouncing along, came a line of over a dozen children – boys and girls, all races – no older than twelve, chanting, 'Yes we can! Yes we can! *GO*!-BAM-A! *GO*!-BAM-A!' People stopped and stared and many smiled and some shouted encouragements.

'It's looking real good for Obama,' Max said finally. The election was four days away.

'Can't believe you're not even arguing for McCain,' said Joe.

'I'd sooner argue for a third Bush term. I mean, *Sarah Palin* ... Fuck no.'

'Hell just froze over.' Joe smiled for the first time that evening, his gloomy demeanour momentarily lifting.

Politics had been their one and only other regular argument, after the merits of Bruce Springsteen. Until recently, Max had been a lifelong Republican. Joe was and always had been a staunch Democrat. They'd argued the 2000 election until they were hoarse, Joe insisting Bush stole it, Max saying Gore voters were too dumb to punch the right hole. 9/11 had briefly united them, but the war in Iraq had once again got them arguing, Max buying the government line about Saddam's WMD, Joe saying that was all bullshit, that it was about oil. Max had continued supporting the war, right up until Abu Ghraib. After the government's inaction during Hurricane Katrina, for the first time in his life he would have voted Democrat if he could – except his criminal record prohibited it.

'The whole family'll be watching the results round my house,' said Joe. 'You're invited.'

'I accept.' Max made a show of studying the menu, despite the fact that he invariably had the same thing here, his favourite – *lechon asado* (roast pork, marinaded in orange, garlic, onion and olive oil), *maduros* (sautéed sweet plantain) and *moros y cristanos* (literally 'Moors and Christians', figuratively black beans and rice).

Joe was determined to try everything on the menu and always varied his dishes. 'You know why the mariposa's the national bird of Cuba?' he asked Max.

'Because of its colours? Red, white and blue?'

'That too,' said Joe. 'The real reason is you can't cage a mariposa because it dies. It's a symbol of freedom.'.

'Freedom? *In Cuba?*' Max laughed. 'Is that some kind of joke?'

'There are many kinds of freedom.'

'Like the freedom to give up your basic freedoms?' Max chortled.

'You ever been there?'

'No. Of course not. Have you?'

Just then the waitress came over to take their order. Max gave his. Joe took his time. From the way he was fussing, uncommonly, Max wondered if it hadn't hit a nerve, and he was trying to cover it up. Had Joe been to Cuba? He decided not to pursue it for now.

He glanced across the restaurant, at the black-and-white tiled floor, and the walls, decorated with mariposa frescos – the birds in flight, the birds singing; the country's symbol of freedom appropriately frozen in midflight, on hold, its mouth open, its voice unheard.

Max remembered the shell casing Lamar Swope had given him and took it out of his breast pocket. He ran down his day, told Joe what he'd found out.

'The shooter's black, has a hare lip. He was wearing a black shirt with bird patterns on it. And he has an accomplice, a driver, white. Not sure if the driver's male or female. The car's a brown Ford Sierra,' Max said. 'You should pull any camera footage you can find from 7th and 8th Avenues, between MLK Boulevard and 54th Street.'

'Great work.' Joe pocketed the bullet. 'Bet you got the taste back today, right? For police work?'

'Yeah.' Max had got the taste back all right, enough to miss every damn thing he'd left behind, to regret every wrong turn, every misstep. Being out there, looking for Eldon's killer – and doing real work again – had energised him, given him purpose, made him forget what a slow-leaking boat his life was. He didn't want to give up what he'd just started.

Joe seemed to read his mind.

'Let it go now, Max, d'you hear?'

'I'd like to know what's bugging you.'

Joe looked at him. 'I shouldn't have involved you.'

'But you did.'

'Now I'm telling you to back off, all right?' As he said it his face darkened a touch and Max knew that he wouldn't get anything more out of him, that the subject was closed.

A heavy silence settled between them. Max thought it best to let the matter rest for now.

64

The waitress brought over their food. She was called Samantha, or at least that's what her name tag read. Tall, with long, blonde-streaked dark hair and a full mouth, she would have been a knockout if she hadn't looked almost permanently pissed off. The first time Max had seen her – a year before – he'd attributed it to anger at the possibility that she would be waiting tables for the rest of her life. Then she turned around and he saw what was probably the cause of her unhappiness. Her ass. High, pert, bulbous and firm, it was one of the finest asses he'd ever seen. It was barely contained in the knee-length black skirt that she wore. Men would stop in the street and stare at that ass and then moments later they'd be sitting at the restaurant. It was a customer magnet. He felt sorry for her. He tried not to look at her ass, but he couldn't help himself, so to compensate he was as friendly as possible to her and always left a generous tip. It only made her scowl harder.

Joe had followed Max's eyes.

'You still God's Lonely Man?' said Joe. He'd ordered *picadillo a la criolla* with a side of boiled green bananas and a mixed salad.

'Of course.' Max nodded. He'd been single since Hurricane Tameka. Not that he'd exactly been inundated with offers. In fact, the only women who looked at him twice were prostitutes he accidentally made eye contact with.

'What else is going on with you – in the bedhopper business?' Joe asked.

Max told him about Emerson Prescott and what had happened at the Zurich Hotel. Liston howled with laughter when Max got to the part about the DVD. He laughed so hard neither of them could eat until he'd stopped.

After Joe had recovered, they picked at their food and watched people idle by on the street, making occasional comments on the pageant of freaks. No one seemed in a hurry. Opposite, half a block down, a young kid with a pudding-bowl haircut was playing electric guitar and singing 'Brown Sugar' with a heavy Spanish accent. A small crowd had gathered and were tossing coins into an upturned baseball cap and filming him on camera phones.

Then Max saw Joe's expression change. The humour drained out of his face and his eyes moved to Max's right, over his shoulder, fixing on something behind him.

'What are you lookin' at?' Max asked.

Joe didn't answer. He glanced at Max. He looked puzzled and worried, like he'd just seen something he didn't believe or understand. His eyes moved back over Max's shoulder.

Max turned around. He didn't see anything out of the ordinary.

'What did you see?'

'Some creep,' said Joe, glancing over Max's other shoulder, at a point past his neck.

'Which one?'

Joe chortled.

'It was the strangest fucking thing,' he said. 'I just thought . . . Forget it. Carry on.'

Max went back to Emerson Prescott, to trying to understand what the fuck it was all about, but Joe wasn't listening. His troubles were refusing to time out.

'Joe,' said Max. 'Why don't you tell me what's up? What am I gonna do – apart from listen? You were willing to go up against the department just yesterday. Risk your livelihood. You asked me to help and I did. And I'd do it again. You know that. So why don't you just tell me what's up? I'd tell you.'

Liston looked at Max for a long moment.

Then he put his cutlery down, wiped his mouth on a napkin and rested it near his plate.

'They say the best way to keep a secret is to tell no one. And this is one I've been living with longer than I've known you. I haven't even told my wife – and I tell her everything,' he said.

'Except this?'

'That's right. Does the name Vanetta Brown ring any bells?'

Max's immediate thought was, No. But in the back of his mind, there was a faint chime of recognition.

66

'The name sounds vaguely familiar.'

'Well—' Joe started and stopped. His eyes suddenly moved back to scanning the crowd behind Max.

As Max was about to turn and look around again, a thunderous boom reverberated right behind him, very close, close enough to deafen him. It was a huge sound, that of a shot being fired just above his ear. He felt it right down to the tips of his toes.

Joe's head rocked back sharply. The people behind him were splattered with blood.

Liston pivoted on the chair's hind legs, balanced an instant, and then fell back, his legs upending the table.

Max had dived off to the side, instinctively, reflexively, away from the sound.

He rolled over on his back and looked up, but all he could see were people running in different directions, falling over each other. Through the din in his ears, he heard screams and shouts, glass and crockery shattering, panic.

He scrambled over to Joe.

His friend's right eye had been shot out. He lay motionless. Max grabbed his wrist and yelled his name. No pulse. No motion. The hand was still warm. But it wouldn't be for much longer. Blood was seeping out of the back of his head, thick and dark red.

Max grabbed Joe's gun out of his holster and stood up.

He heard crying, people screaming. Everywhere, people were running, ducking into doorways, stores. The front of the restaurant had emptied. Tables had been overturned. Food all over the floor. Customers cowering behind the bar, looking at him, terrified.

He couldn't move. He had gunsmoke in the back of his throat.

'Drop your weapon!'

Cop's command at his ear, behind him.

'Drop your fucken' weapon!'

He dropped Joe's gun and put his hands in the air. Someone

grabbed his arms and locked them behind his back. He was forced down on the ground, his face almost touching Joe's feet. His hands were cuffed. He was patted down. Cops surrounded him. He heard sirens, the sharp crackle of police radios and, in his head, the echo of a gunshot.

7

He'd been here before, on the wrong side of the interrogation room, getting grilled about murder. Only this time he hadn't killed anyone.

They were treating him like a suspect, keeping him in this white room with its bolted-down furniture. The chair he sat in was slightly lower than the one opposite and a good half ass-cheek too narrow for basic comfort. The table surface, knuckle-dented and fogged with graffiti and bored scratches, resembled the inside of an old tin pan. Cast iron loops for chains had been bolted to the floor and presiding over the whole dull scene were black cameras, bracketed high on adjacent walls.

No one had said a single word to him.

Two hours in and he was still waiting.

Joe was dead.

A uniformed cop had confirmed it. He walked in, put a picture on the table and pushed it over to Max without saying a word. Then he walked out.

Max stared at the picture.

Joe.

A single bullet to the head, clean through the eye.

It had been taken within an hour of the shooting – the glow of life hadn't fully faded from the flesh. Joe didn't look dead, more the victim of a grim Halloween prank – like someone had put make-up on him in his sleep.

Ha ha ha. Not funny. Not funny at all.

Max knew his friend was gone.

For ever.

And he felt sick.

Then came deep disorientation. Compass points had been switched around, gravity realigned. A few hours before, they'd been having dinner, talking, like two regular guys on a night out. He could see the edge of a Mariposa menu in the corner of the picture. That was their last ever time together.

Max couldn't feel anything.

No sorrow, no anger – no emotions of any kind.

The grief would come later, he knew. You never got over losing those closest to you. You made room for the emptiness and you learned to live with it.

He wanted to call Lena – Joe's wife – and go and be with the family.

He thought of Joe's children. He thought of how Joe had been just seven months away from retirement. He thought of the grandchildren Joe would never see.

That name.

Vanetta Brown.

Still a mere chime, a distant bell tolling in the fog of memory.

Joe was about to tell him who she was. Then he was shot.

Through the eye.

Shot like Eldon.

Shot by Eldon's killer.

The cops had arrived at the scene in under a minute. Four of them had jumped him, knocked him down, frisked him, cuffed him. Sheer panic everywhere. The make-believe monsters had fled in terror. The real one had gotten away.

The Miami PD hadn't changed their game much since his time. Same old shit. Tired playbook. Stick your suspect in a room and leave him there alone for two or three hours. Let him stew in what he's done, let him get a foretaste of captivity. Meanwhile they watched you for tell-tale signs – twitching, fidgeting, crying, sleeping. That gave them angles to use – soft or hard, loud or quiet, empathy or aggression, good cop-bad cop/good cop-indifferent cop/bad cop-worse cop. It all only really worked on newbies. Seasoned pros knew they were heading to prison anyway and rode the routine out for the hell of it, making the most of comparative freedom.

Some guys in the force loved going brain-to-brain with suspects, trying to trip them up and getting them to incriminate themselves. These same guys were aces at crossword puzzles and chess, but were too dumb to get into the FBI. Max and Joe never had the patience for epic interrogations, Max especially. If he was sure the perp was guilty, but the guy was being a wiseass or was holding out, he used oranges in a bag to get a confession. If he couldn't get oranges, he went for a phonebook. Not the Miami one, that was too slim. He favoured the big cities – LA or New York. Hefty things, maximum impact, negligible bruising.

He'd have been thrown into prison and the force sued down to its last dime if he was a cop today and pulled that kind of stuff. He remembered a conversation he'd had with Joe the month before. They'd been talking about how divorce and drinking were way down in the PD. They put it down to the counselling cops got after being in traumatic situations – especially fatal shootings. Joe quipped that Max wouldn't have liked it, that he would have been better off in the army, working for the waterboarding unit.

Max had laughed then and the memory made him smile now.

For a moment.

Then it hurt him deep – real deep. Like he'd burst a bunch of stitches somewhere inside.

Joe was gone for good.

He noticed the air con had come back on. When they brought

71

him in it was cold in the room. They'd turned it off and the place had become stiflingly hot. More tired playbook. Now it was cool again, but comfortably so. The light above had become a little brighter.

He guessed they were about to start questioning him.

A tall, thickset, olive-skinned Latino detective walked in with a fistful of forms. Wavy salt-and-pepper hair, pocked skin, tired eyes. Late forties, maybe older. Dark-grey suit, white shirt, grey tie with black diamonds on it.

'I'm Lieutenant Perez. Miami Beach Homicide.' He held out a large hand. 'Sorry for your loss. Joe Liston was a good man and a good cop.'

'You know him?' Max asked. Wrong tense, he realised immediately, but for him bereavement came in short, sharp increments. It would take a while to admit and then accept that Joe was gone.

'We worked together a few times,' said Perez.

Which meant Joe had probably called him when a tourist had come to harm in mainland Miami – perhaps an out-of-towner trying to cop in Liberty City or Little Haiti, maybe throwing in some patronising rap jargon and gang-signing for good measure, getting well out of their depth in the process. Joe had been joking about the Beach police for ten years. He called them 'The Baywatch Cops'. All they had to do was look good in uniform and save people from drowning in sex and drugs – and then only if they called out for help.

'I'm sorry to have kept you waiting. We had to eliminate you as a suspect. Took some time. We had a lot of witnesses to talk to.'

'Have you ID'd the shooter?'

'Physically, yes. We've got a good description. He got away, but we're on him,' said Perez.

'Black guy, over six feet tall, hare lip, bird-patterned shirt?'

'That's right. You got a look at him too?'

'No,' Max said. Perez frowned. 'He's the guy who killed Eldon Burns.'

'How do you know?' Perez glanced at the camera above Max.

'Same MO. I've been looking into Eldon's murder.'

'You've been looking into Eldon's murder? No disrespect, Max, but you haven't been a cop in near thirty years. Which means you're a civilian. Which means you're interfering with an official police investigation.'

'No disrespect, Lieutenant, but it's not much of an investigation.'

'What do you mean?'

'The guys working Eldon Burns aren't exactly being thorough.'

'How so?'

'Did you recover a shell casing in a glassine bag from Joe's body?'

'Yes, we did.'

'I gave that to him tonight. The owner of Swopes bookstore gave it to me. The store's a few blocks down from Eldon's gym. A few minutes after the shooter killed Eldon, he almost ran over a homeless guy called White Flight in the alley behind the store. White Flight tried to attack the shooter in his car—'

'You got a make on the shooter's *car*?' Perez was surprised. He looked at the camera again. Max was tempted to ask who was watching them on the monitor, but he just wanted to get out of there as fast as possible.

'A brown Sierra,' he said. 'I talked to White Flight in hospital today. The shooter put a bullet in his throat, but didn't kill him.'

'White Flight?' Perez made a note. 'That's the name he's registered under, at the hospital?'

'Yeah. He told me the shooter wasn't driving the car. He has an accomplice.'

'That we already know,' said Perez.

'How?'

'Her prints are all over the casings.'

73

'*Her* prints? The shooter's male.'

'The prints aren't.'

'Is the accomplice's name Vanetta Brown?'

Perez looked stunned.

'Joe tell you that?'

'He mentioned that name right before he was killed. He didn't tell me anything else,' said Max. 'Who is she?'

'We think she's behind this.'

'Who is she?' Max repeated.

'I guess it was before your time. It's certainly before mine,' said Perez. 'Broad strokes: she ran a group called the Black Jacobins in the sixties. Based in Miami. They were like the Black Panthers of Florida. She shot and killed a cop in 1968. Escaped to Cuba where Castro gave her asylum. Up until now, we believed she was still there.'

That didn't make sense to Max. No sense at all. He was about to voice his doubts, but Perez read his face and held up a hand.

'I've already told you way more than I should, Max. I'm sure you remember the policy. Now, I need to take your statement.'

Perez placed a witness form on the table and uncapped a pen.

'Why don't you talk me through what happened tonight. And tell me what else you know. For the record.'

Max rewound back to the moment he'd met Joe outside Mariposa, Liston sitting there at the table, his shirt untucked to hide his gun, jacket slung over the back of the chair, his face a sea of turmoil. Then Max went forward: Joe's eye imploding, the back of his head spraying the diners behind him, the salt and pepper shakers flipping up in the air when Joe fell backwards, the plates of food crashing about his head, lettuce spinning in rivulets of blood. Perez wrote everything down.

Ninety minutes later they were done. Perez numbered the eleven pages Max's statement had run to. Then he gave Max his card.

'Now please do me, the police and yourself a great big favour,' he said. 'Keep well out of this. Let us handle it. I know Joe was

74

your friend. And I know Eldon was too. But this isn't your investigation or your responsibility. We'll find the killer. And we'll find Vanetta Brown. We don't need you tear-assin' around Miami too, you understand?'

'Sure,' said Max, but he was already thinking – about Eldon, about Joe and about Vanetta Brown.

8

It was past 1 a.m. when Max pulled up outside the Liston family home in Biscayne Park. The lights were on.

Nate Rollins, the family pastor, opened the door. He'd married Joe and Lena and baptised their children. He greeted Max with a handshake that started firm and hardened into an unbreakable grip as he looked at Max without speaking a word, his eyes silvering, his jowly face quaking with emotion and pent-up grief. Max imagined the pastor had been there all night, stoically soaking up the sorrow and dispensing what comfort he could, all the while holding down his own feelings. He'd obviously needed this moment of release. They stood together at the entrance as the old man regained his composure. He took Max's arm and led him inside.

Everyone was gathered in the living room, over thirty people stood or sat around, considerably diminishing the large and usually open space, pulling the walls in and the ceiling down. Max recognised them all by sight, if not by name – cousins, friends and colleagues he'd met at parties and get-togethers. The halting, respectful conversations petered out completely as heads turned his way. No one could meet his eye. It wasn't out of shame or hostility. It was that everyone in the room knew he'd been with Joe when he was murdered, that Max had seen it happen, that it could have been him instead, that death had missed him by inches. No one had the right words for that. And no one wanted to be the first to say the wrong thing.

Max searched the room for Lena and the children. He

negotiated the space before him as if it were a narrow, wind-blown ledge above a deep drop. Bodies stepped back and away. He caught sight of Joe's brown-leather La-Z-Boy recliner, big enough to sit two people comfortably, but empty. The flatscreen TV playing CNN's election coverage on mute. His eyes roamed the oak-panelled walls hung with plaques, cer-tificates, commendations and plenty of pictures – one of the largest being of Joe and Bruce Springsteen backstage at the AmericanAirlines Arena three years before. Max had taken that. He remembered how tongue-tied Joe had been when he finally met the Boss. Joe had wanted to tell Springsteen how much his music meant to him, but the words got stuck in his throat and all he could manage was a nervous smile and a handshake. To his credit, Bruce thanked Joe for coming and seemed to mean it. Joe's daughters later asked if the picture was of him and Max when 'Uncle Max had hair'. That made Joe boom with laughter.

The whole family had gathered around the long sofa. Lena sat in the middle with her arms around her teenage twin daughters either side of her, the girls' heads on her lap. Two of Joe's sons – Dwayne and Dean – were perched on either arm of the sofa, while behind them all stood Jet in his dress blues. He was the spit of his father, forty years ago. It was uncanny and discomfiting seeing him there. Max was reminded of the first time he'd met Joe. Eldon had introduced them in the locker room.

'Max, this is your new partner,' Eldon had said. 'Look, listen and learn. Listen to Liston – *hell!* – I could be in advertising.'

Eldon and Joe. Both dead.

Max took them all in, Joe's surviving family, his legacy, proof that there was some goodness in the world. Lena's eyes lit up when she saw Max, as though he was the person she'd wanted to see more than anyone else.

He didn't know what to do.

Where to start?

What to say?

They'd taught him how to handle death as a cop. And they'd taught him well. He'd learned to be familiar with it, to expect it to be everywhere he was likely to be: behind a locked door, round a dark corner, under the dashboard of a pulled-over car. Then he learned to greet it in the morning when he left his house and give it the finger at night when he got back. Eventually, he grew indifferent to it. They didn't teach him that. They didn't need to. It happened naturally, the loss of visceral feeling, the jadedness in the face of horror. Death was something that happened to other people: people whose doors he knocked on to tell them their missing loved one was dead, cops who died on the job. Other people.

The silence was stifling. It wasn't even quiet; it was the polar opposite of noisy, a spot where sound simply didn't exist and had no possibility of coming into being.

He opened his mouth to say something but nothing came out. His throat was sealed, his tongue a concrete sculpture. His lips formed the words he thought he wanted to say like a fish drowning in air.

Then Ashley, one of the twins, got up from her mother's side and came over and wrapped her arms around him. She held him tightly. He bent his head to kiss the top of hers. A tear he hadn't felt dropped from his eye into her hair. Ashley's sister Briony joined them, hugging Max with as much force from the other side. Then Lena came over and hugged him and buried her head in his neck. And the three boys closed around them. Gradually, the people in the room added themselves to the family and things went dark around him – not a mirthless lonely dark, but a respectful one, a dipping of lights.

He was back in time with Joe in the locker room. He remembered already being slightly awed by his partner-to-be: the way Joe had looked at Eldon, not in that deferential, ass-kissing way everyone else in the department did, but with professional suspicion and wariness, and just about enough respect to get away with it. Joe was always polite, even to racists. That was his thing, his way with people. Never get down to their level, always look down on it from several leagues up. 'Please' and 'thank you' to everyone. He remembered the first proper words Joe had said in the prowl car: 'You Eldon Burns's boy, the fighter? Don'tchu expect no special treatment from me, Punchy. In these streets, everyone hates us. We our own race out here. You dig?' They were black and white in a town that was black or white, when it was all a big deal. Black cops didn't trust Joe because he rolled with Max. White cops didn't trust Max because he was learning from a black cop. Not even a badass legend like Eldon Burns could level that playing field. The divisions had made them close, the job and the shit they went through as good as welded them. He remembered times they'd got drunk and stoned, the tail they'd chased, the intimacies they'd shared. The cases they'd solved. He remembered laughing a lot. He recalled the arguments, about music and politics. Bruce Springsteen versus Curtis Mayfield. Nixon, Ford, Carter, Reagan, Bush the Father, Bush the Son. They'd finally both agreed on Obama.

And he was weeping now, safe in all that abundant, womb-like warmth, alone and in public, surrounded by more love than he'd felt in a long time. It made him feel sadder for Joe, who would never know any of this again.

9

Max went home in the rain. A straight and steady downpour, with barely a breath of wind behind it. It was 4.30 a.m. and Washington Avenue was busy with people dashing out of clubs, jackets and handbags over heads, jumping into cars and cabs and those rent-by-the-hour, block-long white limos with blacked-out windows. Drunk and drugged-up partygoers stumbled along the sidewalk, hand in hand, shouting, screaming, singing, laughing, falling over, oblivious to the weather. A bum with a tattered umbrella was making like Fred Astaire. A man in military uniform stood to attention, saluting a flashing neon Stars and Stripes in a souvenir store. A girl in a silver dress puked her guts out while a man tenderly held the hair off her face with one hand and her shoes in the other. He guessed they were Brits. A dull, repetitive dance beat thudded away at the air, a single bass note making the raindrops on his windshield jump and run, run and jump. It sounded as if every single one of the clubs was playing the same damn song in sync, each note meshing into a kind of anthem for twenty-first-century Western youth – all computer-generated, wordless, voiceless pre-fab music celebrating cataclysm without deliverance, marching music for sheep.

He had to hit the brakes hard as a line of people spilled out into the street in front of him, conga dancing under a single sheet of clear plastic, close to fifty or sixty of them, men and women in Halloween costumes bobbing up and down across the street like a translucent, headless Chinese New Year dragon. The car

80

behind sounded its horn. A woman in the procession turned, unzipped the front of her sequinned dress and shook big, tassel-covered tits at him – only, she had implants, so it looked like the tits were shaking her.

Sitting in his Acura, waiting for the lumpy human snake to slither off, Max felt like an alien in a space pod, visiting this slightly threatening and thoroughly unwelcoming place for the first time. He couldn't imagine staying here much longer. His time was almost up. He could feel it. He and this town were done. It didn't want him. It had no place for him.

No easy way to put it. Miami was fucked. The high times had peaked. Sure, it had always had cycles, its culture of death and rebirth, twenty-year booms and ten-year busts; but something told him it wouldn't recover from this one, that he was watching the last big party before the end of something major. People were boogieing on credit-card-thin ice atop a vast dark ruinous hole, hastening its collapse with every frenetic stamp of their designer heels. But they hadn't noticed because they didn't care; and if they'd heard the cracks forming, they'd just pushed their dinky white *i*Headphones in a little deeper and turned the music up louder. His generation had known hardship early, and because of that, they'd bounced back. This pampered, overindulged, maxed-out bunch of pricks knew nothing. When they hit rock bottom, they'd probably mistake it for another dancefloor.

The city had been here before, many a time. And he'd been there for some of it, its unwitting barometer, riding out the down-wave, surfing the up-wave, adjusting his eyes from daz-zling to dark and back again. He'd been born at the time when Miami was America's playground, a tourist magnet. He'd grown up when the playground had gone to seed and the art deco hotels closed. The city had recast itself as 'God's waiting room', the hotels had reopened as quiet retirement homes for East Coast Jews, the garment district refugees, heading for the Promised Land of sunshine and low rent and death. He'd been a cop in the dead-zone seventies, when the Freedom Tower was a homeless shelter and Ocean Drive a refugee camp. That same decade he'd gun-battled the Cocaine Cowboys whose multi-millions made the city fat and corrupt. During the busted-flush comedown that followed he'd been a private detective, looking for the abducted, the kidnapped and the runaways, their disappearances always dollar-indexed. Then he'd watched film crews renovate one derelict hotel after another as a TV show – *Miami Vice* – fed a primetime version of his home town so removed from reality it made him laugh. Within a year, the tourists were flocking to the movie-set hotels, paying top dollar to swagger down the same corridors Don Johnson had. The dying Jews were supplanted by dying gay men, Aids sufferers ostracised by the richest, most medically advanced nation on earth, who'd come to Miami to die somewhere they could afford to live. They breathed their last gasps into Miami's defunct club culture, reinflating it, making it fashionable again. When he came out of prison, he saw their legacy in full bloom: South Beach all hip and glitzy, back to its fifties place-to-be pomp, straight with a gay edge, a fashionista magnet presided over by its crown prince, Gianni Versace, from his gaudy mansion on Ocean Drive. When Versace was gunned down on his doorstep in 1997, the party didn't stop. It just changed frocks. Versace's memory was toasted and then drowned in Cristal, the gay scene relocated to Fort Lauderdale and his old home became a luxury hotel. Class gave way to vulgarity but there was no one around to point out the great big difference. So Miami was long overdue another slump. It would be slow and painful. The neon would cede to darkness, the noise to silence, and the waves would no longer hum lullabies but make hissing erosive sounds as they ate away at the pre-fab postcard-perfect beaches.

He didn't want to be around for any of that.

He didn't know where he'd move. He had nowhere in mind. Just a vague notion of what might suit him best – somewhere quiet and warm, without too many people to fuck things up. Maybe the Utah desert.

He thought of Joe's blood on Lincoln Road and how all trace of it would most likely have been washed clean away now. The restaurant would reopen in a few days' time and people would sit and eat at the very spot his best friend had died. Life would go on regardless, the infinite cycle.

10

Home. Kitchen.

Back in his drinking days he would have crawled deep inside a bottle for comfort. Now all he had for kicks and relief was coffee.

He turned on the espresso machine and watched the Bustelo drip thick and black into a chrome cup; the badass brew, strong enough to wake the dead.

He was tired and running on fumes, eyes red and puffy, vision blurry, weariness deep in his bones, skin heavy on his back like chainmail.

He could have laid down on the floor and gone straight to sleep, conked out for his regulation four to five hours. He could have stopped everything and made space for grieving, for reflection, straightening things out in his head, being there for the family, whatever they wanted, whenever they wanted it.

But that would have to come later.

He had to find out about Vanetta Brown. Who she was and why she'd had Joe and Eldon killed . . . If she really had.

He wasn't sure.

It didn't fully fit.

Why kill Eldon *and* Joe? They'd been complete opposites. Joe was by the book. Eldon lived by his own rules: he'd bullied, blackmailed and intimidated his way up the ranks and then run both his department and the city in much the same way.

Max couldn't see the common ground, outside of the fact that Joe had worked for Eldon.

Plus, why wait so long?

In his office, he checked his email.

Just the one message, but completely unexpected.

It was from Jack Quinones, a pal of Joe's, and a former friend of Max's. Quinones was the only Fed he ever got along with – back in the day. They'd worked cases together and shared information without going through rolls of bureaucratic red tape and jurisdictional one-upmanship.

Now they didn't get along at all. Quinones despised him – as did everyone he'd known in law enforcement, outside of MTF. He'd never fully understood why Joe had stuck by him. He wasn't sure Joe knew – *had known* – himself either. When Max had asked him, Joe had shrugged and taken his time scrounging up some words. In the end all he'd said was: 'Hitler had friends too.' That hadn't exactly made him feel better, but it had made him laugh.

Max,
Heard about Joe. Very sincere condolences.
We need to talk. Drop me a line asap.
JQ

They'd last seen each other by accident at Joe's house around the time Max was setting up Pétion-Mingus Investigations. Max had arrived early to see Joe. Quinones was there and he hadn't even bothered to be polite. He looked at Max with disgust and left. He knew what every cop in Miami knew – that Max had killed in cold blood and walked free after seven years, that Eldon Burns had pulled strings and favours, that he'd leaned on the DA and paid for the judge's house. Would Quinones have liked him more if he'd been doing life? No. But that wasn't the point.

*

85

Max went on the web and searched for 'Vanetta Brown'.

The information was scant – six hits on twenty-three pages.

The first two linked to essays about the Black Power movement, with very brief mentions of 'the Black Jacobins in Miami'. They were described, almost dismissively, as a fringe group, one that didn't share the separatist ideals of the Black Panthers – 'Panther Cubs', 'Black Flower Power' and 'Age of Aquarius Niggaz' were some of the phrases used. The pieces mentioned Vanetta Brown killing a Miami police detective called Dennis Peck in 1968 and absconding to Cuba, seemingly the only thing that she did of note.

Next he found a site called 'Cuba: Gangsta's Paradise', which listed ninety-four US criminals given asylum by the Castro regime between the 1960s and the 1980s. The list was subdivided into five categories: cop-killers, murderers, hijackers, robbers and fraudsters.

The name 'Vanetta Brown' headed the cop-killer roll. Alongside it, a blue link: 'DT'. Max clicked on the letters and the 'FBI's Most Wanted' site came up in a separate window. It categorised Brown as a 'Domestic Terrorist' and briefly detailed her crime, present location ('Havana – unconfirmed') and the government bounty on her head: '$500,000'.

Then he came to Justice4Dennis.com – a site devoted to the memory of Dennis Peck. The home page presented an official police photograph of Peck in dress blues – a fresh-faced, ginger-haired twenty-two-year-old with freckles, dimples and blue eyes sparkling with that familiar rookie glow, right before they hit the street and got the shine scared out of them. Max felt those eyes could have been his own, a mirror throwing all that unfulfilled potential and all those broken promises back at him with a single question: why had he fucked things up so badly?

Below the picture were Peck's dates of birth and death: 'November 9, 1934 – June 4, 1968'.

Thirty-three years old when he died.

Max found an account of Peck's murder on the site. In 1968, Vanetta Brown had fled during a police raid on the Black

Jacobins's headquarters in Overtown. Dennis Peck had been one of the detectives involved in the raid. Four eyewitnesses described seeing Brown shoot him as she escaped through a back window.

The raid netted a big cache of heroin, money and guns.

Captain Eldon Burns and Lieutenant Abe Watson led the operation.

Vanetta Brown went into hiding and evaded a nationwide manhunt. In 1971 she resurfaced in Cuba, where Fidel Castro described her as an innocent victim of racist, imperialist America. They were happy to give her a permanent refuge, he said. She was granted asylum.

Peck's family and colleagues formed the Justice4Dennis movement, devoted to bringing Brown back to the US to stand trial for her crime. They'd been writing to Castro every year since 1972, requesting her extradition. The family also wrote to Pope John Paul II in 1997, asking him to raise the matter with Castro when he visited the country the following year. No dice. Castro hadn't budged.

The site included a slideshow of family photographs: Dennis Peck graduating from police academy, on his wedding day, and multiple portraits of him with his daughters, Wendy and Thelma. Wendy was the eldest. Images of her wearing her father's police hat, playing with a toy police car, sat at the wheel of a real one, complete with a pair of sunglasses too big for her head. Then came her first Communion, followed by a family Christmas on the beach. The last photograph was of both daughters, now grown up, standing by Peck's grave, holding hands.

The final search link was the *Miami Herald*'s online picture archive, where Max found two related photographs, the first of Vanetta in 1967 – a posed, black-and-white studio shot. She could have been a model or a blaxploitation movie queen. She was striking – dark skin, high cheekbones, full lips on a wide mouth – but so angry and defiant with it, any suggestion of sensuality was choked out of her features.

The second image was a US government photo-portrait of Wendy Peck, taken in 2006 and issued to the press on the day of her appointment as head of Miami Homeland Security. Shoulder-length auburn hair, blue eyes and a smile more formal than friendly. She favoured her father.

Max looked over his notes.

Questions:

Joe – what was his involvement? He'd been in Patrol back then.

What were Robbery-Homicide detectives Eldon Burns and Abe Watson doing on a drugs raid?

He paused there.

This wasn't going anywhere good.

He knew Eldon had been neck-deep in shady shit from the jump, doing the bidding of Victor Marko, the political fixer. It wouldn't have surprised him in the least if the Black Jacobins bust had been a proto-MTF fit-up. Find a perp, plant the evidence, arrest or kill on sight. Above all: *make it fit, make it stick.*

But Joe?

If Max left it here, he'd never know. And that would be for the best. Ignorance was bliss and he'd smile with the best of them. He could still preserve his memories.

Yes, he *could* do that.

And spend his life getting eaten up by doubt, by the not-knowing?

Yes . . . at a push, he could do that: his memories were all he had left now.

He looked back at his notes.

He'd written 'FBI/COINTELPRO', and circled it twice.

Max tapped out an email to Jack Quinones: *What do you know about Vanetta Brown?*

He sent it and printed off the *Herald* pictures. He took two prints of Vanetta Brown's studio shot. He stuck one on the board in his office.

He was dog-tired, but he knew he wouldn't get any sleep, that he'd just lie there seeing Joe get his brains blown out right in front of him.

He took a shower and made more coffee.

He turned on the TV. Local news reported Joe's murder and issued a description of the shooter. No mention of Vanetta Brown.

Then he thought of Emerson Prescott.

Prescott still owed him for the surveillance job. The sum of $5837 – plus $1200 expenses. That it had turned out to be bogus and he'd been made to look and feel a fool was neither here nor there. He'd played his part in whatever sad-sack postmodern porno pantomime Prescott had going on, and he was going to collect.

He needed to take his mind off Joe. There was nothing he could do right now but leave it to the police, be there for the family . . . and find out some more about Vanetta Brown.

He went back to his office and fed the Zurich Hotel DVD into his computer.

11

Max had never been into porn, never got the appeal. He found it pathetic and grubby, the preserve of the complacent and sexually short-circuited. His was a childhood-old repulsion. He'd seen his first strokemag when he was ten. It had been lying open in the middle of the sidewalk. Two thick rectangular humps of glossy paper with a faintly plastic smell. The mag was called *Farmers' Daughters* and consisted of gyno shots of fat Midwestern girls sprawled on bales of hay. He felt like having a wash and then burning the shower down after seeing it.

So he'd never used strokemags. Not even tame ones like *Playboy* and *Penthouse*; not even in his teens. He had boxing instead. Eldon Burns used to buy his fighters hookers every time they won a trophy. The night he won the South Florida Golden Gloves, he popped his cherry on Eldon's dime. When the hooker found out it was his first time, she stroked his face and hugged him and told him her real name was Evangeline. She said she'd always wanted to be remembered in a good way by someone. He never forgot her, even though for all he knew she said the same thing to all her virgins. Nine years later he busted her on Washington Avenue. He promised himself to let her go with a warning if she recognised him. When she didn't, he took her in. After she'd been booked and processed, he told Joe about their shared past. Joe laughed and called him a heartless asshole. Truth was, the sex hadn't been all that great. For a while he'd even wondered what all the fuss was about, until he started winning more titles. And getting girlfriends.

90

These days porn was everywhere, diluted and used to sell everything from soap to music. And it reminded him of prison. Porn had wallpapered practically every cell in Attica. Everyone jerked off in the Big House. It was the only thing they had in common – apart from the fact that they were massive fuck-ups. Masturbation was the great leveller. Blacks, whites, Latinos, Asians; lifers, short-timers; big men and their bitches. Everybody did it. His cellmate, Velasquez, had elevated it to a kind of theatre. He painted the nails of his left hand red and let them grow, relieving himself with the manicured paw after sitting on the hand for an hour to deaden it. When he closed his eyes, he explained, it was almost like his *mamacita* Melyssa was right there pulling his pud. She gave the lousiest handjob in Harlem, he said. But he still used to cry when he was finished. That was some sad shit.

As the film started Max realised it was the first time he'd thought of Velasquez since leaving prison. They'd spent every day of seven years and change together. He even liked him, as much as he allowed himself to like anyone in jail. Velasquez was several sets of irritating, but he didn't care that Max had been a cop. Mingus wondered what he was doing now. Probably back inside, jerking off.

The DVD started with a shaky shot of an American Airlines plane coming in to land at Miami International, sunlight flashing in and out of the frame, as if it had been filmed on a cellphone. The picture briefly cut out. He saw a bright flash on the screen and heard a garbled noise – a short, low-pitched moan like a cassette tape of bass notes being chewed up. Then the picture returned and he heard the unmistakable crepitations of a needle on vinyl. As the aircraft's wheels bounced on the runway, the music kicked in. Mid-tempo, mid-eighties generic rock bombast – every instrument turned up way too loud, echoing electronic drums and guitars wailing like suffering cats – bringing back memories of music videos of gurning men in Davy Crockett mullets and Sonny Crockett half-beards. To his ear, the music seemed better suited to an action movie sound-track from the era, something starring Dolph Lundgren or some other semi-literate Eurotrash beefcake. But out of nowhere, a saxophone undercut the synth metal with sleazy honkings, bonding film to genre.

What was it about sax and sex in movies? Surely, more than just a misplaced vowel.

On the screen the woman he'd known as Fabiana Prescott strutted out of arrivals in high heels, a sprayed-on white suit, big sunglasses and a broad-brimmed floppy black hat with a white polka dot band. No bags. The camera zoomed in and out on Fabiana's pneumatic tits and round ass. She went up to the chauffeur, who was stood close to the exit in cap and black suit.

Está usted mi chófer?

Yes, mam. I haf big car.

The following ten minutes comprised a medley of scene-setting (cue palm trees, the beach, girls on the beach, girls under palm trees) intercut with front and side shots of a Lincoln Town Car, and interiors of Fabiana and the driver exchanging suggestive looks. Plenty of zooms down Fabiana's cleavage, close-ups of her giving come-hither stares and licking her collagen-plumped lips. The chauffeur arched a brow and loosened his tie, as he pretended to drive the car, which was apparently stationary and parked next to a convenience store. Max guessed the budget didn't extend to CGI.

The sequence ended with the limo stopping outside Tides on Ocean Drive. Fabiana got out and walked up the stairs. At the top she turned and beckoned suggestively to the chauffeur leaning against the car. That last touch made Max smile. Every time a movie set in Miami featured a hotel sequence where one or more of the characters was rich and classy, it was filmed at Tides.

Now the couple were in familiar territory, getting it on in Room 30 of the Zurich. Max recognised Fabiana's dialogue by tone and intonation, having committed every vocal inflection to memory when he'd timed them.

There were only about forty more minutes of this crap to sit through and that pleased him no end.

Eventually when they were done they laid on the bed, sweat basted and breathing hard. Fabiana told the chauffeur he had a magic wand.

Call me Harry Focker, baby.

She laughed shallowly, but loudly and on cue.

They took turns to shower. The camera stayed in the room and filmed the steamed-up bathroom mirror through the open door. It didn't move. He saw the chauffeur's feet. He had thick, opaque toenails. A couple of flash cuts and that snippet of sound broke up the monotony.

Fabiana dressed and left. The chauffeur went in the shower and closed the door. The camera didn't move.

The screen went black.

Max was angry, but he didn't know why or at whom.

Why the fuck hadn't he noticed anything?

Simple – because there was nothing *to* notice. Everything about the case had seemed straightforward. Trophy wife cheats on sugar daddy. Sugar daddy wants photographic proof. Max had done his job. Or, rather, he'd played his part.

He weighed up the options.

He couldn't afford to forget about the money Prescott owed him. He had bills to pay. And he wanted the answer to a simple question: why had Prescott picked him? Was it random or design?

He called Prescott's number and got a looped recorded message.

'Sorry. This number is unavailable.'

Max rang off. Was Prescott even who he said he was? His 'wife' certainly wasn't.

12

'Moved out last week. Eight months left on the lease. All paid up. Weird,' Dan Souza told Max. Souza was the letting agent of the Tequesta Building, where Prescott's practice was located on the tenth floor.

Everything was still there – furniture, computer, phone, plants, water cooler, the magazines on the table – but the place had the definite feel of abandonment to it. Max noticed it as soon as he stepped out of the elevator: the silence, the way his steps seemed to echo about the walls, the way he could hear every creak and pop of his body. Which was pretty much how he felt in his own home when he woke up some mornings. Not this morning though. Because he hadn't woken up. He hadn't been to sleep. And he hadn't changed his clothes, showered, shaved or even brushed his teeth.

Souza had arrived a few minutes after him, pen and clipboard in hand, a who-the-fuck-are-you look on his face as soon as he saw Max.

'What did he say to you?' Max asked.

'Just that he was closing down the business and moving on. He told me to keep everything. There must be, like, at least $15,000 worth of stuff here and in the office. And I haven't even seen inside the other offices yet.'

Souza was a short guy who looked at the world through steel-rimmed glasses. Late thirties. Blue blazer, beige pants, black loafers. His hair was too black, his skin too tanned and his teeth too white. His handshake overcompensated for soft hands. He wore a wedding ring. Not that it meant he was really married.

'Are you a cop, sir?' he asked Max.

'Private detective.'

'You'd been a cop, you would've "badged" me, right?'

Too much *CSI*, thought Max. Probably believed cops told people to 'lawyer up' too. Only last month Joe had been complaining about the new generation of cops talking just like cops did on TV, imitating the imitators.

'What's your business here?' he asked.

'I was working for Prescott. He didn't tell me he was leaving.'

'He owe you?'

'Yes,' said Max. 'He owe *you*?'

'No.'

'He leave a forwarding address?'

'No.'

'Do you have a home address for him? Landline?'

'Just his cell and email. Only I can't give those out. Even if you were a cop, you'd need a warrant.'

'How did you meet him?' Max asked.

'Same way I meet all potential customers. He called me, made an appointment, looked around the premises, paid his deposit right there and then. Easiest sale I ever did. I mean, I didn't even have to spiel the place.'

'Cash or cheque?'

'We're not a cash business, Mr Mingus,' said Souza, affronted.

'What bank was the cheque drawn on?'

'I can't remember that. And I'm under no obligation to tell you either.'

'Of course you're not,' said Max. He didn't want to lose him, didn't want to get kicked out.

But . . .

Christ – was this guy a prick.

The fun I would have had with your petty bureaucratic ass, Max thought with a hint of nostalgia. His mind went back to his

95

cop days, and he imagined bracing this idiot, shaking the information loose with implied threats. He'd never had to get rough with these white-collar jerks. They took one look at him and saw everything they had to lose – past, present and future – flashing by, and they gave up the goods. Of course, he couldn't do that now. He'd get locked up for assault and this little asshole would sue him. But a badge made a difference.

'Did he come to see you alone?'

'Yeah,' Souza said, impatiently manipulating the clipboard, keen to get along and tot up the contents of the office for a fire sale.

'You ask for references?'

'Benjamin Franklin's good enough for me. Look, the cheque cleared. Space doesn't come cheap here.'

'How much?'

'This? $250,000 for the year. And he paid in advance.'

That was a lot of money to spend on a scam, Max thought. But what was the scam? Paying him to waste his time? Was Prescott using him as an alibi for something?

'Is that normal? Paying it all upfront?'

'No. It isn't. In fact, it's the first time that's happened to me. And I hope it won't be the last.'

'It occur to you this guy could've been a criminal?'

'I thought like that every time, I'd be out of a job,' he said.

Typical Miami business logic. Back when the cocainistos had invested their money, they put it in property. No one cared. Most of the skyline, Midtown to Downtown, had been built on coke and baptised in blood. No matter how glamorous and alluring it looked at night, dressed up in its twinkling lights and neon washes and spotlights, Max couldn't help but think of gigantic tombstones whenever he saw it.

'Did you ever visit? You know, to check up?'

'Yes, as a courtesy, two weeks after they moved in.'

'Who was here?'

'Mr Prescott, obviously, a visitor, and the receptionist.'

'The receptionist who looked like jailbait?'

Souza blushed and nodded.

'See any of these people here?' Max gave him a couple of stills of Fabiana and Cortland.

Souza looked at them. Fabiana didn't register, but he frowned at the chauffeur's picture. Looked closer. Frown eased.

'The guy was here,' he said. 'He was the visitor.'

'Did you talk to him?'

'No.'

'What was he doing?'

'Sitting in reception.'

'What did you and Prescott talk about?'

'"Is everything OK? Lights working? Water running? Toilet flushing?" That kind of thing. He answered yes to everything. Like I said, he paid upfront, in full.'

'What did he tell you he did?'

'He said he was an architect.'

Max chuckled and shook his head.

'He wasn't?'

'He told me he was a cosmetic dentist.'

'Is he some kind of criminal?'

'Maybe,' said Max. 'I don't know. Say, you mind if I have a look around? I'll only be a few minutes.'

'Be my guest.'

Max went into Prescott's office. It was almost as before, except that the desk was bare. The laptop and phone were gone. He checked the desk drawers and filing cabinet. All empty. Nothing.

Back in reception he star-69'd the phone. No outbound calls made.

He checked the answering machine. He heard the four messages he'd left for Prescott.

'I don't ... get it,' said Souza, flustered, bewildered. His skin had lost its glow and there was perspiration on his upper lip. He'd seen the empty offices. 'Who was he?'

'I don't know yet. But he had a lot of money to fool the two of us. This could be nothing – some harmless eccentric with more money and time than sense and purpose.'

'But you don't believe that?'

'No.'

Yet what did he believe? The whole thing had been about role playing – Fabiana, the younger trophy wife fucking the chauffeur; Prescott, the wealthy older cuckold who hires a private eye to catch them in the act. It was a classic, worn-at-the-heel scenario. Like a bad movie. Or a *porn* movie. What if that was Prescott's intention, shooting his own porno, only with a real private detective either in it or somehow involved? *Gonzo shit*, he'd said he wanted. Maybe Fabiana wasn't even Prescott's wife, but a porn actress.

'What do you suggest I do?' Souza asked.

'Nothing. You didn't do anything wrong. But you could let me know his bank details.'

Max handed him his card. Souza studied it.

'How do I know you're a real private detective, Mr Mingus?'

'You don't.'

13

Lamar Swope was stood behind the counter of his bookstore talking to a pretty woman when Max walked in. She was smiling, hanging on his every word with a sparkle in her eyes.

'When Napoleon invaded Egypt in 1798, he came across the Great Sphinx of Giza,' Lamar was explaining, holding a coffee table book open in front of them both. 'See how the Sphinx in this painting has distinct black features? The theory goes that when Napoleon saw the huge black face looking down at him, and the great pyramid of Khafre behind it, he realised that black people had built it. He couldn't handle the thought of that because back then black people were thought of as fit only for slavery or slaughter. So he had his soldiers blast the Sphinx's face off.'

Max smiled to himself. He knew that was a bullshit theory, sometimes also posited on the British and the Arabs. Scientific tests had shown that the Sphinx lost its nose – and beard – some four hundred years before Napoleon. The only debate was whether it had been caused by wind or water. He'd read about Egyptian history when in prison, after Sandra had begun planning a round-the-world trip for them both after he got out. Egypt had been on their itinerary.

Lamar acknowledged Max with a quick upward tilt of the chin. Max cast another glance at the woman, whose hips spilled over the edges of a stool she was practically driving into the ground. Every breath she took stretched her dark-blue Obama T-shirt critically close to bursting point.

Max searched through the bookshelves for something about

99

Vanetta Brown. The single other customer in the store, a man with long grey dreadlocks and purple sunglasses, was leafing through a book about Tookie Williams, shaking his locks and tutting disapprovingly at every page. He looked up and caught Max's eye.

'I don't get this store,' he growled. 'I come in here looking for something on W. E. B. DuBois and Lamar don't have nuttin'. Instead he got *five* different books about this scumbag. And what did he do? He founded the Crips. The Crips've kilt mo' black people than the KKK and the poh-lice put together. And this guy, this writer? Talks about him like he a *heee-row!*'

'Maybe the reason those books are there is that no one's buying them. People feel the same way you do.'

'Nah man.' The dread put the book back. 'Reason this crap be here instead of somethin' 'bout a real hero is 'cause Lamar gotta *eat!*'

The dread walked off, nodded to Lamar, who nodded back without breaking his flow of conversation.

'People say Napoleon's downfall was brought about by his failure to conquer Russia, but he also got his ass kicked by Toussaint L'Ouverture in Haiti. That probably hurt more. Here's this guy, meant to be a *military genius*, and he goes and gets out-thought and outfought by an escaped slave in his own colony. Imagine how that played back home?'

'That's just amazin', baby, you knowin' so much,' the woman sighed.

'I do my best.' Lamar excused himself.

He came over to Max, took him by the arm and walked him over to another part of the store.

'You see White Flight?' he asked.

'Yeah, I did.'

'How is he?'

'He won't be able to talk again, but he'll live.'

'Some life,' Lamar said. 'What can I do for you today?'

'Have you heard of Vanetta Brown?'

'Of course. Saw her speak a couple of times in Overtown,' he said.

'What was that like?'

'Inspiring. Kind of the way Barack is now, only angrier – way angrier. But then times were different.'

'Sure.'

'You know what surprised me though, when I saw her? It wasn't all just black people. White people were there too. Not big numbers, but enough to make you notice. Decent, committed people. Not like those typical hypocrites you get nowadays either – you know, act all liberal, tell you they feel your pain, talk all that hip hop jive, then when their cars get jacked and their daughters start steppin' out with Mister Tibbs, they put on the white sheets and want to bring back segregation.'

'Principles only count when they're inconvenient,' said Max.

'Word!' Lamar grinned. 'Why do you want to know about Vanetta?'

'Background.'

'Background for what? That thing you're lookin' into?'

'Yeah.'

'Think she had something to do with it?'

'I don't know.'

'Far as anyone knows, she's in Cuba.'

'I know. Let's just say I'm tracking down a lead.'

'Sounds like someone's pullin' on yours. Anyway, I do have a book on Vanetta here, if you're interested,' said Lamar.

'Sure.'

'Only ... I ain't strictly supposed to have it. So if I sell it to you, you ain't gonna say nothin' to your buddies on the force.'

'I don't have any buddies on the force. What's so special about this book?'

'It was published in Cuba.'

'Don't worry about that,' said Max. Half the people in Little Havana drank Cuban rum and smoked Cuban cigars. 'How d'you get it?'

'This Canadian brother I know. Runs a black bookstore in Montreal. He knows this publisher in Havana, a French guy called Antoine Pinel. He publishes books about the Panthers – autobiographies mostly. Cuban X-Press, his company's called.'

Lamar went back to the counter and ducked down behind it. He re-emerged a few moments later with a hardback book by Kimora Harrison titled *Black Power in the Sunshine State*. On the cover was a photograph of Vanetta Brown making the power sign with the Freedom Tower in the background. The book was old, the edges of the pages tinted amber, and when Max flicked through it, the volume released a faintly musty smell.

'You know anyone around here who was in the Black Jacobins – or knew her well?' he asked.

'Not any more. They're either dead or gone, one way or another,' said Lamar. 'Tell you what everyone was agreed on though: she didn't kill that cop.'

'No?' Max wasn't surprised. Castro thought she was innocent too. 'Who did?'

'The Man.' Lamar smiled sardonically. 'The Man did it. The same Man does every bad thing to every good black person in America.'

14

Max settled down on his couch with a notebook and pen, and read *Black Power in the Sunshine State*.

Vanetta Brown was born on February 17, 1936, in Overtown, Miami, to an affluent family. Her father, Medgar, was a doctor. Her mother, Nirva, was a secretary, originally from Haiti.

Vanetta was an only child. Before she turned twelve, she had visited Haiti, the Dominican Republic, Cuba and Brazil with her parents.

Her mother was her formative influence, reminding her daughter never to forget that she was black *and* Haitian in America. Nirva also taught her about Toussaint L'Ouverture, the former slave who, by educating himself and learning military strategy, had overthrown French rule in Haiti and freed his people. At the age of thirteen, Vanetta read the key book about Toussaint and the Haitian revolution – *The Black Jacobins* by C. L. R. James.

On March 28, 1954, mother and daughter attended a civil rights rally in Overtown. Although peaceful, the march was broken up by cops using fire hoses and dogs. Nirva took a direct hit from a hose and cracked her head open on the sidewalk. She went into a coma and died ten days later. Medgar Brown never recovered from his wife's death. He fell into a deep, alcohol-assisted depression and committed suicide in 1957.

In November 1955, Vanetta saw Fidel Castro speak at the Flagler Street Theatre in Miami. There she met Ezequiel Dascal, the son of Miami-based Cuban activists and prominent Castro fundraisers, Camilo and Lidia Dascal.

In February 1960, Vanetta married Ezequiel. Their daughter, Melody, was born that April.

In 1962 Vanetta and Ezequiel formed the Black Jacobins, originally as a charity to help newly arrived Haitian and Cuban immigrants in Miami. Based in a disused warehouse in Overtown they named Jacobin House, they provided food, shelter, legal advice and English lessons.

The Black Jacobins were politicised in 1963, following the bombing of a black church in Birmingham, Alabama, which killed four children. Vanetta Brown started giving speeches around Miami and actively recruiting new members. Unlike the Black Panthers, who advocated separatism, the Jacobins were a multiracial organisation, with significant numbers of Hispanics and whites in their ranks – this was in keeping with Toussaint L'Ouverture's original vision of a free Haiti as a multicoloured, multicultured free republic.

The Black Jacobins became increasingly popular throughout Florida and then the South. Vanetta Brown was a passionate orator. Her fame and media profile rose accordingly. The media dubbed her 'The Black Red', and alleged that Fidel Castro was funding the group.

In 1965 heroin hit South Florida. High-grade Golden Triangle smack was smuggled almost daily into the US by military cargo planes flying from Vietnam to Florida's army bases. Heroin became the drug of choice in Miami's ghettos. The crime rate spiked.

The Black Jacobins declared a 'war of shame' on the dealers, the kingpin being Daniel Styles aka Halloween Dan. Their tactics included putting up wanted posters of known dealers all over town, picketing dealers' homes and well-known drug spots, and forming human barricades in front of shooting galleries, forcing them to close. They also opened a free rehab clinic in Liberty City. The programme had an 80 per cent success rate.

Within two months, drug dealing and drug-related crimes in inner-city Miami dropped significantly.

On June 4, 1968, Miami police raided the Jacobin House. There was a gun battle and the building was set on fire. Ezequiel and Melody Dascal were killed in the blaze, along with five Jacobins.

Vanetta Brown allegedly escaped through a back window after shooting and killing Detective Dennis Peck – except that at least three eyewitnesses reported seeing Vanetta Brown several miles away in Miami Springs at the time of the raid. This contradictory evidence was buried in favour of that given by the two decorated and respected officers who led the raid – Eldon Burns and Abe Watson.

Over the course of the following week these officers found over a hundred kilos of heroin, $750,000 cash and numerous semi-automatic weapons in properties said to be tied to the Black Jacobins – although no corroborative evidence was ever presented linking buildings and group.

Vanetta Brown evaded a nationwide manhunt and seemingly disappeared. Then, in December 1971, Fidel Castro confirmed that she was living in Cuba, one of an estimated ninety-four US criminals the Cuban regime has granted asylum to since 1962.

Vanetta kept – and continues to keep – a very low profile. She is never seen in public and there are no known photographs of her in Cuba. She is believed to be alive and living in Havana.

The Cuban government pays $13 a day towards her living expenses.

15

Three and a half hours later Max was reading through his notes in the kitchen, waiting for the espresso machine to heat up.

The book had stirred up old memories.

Old, *old* memories.

His MTF days . . .

The raid on the Jacobin headquarters and the stash houses bore all the hallmarks of a classic Eldon Burns op. Max had had a hand in enough of them to know one when he saw one. The only difference was that this time it had been messy – a child had died and a cop had been killed. That never happened in his day, but by then Eldon had become so practised at stitching people up he'd got it down to a fine art.

Max thought back to Abe Watson. Joe had always despised him. Never explained why. It was there in the defensive-aggressive body language Joe adopted and the way he clamped his mouth extra tight whenever Abe's name came up, like someone biting their tongue and trying not to vomit at the same time. Max had heard plenty of stories about Abe, most of them from Eldon: Abe and the lead-filled sap he christened his 'nigger knocker', Abe and the way he was *extra* harsh on black suspects, Abe always out to prove he was blue before black.

Halloween Dan. Max remembered Styles all too well from his days in Patrol; the sight of him, decked out like a dayglo pumpkin. The bright orange Caddy he'd driven, with orange-walled tyres, orange seats, orange-tinted windows. He always rode with four women – three in the back, one in front; black, white and brown, all in spray-on orange dresses.

Everyone in Miami knew who Halloween Dan was and how he made his money, but no one could touch him. He always avoided each potential bust. Evidence and key witnesses in cases against him would routinely disappear. Rumours abounded: that he was a snitch, that he was selling his high-grade smack for the CIA or the Feds, that he had himself some powerful friends.

Then, one day in 1973, he just disappeared. He was presumed murdered, hacked up and dumped at sea for the sharks and the lobsters. The drug trade in Miami was subsequently taken over by the Colombians, the Cubans and the Haitian, Solomon Boukman.

Of course, Max *could* have been wrong, and Vanetta Brown and the Black Jacobins really had been dealing heroin, but he'd known Eldon and just how bad he was.

He guessed the following: Eldon's political paymaster – Victor Marko – and maybe the FBI as well – wanted rid of Vanetta Brown and her organisation. They gave Eldon the job in exchange for more power, more influence, more money. He gratefully accepted.

If Brown was innocent and the drugs, money and guns had been planted, she still had a motive to kill Eldon. A solid one. Her husband and daughter – her family – had died in the raid.

She would be seventy-two now. She could have paid a hitman to kill Eldon. That was feasible. Revenge never got old.

But what about Joe? In 1968 he was an ordinary Patrol cop.
Where did he fit in?
What had *he* done to her?
Something wasn't right.
Max's phone rang.
It was Jack Quinones.

16

'How are you, Jack?'

Max pulled up a chair and sat down.

'I don't like Miami any more,' Quinones said.

'I know.'

'I like you even less.'

'I know that too.'

They were sitting outside a busy Creole restaurant in Bayside Mall. The place had a great view of the marina, which was clogged with tourist boats swallowing and disgorging groups of people. The operators offered tours of the tiny surrounding islands, where the rich and famous lived. At a loose end Max had gone on one to see what tourists were spending their money on outside of clubs and coke. When the boat stopped outside a celebrity's house, the loudspeakers blasted a snatch of something appropriate – a movie theme, a song, a catchphrase. At Sylvester Stallone's place they played the theme from *Rocky* at full volume. It had made him thankful he'd never been famous.

Quinones looked terrible. It had taken Max a hard look and a double-take before he recognised him. He'd withered since their last encounter. Eleven years ago he'd been swarthy, black-haired and goateed, his body heavy. Now he was thin, sallow, sunken-cheeked and clean-shaven. His lined face looked like it had been painstakingly glued together from a thousand fragments. His hair was the colour of ash on snow.

Quinones had been through hell recently. His wife died of cancer in 2004. He watched the disease take her away very slowly, piece by piece, over three years. Every night she woke up in extreme pain, screaming and crying, the illness fighting over her insides. It was a tug-of-war with tightly clamped jaws filled with sharp and serrated teeth at both ends. One night she ran out of morphine. The pharmacies were shut and she was in agony. Jack needed to do something quick so he went out and scored smack on the street. That helped her through the night.

The next day he told his boss about it. He was disciplined and demoted to a teaching post. So much for honesty. Not that Jack minded. In fact, it was what he'd wanted, because his new role let him spend more time with his wife.

'Far as I was concerned, the last time I saw you was the last time I'd see you,' said Quinones. 'But Joe was a good friend and he asked me to talk to you if something like this happened.'

'Did he have reason to think he was going to get killed?'

'No. He just asked and I promised.'

'I didn't know you two were that tight.'

'There's a lot you didn't know.' The only thing that hadn't changed about Quinones was his voice – its natural Latin lilt held in check by buffers, officious and gruff.

A waitress came over with a smile, a spiel and two menus. Max knew they weren't going to be eating even before Jack cut her off at the specials and asked for water. Max ordered coffee.

'Joe ever tell you how we met?' Quinones asked.

'Didn't I introduce you?'

'We were on first-name terms long before you put on a uniform.'

That surprised Max and he didn't try to hide it. For a few moments his mouth hung open like that of a beached fish.

He had first met Jack in the summer of seventy-six. He was impressed: Jack wasn't your typical Fed bureaucrat, looking down his nose at local law enforcement, using his smarts to reflect your perceived stupidity; he was simply interested in doing his job and catching criminals.

Quinones was investigating an IRA gun-running operation.

The weapons had all come from Argentina and been re-routed to Ireland via Miami. By chance, Max and Joe were investigating an Irishman who'd absconded first to South America, then to Miami after being caught in a credit scam in Cork. They teamed up with Quinones, pooled resources and brought down a small network of smugglers and money launderers.

Max introduced Joe to Quinones one night while they were working on the case. Or so he thought. The two certainly acted like they didn't know each other. The tentative small talk, searching for common ground to build a conversation on. Boxing had been that junction, and booze brought them closer. Now, Max couldn't help but feel hurt. He and Joe had shared everything. There'd been no secrets between them. Supposedly.

'Where's this going, Jack?'

'Why are you involved in a police investigation?'

'Who said I was involved?'

'Don't fuck with me. Your best friend gets killed right in front of you, and you're doing what? *Nothing?* Yeah, right. You knew who it was, he'd be dead already.'

'Who said it was a he?'

The waitress brought the drinks over. Quinones waited until she was out of earshot before continuing.

'Word is Vanetta Brown's in town,' he said.

'You know her?' Max asked.

'I'll talk, you listen. When I'm done, we're done. No questions. Understood?'

'Yeah.'

'When she was still in Overtown, I was working a COIN-TELPRO for the Bureau here in Miami. The dirty tricks brigade. We were undermining Black Power groups. Not just them. We targeted the Klan and the American Nazi Party too. We were equal-opportunity mischief-makers. We'd plant undercover operatives in the organisations and keep tabs on them. And we did other stuff as well, fun stuff, like undermining reputations with rumour and unsubstantiated gossip. If we couldn't get them

110

on crime or Commie ties, or any kind of sex, we just made it up. Some of the stuff even became true.' Quinones smiled. 'The public are basically fucken' dumb. They'll believe anything. That's why they voted for Bush the Second.'

'You're some Fed, Jack.'

'I'm getting used to the idea of retirement.'

Max finished his coffee.

'I handled the operatives within the Black Jacobins – Brown's group,' Quinones said. 'The local membership was young. And angry. Black kids brought up by parents who remembered the Liberty City wall. Parents who remembered redneck cops calling them 'nigger' and 'boy'. Parents who'd tried to fit in their whole lives, trying to be white with their hair-straightening parlours and Uncle Tom obsequiousness. But they still had to sit in the back of the bus and drink out of segregated water fountains. Their kids grew up and thought, Fuck that – that ain't gonna be me.

'The way we infiltrated the Jacobins was by getting a handful of young black guys fresh out of police academy, right before they got assigned. They'd already had the basics drummed into them. We took them and turned them into spies. We promised them Bureau jobs or a fast track to detective. Joe Liston was my guy, my operative.'

'*Joe . . .?*' Max started but shock choked his voice.

'He saw what looked like a good opportunity and he took it,' said Quinones.

'Joe? Sell out his own people? I don't fucken' believe you, Jack.'

'That's not the way it was. First up, Joe didn't 'sell' anybody out. You think Hoover would've created COINTELPRO if he didn't have just cause? And it wasn't about race either. Hoover came down on white extremists as hard as he did on blacks – Panthers, Klan, Nazis – they were all the same to him. Like I said, equal fucken' opportunities. Get over it. Extremists are all as bad as each other.'

'What about Martin Luther King? He wasn't an "extremist"!'

'Back then, to us, he was,' said Quinones. 'But so was Jesus in his time, if that's any consolation. And look what happened to him.'

'When did you recruit Joe?'

'Nineteen sixty-five. He didn't volunteer. He'd lied on his police application form, said he didn't have a criminal record. He had two unpaid parking tickets. He said he'd forgotten to pay 'em and blah-blah, but that was basically his career fucked in the womb. Cops have to be honest and law-abiding. At least, they did then.' He winked at Max. 'So we gave him a choice: work for us for a while and we'll wipe the slate clean. Joe worked for us for a year and a half. He reported directly to me. I was his only contact.

'He got close to the inner circle. Vanetta Brown trusted him. He never found any evidence of criminal wrongdoing the whole time he was there. Neither did any of our other guys.'

'So Joe stopped working for you in, what, sixty-seven?'

'Yes and no. He said he couldn't see the point of our operation. The Black Jacobins weren't a threat to national security. They were doing a lot of good in the community. Which was absolutely true. He joined the Miami PD. He could've had a Bureau job if he wanted one. He had the right temperament for it. And the smarts. Or he could've gone to another state, but Miami was what he knew, what he wanted. Didn't even want the fast-track option either. That was the way Joe was. Honest and principled to a fault.'

'What about the drug dealing?'

'Joe never saw any of that. Neither did any of our other operatives,' said Quinones.

'Are you saying that smack was planted?'

Quinones didn't answer.

Which meant yes.

Max wasn't surprised.

'What about the ties to Cuba, the money the Jacobins supposedly got?'

'We planted those rumours in the press,' said Quinones.

'None of it was true?'

'No.'

'Why d'you do it?'

'It was my job to,' Quinones said. 'Two colours white America hates: black and red. Mix them together and you get some kind of dynamite. Look at what the right-wing media are saying about Obama now – that he's a "socialist". Black and red again. Never stops, never fails.'

The waitress came and took away Max's cup. He ordered more coffee.

'How did that work? Joe just leaving an undercover gig and becoming a cop – on the same streets he'd marched through?'

'Joe told Vanetta Brown he was leaving to join the police.'

'What?'

'That was his idea. Joe sold it to her like he could do some good on the inside, take the lessons he'd learned and apply them in the force. He said he'd spy for her too, let her know what was coming down. She was all for it. She gave him her blessing. The Black Jacobins were never anti-police. Despite everything that had happened to Vanetta Brown. She believed in reform, not revolution.'

'So she never suspected?'

'She never knew he worked for us, no. And that's all I'm going to tell you, Mingus, because that's all Joe *asked* me to tell you.'

'You mean there's more?'

'There's always more. But as far as I'm concerned, your bowl's full. The check's on you.'

Quinones got up.

'One more thing: I'll be coming to the funeral next week. Do me a favour. Don't sit next to me, don't talk to me, don't look at me. Goodbye.'

'Yeah, and fuck you too, Jack,' Max said to Quinones' departing back.

He stared at the tiny black puddle at the bottom of his cup, looked around the restaurant. The crowd had thinned. The background muzak became more prominent. As did the sounds of the gulls squawking over tourist conversations.

Sitting there, he felt hollow and dizzy. It was all crashing down around him. Everything he'd known. Everything he'd been sure of. None of it still standing.

17

Max rested against a palm tree and dug his bare feet into the fine warm sand.

He never came out to the beach any more. It reminded him too much of Sandra. She used to like going there when they lived together in his condo on Ocean Drive. She'd lived in and around Little Havana all her life before she met him; a trip to the beach had been a treat, a place she'd had to make an effort to get to, something she'd only done with family or friends on holidays or weekends. Having a place so close to the sea was a novelty for her. And it never wore off.

He liked thinking about Sandra but he didn't like being reminded of her. Thoughts he could control, memories he couldn't. They were happy memories, but they left the bitterest taste. He knew what came next, where they led to.

Max wasn't angry at Joe for not talking about his past. Maybe he'd even been leading up to it when he was killed. It didn't matter. It didn't change a thing about them or the way they'd been.

But . . .

Why had Vanetta Brown put a hit on him?

Had she found out about him being an FBI informant?

Eldon led the raid on the Jacobin House. Vanetta Brown lost her husband and her daughter that day.

The motive wrote itself.

It all made sense.

Too much sense.

Like Quinones said, there was always more.

But . . .

Wouldn't it be best just to leave it here, cherish the version of Joe he remembered and accept it as definitive, as some kind of truth?

He sensed that if he went deeper, he'd find out the kind of things that would redefine his memories, sully them, warp them. He didn't need that, not now, not at his age, not when he had so little to look forward to and so much to look back on.

His phone rang.

It was Dan Souza.

'I checked Emerson Prescott's account details. Payment was made from a Bank of America account in the name of RMG Ents. I don't know what the RMG stands for. Ents could be Entertainments or Enterprises.'

'Or both. Or neither.'

'Sorry?'

'Nothing,' said Max. 'Thanks for your help.'

'You're welcome.'

Max headed home via the walkway that ran between the beach and the backs of the hotels. It was part living breathing billboard, part scenic route, part pink-and-white concrete vein sluicing tourists, joggers, dogwalkers, couples, manual workers, bums and cops on bicycles from the top of Collins to the end of Ocean Drive.

He noticed the man following him. Short dark hair, linebacker build, sharply creased slacks, black leather shoes, short-sleeved white shirt, tie, RayBans and a cellphone he mumbled into intermittently. He was hanging back, trying to blend in with the pedestrians. Max had made him on the beach while talking to Souza. He'd been standing by a lifeguard hut as though buying water, clocking Max the whole time. He wasn't a cop. A cop would know better than to dress like a Bible salesman trying to find his way out of Gomorrah.

Max stopped and sat on the wall and stared down the tracker. The man's face showed confusion and then irritation, before he stopped and consulted his phone.

When he'd finished the call, he walked over to Max with quick, bold strides.

'Max Mingus?' the man asked. 'Agent Joss, Homeland Security.' He showed his badge.

How long had they been following him?

'Could you come with me please?'

'Why the elaborate tail?'

'I wasn't tailing you. I was trying to catch up with you.'

Pride before patriotism, Max thought.

'Am I under arrest?' he asked.

'Someone wants to talk to you.'

'Who?'

18

Wendy Peck stepped around her desk to greet Max with an extended hand and the same smile she wore for her official photo – the projection of pleasure they taught on the body language module of MBA courses; that pleased-to-meet-you, tooth-sheathed inflection that started and stopped at the corners of the mouth and was designed to be summoned or lost in an instant.

The small office in Little Havana was above a launderette, directly opposite the white art deco Tower Theatre, a building whose spire made it look more like a modern church than the cinema it really was.

The interior was low-budget functional: two grey plastic chairs, a wooden desk, a floor covered with carpet tiles. Everything looked and smelled new, the set-up feeling about an hour old. No plants, no phones, no lamps, no flag, no photo of the President. This was going to be the sort of meeting that had never happened; just his word against the state's.

'I'm sorry we had to do it this way, Max. But I'm sure, once we've talked, you'll understand why,' she said in lieu of an introduction.

Her photograph had made her seem robust, the first line of offence in America's War on Terror. But in person she was slim going on petite. She wore a pale-blue blouse and a dark-blue skirt and jacket. No flag pin. She hid most of her wide, lightly lined and prominent forehead behind a fringe that stopped short of dark eyebrows and rimless rectangular-lensed glasses.

She wore no rings and, aside from two small gold studs in her earlobes, no other jewellery. Minor make-up, most of it on her lips, which erred towards the thin. Not unattractive, he thought, but there was a remoteness about her, a frozen-over distance that wouldn't thaw. He wondered if she had a family or a partner, or anything at home outside of the job she left it for.

She motioned to the chair opposite the desk and sat down after he'd taken his place.

'Can we get you anything before we start? Water? Coffee?'

Empathy ploy, Max thought. First names, make the unpleasant a little less so. A preflight beverage before the bumpy ride started. He tried meeting her eyes but his attempt was rebuffed by the bright-white reflection from her glasses.

'I'm good,' Max said. She motioned for Agent Joss, who'd followed him in, to leave the room.

To Max's left, there were two green box files on the desk, one on top of the other. She opened the first and pawed and pulled her way quickly through the contents, bunching printed pages aside like fabric samples in a swatchbook, until she found what she wanted: a single page. She placed it in front of her, glanced down it and then up at Max.

'Why are you investigating Vanetta Brown?' she asked, folding her hands together and leaning forward.

'I wouldn't call it investigating,' he said. He'd known this was coming the minute they'd picked him up.

'What would you call it?'

'Trying to understand her motive for killing two of my friends.'

'Do you?'

'I'm getting there.'

'You met with Special Agent Quinones a few hours ago. He filled you in on Captain Liston's past as a Bureau informant. Yesterday you bought a banned book – *Black Power in the Sunshine State* – from Swopes bookstore.'

She spoke with the same modest Southern twang he did, taking the long way around vowels, but there was precious little Floridian warmth to her voice. She sounded like she'd spent serious time and effort ditching Dixie.

'Why've you been following me?' Max asked, feeling the screws tighten. He wondered if they'd report Jack to the Bureau. He was surprised he even cared, but he did. A little.

She ignored the question. This was her show. She looked at her sheet of paper again.

'You've been spending a lot of time on the internet at home, reading up about Vanetta Brown.'

'How do you know what I've been looking at?'

'How do you think?'

That jolted him, that he was being spied on. And then it started scaring him. How much did they know about him? How far back had they gone? He suddenly thought of Eldon. Eldon and the piles of dirt he'd salted away. His 'insurance policy', he'd called it. Had she got hold of that?

He corked his turmoil. He reminded himself he'd done nothing wrong. And that pissed him off. The fact that he was even here. Being talked to like this, being investigated.

'Don't you need a warrant?' he said.

'We have one. It's called the Patriot Act.'

'This was murder not terrorism.'

'What's the difference?'

'Terrorism is murder for a cause or an ideology – political, religious, whatever,' said Max. 'I don't see any kind of cause or ideology behind what Vanetta Brown did. I just see someone getting even.'

'Look again,' she said. 'Brown is a fugitive from American justice, a cop-killer living in Cuba, a rogue state. She contracted an assassin to murder not one but two Miami cops. See where this goes? Cuba as a state sponsor of terror and all that?'

She smiled, not her camera-ready smile, but one she meant: a wry and mirthless grin telling Max that yes, that's not necessarily the way it went down, but that was the way it would go down if she wanted it to.

'How well did you know Captain Liston?'

'You should know.'

'Tell me anyway.'

'We were best friends for close to forty years,' he said. 'I guess that means I knew him better than most.'

'But not as well as you thought.'

'Everyone's entitled to a secret or two.'

'Depends on the secret. Why do you think he never told you?'

'Maybe because he thought it wasn't relevant. Maybe because he'd taken an oath of silence. Or maybe because it was none of my business. I don't know. And, frankly, I don't care.'

'Why not?'

'Because he's dead and he took the answer with him. All that's left is speculation.'

'How do you feel about him being killed like that, right in front of you?'

'How did you feel when your daddy never came home?'

That stopped her. She flinched, then gave him a fierce look. And that was when he saw her eyes, hard and grey-blue, with the emphasis on the grey, the colour of icicles reflected on stainless steel. Her fingers tensed up into talons and the edges of the paper shrivelled under her touch. Outside, he heard wheels screech in the road and the beginnings of a dispute in Spanish. He felt sweat prickling on his back.

'Why don't you cut the shit and tell me what I'm doing here,' Max said.

She stared at him a moment longer, weighing up personal rage against professional commitment, the what she wanted to do to him versus the what she wanted him to do for her. It took a while for her to tilt and settle in favour of the latter, but she did, turning back to the open file and extracting some photographs.

'The police aren't going to catch the man who killed Captain Liston and Eldon Burns,' she said.

'Why not?'

'Because he got away. Like all good assassins, he split town as soon as his job was done,' she said. 'While you were waiting to give your statement to Detective Perez, the shooter and another man were getting on a speedboat in Miami Harbour. By the time you'd finished talking, they were transferring to another boat about fifteen miles offshore. That boat took them to Cuba. See for yourself.'

She dealt out half her sheaf of photographs and pushed them over.

The shooter's face slid across the table. He was staring straight at the camera, straight at Max. Black eyes, a face so thin the features looked painted on to his skull, and then that cruelly hare-lipped mouth, a disfigurement so prominent and acute, at initial glance it appeared that the photograph was damaged; as if someone had cut diagonally across the right corner of the picture, taking out half the nose, mouth and chin, and then clumsily pushed the parts together, the segments misaligned, the physiognomy askew. Max covered the mouth and studied the face. The shooter looked young, late teens, barely a man.

The next picture was the uncropped original, the killer in context. He was standing on a pier, looking over his shoulder, wearing surgical gloves and a black short-sleeved shirt patterned with light-coloured, upward-flying birds. To his left, sitting at the wheel of the boat, was the accomplice – fuller in build, shoulder-length hair, face silhouetted in perfect profile against the pale boat.

The ensuing photograph was a cropped blow-up of the profile. Although the features were obscured by poor light and shadow, Max could make out the driver's prominent, Armenid nose – curving out at the top, bulging in the middle, following a straight line to the rounded tip. He also noted the arrow-shaped depression in the middle of the forehead. The driver looked distinctly male.

'Did you run facial recognition?' Max asked.

122

'Yes. We got nothing.'

The rest of the photographs were satellite captures of the speedboat cutting across the ocean, rendezvousing with another boat, two figures boarding, the second boat disappearing. Then the speedboat was on fire, burning in stills – a blast turning successive images into radiant Rorschach blots of differing size and interpretation, before ending at the flame-defined outline of the jutting prow sinking into black.

They'd burned the boat to remove all forensic evidence. Which meant they didn't want to be identified. Which meant that their details were on file, somewhere.

Max went back to the first photograph and looked into those blank, inky eyes staring back at him. This was the face Eldon and Joe had seen right before they died.

Wendy Peck pushed another glossy his way.

'Recognise that?'

It was a blow-up of a bullet casing next to a ruler.

'Lamar Swope gave it to you. Take a good look at it.'

A small black mark at the centre of the casing immediately caught Max's attention. It could have been two halves of a broken heart, but the shape was slightly wrong: the upper part didn't fully bulge out and the inner edges were smooth, while the outer ones were ragged.

Another photograph slid across the desk, the image now magnified.

And he was seeing a pair of long black wings, folded, at rest. They were shaped like vicious pincers, about to grab their prey, but they also had a tenuously human aspect. The upper part wore a kind of face in silhouette – he could make out a puckered mouth, the hint of a chin, a sharp nose and a brow – yet the overall shape was leonine. The rest of the wing was layered, a thick section, then a thinner one, tapering to a long curving point.

'What is this?' Max asked.

'*Las alas negras*. Black wings. The mark of the Abakuás.'

123

'Who?'

'The Abakuás,' she said and spelled it for him. 'They're an Afro-Cuban sect, a secret society that's been on the island for over five hundred years. They started during slavery and endure to this day. They're a people within a people. They live in Cuba, but they're apart from it. They're no friends of Castro and never have been. They hate his revolution and they hate the regime.'

'And the shooter's one of them?'

'Maybe,' she said. 'Most likely, yes. The Abakuás do contract killings – among other things. Their triggermen are all ex-Cuban military. Highly skilled.

'The Abakuás do most of their work in South America, but they've been active here, in Miami and in Trenton, New Jersey, and as far away as Spain, France, England and Russia. The MO rarely varies – bullets through the eyes, the calling card at the scene, the black wings. It lets people know who did it. At one time the CIA tried to recruit them as counter-revolutionaries. It ended badly.'

'How badly?'

'The first few times, only badly. As in a lot of time and money got wasted while one operative after another got led down a blind alley. You see, no one knows who the Abakuás actually are. They don't ever identify themselves. You could be having a drink with one and you wouldn't know who they really were.

'In 1975 an operative got very close. Scott Colby, his name was. He's believed to have made contact with a leading Abakuá, only this was never confirmed.' She paused to sort through more photographs.

'What happened?'

'That's the one that ended *very* badly. Colby disappeared,' she said. 'He was found after a month, in his hotel room in Havana.'

She handed Max more photographs, black and whites, sourced from the Cuban police.

A bearded white man slumped in an armchair, his arms dangling over the rests, fists clenched, head tilted back. He looked asleep, like he'd been up for days and conked out as soon as he sat down. The ensuing pictures were of his face: bloody star-shaped wounds instead of eyes, dried blood in his moustache, his mouth half parted over buck teeth. Then a close-up of his hands, the fists having been broken open by the coroner, revealing a shell casing nestled in each palm. Both were stamped with the black wings, confirmed by the next two photographs: close-ups of the jackets, the markings stuck to the metal like crushed insects. Finally, there were the morgue pictures. Colby had been tortured, his chest and legs fist- and boot-bruised, his left ribcage staved in, his back lacerated with long slashing cuts of varying depth, like whiplash marks. There were burns on his scrotum and most of his fingernails had been torn off.

Max had seen worse, but not for a long time. The sight of the body and what had been done to it made his stomach spasm.

'He wasn't killed in his room. He was put there, after the fact. This was a busy hotel. No one saw anything,' said Peck. 'Before they shot him, they found out what he knew about them, includ-ing the names of all the people he'd spoken to. Those contacts disappeared the same day. August 8. Over the next few weeks, bodies began washing up on the coast. All shot through the mouth. That's also the Abakuá way. If someone identifies one of them, they're shot through the eyes. If someone names them, talks about them, they're shot through the mouth.'

'What did Castro do when the bodies started turning up?'

'The Cuban government said that they'd drowned trying to get to America. That's what always happens. Sometimes the Cuban police will even dump the bodies of Abakuá victims in the sea themselves.'

'And Castro can't do anything about them?'

'Castro has never been able to get at them. Like I said before, they're a secret society. And secret in Cuba *means* secret. It's fair to say that he fears them – more than he fears anyone,' she said. 'And with good reason. The Abakuás have infiltrated every corner of Cuban society, every rung of the regime. They're in the government, the hotels, the military, the police, the taxis, the hospitals. They're the uniformed cop on the street and they're that cop's superior, and they're that superior's boss. They've spread through the regime like cancer. They could easily overthrow it.'

'Why don't they?'

'It's not in their interests. They've got a sweet deal going on. They've got a monopoly on the black market, which is how they make their money,' she explained. 'When Communism collapsed, Russia stopped its subsidies to Cuba. No oil, no machinery, no food. The country was in dire straits. Castro announced what he called the "Special Period" – which meant Cubans had to make do without basic essentials. One month it was soap and toilet paper, the next it was rice. The Abakuás had seen this coming and been stockpiling food and toiletries while the Eastern Bloc crumbled. They sold the goods on at inflated prices. They made a fortune. It was even rumoured, at one point, that they supplied government bigwigs with meat.

'They also foresaw that Castro would have to open up the island to tourists. They got in at ground level. They now supply every bar, every restaurant, every hotel in the country.'

'So what's their connection to Vanetta Brown?' Max asked. 'She's not one of them. She's not even Cuban. And they're against the system that's protecting her. They're enemies of the very man who gave her asylum.'

'Money makes the strangest alliances,' she said. 'We believe she paid the Abakuás to kill Burns and Liston and they did. When revenge is on your mind, you do what you have to do, use whatever you can.'

'Or whoever you can,' Max said, and looked at her pointedly.

He could have voiced the doubts mushrooming up in his head, the reasons the evidence against Brown now suddenly seemed so flimsy, but he knew whatever he said wouldn't matter to her. She hadn't brought him here to discuss a murder case, or even help solve one. She didn't care about Eldon or Joe. This wasn't about them. It was about her father.

126

He felt the room's walls move in a little closer, the floor rise a little and the ceiling lower commensurately.

He knew where things were going. And he knew Wendy Peck was holding something over him.

She was studying him, watching his mental tumblers fall into place, hearing the doors opening and realisation barging in.

'Will you do it?' she asked.

'Do what?'

She smiled again. Only it was a nice smile, one that changed her face and put a permanent crack in her austerity. He got a glimpse of how she might be in private, away from her desk and the constant pressure: a fun person who maybe told crude jokes and drank beer from the bottle.

'Bring Vanetta Brown back to Miami to face justice.'

'I believe that's called kidnapping,' he said. 'And that's not what I do. I handle divorces.'

She replaced the photographs in the file she'd been going through, closed it and moved the box to the opposite corner of the desk. She opened the second box file and began sifting through its contents.

'You used to find missing persons. You were good at it. The best, some say. You never gave up.'

'That was a long time ago. The world's changed. And I've changed too. But not necessarily with it.'

She pulled out a thick wedge of paper and set it before her.

'You found that Carver boy in Haiti, didn't you?'

'Yes.' Max tensed.

'I remember that business,' she said. 'The family advertising in all the papers, on local TV. They put a lot of money into it.'

Max tried to swallow, but his mouth was dry.

'How much money did they pay you for finding the kid? Or should I ask, how much did you bring back from Haiti in 1996, Max?'

And there it was. No carrot, no incentive, no this-is-what's-in-it-for-you. Just the stick. How did she know about that money?

Who'd talked? Who'd told her? Again the room got smaller and tighter, and he felt himself shrinking before her.

'It was $20 million in drug money,' she continued. 'Which makes you guilty of money laundering *and* tax evasion. If we can't get you on one, we'll definitely get you on the other. You deposited $6 million in trust funds for Captain Liston's children. That'll be frozen by the DEA and seized by the IRS. You own a $565,000 penthouse on Collins Avenue. That'll go too. And that's before you even make it to court. You see where this could go? It's open and shut. With your record, you'd be looking at double-digit jail time, and, at your age, you'd die there.'

Max glanced out of the window. It was his only way out. Head first and into the street.

'This thing you want me to do – this is something you need a professional for. Ex-CIA or military. Doesn't even have to be an American,' he said.

'Don't you want to bring the person who killed your friends to justice?'

'Yes, I do. But I can't do that personally. Look at me. I'm old. I don't move as quick as I used to. And I haven't held a gun in twelve years. I had my last good day ten years ago. Are you sure I'm your man? Because – put it this way – I wouldn't hire me.'

'I'm not *hiring* you,' Wendy Peck said.

He had to hand it to her: she was a straight-up nasty piece of work, almost as bad as he'd ever been. *Almost* . . .

Max smiled at her bitterly.

How would the conversation have gone if he'd been more co-operative, played along? Would she have sold it to him as a patriotic mission? Talked about potential rewards if he was successful? The finder's fees from her website and the FBI? The talk show appearances, the book deal, the movie of the book, the computer game of the movie? The end result would have been the same. He still would have been going to Cuba.

'I want a few days to think about it,' he said.

'Who says you have that luxury?'

'Lady,' Max leaned towards her, 'what you're doing right now is completely illegal. And you know it. You're abusing your position, abusing your authority and bringing your department into disrepute. You're also wasting your department's time and money. You're supposed to be catching real terrorists and keeping this country safe, not conducting some private manhunt on the taxpayer's dime. You're way beyond your remit. You're pulling the same rogue shit I used to when I was a cop – the secret location, the extra-curricular surveillance, the coercion, the threats. The difference between you and me, now and then, is that in my day, I could get away with it – and I *did*. But you can't.'

She stared at him. But she was smiling again.

'I'll call you on Tuesday,' she said.

'That's election day.'

'You're a convicted felon, Max. You can't vote.'

19

Agent Joss dropped him off outside his apartment. He didn't want the ride, hadn't asked for it, tried to refuse it, but they'd insisted; their way of telling him where his leash started and stopped.

He turned on the coffee machine and then his computer. He knew Wendy Peck would be watching his every keystroke and he didn't give a fuck. He fed her name to the Google dog and hit search.

Older than she looked – forty-nine – which made her thirteen when her dad had been murdered.

Immaculate career: graduated top of her class in law school, joined the DA's office, prosecutor, Assistant DA. Put a lot of people away. Not surprisingly, she had a hard-on for cop-killers. Always sought – and generally got – the death penalty. Career paths like hers – standing up in a courtroom on behalf of the state, pleading her case, putting passion into an argument – usually led to politics, but that wasn't for her. She didn't have the populist touch. She switched sides, went private, became a highly successful defence attorney.

Launched Justice4Dennis.com website in 1996.

Joined the Department of Homeland Security in 2005.

Personal life: married 1980, divorced 1998. One daughter, Joanne.

*

Why had she picked him?

Not hard to figure out.

It wrote itself.

He was exactly the right person for the job.

If it went wrong, the story would read something like this: Vanetta Brown had had two of his friends killed, so he'd gone to Cuba for payback. It fitted his behavioural profile: he'd pulled this kind of stunt before – three revenge kills that had earned him seven years in prison. Unreformed, unrepentant. If he got caught and started talking about Wendy Peck, she'd deny everything. They'd never met, never spoken, never corresponded. His word against hers. And he was an ex-con.

If he succeeded, she'd still deny any connection. He'd gone there of his own accord, on his own initiative, frustrated by his government's inability to extradite criminals from a country so close. The conservative media would pick up on the story and make him out to be an American hero. He'd be the toast of Little Havana. A year later Vanetta Brown would go on trial for the murders of Eldon Burns, Joe Liston and Dennis Peck.

It was win-win for her.

He did a search on 'Abakuá'.

He got back a few articles on a Cuban dance troupe touring Europe and something about the Abakuá influence on Cuban music.

It was possible that Brown was behind the murders.

She'd carried heartbreak and hatred with her into exile.

They'd fused and festered.

She'd bided her time, but time was running out. Not just for her, but for the men who'd ruined her life.

She had turned seventy-two in February. Eldon, she would have known, was in his eighties and not long for this world. Joe was close to retirement. Either she punched their clock or God did.

131

Time to get even. Now or never.

But the fingerprints on the casings?

That was stupid.

Unless she had nothing to lose, in which case it didn't matter.

Or . . .

Maybe Vanetta was being framed – possibly for a second time.

Someone had got her prints on the bullets. The casings had either been placed in Eldon's hand as a calling card or to make sure the cops found them.

If that was so, then who was behind it?

One way or another, the answer lay in Cuba.

He had two days before Wendy Peck called for an answer. He already knew what he was going to tell her.

But, first, he had unfinished business to clear up with Emerson Prescott.

20

Max didn't usually research his clients. It was an unspoken part of the PI code. He was paid to be on their side, and his trust was covered by his fee; so their probity was taken for granted and they were off limits.

But Emerson Prescott's invoice was overdue. And he'd never liked the motherfucker anyway.

He sat at his computer and did a search on his client's name. He got an immediate hit on an Emerson F. Prescott, co-owner of Prescott & Lamb Dental Services, with offices in LA, New York and Miami.

They had a website. Sleek, professionally produced but very simple. The logo was large brown-and-blue lowercase letters on white. Then below came a list of services – dental and cosmetic, skin treatments, spas – followed by a mission statement, FAQ, locations, bookings and staff. He clicked on 'staff'. He went through to another page: the logo again, then a vertical list of names. Emerson F. Prescott and Arielle Lamb were listed at the very top.

He clicked on Prescott.

A photograph and a bio. Emerson F. Prescott, a dentist with twenty-one years' experience and numerous qualifications after his name, looked nothing like his client. Emerson F. Prescott was black.

He could have done another search, just to make sure, but he knew he'd find nothing.

He typed 'Fabiana Prescott' into the search engine and got back a thousand separate listings for 'Fabiana', and ten thousand more for 'Prescott', but not a single joint match.

He tapped in 'RMG Enterprises' and up came a link for an independent car dealership in California.

He tried 'Fabiana Prescott' and 'RMG Enterprises' together and found himself looking at a bunch of pages in Chinese and Russian, and a pop-up window asking if he wanted to download the Japanese text option. He hit 'OK' without thinking and had to wait twenty minutes for the program he didn't actually need to load. Then he had to restart the computer.

'Fabiana Prescott gonzo porn' was his next attempt.

Big mistake.

Ask the internet for porn and that's a billion pages.

Ask it for gonzo porn and the billion gets halved.

And there were plenty of women called Fabiana or Fabiane or Fabbie or Fab or Fab Annie doing gonzo porn. Not to mention the ones called Prescott, Prescot, Prescotte, Press Cock and Pressed Cock competing with them, the last two being male.

But no Fabiana Prescott.

So he tried typing in everything he had.

This time he got back the one page, and that with only a single porn-related listing on it – a site reviewing adult DVDs.

Fabiana Prescott went under numerous aliases, the most common being Sharona S. Bliss.

She was also called Sexxx Bliss/Sexy Bliss and BJ Bliss.

She was very popular. There were over ninety websites featuring her.

Her real name was Gilmara Vendramini. She was born March 28, 1975 in Sao Paulo, Brazil. She moved to Lubbock, Texas, with her parents in 1986.

She played basketball for Texas A&M University. Dropped out at the age of twenty-one and made her film debut in a flick called *Dirrrty Dreamz 4*. She initially only acted with her then husband, Herc Ho'gan. She'd won three AVN awards – the porn trade's Oscars – for best female starlet in 1998, and an unprecedented two the following year for Best Actress in a

134

Video and Best Actress in a Film. In her tearful acceptance speech at the 1999 ceremony, she thanked her parents for their support. Her parents weren't in attendance.

In 2000 she divorced her husband and got engaged to director, producer and owner of the Prêt-a-Porno film studio, Rudi Milk. She was under exclusive contract to the company. They had yet to marry.

She'd starred in over 350 porn films.

He looked at pictures of her over the years. She started out pretty in an unremarkable, girl-next-door kind of way. There were photos of her playing basketball, as well as a team shot from 1995. He wouldn't have even noticed her if her face hadn't been circled. Nothing really stood out about her: a plain, sweet-looking girl with a friendly smile, short brown hair and a nose that was on the bulbous side. Within two years her nose had gone down a size and her breasts up three.

He looked up Rudi Milk.

Anthony Rudolph Milk. Born November 17, 1949, Hoboken, New Jersey. Initially a music and boxing promoter, in his mid-twenties he started running strip clubs in Fort Lauderdale, before moving into porn films. He did both mainstream (full-length movies with a semblance of script and plot) and specialist stuff (bondage, humiliation, assorted fetish from feet to food). In the mid-eighties, he launched two companies: Prêt-a-Porno and B-Spokeporno. The second made one-of-a kind films to wealthier fans' specifications, which could include 'performing' with their favourite stars.

The home page of the Prêt-a-Porno website featured a cartoon of a naked, curvaceous black-haired woman in profile. She was lying on her front, one foot in the air, lapping at a gold bowl. B-Spokeporno.com had the same woman, only seen from the front and on all fours, leaning over the bowl, licking her lips.

When he clicked on her, he got a page with the following message:

B-Spokeporno
The ULTIMATE in interactive adult entertainment!

Your very own adult film!
Tailored to your desires!
Tailored to your tastes!
Tailored to your needs!

Yours and only yours!
Made by us – for you!

That's right!
A truly UNIQUE video –
Made specifically for you!

Only one copy will ever be made –
Yours!

Choose your stars!
Choose what they wear!
Choose what they do!
Choose who they do it with!

REMEMBER –

Only YOU will ever see this.
Only YOU will ever own this.
Your very OWN unique, individual,
one of a kind adult film.

He clicked through to an online form: name, address, email, telephone, and a box to fill in basic requirements. No girls were advertised. No prices were listed.

Max noticed minuscule, illegible print running along the bottom of the form. He magnified the text.

It was the company's address: Rudi Milk Group Entertainments, Floor 2, Cavanaugh House, 21361 Pennsylvania Avenue, Miami, Florida.

Pennsylvania Avenue was off Lincoln Road, not even fifteen minutes from where he lived.

He continued searching on Rudi Milk, looking for a photograph.

He kept on looking.

And looking. The sun went down in front of him and the city slowly lit up as darkness fell. Traffic snaked across the bridges, every one of those jaundiced sparkles bringing more weekenders to the beach.

Then he came to Phatboyzusa.com

Phatboy was a self-confessed 'porn mentalist' from Nebraska. His 'heros' were Larry Flynt, Hugh Hefner and Rudi Milk, his favourite stars Jenna Jameson, Tera Patrick, Midori, Crystal Knight and Sharona Bliss. He described himself as an 'equal opportunities onernist'. He had a picture gallery called 'Meat Your Heros & Heroins' – more than two hundred photographs of him crossing the porn Rubicon and meeting fuck-flick illuminati through the years. Max went through them. Phatboy had been at this for a good long while. There were older pictures of him with 'legends' John Holmes and Marilyn Chambers. Both had that red, runny-eyed hayfever *in excelsis* look of the habitual coke funneller. Holmes had a gold soup-spoon pendant around his neck. Phatboy had been a million and one cheeseburgers lighter then.

Come the late nineties and the new Millennium, terminal masturbators like Phatboy went to conventions to meet the objects of their fibre-optically connected fantasies – yup, ugly fuck-ups like him could actually talk to a hot-looking chick without her telling him where to go or getting her NFL-built boyfriend to kick sand in his face. The world, according to Max Mingus, was officially fucked and, thinking about it, he was glad that one day soon he'd no longer be part of it.

At the end of the thumbnails was a folder marked 'Godz'. More pictures.

Phatboy with Hugh Hefner in his silk dressing gown; Larry Flynt in his wheelchair, legs covered by a silk blanket; Bob Guccione in his silk hospital bed; and, in a black silk suit, Rudi Milk.

Max clicked and enlarged the picture.

He recognised Rudi Milk immediately.

'Emerson Prescott.'

He wasn't in the least bit surprised.

Just angry.

Real fucken' angry.

21

Rudi Milk's receptionist was about to take a sip of whatever con-coction was in her Starbucks takeout cup when Max came storming through the frosted-glass doors. Her face went from startled to petrified in the two seconds it took for recognition to hit. Her hand stopped mid-raise, fingers holding the cup by its dinky cardboard handle.

'Where's your boss?' Max asked, crossing the space to her desk in four quick strides. They'd met several times before in the fake office, where she played the same part. She'd been pleasant and polite, making small talk about the weather and sports and offering him water in between fielding incoming calls and book-ing fake appointments. She always said goodbye to him when he left, which he thought was a nice professional touch. Most recep-tionists didn't. Not that any of it mattered now.

'He's not here,' she said. 'I haven't seen him all week. And I haven't heard from him either.'

'When did you last see him?'

'A few days ago.'

'Be specific. Was it before Halloween?'

'No,' she said. 'The last time I saw him was *on* Halloween. He came in in the morning for a couple of hours and left.'

'Does he have another office somewhere – a real one?'

'No. This is it.'

Max went round to her side of the desk and stood a couple of feet away, looking down at her, at the grayish swill in her cup, seeing how tiny she was. He gave her his full, unblinking, don't-lie-to-me-because-I'll-know-if-you-are stare. Her eyes were deep green with a hint of gold, a nice shade of shallow ocean and the sand beneath. She couldn't reciprocate. She looked at his nose, mouth, throat, anywhere instead of those hard cold beams he'd fixed her with. She was scared witless – and he didn't blame her – but at least he could be sure she wasn't lying.

He could tell she was alone in the office. She'd been getting ready to go out when he came in. Her make-up was freshly applied and her perfume pungent. She was playing music on her big-screen iMac – overproduced, oversung, underwritten dreck that dared to call itself R & B or modern soul, or urban soul, or ghetto smooch, or whatever the fuck they were branding it.

'Turn that shit off.'

She put down the cup and clicked on her mouse. The torture stopped and silence rushed in all around them like air to a vacuum.

Max looked around the reception area. Everything about the place was tasteful and understated, none of the porn-set vulgarity he'd expected. Tall palm plants either side of the door, pastel-blue walls, grey carpet. Comfortable black leather sofas, a glass table in between with three neat piles of magazines for the upwardly mobile: back issues of *Ocean Drive*, *GQ* and *Cool Fast Cars*. On the nearby wall was a rack with the day's newspapers. He could have been standing in the antechamber of any white-collar business. That was, he supposed, the whole idea. Make it all seem like a successful business, nothing furtive or sleazy.

'Where'd he go?' Max asked.

'I don't know. He does this all the time. Just takes off,' she said. 'He calls them his "scouting trips".'

'*Scouting?* As in scouting for girls?'

'Yeah. He goes to South America a lot. Brazil mostly. Those are the in-girls right now. That's all guys want. White girls built black. Big asses and tan lines. You like Brazilian girls?'

Max ignored the question. A nervous reflex on her part, he

was sure. She was the sort who talked a lot when she got stressed.

'Doesn't he ever call in to let you know where he is?'

'No.'

'That usual?'

'He does this *all* the time. Says, "See you tomorrow," and doesn't come back for a while.'

'How long's a while?'

'A week, ten days. Never more than two weeks. Right when I'm starting to panic and thinking of calling the cops, I'll get a call or an email from him.' She said all this with fondness, like she was talking about an eccentric but lovable relative.

'What about his ... his fiancée, Sharona, Gilmara, Whatever-a? She go with him on these trips?'

'No.'

'Where is she?'

'I dunno. Maybe at home. I really dunno. I don't have too much to do with her. Rudi says they have an open relationship.'

'You don't say. Where's home?'

'You want their address?'

'That's right,' said Max. He could tell she was going to try refusing, so he moved in a little closer, crowding her, giving her no option but to comply.

'I'm not supposed to give that out.'

'The address.' Max held out his hand. Her eyes were moving now, panicked. 'And don't even think of giving me the wrong one.'

'He'll fire me.'

'Only if I tell him where I got it.'

'What are you gonna do to him?'

'Ask him some questions.'

'Just that?'

'Just that. I promise I won't touch a single hairplug on his head.'

That made her smile a little. She started rifling through a

Rolodex. Max took it from her, found Milk's home address: Aledo Avenue, Coral Gables.

'What's your name?' he asked her.

'Petra Sorenson.'

'How long've you worked here?'

'Two years in January. I was a temp. Rudi liked me, I liked him. I stayed. It's a great job. It pays well. Benefits are great. And Rudi's a good guy.'

'That's nice,' he said. 'I'd like a guided tour.'

They went down a corridor to the right of her desk, past open rooms, a stationery cupboard with a photocopier and fax machine, a spotless bathroom and shower.

In the opposite corridor, the first office they came to was locked. As she opened it, she said it was the projection room, where Rudi watched his forthcoming films. It was a windowless space with a flatscreen TV in front of a recliner.

The next two offices were almost identical.

All empty.

'Why do I get a feeling of déjà vu?' he said. 'Like there's no one actually employed here?'

'I'm Rudi's only full-time employee. He uses freelancers to do everything else – film-editing, marketing, distribution, publicity, accounts.'

'So why not get a smaller office?'

'This is for show, to impress clients and investors. When they come round we just get some people in to look busy.'

'Kind of like the scam you pulled on me?'

'It wasn't a scam . . . OK, it *was* kind of a scam, like you were deceived, but you got paid. A lot of money too. Why are you so mad?'

'He still owes me for two weeks – plus expenses,' Max said.

'He'll settle, I'm sure. He always pays his bills.'

They went into Rudi Milk's office. At first glance, he thought it was an exact replica of the one Milk had in the Tequesta Building – the same wood-panelled walls, thick

142

carpet, huge mahogany desk. Yet he noticed small but significant differences: its distinct smell of vanilla, the large square scented candles on the window sill, and a set of coasters in the shape of jigsaw pieces on the coffee table. The furniture looked a couple of years old. A ragged and filthy Stars and Stripes hung in a glass frame. The office had life to it, a sense of long hours passed, of ups and downs, triumphs spiked by setbacks. There was a photograph in the corner of a fireman carrying what Max guessed was the same flag away from the ruins of the World Trade Center. A gold plaque below it read 'Never Forget'.

'Rudi bought that on eBay,' Petra said, pointing to the Star Spangled Banner.

Max lifted the frame back to check for a safe. Nothing.

As with everywhere else, there wasn't a single hint as to how Rudi made his money. Max wondered if he wasn't embarrassed about it. Milk revelled in the financial rewards and the image of respectability, but he refused to acknowledge the source.

Max motioned for Petra to sit down in one of the two chairs facing the desk.

'Did someone pay to have me – specifically me – involved?'

'I don't know, I really don't.'

'You're his PA and you don't know? Bullshit. You were in on it.'

'First of all, I'm not his PA,' she said. 'I just answer the phone, take messages. Second, I wasn't "in on it". He told me what to do and I did it.'

'Did he tell you why?'

'Yeah. He said it was all part of a movie he was shooting, and that you didn't know.'

'But I wasn't *in* the movie,' said Max. 'It was already filmed.'

'What?'

He told her what had happened at the Zurich Hotel.

'That's kinda weird,' she said, frowning. 'But kinda tame too, compared to some of the stuff I've seen and heard here.'

'Rudi know anybody I worked for?' Max reeled off a few names of past clients.

'I don't know any of his friends.'

'None of those names sound familiar?'

'No.'

Max sighed heavily. She was telling the truth. Best to finish up here and go to Coral Gables.

He picked up the keys from the table. They went back to the projection room. He told her to sit and he checked the room for something he might have missed.

'Where's your cellphone?'

'In my bag outside.'

'You're going to have to stay here until I get back.'

She stood up.

'What? No. No! You can't do this!'

'And walk out of here and let you call Rudi? I'll come back for you soon as I'm through talking to him.'

'But I've got a *date*.'

'If he loves you, he'll wait.'

22

Porn pays, thought Max as he stepped away from the porch and stared up at Rudi Milk's home. It was a three-floor red-and-white villa with stuccoed walls, dolphins and conch shells etched into the plaster, balconies hung with bright flowers, recessed windows framed by arches, a shamrock keystone over each. He supposed it was one of the first residential properties in the area. The architecture was of the same Mediterranean Revival style as the first Coral Gables buildings. The place had both the solidity and the discreet opulence of a bygone era about it; a monument to a time when class was something you couldn't buy or acquire, you either had it or you didn't.

Shame, then, about its current owner.

Who wasn't coming to the door.

He tried the bell a third time. Those ding-dong chimes again, faintly, their resonance soaked up by the thick walls. He looked through the windows into a vestibule with a shamrock mosaic floor. A chandelier hung from the ceiling. The only piece of standing furniture was an eight-foot-tall wooden object to the right, one he originally mistook for a grandfather clock, until his eyes adjusted to the gloom, and what he had thought were edges and lines became the hourglass contours of a varnished sculpture of a woman, her face to the wall and big, high round ass to the world. On top of the woman's head was a stuffed seagull. He found it about as fitting as it was utterly tasteless – while the house's original owner had chosen to incorporate Irish heritage into this symbol of their success, Milk had created a monument to Brazilian (he guessed) *bunda*. He wondered if the sculpture had come with the gull.

He looked at the security camera, bolted to the left wall, trained on him. He stared into its oblong eye. He waved. He smiled. He mouthed, 'Hello, remember me?'

He stabbed at the bell twice more in rapid succession. He knew it was useless. Either there really was no one home or no one was going to open up.

The late-afternoon light was starting to thicken as it faded; a soft, buttery yellow with a brown hue giving the overhanging leaves of the palm trees a golden tinge and making the grass sparkle. There was a mild scent of lemon in the air.

He looked back up the short gravel path and the open gate he'd come through. A sign on the gate warned of dogs on the premises. He'd assumed that a property this size might have more than one dog guarding it, so when he'd stepped out of the car, he put a collapsible baton and a can of mace in his pockets. But no dogs had come for him so far. He hadn't even heard any barking.

He glared at the camera again, its eye immobile, fixed on him. He imagined Milk sitting somewhere upstairs, looking at him on a screen, smirking, maybe even recording it for a future flick.

Christ, he missed being a cop. The badge, the right of entry. And he missed being young, those reckless, thoughtless impulses that would have had him picking or shooting out the front-door lock.

And then he saw something pale flit across the window, like a face appearing at the glass for a furtive glance.

He peered inside.

Nothing.

He knocked on the window.

'Milk, I need to talk to you,' he said. He looked up and down the empty vestibule. There was something different about it. He wasn't sure what. 'Come on. Open up.'

He banged on the window some more.

His eyes moved to the sculpture.

And to the bird on top of it.

It was gone.

He searched for it. It wasn't anywhere on the floor and it wasn't flying around.

He looked up at the chandelier, which was swaying slightly. The gull was on top of it, looking right down at him.

It jumped off, fell heavily a couple of feet, before swooping up, then dipping and gliding gracefully in a smooth arc towards the sculpture. It reclaimed its position on top of the woman's head, trotted a little and stood still.

Max stepped off the porch and walked around the house. He found the gate to the back. It swung open with a simple push.

He followed a brick path to where it stopped, at the edge of a long wide garden, bordered with roses, bougainvillea and banana palms. Three lemon trees stood at the very end, the fruit ripe and full, much of it on the ground.

Stone steps led up to the white French doors of a conservatory. He was about to try and open them when he spotted dried blood smeared on the edge of one of the handles. He wrapped a handkerchief around his fingers.

The door was unlocked. He walked in.

He noted the thin film of dust on the bar-top and stool seats. He moved towards the sliding door – also white – connecting the conservatory to the rest of the house. Dried blood there too, a fingertip-sized smudge close to the handle.

He came to the kitchen. Spacious and sleek, everything built into a long glass-topped counter. The window above the sink was wide open. That was how the gull had got in. At the very end of the counter was a silver tray with six champagne flutes on it. Next to that, a big silver bucket with an unopened Bollinger magnum floating in a puddle of water.

The trashcan was empty. No bag.

Max headed for the steps leading out of the kitchen and down into a sunken den in the middle of house.

147

He trod on something that scraped under his shoe.

It was a spent shell casing, which from above looked like a gold molar because of the way its ends were pinched together. He picked it up with his handkerchief and checked the base: 9 mm Luger. He scanned the casing for markings. None. He dropped it into the breast pocket of his shirt. His stomach tightened and his heartbeat quickened; his wrists started to throb, the watchstrap above his left hand tightening with his pulse.

As he reached the steps, he caught a glimpse of what lay at the bottom and his right leg froze, his foot hovering in mid-air, stranded in a half-step.

Jesus.

Explosions of dried blood covered the couch, the walls, the floor. The coffee table was upended and cracked right down the middle. Bullet holes absolutely everywhere. Furniture burst open to stuffing and springs. Spent shell casings covering the ground, glowing like disembodied lightbulb filaments. He walked down. Slowly.

The air was rank and sour with blood and stale gunsmoke. It was impossible to tell for sure how many had died right here. From the amount of blood on the couch, the wall behind it, and on the floor, he guessed three. A fourth person had been shot – probably afterwards – near the main stairs. There were more bullet casings around the coffee table. He didn't know how many that made; he'd lost count at thirty-two.

Six champagne flutes. So how many dead?

Had the killer been a guest?

And where were the bodies?

No drag marks on the floor.

In the corner, by the steps, half covered in dried blood was a stack of wadded $100 bills. Around forty or fifty notes with a plain pink band around them.

He moved deeper into the rest of the house.

The gull, still on top of the wooden statue, looked at him as he walked into the vestibule. He saw its body bunch up. He

148

examined the wooden woman: she was covering her face with her hands and her breasts with her arms, as if in shame – real or mock he couldn't tell.

The next room he checked was completely empty. Bright white walls with a silk finish. A spotless white floor.

He heard a loud squawk close by and the flap of wings.

He looked around the door and saw the gull flying out of the house, its wings first flapping then straightening out, as the bird drifted low across the grass.

The sun was setting and it would be dark within the hour.

The gull alighted on one of the lemon trees at the end of the garden and shuffled around noisily, rustling the leaves as it did so, stopping to look back at the house.

Then the bird flew off and away, dislodging a small rain of bright yellow fruit as it went. A dozen lemons thudded on to the grass. Max watched them land, bounce and roll left and right. He noticed the way the other fallen fruit had massed in two opposing piles. He found that strange, how there seemed to be a large hump in the grass between them, how one particular area was higher than the rest.

'You gotta be fucken' kiddin' me!'

Max lifted back the turf and exposed an area of dark soil, six foot wide by eight foot long. It had been bashed flat with a shovel. He made out rhomboid imprints. He found the shovel at the far end of the garden, leaning against three dog cages. Milk had had Dobermans, but they were long dead, their bodies stinking and fly infested in the cages. No blood. They'd probably been poisoned.

He went back to the trees and began to dig.

He dug fast, throwing the soil back. As he dug, his arms, chest and lower back stiffened with stress and pain. He ploughed himself lower and lower into the ground, sweat slaking off him, mosquitoes biting at his face and hands. The light was fading fast now. Stars were appearing in the purple-blue sky. Night was falling. He went faster. The stink from what was below started to rise and stick to the back of his throat. Lemons dislodged by the flying dirt fell on him. He mashed them up with the shovel as he dug, the zesty tang mingling with the mounting stench. He knew he'd never be able to drink or smell or look at lemons again without thinking of this moment.

The first thing he found was money. Stacks and stacks of $100 bills in pale pink bands. He shovelled them out and threw them over to one corner, hearing them land with a thud. He figured there was at least two, maybe three million dollars here.

Why bury money?

He dug down more. He was now up to his thighs.

And then he hit something solid.

Thunk.

Down on his knees now, sifting the soil away with his hands, clawing into the ground, fistfuls of dirt flying over him.

It was a black body bag. He felt around it. It was a head. He squeezed the nose without meaning to. He pushed away more dirt until he found the bag's zip.

A woman he didn't recognise, Latin. She wore a maid's white uniform. A dozen bloody holes in her front, part of her head missing, half her hand gone. She was still wearing white espadrilles, which had somehow stayed spotless.

He had to pull the body out of the hole to get at the others.

He found Rudi Milk next. Shot through the neck and chest.

Then the woman he'd known as Fabiana, killed the same way. He guessed they'd been sitting next to each other.

Then came the man who'd played the chauffeur. Max almost didn't recognise him. His lower face was missing. Bullets had ripped chunks out of his upper arms. Others had gone through his stomach, groin and legs.

The fifth body belonged to Teddy, the night manager of the Zurich Hotel. His torso had been shredded.

Max closed the bags and crawled out of the pit.

He lay on his front, exhausted, unable to move.

With great effort, he managed to get to his feet. He was caked in dirt. His trousers and bare torso had gone black and he reeked of death. Death was in his nostrils, in his throat, in his mouth, all the way down in his pores.

All so familiar, all so terrible.

Two wads of bills lay on the ground in front of him. He picked one up, ran his thumb down the corner. Specks of dirt flew out. Five grand there, all in hundreds. If he took the other deck, him and Prescott would be more than square.

He threw the money on the ground, disgusted at himself for even thinking that way. Is that how low he'd gotten – a fucken' *graverobber*?

He'd already irreparably fucked up a crime scene. His DNA was all over the bodies.

He had to get out of here.

He drove back to Miami, taking that smell of death into his home. After particularly brutal bouts, Eldon Burns had made him take ice baths. Said it repaired the body faster. They kept cadavers on ice too. To stop them rotting. It was all relative. He started the bath running, then shut off the hot tap and turned the cold to full. It wasn't cold enough. He scrubbed and scrubbed himself until his skin burned. Then he scrubbed again.

After, he bagged his clothes and dumped them in an incinerator.

Then he took his car to a twenty-four-hour gas station and had them wash and clean the inside. While they were vacuuming up the dirt and soaping the stink out of the seats, he went and got Petra. She'd fallen asleep. Max shook her awake. She started, gasped, blinked.

'Did you see Rudi?'

'No one home.'

The car wasn't ready. So he walked up Collins, then down Washington, then up Lincoln Road. He heard the pre-recorded bells chiming from Miami Beach Community Church. He stopped by the gates and looked at the stained glass with the gold light behind it. He thought of going inside for a while, just like he used to do when he needed space and quiet to think. Close by was an Irish bar. Lots of people sitting outside. Drinking, talking, looking. He could have done with a drink about now. He as good as needed one. But one had never been enough. One had always lead to two, three, four, five, eleven, twelve. The math of oblivion. He felt the ghost of those old addictions, the lure of the pacifiers, tugging at him, beckoning. They'd never let him be.

He wasn't going there either.

The Mariposa was open for business, people eating at the very spot Joe had died, just like he knew they'd be. The Miami Money Train never stopped. Just rode roughshod over all and sundry.

Eleven p.m.

He dialled 911 from a payphone.

He told the police operator where to find five bodies and a lot of money.

23

November 4.

Election day.

Morning TV on local news. Sound low. Nothing but weather and then pundits predicting a high turnout and how Obama would take Florida by a slim margin – and therefore win the Presidency. Sarah Palin at a rally the day before. John McCain at another.

He thought of Joe. An African-American might be elected President later today. Joe had been so excited about Obama, hadn't quite believed it when he started beating Hillary Clinton in the primaries, had cried when he got the nomination. Moments before he was killed, Joe had invited him to watch the election with the family. The invitation still stood. And he'd be there.

Max wanted Obama to win. Not for the good of the country, not even for what it would mean to millions of black Americans, the descendants of second-class citizens in the Land of the Free, but for Joe, his best friend, not yet in the ground, and for the memory of Sandra.

He closed his eyes and tried to think of her, but all he could see were those bullet-ridden bodies, buried in dirt and money. Who'd killed them? And why bury all that money? Maybe they were counterfeit bills. Maybe Milk had been mixed up in way more than porn.

And how much was *he* – Max – involved? Were the murders related to the film or not?

The police would want to talk to him. They'd find his DNA on the bodies, on the money, on the shovel. And Petra would tell them he'd been to the office, pissed, looking for Rudi. He pondered whether to turn himself in as a witness. He couldn't decide now.

Somehow he pushed all this out of the way and found sleep.

When he awoke it was broad daylight.

And there, on the TV he'd left on, was footage of bodies being stretchered out of Milk's house, intercut with footage of Milk and Sharona at an AVN ceremony.

'Coral Gables Massacre.'

He turned up the volume. The reporter – a woman – said that two black men were already in custody. The screen cut to the detective in charge being interviewed outside police headquarters. He gave more details. Patrol cops had spotted the men driving a stolen Lexus. They'd refused to pull over and there was a short freeway pursuit, which ended after the getaways rammed a Ford Bronco and flipped over. When officers looked in the trunk, they found a MAC-10 and about two hundred rounds of ammunition. Ballistics matched the Coral Gables slaying.

Then the news went back to live election coverage, long lines of voters stretching around blocks.

His cellphone started ringing. 'Private' flashed up under caller ID.

'Hello.'

'It's decision day, Max,' Wendy Peck said. 'What's your answer?'

24

'I'll be going away, after the funeral,' he said.

He sat with Lena and Jet around the Listons' kitchen table. The rest of the family was gathered in the living room, watching the election results. A small TV was playing on the counter, tuned to CNN, the sound down to the meagre murmur of men in suits and studio make-up around a desk.

Max had got to the house around seven, the last to arrive. Everyone was dressed in dark-blue Obama T-shirts, a thermo image of the candidate's face dominating, the set jaw and sky-ward gaze rendered in lysergic-bright national colours. Lena gave Max one of his own to put on. It squeezed him like a corset, but the sight of him raised a laugh, the way he looked like a dweeb trying desperately to blend in. The family all joined hands in prayer before sitting down to eat. They talked politics, polls and projections the whole time, no mention of Joe, no one even asking Max how he was doing. He didn't mind because he understood: it was all too close. He hadn't taken much food off the table and pecked at the morsels on his plate, the tastes indistinguishable. Around 8.30 p.m., they turned on the TV and sat down, everyone close to Joe's La-Z-Boy, but no one touching it, let alone sitting on it. Max stole glances at it, that bought-in-a-store slothbucket male recliner with built-in cooler. He could see the ridges the big man's arms and back and haunches and feet had pressed into the leather over time, a record of his presence, a trace of life. Max imagined, for a moment, that Joe was back among them; he swore he even sensed Joe's presence, almost caught a glimpse of him. Then he remembered the promise they'd made each other, the sign they'd pledged to send. What was taking him so long?

The Obama victories started coming through quickly. Illinois, Ohio, Pennsylvania, the old red map turning blue. No fuss, no recounts, no hanging chads. McCain was in the toaster and history was in the making. No one could quite believe what they were seeing, what they were on the verge of living. Apart from Lena. Max had watched her getting quieter and quieter, shrivelling, disconnecting, getting further away, the corners of her mouth drawing down to her chin. He knew she was thinking what he was thinking. Where was Joe and that way he'd dart up out of his chair and scream victory or howl defeat at the screen? The bigger and more significant Obama's victories, the sadder and smaller she became. When Florida appeared on the screen and the room cheered and someone started singing 'The Big Payback', Lena had stood up and gone to the kitchen. Max followed her out a few moments later. She was crying by the sink, the tap running hard to drown out the sound. He wondered if Joe hadn't told her about that old tactic suspects used when they thought they were being bugged. Blast the taps and turn up the TV. Max had held her for a good while. Then she made coffee and they sat at the table over their steaming cups and said nothing. Jet walked in, smiling, saying Florida was looking good. He saw them sitting there like two neighbours who'd lost everything to an Act of God. Lena asked him to turn on the TV and sit with them.

'Where are you going?' Lena asked.

'Just away,' said Max.

'How long for?'

'A while.'

'Has this got anything to do with Joe?'

He could have lied and said no, he just needed a break, but that would have been callous in every way. So he told the truth with a nod.

Lena closed her eyes, bowed her head and let out a slow, quiet, exasperated breath.

'What have you found out?' Jet asked.

How much did Jet know? His eyes and expression indicated that he knew next to nothing. He hadn't heard the name Vanetta Brown. That was being hushed up from on high, nothing filtering down: the code of silence. For now, it was best to keep it that way. Max didn't want to be the one to tell about Joe's past.

'It's out of your jurisdiction,' Max said.

Mother and son looked at each other. Jet took his mother's hand and held it. Then Lena looked at Max, into his eyes, down at his forearms and the faded blue tattoos on the inside of each. They were relics from the MTF days, permanent reminders of the mistakes of his youth. On his left arm he had 'Born to Run' written in what were once block blue capitals. Time and the loss of elasticity in his skin had blurred the script so that the letters ran together in a solid smear. On the other arm he had the unofficial MTF emblem – a shield bearing a skull and two crossed six guns, with the legend 'Death is Certain, Life is Not' scrolling around it. Everyone in the unit had one – apart from Joe, who objected to being branded. It was typical of the fatalistic attitude Miami cops had back in those days, half-expecting to die on the job. The emblem tattoo was more legible, although it had faded from dark blue to a varicose pale green that reminded him of mould.

'Haven't you done enough?' she said, her stare liquefying. Max took out his handkerchief and offered it to Lena, but she wiped away her tears with her hands, smearing her cheeks with wet silver.

Max looked into his half-finished cup of coffee, at the fine rainbow film on the surface. That was how drunken evenings had sometimes ended at Joe's old apartment in West Miami – in the kitchen, over cold unwanted coffee, after too many cigarettes and cigars, the world put to rights and making sense in the wee small hours only to get fucked up and senseless again by sun-up.

'Joe always said you were the worst one. You knew where the line was and you used it as a starting point,' she sighed. 'But I knew that anyway. About you. I knew you were no good. The first time I met you, you had blood on your collar. You'll always have blood on your collar.'

He remembered that day all too well, Joe introducing Lena as his fiancée. She'd been frosty from the moment they shook hands. By the end of the night she wasn't even looking at him, let alone talking to him. The blood was that of a suspect he'd interrogated earlier that day. He hadn't even noticed it.

Things got worse between them after a disastrous double date with Sandra. Joe didn't tell her Sandra was black, or that all of Max's girlfriends had been black. As Max found out that evening, Lena didn't mind white people, as long as they stayed in their own beds. Relations started gradually thawing after Jet was born and Max took his godfatherly duties seriously. He didn't think she'd let him darken her door after he came out of prison, but by then she'd mellowed quite considerably. They were now good friends. Time eventually destroys everything.

'Blood doesn't wash away blood,' Lena said.

'I know.'

'No, you don't.'

Max wanted to say something to that, but neither thoughts nor words came to him. He said nothing and neither did they. And that's how the three of them stayed for a long time.

The sounds of the TV in the living room were coming into the kitchen, louder than those from the set in front of them. Then there were the excited sounds the rest of the family were making. Happy happy sounds. Those of a party without music.

He glanced at the screen and saw talking heads. Behind them the country map was bluer.

The living-room door opened and Ashley came quickly into the kitchen, a big smile on her face.

'Barack won!' she said.

Her happiness withered in the room. Ashley looked lost, like she'd done something terrible without realising it.

Lena didn't react, didn't turn around to look at her daughter, to look at anyone. She was crying again, very very quietly, and Max couldn't tell if it was because of what he'd said or because of Joe, or because of the result. Maybe it was because of all these things.

Ashley slunk out, head bowed.

The TV was broadcasting live scenes from Grant Park. Obama was about to make his victory speech. A crowd of over a hundred thousand, then a cut to a single face – that of Jesse Jackson; there on the balcony when Martin Luther King was gunned down, a two-time Presidential candidate, the trailblazer, the instigator, bawling his eyes out while clutching a small American flag: the dream had finally been realised.

Jet got up and turned up the volume as the Obama and Biden families strode across the stage, hand in hand.

The President-elect spoke behind a rain-speckled bulletproof shield, and when the new first families walked away, hand in hand again, Bruce Springsteen's 'The Rising' played over the PA. Barack and Bruce, Max thought; Joe would have been weeping like Jesse about now. The TV split-screened to scenes of jubilation all around the world. He'd never seen anything like it. He wondered if they were celebrating in Cuba or Haiti. He wondered if they were celebrating in prison. He wondered what Vanetta Brown was thinking.

'I'd best go,' said Max. Lena didn't look at him.

He stood and started walking out of the kitchen.

'Max ... ' she called after him. He stopped in the doorway and looked back, meeting her puffy but hard eyes. 'Not in our name, d'you hear? *Not* in our name.'

He parked his car outside the 7th Avenue gym. He hadn't wanted to stop there specifically, hadn't wanted to stop anywhere at all, but he couldn't go any further. The street before him was blocked with a massive surge of people, thousands of them it seemed, bobbing down the road, heading away from him, chanting 'Yes We *Did*! Yes We *Did*!' and 'O! – BAM! – *AH*! O! – BAM! – *AH*!' He'd never known Liberty City like this – exuberant and vibrant, and so full of people at night.

He walked towards them and was soon deep in the crowd. Hands reached out to shake his. A woman kissed him on the cheek. At least he thought it was a woman. It didn't matter. He saw young and old, men and women, black, brown and white. Booze was being passed around, joints and cigarettes too. He felt himself swaying slightly from side to side, borne down the street like a cork in a slow-flowing stream. He had no idea where the people were going, and he wasn't sure they did either. But he let himself go, smiling all the way into the darkness.

PART II

THE OUTPOST OF TYRANNY

25

Havana.

La Habana.

It was stormy on his first afternoon. Max stood at the edge of the Hotel Naçional's grounds, looking out across the sea, a roiling, slithering mass of dirty-grey turbulence and delicate white foam. Big waves crashed on the rocks and vaulted over the Malecón wall, drenching the sidewalk and washing right over the wide road, saturating the crumbling infrastructure, seeping through its fissures and holes, getting deep into the foundations, attacking the city from within.

People were out walking; locals, not tourists. They knew the sea, how it was when it got angry. They could tell the waves apart, the ones that would make it over the wall from the ones that wouldn't. When a jumper was coming, they'd slow down, let the water do its worst and then continue along their way. They never ran. They never retreated. They never ever stopped. They kept on going, in spite of everything. Just like the country itself.

He felt the wind on his face, the warmth then the chill then the warmth again; the brine on his tongue worming its way to the back of his throat, the aftertaste reminiscent of stale tears. Above him the Cuban flag flapped in the air with a sound like muffled slaps. Lone star on red, blue stripes on white. It reminded him a little of the Texan flag, just like so much here reminded him a little bit of home. Those vintage American cars

163

in particular. A few were well preserved, but most were held together by wire, tape, hope, rust and mismatched licks of paint – Bel Airs, T-Birds, DeSoto coupes, finned Caddies, Willys trucks, four-door Plymouths, Super 88s, Skylarks – a clanking, creaking, backfiring, smoke-belching, wobbly-wheeled parade of the bygone.

To the right Havana's skyline stretched out in a claw-like curve, ending at the Castillo El Morro lighthouse. The buildings were mostly low-rise and solid, with a few flimsy-looking, garishly painted high-rises breaking the uniformity.

To the left was the US Interests Section in Havana – the US's embassy without an ambassador. It was an unremarkable concrete-and-glass building ringed with a high steel fence and a permanent guard of Cuban cops. Here the Cold War was alive and well and being fought out daily and especially nightly. When the sun went down – as it was doing now – the building became an electronic billboard. Big red digital letters scrolled across a black strip under the windows of the upper floors, spouting anti-Castro slogans and quotes. The regime had retaliated by planting a small forest of gigantic flagpoles opposite the building. The poles flew black flags with a single silver star on them – meant in part to commemorate the victims of the Bay of Pigs, the 1976 Cubana Airlines bombing, and the hotel blasts of the 1990s, and also, more practically, to obscure the enemy propaganda and keep it from the people. If that wasn't enough, the cops used whistles to warn passers-by from looking up too long and too hard. The whistle hoots were frequent and shrill, louder than the sound of the shattering waves, the wind and the cars.

It was a mere ninety miles to Key West.

A week before, he'd attended two funerals in as many days.

Eldon was cremated. No family. No friends. Just Max and a man he didn't recognise – Latin, fifties, grey hair and a snow-white goatee offset by a deep olive complexion.

164

He knew Max. He introduced himself with a handshake and a card.

Sal Donoso, Eldon's lawyer.

'We'll have some things to talk about in a week or two,' Donoso said.

'I'll be out of the country for a while.'

'I'll be in touch,' the lawyer said.

Joe was buried the next day. The funeral was a media circus, which meant the Mayor came and the Chief spoke. There was a rifle salute, a crisply folded flag and every cop turned out and sweated in their dress blues.

At the wake, all but the family avoided him. The Chief looked through him. He felt like the cork stopping a release. He made his excuses and left as soon as he decently could.

Four hours before, he'd landed in Havana from Montreal.

Terminal 2, José Martí International Airport: flags from every nation hanging from the rafters, dusty and a little worn. He'd looked for the America flag and found it. The message, clear and simple: everyone was welcome – no exceptions.

There were plenty of Americans with him; by his reckoning at least a third of his fellow travellers. Couples mostly – white, between thirty and fifty, educated, comfortably off – the kind who travelled regularly all their adult lives and wanted to broaden their horizons. The single travellers were all male. Some were business types, but the majority were the sort you got on every flight to an impoverished Third World country: overweight middle-aged droopers out for some cut-price pay-to-play. None of his countrymen spoke too loudly or made eye contact for too long. They didn't draw attention to themselves. He found that ironic, and sad and funny too. Here they were, citizens from the Land of the Free, travelling to the home of that blood-drinking repressive commie Castro – for some sight-seeing and bragging rights in the Axis of Evil – and they were scared of their own government finding out and locking them up.

The customs official had looked from his passport to his face, checked his ticket and let him through. No big deal.

'*Bienvenido a Cuba.*'

'*Gracias.*'

At baggage reclaim, female security guards stood around in tight beige uniforms – short skirts, high heels, fishnet stockings, gunbelts and full make-up. Their faces were hard – not-enough-money-hard, too-long-hours-hard; beauty etched in granite.

Max couldn't help himself. He smiled at one. She smiled back.

He wished for a second that circumstances had been different. Or that he'd come here sooner.

The arrivals were transported to their respective hotels in a flimsy Chinese bus that was like a mutant plastic toy, designed to be grown out of and discarded. The vehicle creaked and rattled and the windows almost shook themselves free at every bump; the air conditioning was temperamental, and the seats were too hard and too small.

The first glimpses of the forbidden country blipped by the window, monochromatic vistas with sporadic dashes of sharp colour. It was just as he'd imagined it, and then nothing like it at all. The buildings were a mixture of the ancient and the not so new. It wasn't falling apart exactly, but everything appeared on its last legs, badly in need of repairs and a facelift. The few construction sites along the way looked unmanned and neglected, the machinery ancient and inadequate, so it was hard to tell if something was going up or coming down. Traffic was sparse, most of the cars running slow. He noticed the complete absence of corporate advertising, no one telling you how to spend your money. State billboards proliferated instead. They hailed *La Revolución* and damned *Imperialismo*, but even here they were in thrall to fifties Americana. The propaganda was styled after drive-in movie monster posters: George W. Bush depicted as *Bush-zilla*, spitting fire on Iraqis, *Bush-acula*, the red-eyed, bloody-fanged vampire, or *Bush-enstein*, the flat-headed dollar-green ghoul. The sight of these raised a few laughs and cheers from the non-Americans on the bus, but it made his countrymen uneasy. They stiffened in their seats and pretended not to notice. He found the billboards crude but funny – and impossible to take seriously. He thought they were aimed at children. Catch 'em young, twist their soft impressionable minds into paranoid knots. The only graffiti was state-sponsored, and there was lots of it. Long, carefully painted quotes from José Martí, Che Guevara and Fidel Castro babbled from the tallest, most prominent walls; while elsewhere buildings wore murals of flags and men in berets, beards and fatigues – the conquering heroes as militarised hippies, waving clenched fists instead of peace signs, rifles instead of bongs. Wandering through this rhetorical overload were the people – on foot, on bicycles and mopeds, in the back of horse-drawn carts – skin tones ranging from black to white, a weathered deep olive the commonest shade; a nation of golden brown. They looked exhausted but healthy. He thought back to his first views of Haiti: the potholed roads, the blighted, waterless landscape, the dazed people wandering about, bodies draped in rags, swollen naked feet on sharp stone, the victims of some horrific natural calamity. Cubans may have been breadline poor, but they didn't seem that desperate, just weary and resigned to a lifetime of state-imposed hardship.

He sat at the counter of the Vista del Golfo, one of the Naçional's six bars. Photographs of the hotel's famous guests covered its walls – a hall of fame of actors, politicians, musicians, athletes and ne'er-do-wells, their photographs hanging on frames or arranged in themed montages, set into recesses and bordered in bright pink. A gold Wurlitzer jukebox stood in a corner like a neon sarcophagus and random heirlooms sat proudly displayed behind glass cabinets – a record player that had belonged to Ava Gardner, a crumbling Underwood typewriter long gone green, one of Michael Moore's baseball caps,

Lucky Luciano's monogrammed shaving kit and Gary Cooper's cigarette case.

The place was crowded, the air dense with cigar smoke and murmured conversation. The only available seats were at the bar itself, where a set of stagnant-looking red, white and blue cocktails were laid out, with national flags sitting in them instead of umbrellas.

The barman welcomed him with an effusive greeting and a handshake. Max ordered coffee, expecting a Cuban coffee like they served in Miami – an espresso so thick and sweet he could stand his spoon in it – but instead he got a regulation black coffee in a small cup. He was disappointed when he tasted it. Bustelo was better. Bustelo ruled.

Two women sat either side of him, the one on his left eating a pork sandwich and drinking beer from a bottle; the other, in make-up and a tight green silk dress with a tiger and palm tree pattern on it, looked like she was on a hot date. He felt himself being appraised in stereo. He kept his eyes pointed right ahead – except his gaze met a wide slanted mirror hanging on the wall above a row of bottles of Havana Club rum. Both women were looking at him.

The woman eating the sandwich caught his eye first, smiled and said, '*Hola.*'

Max turned slightly and nodded.

'Inglish?' she asked.

'No.'

'Where you frahm?' Her accent was pure Tony Montana School of English – with honours. She was light brown and stout, a circumference of belly made a gap between her loose T-shirt and long denim skirt. The woman to his right shot her a foul look: he was the prize who'd gotten away.

'Canada,' he said.

'Nice condree.'

'You been there?' Max asked. Very few Cubans were legally allowed to travel abroad. In fact, until recently, Cubans hadn't even been allowed into the hotels. Times had changed with Fidel Castro's retirement. The hotel ban had been lifted, but this was purely symbolic. The average Cuban, earning eighty cents a day, couldn't afford to stay in them.

'I meet Canada peoples many tyme. Nyce peoples. *Mucho simpatico.* So I teenk – nyce peoples, nyce condree.' Her teeth reminded him of a shanty town, every one of them grey brown and leaning against the other for balance. 'You arrybe today, yes?'

'Uh-huh.'

'Firss tyme you com to Cuba?'

'Yup.'

'You like?'

'So far, yeah.'

'What you name?'

'John.'

'*Qué coincidencia!*' She clapped her hands and, in a single move, brought herself, her stool and her food and drink a few inches closer to Max. 'You name in Espanish is Juan. My name is Juanita.'

'That's nice,' he said. He noticed the barman watching them intently. There was no hint of disapproval on his face. He caught Max staring and broke into a smile.

'You 'ere wid you wife?' She was looking right at his wedding ring. He'd put it on before he left Miami, the first time he'd worn it in nineteen years. It still just about fitted.

'No. She's dead.'

'*Muy triste.*' She pulled down the corners of her mouth and looked like she was about to cry.

'It was a long time ago.'

'But you still sad, yes?'

'I cry every day,' he said dryly.

'You muss no' cry.' She patted his forearm, then rested her podgy hand on it, before removing it with a subtle stroke. 'Is no good to cry.'

The woman and the barman exchanged a look. He raised his eyebrows and she gave him an almost imperceptible shrug.

'You 'ere wid girlfrenn?'

'No.'

'You 'aff girlfrenn?'

'No.'

'You come to Cuba to fyne one?'

Max shook his head. He scoped out the bar in the mirror. Nearly every man there was middle-aged, white and in various stages of physical decline. Many looked like him – bald and thickset. Sitting with them, sometimes in pairs, were Cuban women. They were stunning, well dressed, and much younger than their companions. Some might even have been teenagers. He could tell some of them had been paired off for a week or two, because their men were carefully suntanned and they were barely speaking, each in their own universe, each looking for someone better. Watching over this meat market were several of the hotel's security guards. They wore heavy black moustaches and loose blue blazers that covered paunches and guns. A security man stood in a corner to Max's left, watching the barman. Max guessed that they were running the hookers, watching who went off with whom.

'How long you stay in Cuba?'

'Two weeks.'

'A long tyme! You can meet girlfrenn.'

'I don't want to meet a girlfriend.'

'No' fo' love an' marry. No' fo' serious. Juss fo' fun, you know. Two week.'

'Not interested.'

'So why you come to Cuba? You come fo' beezniss?'

'Whatever.'

'What that? "Whatever"?'

'It's not important.'

'*Mysterioso.*' She sighed and shrugged at the barman, this time more obviously. He looked at the security guy and moved his head slightly from side to side. They weren't sure what Max was there for.

She picked a small morsel of pork out of her teeth and pulled herself as close as she could to Max, so that they were almost touching. He could smell perfume and onions on her.

'So you no' want say why you here?'

'Nothing to tell,' Max said. 'I'm a Canadian tourist.'

'You no' want to tell me because you are – how you say – *timido*? But I know you 'ere fo' some fun weev lady. Is OK. Lotta Canada people com 'ere fo' fun weev lady.'

'Furthest from my mind.'

She lowered her voice.

'You no' like lady?'

'I didn't say that.' He'd finished his coffee and he didn't want another.

'You like man?'

'What?'

'You like man – you know? Haff fun with man?'

Max laughed at that. 'No. I don't like that either.'

'What you like? You no' like woman, you no' like man?'

Then he thought of something.

'You want a drink?' he asked her.

'A drink?'

'*Uno más cerveza.*' He nodded at her empty beer bottle.

'No. Drink is fye peso. That a lot money.'

'It's OK.'

'No. Is no' OK. Is fye peso.'

'You don't want a drink?'

'Instead you buy drink, why you no' gi' me fye peso.'

'You want five pesos?'

'Si. Fye *tourist* peso. No' Cuban money. Cuban money is fo' toilet, you know. *Papel higienico.*'

There were two currencies in Cuba. One for tourists and one for locals. The tourist peso was convertible and worth twenty-five times the local peso. So much for socialism.

Max opened his wallet. He saw her eyes widen at the thick stack of bills. He gave her a ten-peso bill. She took it, looked for the barman, but he was serving a customer. She slipped the note into her waistband.

'*Gracias*,' she said.

'*De nada*.'

'You haff chil'ren, John?'

'No.'

'Me. I haf son. Him birthday tomorrow. I no' haf money to buy he present.'

'How old is he?' Max knew what was coming next.

'Six.' Without him asking, she took out a picture from a battered black leather wallet she wore on a thick chain. The kid looked about twelve and didn't resemble her at all. Plus the picture was old, creased and flaking.

'What's his name?'

'Angel.'

'Angel?'

'I need money fo' present, John.'

'I see,' he said and laughed.

She got angry.

'You tink I prostitute?'

'I didn't say that.'

'But you tink I prostitute?'

'No,' he said. If she was a hooker, she was the shabbiest, ugliest one there. Maybe that was her appeal, her hustle, her way of doing things. Or maybe she was the sort who talked money out of people with sob stories, played every note of the First World Guilt Symphony.

'I tell you what,' he said. 'I'll give you money for your son, if you do something for me.'

'Yes?'

'I want a phonebook. A Cuban phonebook.'

She frowned.

'*Uno libro de telefóno*,' he said.

'Why you want that?'

'I collect them. I go to a new country, I bring back a phonebook. Souvenir.'

'*Si?*'

'*Si.* It's my hobby. *Es mi mania.*'

'*Mania loca.*'

'Whatever,' Max said. 'Get me a phonebook. I give you some money.'

'I see you in fye minute.'

26

In his room he started checking the list of American fugitives against the Cuban phonebook.

Thirty-nine were listed, seventeen of them former Black Power activists. He'd researched them all, memorised their lives. No Vanetta Brown, but he'd been expecting that.

Max began calling. It was a slow process. Some numbers were disconnected. Others rang interminably. Some would be answered and then cut off. All the while he'd hear echoes and clicks, faint fragments of other conversations. The phone was tapped, and crudely so. The state wanted you to know you were being listened in on.

When he did manage to get through he started his spiel. He gave his real name and said he was a freelance writer researching a book about political exiles (his term) living in Cuba in the age of Obama. Would they maybe like to meet up and answer some questions? He was hung up on or told to fuck off. He was accused of being a mercenary, a Fed, or a private detective. He was told he sounded white, despite his black name, so what the fuck did he know about the black struggle?

He felt tired. He was hot and sweaty. The feeble air con whined and the room reeked of stale cigars and cleaning products. He lay down on the bed for a quick rest and ended up falling asleep for an hour. When he woke, he stretched and rolled his neck. He did a hundred push-ups straight off, then splashed cold water on his face. Out the window he could see girls in leotards practising dance moves by the illuminated swimming pool. Beyond the hotel grounds the city was dark, no lights.

He resumed his calls.

He turned on the Russian TV set as a distraction, the volume down low. The satellite channels were relatively clear. The local ones were temperamental and the image alternated between fuzzy and snowy.

He tried the disconnected numbers again, then the dropped calls.

Then he reached Earl Gwenver.

Gwenver had been a Black Panther. He fled the US when he was twenty-two. He'd shot a night clerk in a liquor store in Encino and was making his way to Mexico via Texas with his on-off girlfriend, a white med-school dropout. They were both high on reefer and the booze they'd stolen, when they stopped off at a gas station. There, an off-duty state trooper was cleaning the remains of a coyote off his car. According to the attendant, the trooper smelled the reefer and asked Gwenver and the girl to step out the car. Gwenver pulled a gun and shot him in the chest. The trooper fired back, hitting the girl in the stomach. Gwenver later claimed she shot the trooper after he called her a nigger-loving whore. According to Gwenver, his girlfriend had also held up the liquor store and shot the clerk because she was 'on some Patti Hearst trip'. He'd tried stopping her, he said. She was later found at the side of the road, a few miles from the gas station. The police reported that her body had additional wounds, fractures consistent with having been pushed out of a moving car. Again Gwenver cried foul and insisted he'd driven her to a nearby hospital.

'What you say your name was?' Gwenver asked him.

'Max Mingus.'

'Any relation to Charlie Mingus, the jazzman?'

'Not by blood. My father was a jazz musician. He changed his name to Mingus. As a tribute, I guess.'

'And you never changed it back?'

'No.'

Silence.

'We have a pie meetin' every Thursday – as in tomorrow. Why don't you come along?'

'What's a pie meeting?'

'P-I-E. "Panthers in Exile". We got our own support group.'

27

If he'd taken them all in and turned them over to the FBI, the thirteen men and women in the room would have netted him close to one and a half million dollars. Each and every one of them had shot and hijacked their way out of America. A few had killed more than once, and all but one of that number had killed a cop. The FBI knew exactly where they were, but hadn't gone after any of them. Every year the Bureau put in formal requests for extradition through US Interests, and every year the Cuban government turned them down.

The Panthers in Exile were gathered around a big wooden table with a jug of ice water in the middle and a ring of upturned glasses. They were dressed in black T-shirts, fatigues and boots. Some wore matching berets. They were close to unrecognisable from their mugshots. Age had atrophied or bloated them, made them bald and grey, bent their backs, frozen their hands, and shattered their features. Thirty-plus years in Cuba had applied the finishing touches. Their expressions were the same as those of their adopted countrymen – that look of knowing disillusion worn by old and young alike, the certainty that the pot they'd find at the end of the rainbow wouldn't even be fit for pissing in.

Earl Gwenver was the exception. Earl Gwenver looked good. Medium height and build, head shaved and gleaming, face thin and hard. He was the youngest at the table, pushing sixty but looking ten years younger. It wasn't good genes. They counted for nothing in a poorhouse country. Gwenver was making plenty of money at something – a lot more than the average official salary of peanuts and change. His Panther garb was made by Nike, the white swooshes on his breast and thigh mirroring the furry ticks he had for eyebrows. The twinkle in his eye matched the gleam of the gold studs in his earlobes. Instead of boots, he wore black-and-red Nike Shox, offsetting the black-and-red bead bracelet on his right wrist.

He'd met Max at the entrance of a three-storey building close to the Grand Theatre on the Prado, the main drag running through the heart of Old Havana. The building had once been painted pastel blue, but the façade had cracked years before and parts of it had fallen away, exposing big patches of grey and brown. Flower baskets and trays hung from the balconies on each floor, possibly to distract from the sagging clothes lines and the warped and rusty metal balustrades whose fittings were pulling from the stone.

Gwenver led Max inside, where it was peeling hot and crowded, families crammed into every space, businesses being run through the gaps. All the doors were thrown wide open for ventilation. He passed a makeshift art gallery cum studio – unframed bright and gaudy canvasses fixed to the walls with small nails. In the middle, three women sewing garments, children eating, and an old man watching television. The first floor was noisy – two bands were rehearsing in adjoining rooms; a salsa ensemble whose musicians were spilling out into the corridor and a teenage rock group doing 'Smoke on the Water' in Spanish. In an adjacent room, a man and woman were working on a car engine, while three children sat on the floor rolling a toy car to each other with accompanying sound effects.

Gwenver was explaining the history of the group as they walked.

'We started up around seventy-three, seventy-four. It was like a support group. We looked out for each other. Taught each other the ropes and the lingo, talked about shit back home. It was strictly for militant black folk, mind. We didn't let none o' that

178

common criminal element join, you dig? Castro took to lettin' in all kindsa riff-raff, anyone who could jack a plane and spout some Marx simultaneously. He had a real soft spot for fraudsters and conmen too. White-collar thieves. Ain't much left of our group now. A few dead, a few as good as, a few just stopped comin'.'

In the meeting room, he introduced Max around as a book writer.

Max was met with shrugs, grunts and plenty of suspicion. He recognised the names, recalled the crimes and dates of flight. He hadn't spoken to any of them the previous night because they weren't in the phonebook. Yet he sensed that word had spread, that they knew of him already and they didn't like what they saw. Maybe they'd smelled out the cop in him. Maybe it was because his white face didn't fit his black name. Or maybe it was simpler – the close-knit community's suspicion of the outsider.

The only people Gwenver didn't introduce him to were two stern-faced men stood at the door, legs apart and arms folded, thick, muscle-ridged forearms, overdeveloped club-bouncer physiques crammed into full Panther regalia. They didn't intimidate him. Bodybuilders couldn't do much when it came to fighting. No flexibility. Meat too heavy on the bone. One tap on the jaw button and they were down and out.

Apart from the round unvarnished table and chairs, and a dusty fan that wasn't working, the room was bare – just dirty floorboards, some loose and bent upwards; partially paint-stripped walls, the room's previous colours showing through – white, blue, green and possibly yellow.

The newest thing there was a black-and-white picture of Che Guevara – the same iconic Alberto Korda picture reproduced in giant relief at the Plaza de la Revolución: Che in his starred beret and wispy beard, his faraway windswept look, a hint of a smile on vaguely simian features. The very same image was on sale as a T-shirt, postcard, poster, button, bandana, signet ring, coffee cup, blanket and pillowcase in every souvenir shop and on every street corner. Rebellion turned into convertible pesos. And there was one of these photographs hanging in every Cuban building. It was a quasi-obligatory ornament. Just as it had been de rigueur for young Western radicals in the sixties and seventies, except that they'd had a choice. In Cuba, not to have Che on display meant you were against the fundamental principles of the state, against the very revolution it was built on. Che was a nursery rhyme, learned in kindergartens. Che's life was taught at school and analysed in college. God wasn't officially worshipped in Cuba, but Che was. The real Che was probably turning in his grave now.

Max was shown to a chair by an open window. Beyond, he heard traffic mingling with the sound of horses' hooves, the voices of children rising above those of adults.

The meeting started. Everyone stood and raised a clenched fist.

'Say it loud!' shouted Gwenver.

'I'm black and I'm proud!' came the reply.

'*Saaay* it *loud*!' Gwenver raised his voice.

'I'm *black* and I'm *proud*!' a dozen old Panthers responded, although no louder than before. Max noticed one of the fists trembling, palsied, like the head of a withered rose about to fall off in a gentle breeze.

'Brothers and sisters . . . You gotsta . . . *say it loud*!' thundered Gwenver.

'*I'm black and I'm proud!*' they yelled back, voices ragged, the volume dropping, the effort provoking wheezes and coughs.

Gwenver had mercy on them.

'Right on, brothers and sisters, right on, right on. Please sit yo bad selves down.'

They took their places, looking relieved and exhausted. The jug of water got passed around. It was empty by the time it made it back to the middle of the table.

'Last week,' Gwenver began, 'America elected its first-ever

180

black President. A *black* President. A genuine *African*-American. What y'all think this'll mean for us?'

'As black Americans or "domestic terrorists"?' asked a woman.

'Same difference,' a man quipped. He had a battered walking stick propped up in front of him.

'I say it's wack, brother,' said the man next to Gwenver. He looked fresh off skid row. Max had smelled booze on him when they were introduced. Not just on his breath, but coming out through his pores, distilled in his sweat. A few days' uneven beard growth sanded his puffy face and he wore a pair of thick-lensed glasses with both arms crudely taped to the frames. 'Obama's talkin' 'bout dialogin' wit' tha' enemy. Which means Cuba. Which means we at risk o' extradition.'

'If only the *other* guy'd won,' said another woman.

'Right on!' a male voice agreed.

'Bush was good for us,' said Stickman.

'Bad for the world,' a woman grumbled in a raspy voice.

'This ain't '*bout* the world, sister, this 'bout *us*!' said Glasses. 'Republican gunments always tighten up that ole embargo. Democrats get the White House, they start makin' sweet wit' Fidel. Travel restrictions come off, money comes in, then they conversate. Carter did it. Clinton too. Obama'll do more of the same. And we ain't even got Castro to have our back no mo'.'

Max wanted to laugh at the reasoning and its attendant irony, but he kept a straight face.

'Nothing'll really change as long as there's a Castro in power,' reasoned Gwenver. 'There'll be a few concessions on both sides, at the most. First we'll get Cuban-Americans being allowed to travel here, then regular American tourists. Then Castro'll free a few dissidents from jail – just enough to look good. That'll take at least two, three years. And *then* Obama'll have a new election to fight. He won't want to upset the Cuban exile bloc by being *too* liberal, so he'll hold back on doin' any-thing drastic before 2013. The most change we'll see here in our

181

lifetimes is loud asshole tourists complainin' about not bein' able to get their McDonald's.'

'So you sayin' we got nuttin' to worry 'bout?' asked the first woman.

'Oh, we always got *somethin'* to worry about, sister. We in Cuba, remember. Somethin's always goin' wrong here,' said Gwenver chuckling.

They took this as a cue to leave behind the politics and get personal. They complained about their homes, their neighbours, their lack of money, their lack of soap, their lack of painkillers. No one offered much in the way of sympathy. They just listened and waited to speak. They reminisced about the good old days, not the good old glory days, but when they'd had the things they missed. A million different kinds of toothpaste, two million different choices of soap. And they talked food a lot. Beef, mostly. Then candy. That was what America was to them now: one big inaccessible supermarket. They swapped personal news, how relatives were doing. A few had graduated, a few had steady jobs, a couple were in jail. The language was vintage blaxplo babble – words Max hadn't heard spoken in decades, words that had changed meaning, been reclaimed and recast and reinvented. Sadness underscored everything they said. He heard plenty of regret and little defiance. They were broken people. They were obsolete and they knew it. Nothing to fight for, just scraps to fight over. Their revolution had been televised, sold as a DVD, uploaded on the internet as a two-minute YouTube clip and promptly forgotten about, in favour of hours of stick-thin celebrities and their stick-thin chihuahuas. They were homesick too. Desperately pining for the country they'd fled, whose government and institutions they'd vowed to bring down. He felt a kind of refracted pity for them: yes, they were murderers; yes, they'd robbed families of fathers and mothers, parents of children; but they hadn't really gotten away with anything. They weren't free. They'd merely run from one life sentence to another. Conditions in Cuba may have been far better than your average federal pen, but the principle remained the same. They were never going home.

'You don't think you'll get extradited?' Max asked Gwenver when they were back outside.

'Last thing I lose sleep over,' he said.

'What *do* you lose sleep over?'

'Mosquitoes 'n' roaches – the important things in life.' He smiled.

'I don't hear you protesting your innocence.'

'Nothin' *to* protest. Someone next to you shoots a cop, they're guilty not you.'

Max could have challenged him on the particulars – but he didn't. He wasn't here for that and he wasn't here for Gwenver; plus he didn't want to risk pissing the guy off and alienating him.

The PIE meeting had lasted two hours. The conversation petered out naturally, until Gwenver called time on the proceedings. He'd taken a small black notebook out of his back pocket and asked a couple of people for their new phone numbers; then he asked if anyone needed anything in the way of food and toiletries. Almost everyone clamoured for toilet paper, and nearly as many were short on soap and toothpaste. Gwenver wrote down the orders, this time in a red notebook. He quoted prices. Everyone complained and a few tried to haggle him down, but they all handed him money. Then it was goodbyes and promises to see each other again the following month; same time, same place. No one acknowledged Max on the way out.

'Your first time in Havana, right?' asked Gwenver.

'You can tell?'

'Sure. You got newbie's eyes. All that wonder at your surroundings. I don't blame you. This place took my breath away too, first time I saw it. Let's walk.'

Havana was a beautiful ruin, a crumbling museum where sightseers had gone for an hour and stayed a lifetime, a well-heeled slum of once-grand buildings turned into hovels. At first glance these appeared condemned and empty, but were in fact full of people, their pale forms visible skirting the dark recesses of windows and doorways and balconies, indifferent to the loud bustle beyond and below them; the flocks of tourists on guided tours, the hustlers, the idling couples, the bike taxis, the dozens of schoolchildren in maroon uniforms, and the passing cops – one every thirty seconds – grey berets, light-blue shirts, dark-blue pants, earpieces, shoulder radios, guns – forever vigilant.

Max and Gwenver cut down side streets where the buildings seemed to bow towards each other, opposing walls practically touching. The road surfaces were buckled and bursting open, or else lumpy and uneven. Every few blocks they'd come across taped-off ruins of indeterminate vintage, hunks of rubble spilling across the street, people circumventing the collapsed mess.

Everywhere they went they saw the Capitolio – the pre-Castro parliament building, and a close cousin to the Capitol building in Washington, its equal in size and stature. The pale white dome dominated the rust-coloured, discombobulated cityscape, re-splendent and apart, as though it had been dropped there intact from another place altogether.

They crossed the Prado and made for a wide paifang arch, which marked the beginning of Dragones Street and Barrio Chino – Havana's very own Chinatown. The arch had been a gift from the Chinese government. In the plaque they'd mis-spelled 'Chino', dropping the 'C': it read 'Barrio Hino'.

They stepped out of the blistering sun and walked down a long arcade, past cracked and chipped curlicued columns. The worn tiled walkway had become grey and glassy, so that their reflections came back faint and dark, like fish gliding beneath the surface of a greasy lake. People were working in every doorway – banging, hammering, sawing, drilling, welding. There were men resoling shoes with strips of discarded tyre, children making sculptures out of old soda tins, women planing tables and var-nishing chairs, an old couple making crockery from a pile of broken china.

A stray rottweiler came trotting towards them. The dog looked bewildered, stunned by hunger and heat, a jumble of bones wrapped in a coat jumping with fleas. Whenever it got close to someone, it swerved sharply away, giving the passer-by a wide berth.

'Dogs scared o' people here,' said Gwenver. 'That's 'cause o' the so-called "Special Period". Back in the nineties there was a food shortage. Meat, specifically. People ate anythin' they could catch – 'cept each other. Most of the zoo animals disappeared and pets ended up on dinner plates. The government took to mass breedin' rodents for food. You ever eat a rat?'

'No. You?'

'Sure have. Tasted a bit like rabbit. Say, you hungry?'

28

They walked on through Havana's Chinatown – once the biggest and most prosperous neighbourhood of its kind in Latin America, now reduced to a single street comprised mainly of restaurants with names riffing around either 'China' or 'dragon', the décor pagoda-lite and chintzy. The menus offered mostly pizza and pasta. At the end of the road they came to a large pale-orange house with immaculate white balconies.

Gwenver rapped on the door three times. A few moments later a voice asked who it was.

'Malcolm X,' he said.

The door was opened by a young, beautiful dark-skinned woman dressed in an ankle-length turquoise Chinese dress with floral patterns running down it. The dress was shoulderless and tight, the sides split up her thighs. She was wearing too much make-up and a pair of heavy glittering earrings that stretched her earlobes to points.

She greeted Gwenver with a smile broken by a slight scrape of lipstick and a fast tumble of words Max didn't understand.

She led them inside.

Max had expected to find himself in a brothel, but it was a restaurant. The walls were all hung with dense crimson drapes, roaring gold dragons stitched into each. Garlands of red paper lanterns, strung across the ceiling, emanated a muted glow, giving the place the feel of a huge luxury coffin with a poorly fitted lid.

A dozen or so people sat around marble tables eating pizza

and sucking up spaghetti. Every last one of them oozed affluence. There wasn't the slightest hint of poverty or struggle about them. They were dressed in designer labels and jewellery. Hair, teeth and skin camera-ready perfect. The men were Latin-lover handsome, the women break-your-heart beautiful. They were young-looking, no one south of mid-thirties.

The woman summoned a waiter and he took them to their table. Like the woman, he was Cuban but dressed Chinese: white tunic, buttoned up to the collar, billowing black pants, black slippers and a black skullcap with a thin black ponytail running down the length of his back. The hair extension had been sewn into the back of the cap.

Gwenver walked ahead of Max. People stood as he neared their tables, or, if he wasn't in their immediate orbit, left their seats and came over to greet him. He gave the men skin and the women kisses. The women made eyes at him, a few whispered things in his ear – in full view of their male companions. There was due deference and due ass-kissing. There were insincere smiles and forced laughter and plenty of backslaps.

They took the table at the very end of the restaurant, opposite a fully stocked bar.

Gwenver sat with his back to the wall and ordered a rum on the rocks. Max asked for the first thing that came to mind. A Coke. He realised immediately that he'd asked for the impossible, but the man had already disappeared behind the bar.

'You don't drink alcohol?' asked Gwenver.

'I quit.'

'Problems with it?' Gwenver's right eyebrow arched up in a snowy arrowhead.

'No. Just lost the taste.'

Gwenver smiled.

There were two menus and a heavy marble ashtray on the table.

Max glanced through the menu. The meals were written in

Chinese first, with Spanish translations beneath in brackets: pizza on one page, pasta on the next, drinks on the back.

'Where do I go if I want dim sum?' he asked.

'Know how you tell a Cuban from a tourist at a Chinese restaurant? The Cuban's the one eating pizza.'

'I didn't know pizza counted as Chinese food.'

'Cubans love their pizzas, man.'

The waiter came back with the drinks. After displaying the Coke bottle – a genuine hourglass one with greeny blue tint – he poured Max's drink with great care and ceremony, as though dispensing fine wine. He was very careful not to make the Coke froth over the side of the glass, before leaving the bottle on the table.

Gwenver mumbled something to the waiter as he set his rum down. The waiter nodded and walked away.

The conversations were quiet and impossible to hear, their particulars inaudible under the sound of busy cutlery on plates.

'What is this place?' Max asked.

'What's it look like?'

'A restaurant. But an exclusive one, the kind you can't just walk into.'

'Then that's what it is,' said Gwenver.

'Not very socialist.'

'That's the thing about Cuba: nothin's as it seems and nothin's as it should be. What you think you know, you don't.'

Gwenver took a sip of his drink.

Max picked up the Coke bottle and scanned it for bottling information. He found it, below the curled logo: Pensacola, Florida.

'You can get anythin' you want here, you know the where to look, the who to ask – and the how to ask.' Gwenver winked.

'Even if it's made in America?'

'Especially if it's made in America,' said Gwenver. He downed his rum. Max had noticed how Gwenver's way of looking at him had changed. Prior to walking through the door, he'd had an open, almost happy look about him: the tour guide eager to share his enthusiasm for the country, the blissfully brainwashed propagandist peddling his manifesto for this threadbare utopia. Now Gwenver was scrutinising Max like he was some rare species of bug he'd trapped under a glass – looking at the way he was put together, working out how hard he'd have to pull to break off wings.

'Via the black market?' asked Max.

'The black market's what's keeping the government in power.'.

'How's that?'

'Dictatorships always collapse when somethin' essential runs out, somethin' people can't do without,' he said. 'Most people will put up with anythin', as long as they have three basic things: food, water and a roof over their heads. Cubans get their food from the state. Everyone has a ration book. Every month they line up outside the government stores and get their allowance of rice, beans, some kind of meat – usually chicken or pork, rarely both. It's their constitutional right to get them things. Castro's equivalent of forty acres and a mule.

'That's meant to last a month, but they're lucky if they make it to week three before one of the staples runs out. And then there's always shortages. The well has a way of goin' dry here right when you're dyin' of thirst. Been that way since the Russians stopped subsidisin' the country and Cuba had to fend for itself. That's where the black market kicks in. People don't like spendin' more than they can afford on stuff, but if it's a choice between doin' that or startin' a riot, finding a few extra pesos is easier, and healthier.'

'Castro knows about this?'

'Sure. He knows about everythin'. Publicly, he doesn't stand for it. Publicly, black marketeers are enemies of the revolution, scum of the earth, *parasitos*. That's the five-hour speech. Privately, he accepts it. He knows no one under forty's a socialist here anyway,' said Gwenver.

'Now, there's two kinds of black market – micro and macro.

189

Micro's your standard solo, money-on-the-side hustle. And there's a million different skins to that onion. One is – say I'm workin' in a government food store. I'll keep a few sacks of rice and beans by and tell the government my delivery came up short and can I have some more? No one bothers to check. Why go through all that trouble for a few pounds of rice? So I get replacement stock. I divide up the food I stashed and sell it privately for one or two times the goin' rate. Sometimes more, if there's a national shortage. Then there's the trade in toiletries. Most tourists leave behind soap, shampoo, toothbrushes. The maids keep it and either use it themselves or sell it. It's a tidy lil' bidniss. Do you know bein' a maid in a big hotel actually pays more than a doctor earns, when you factor in tips and extras? It's fucked up, but it's true.

'You know how they say history repeats itself? Well, the replay started here in the nineties. There's more hookers now than in Batista's time. Full-time hookers, part-time hookers, only-on-weekends hookers. The revolution's made whores of all its granddaughters. The young women now, they use their bodies first, their brains second. Their bodies get them what they want and they use their brains to keep it. The nightclubs and brothels are back. Soon there'll be peepshows, casinos and neon on the Malecón again. Folk are just as broke as they was before and twice as miserable,' Gwenver went on. 'Take a good look around and take a big whiff, 'cause the Cuba you seein' today is all comin' to an end real soon. When the Castros go, that's it. Five, ten years' time, and it'll be another Puerto Rico or Bahamas. The revolution's come full circle, baby. It's over. Played out.'

'That doesn't bother you?'

'Nope.'

Gwenver took an ice cube out of the glass, popped it in his mouth and chewed down on it, making the sound of heavy feet on gravel. He looked over Max's shoulder and waved to someone.

'What about the macro side of the black market?' asked Max.

'Now *that*, my man, is a whole other conversation.'

'That's what you do, right?' said Max, glancing down at the Coke bottle. And that's when he noticed a small red blemish on the first white 'o' of the brand name. When he looked closer, he saw what it really was – a pair of wings, identical in shape to the ones on the bullet casings. The mark of the Abakuás. It didn't surprise him – Wendy Peck had said they supplied every restaurant and bar in Cuba – but noticing the symbol for the first time here chilled him.

Gwenver was working for them.

Max felt his balls shrivel and his stomach tighten.

'Enough about me,' said Gwenver. 'Let's talk about you.'

'What do you want to know?'

'What do you do?'

'I told you. I'm a freelance writer.'

'Yeah, but what do you do *really*? You ain't a Fed 'cause you're too old for a gig like this. And you ain't the CIA 'cause they wouldn't send a white guy here. Be a black spic. Which narrows you down to three: cop, bounty hunter, private dick. Which is it?'

Max heard the sound of windchimes from his left and, out of the corner of his eye, he saw one of the drapes undulating slightly, the hem of the fabric rippling, as if from a draft.

He heard the door behind him close, a key turning in the lock and the snap of a bolt. He turned his head. The restaurant was empty. The plates still lay on the tables, pizzas in various stages of demolition, glasses halfway to empty, the dirty cutlery resting on napkins. He hadn't heard anyone leave. It was as if the clientele had simply been erased.

'You a writer, I'm Donald Duck,' said Gwenver, running his tongue around the inside of his mouth. 'See, I met enough in my time. But I met myself way more cops. So I do know the difference. You walk cop, talk cop, stare cop. You think it wasn't strange no one talkin' to you at the PIE? No one askin' you where you was from, askin' for some back-home news? They knew you wasn't right.

191

'So, let's start this again. Who and what are you?'

'I told you.'

'Right ...' Gwenver sighed, leaned forward and reached behind his back. He drew out a black .38 Smith & Wesson snub-nose, the humpbacked, hammer-shrouded Bodyguard model, ideal for concealment and a quick draw but wildly inaccurate on multiple shots. Not that he'd need more than one, at this range. He placed it on the table, close to his fingers. 'Maybe you wanna rethink your answer.'

Max had exactly two options.

The first was to keep denying it.

Best-case scenario: he'd get thrown out and blow his best chance of finding Vanetta Brown. Gwenver would notify the other Panthers. No one would talk to him.

Worst-case scenario: Gwenver would turn nasty. He could either turn him over to the Abakuás, who'd torture the information out of him, or turn him in to the cops, who might do the same. In short, whichever way it played, if he went with option one, he was fucked.

Option two: play for time, see how serious Gwenver was, how far he was willing to go. When you pull a gun on someone and mean to use it, you point it at a person. Gwenver had taken the gun out and put it on the table, like it had been inconveniencing him all day. He was either showing Max how bad things could get if he didn't talk or else it was a crude display of power – letting him know who was in control.

Max went for the last alternative.

'Isn't carrying a gun illegal here?'

'Quit stallin'.'

'I'm not a cop.'

'OK then, you're retired. Which means you're either a private dick or a bounty hunter. Which-the-fuck is it?'

Max looked at the gun again. It was old. The frame was scratched and there were chips and cracks in the stock. Smith & Wesson had stopped manufacturing the Bodyguard in 1997, he knew, replacing it with a lighter, more accurate model. He scanned the table for a weapon of his own. His glass and bottle were too small. The ashtray was heavy, but too far to reach. Gwenver would get the drop on him.

'I'm a private detective. But I'm here of my own accord.'

'You come *here* "of your own accord" – for *free*?' Gwenver chuckled. 'Who you lookin' for – "of your own accord"?'

Max put his palms to the underside of the table and felt cool marble against his damp, hot skin. He pushed up a little, testing the table's weight and resistance, feeling for its tipping point. It wasn't giving.

'I'm not going to tell you,' he said.

'Why?'

'Because it's none of your fucken' business.'

'Our struggle may be over, but we still a brotherhood, Mingus. You come for one of us, you comin' for all of us.'

'Is that right?'

'You bet yo ass,' said Gwenver. 'And you can play hard to get all you like, but I already got a good idea who you come for. See, the whole time I was walkin' you around, I was figurin' you out. I started with the way you talk. The South for sure, but not that inbred, tobacca-spittin', hillbilly South. You speak poh-lite South. So I'm tellin' myself, maybe this peckerwood was born there and moved away, someplace like the Midwest or the East Coast. Then I broke it down some more. Took in your clothes – lightweight pants, lightweight shirt, the way you ain't sweatin' too much, you're at ease in the heat and sun – and that's when I put it together. You from South Florida. Big city too, from your manner. Miami, by my reckonin'. And if I'm right, which I am, that means there's only one person you could be here for. Vanetta Brown.'

Max kept his reactions in check, his eyes level with Gwenver's. He moved his hands under the table, searching for the fulcrum.

'You missed your vocation, Gwenver,' he said. 'You should've been a cop. Too bad you killed one.'

'Quit tryin' to bullshit your way out of this, Mingus. Bullshit ain't your forte.'

'As you should well know. You might fool the Cubans with that "brotherhood" rap, but you're no militant. You never were. You may be the big man in this glorified pizza joint, but what you really were – and what you are and always will be – is a small-time hustler,' Max said. 'You got busted for cheque fraud when you were fifteen. You got four years. Three in youth correctional, one in San Quentin. When you got to the big house, you knew the score. Same as every teenager who goes there. Either join a gang or be some big man's bitch. All you could think about was saving your ass. Literally. So you hooked up with the Black Guerrilla Family, the Panthers' "military wing". Only you didn't give a shit about the struggle and you cared even less for their Marxist beliefs. You were getting out in a year. You were just doing what you had to do to stay alive. They were a badass gang. They were protecting you. But back out in the free world, you had no place to go. Your mama didn't want you back because that cheque you forged was hers. She was the one who turned you in. All your deadbeat friends were in jail. So you hooked up with the Panthers all over again. You were never about them or your people. You were just about you. And you still are. And for the record, looking at you face to face, I know for sure you killed that state trooper and dumped your girlfriend in the road instead of taking her to the hospital, because that's the kind of two-bit, self-serving cocksucker you really are, *brother*.'

Gwenver had lost his smile and some of his confidence. As Max was talking, he had watched the storm clouds massing in the man's stare, the way his eyes had changed to a darker, denser shade of brown. His bottom lip had started trembling.

Gwenver's fingers closed around the gun.

And Max heaved over the table. The marble edge smacked the pistol out of Gwenver's hand and on to the floor. The ashtray, glasses and Coke bottle followed, smashing. The table landed on its side and split in two, as the cloth fell softly over the mess, covering it like a shroud.

Gwenver sprang to his feet and grabbed his chair. He edged back towards the billowing drapes, stabbing the legs at Max. Mingus grabbed at the chair as Gwenver lunged. He caught a leg and pulled in hard. Gwenver tilted forward, off balance, feet tangled. Max sidestepped and threw a straight right at Gwenver's head, his fist thundering into the man's temple. Gwenver staggered back on rubberised feet, his pupils revolving up into his skull, his mouth dropping open. Max hit him again with a left hook to the chin and put him down cold.

Max picked up the pistol, which felt much lighter than a loaded gun should. He cracked the cylinder. There was a shiny round in every chamber. He upended them into his palm. When he saw what he was holding he almost laughed. The bullets were made of wood: six perfectly sculpted little ammo statuettes, spray-painted gold and copper, coated in varnish, and accurate right down to the make and calibre stamp at the base. The gun itself had been decommissioned – a metal rod was welded inside the barrel and the firing pin had been removed. No wonder Gwenver hadn't pointed it at him.

He patted Gwenver down. He tossed out his wallet – crammed with convertible peso notes – a set of keys and both notebooks. He flicked through the black one. It was an address book. No full names, just initials, addresses and phone numbers.

He looked under B.

AHB, DB, IB, JB . . .

VB.

Address: 87 Calle Ethelberg (Angola), Havana.

No number.

He pocketed the books.

Gwenver's legs twitched. He gasped and groaned. Then he spluttered. Max turned him on his back. There was blood coming out of his mouth and his eyelids were chattering.

Max heard the windchimes again, behind the drape. He got

up and pulled it back. He was staring at an empty kitchen with dirty pots on the cooker and a few dishes by the sink. The breeze was coming through the back door, which had been wedged open a crack, and it was riffling the metal chimes hanging over the window.

He went back to Gwenver, whose eyes were now open and glassy.

When he saw Max leaning over him he looked confused and lost. He started feeling about the floor and looking at his weird surroundings, his scrambled head chasing sense through deep fog.

Then he hit clarity and tried to get up.

Max pushed him back down with his foot.

'Tell me about Vanetta Brown,' Max said.

'Fuck you!'

'When d'you last see her?'

'Fuck you!'

Max grabbed Gwenver in a headlock and started choking him. Gwenver tried to wriggle free, slapping and kicking at the floor.

'Talk to me you piece of shit or I'll snap your fucken' neck!'

Just then the restaurant door flung open and the waiter rushed in. He clocked Gwenver and Max on the floor and stopped to assess the scene, his lips moving wordlessly, as if costing the damage. Other people began to come through the door, men with bats.

Max let go of Gwenver, whose head hit the floor with a crack like colliding billiard balls.

Max fled through the kitchen and slammed out the back door. He was in a narrow alley, a main road at either end, daylight scorching his vision.

He turned right and started running.

Behind him he heard shouting.

He didn't look back.

196

29

Max waited daylight out at the Hotel Naçional.

He couldn't find Calle Ethelberg on any Havana street map and it didn't appear in either of his guidebooks. As for Angola, the only mentions of it were in relation to Cuba's past military campaign in the African country.

He tried the hotel's internet, which was unrestricted to tourists, but he drew the same blank. Vanetta Brown, he concluded, lived in a part of town the state didn't want tourists to see or find out about – either because it was an unphotogenic dump or because it was secret.

He went out shortly after 10.30 p.m. and headed up La Rampa, the main road linking the outskirts of downtown Havana to the Malecón, into which it spilled like a concrete tributary.

Traffic was sparse, but both sidewalks were congested with flocks of young people descending on the seafront in chatty, perfumed waves. The Malecón was where Havana's young hung out, their communal stoop. They filled up the length of the promenade and stood five deep on the sidewalk or sat back to back on the wall, facing the city or the sea, making sure to pick the dry spots, where the waves and sea spray wouldn't catch them. It was a kind of informal street party where they'd break out guitars and have singalongs, read poetry or perform plays and amateur gymnastics; they'd eat roasted peanuts out of paper flutes bought from roving vendors and pass around bottles of white or yellow Havana Club, the cheapest kind. Max kept out of their way, but he couldn't keep himself from looking at them. They might have been poor, but every last one was dressed to kill, the girls in tight jeans, sheer tops and heels; the boys in polo shirts with the collars up, laceless sneakers and pants worn at half-mast. But these Cuban kids were not like their spring-break equivalents in Miami. They were the quietest he'd ever known a crowd of young people to be. He guessed why and had it confirmed. They were being watched and filmed from unmarked cars parked in the sideroads: the state was chaperoning its young like a harsh, possessive and deeply unloved parent – and crushing a little of their vitality along the way.

He turned left at the Calle L intersection and made for the Habana Libre, originally and briefly the country's first Hilton before Castro seized it on behalf of the revolution and transformed its plushest suites into his headquarters. The building was imposing in a drab and functional way, a monolithic blue-and-white rectangle that seemed to have been designed by an architect mistaking Havana for a coastal town in New Jersey.

Parked outside the entrance was a row of taxis, each car painted a shade of eyesore yellow. At the head of the line were four vintage Checker cabs and an Aerobus, both of which Max had only ever seen in old movies. A quintet of Soviet matchboxes followed these, and, trailing back like an interminable series of suspense dots, a line of coco cabs – pod chairs on three wheels powered by moped engines.

Max went up to the first Checker driver and told him where he wanted to go. The driver asked him to repeat the address and when Max did, he shrugged his shoulders and said he didn't know where it was. The next driver, who'd overheard the first, did and said the same thing, but he was a bad actor. He couldn't look Max in the eye any more than he could keep the nervousness from his face. Max bypassed the Aerobus and went up to a man leaning against a Lada, his head hidden by a newspaper.

'I no' take you,' he said softly from behind the paper he didn't bother to lower. 'No one here take you. No' even coco.'

'Why not?'

'We no' go.'

'Why?'

'*Camino muerto.*'

'What?' Max's grasp of Spanish was at best tenuous. A lifetime living in Miami and he'd only recently got to first base with the language, and that purely by enforced osmosis. '*Camino muerto?* That means "dead road"?'

'*Sí.*'

'So – what? – the name's changed? Is that it? I got the name wrong?'

'You can no' go.'

Some people came out of the hotel and got into the first Checker cab.

'What about Angola?' asked Max. 'Where's that?'

'Angola?' The driver lowered his paper and smiled. He had a round face and thin shoulders. 'Angola is in Africa, *señor.*'

'You know where I mean.'

'My brother was soldier in Angola.'

'You don't want to take me?'

'To Africa? I need visa.'

'You're a real funny guy. Look, I'll pay you. I'll pay you well.'

'*No señor. Lo siento.*'

'A lot of money. *Mucho dinero.*'

The driver looked at his paper.

'OK. Why don't you just give me the directions?'

'Try by La Coppelia.' The driver nodded to where Max had come from. 'Is possible you find person *muy desesperado*. Them take you to *Habana nuevo*,' the driver said.

'*Habana nuevo?* New Havana? What's that?'

'*Buenas suerte.*' His newspaper went back up. Max noticed it was upside down.

La Coppelia was a vast ice-cream parlour built on an entire block on La Rampa. Each weekend Cubans of all ages would

199

line up for two scoops and – money permitting – a fruit juice. Service was slow, stifled by demand, and there weren't ever enough places to go around, despite the saucer-shaped parlour's two floors. Once inside, people liked to stay a while. Prospective customers would have to wait, patiently and quietly, sometimes standing in the baking heat for hours, so determined were they to add a small dash of sweetness and colour to lives well short on both. Tourists flocked there too. It was in the Things To *So* Do section of the brochure. They had their own queue, shorter and faster than that of the locals. Most came out disappointed with the quality of the ice cream. It was a microcosm of Cuba, they said: basic flavours, not enough milk, portions too small, every shortfall in composites masked by excessive sugar. Still, they consoled themselves, it was nice to see what ordinary Cubans did for fun.

Max walked around the entire block looking for transport with a desperate soul at the wheel. It was poorly lit, most of the street lamps dead, every few feet a big blue plastic bin on wheels was parked in the gutter, overflowing with putrefying heat-baked trash. Roaches were crawling all over them, fighting each other to get first bite at the filth inside. Every so often a breeze would cut through the heat and blow the foul and fetid smell in his face, making his eyes smart and his gut convulse.

The prostitutes came at him quick and furtive. Even through the feeble light and blankets of make-up, he could see they were too young, that they belonged with the Malecón lemmings. Their approaches were strictly by the book. Some would try to strike up conversations, some asked him for the time or a light, some dropped the pretence and cut straight to the chase – 'You like go with me?' – while a couple, unsure of his nationality, propositioned him in three or four different languages before getting round to English.

After two fruitless turns, he stopped by the La Coppelia sign to reassess. A bike taxi wobbled past, ridden by a tiny, decrepit-looking black man with round pebble glasses and a baseball cap. His feet barely reached the pedals. He looked at Max as he passed, the ambient light turning his specs into two bright white dots. He grinned and waved. Max ignored him. When the driver reached the end of the road, he doubled back. This time he stopped, dismounted and came over. He was in a white vest, white shorts and beaten-up tennis shoes with holes in the toecaps. He was out of breath and sweating hard. He looked about sixty.

Jesus, no, Max thought as he braced himself for the hustle. He was flat out of patience.

'*Hola*, my frenn!'

'*No gracias*,' Max pre-empted him.

'*No gracias?*' The man was surprised. 'Why *no gracias?*'

'No,' said Max. 'Whatever it is you're selling or offering. Thank you but no thank you.'

The man frowned. His face was so furrowed he looked like a prune.

'You no' want taxi?'

'You call that a *taxi*?' The passenger part was a wire-covered trailer hitched to the back of the bike. Its seat was a wooden plank covered with filthy-looking cushions. The bike itself was listing to one side.

Then Max thought about it. He told the man where he wanted to go. The man looked doubtful and very worried.

'I'll give you a thousand pesos.'

'*Tourist* peso?'

'Yeah. Half now. Half when you bring me back'.

The man looked up and then down the road.

'*Mil pesos?*'

'*Si. Prometo.*'

'*OK. Vamos.*'

Down La Rampa they went, bumping and rattling along the uneven road. Max held on tightly to the wire basket as the bike hurtled towards the Malecón, every bounce and hard landing jolting his spine and threatening to throw him out of the seat. The driver – who'd introduced himself as Teofilo – whooped and hollered, sticking his feet out in the air and waving his hands around.

'I like go *fas*'! I like go *fas*'!' he yelled.

When the surface flattened out, Teofilo started struggling. Veins popped out of his slight bare calves and sweat rained down his back, as if his body had sprung a leak. He grunted and groaned, breathed heavily, and cursed frequently. They were overtaken by bendy buses stuffed with sorry-looking passengers, coco cabs, horse-drawn carts, pack horses, a trotting donkey, people on foot.

After an eternity they reached the Prado, which was crowded with tourists going in and out of bars and restaurants, spilling out of hotels, cruising around in open-topped cars, camcorders and digital cameras canning and pickling the view.

They clattered slowly through side streets until the next main road, when an exhausted Teofilo grabbed the back of a passing truck, letting it pull them along. With his free hand, he took a swig of water, wiped his face with a rag and tipped his cap at a group of girls looking in the window of a clothes store.

'You strong man!' Teofilo yelled at Max.

'Strong?'

'Yes, strong man. Drink much beer, yes!'

'I don't drink beer.'

'You drink much milk, yes!'

Max understood what he was getting at. 'You mean I'm fat? Heavy?'

'Yes, strong fat man, hebby man, drink much milk!'

'It's all muscle.' Max laughed.

The street forked off at a set of traffic lights and Teofilo let go of the truck and they went left. The road curved gradually and began to dip. They glided down.

Teofilo turned on the torch taped to the handlebars. The beam bounced and shimmied around, splashing on partially collapsed buildings, ominous-looking and crooked, jutting out of the ground like the hulls of torpedoed ships stuck in sandbanks. Variations of the Angolan flag were painted on every upright surface: red-and-black horizontal bars with either a gold star or a machete crossed over a half-cogwheel in the middle. A smell of smoke hung in the air, under it a deeper stink of trash and decay.

They pressed on. The streets turned to rubble and dirt. The bike responded with a riot of angry clanks, as if telling Teofilo the effort was all too much and it was only going through this as the last of final favours.

There were people all around them, still and soundless, blank expressions on grimy faces, eyes void, their passage reflected but not registered. Normally Max would have been tense and on edge, expecting to be set upon, but these were defeated creatures, as hollow as the buildings they populated. He saw groups of children in the remains of gutted cars, pretending to drive, two legless men on pallets racing each other down a slope, a platoon of people in ragged fatigues, marching in perfect formation, but on crutches. And at every turn small gatherings of Santeria worshippers, dressed head to foot in white, bowed before candle-ringed altars, their devotions watched by packs of weak and hungry dogs.

It took another half-hour to navigate the ruins, the road sometimes so potholed they both had to get out and carry the taxi.

It was Max who noticed the lights first – a row of small emerald bulbs embedded in a high wall, sparkling like displaced cat's eyes.

As they rolled down the street, the surface became smooth and intact, and other buildings began to appear – modern, surrounded by high spiked railings topped with barbed wire. They read descending numbers on the walls, even to the right, odd to the left.

'Is this Calle Ethelberg?' asked Max.

'*Si, camino muerto*,' Teofilo muttered.

203

Apartment blocks followed the gated buildings. There were lights on in the windows.

They reached a crossroads before the numbers went down to double digits. Max told Teofilo to stop.

He got out, took most of the money he had in his wallet and handed it to the driver, who checked and rechecked it, his mouth hanging open before closing around a broad grin.

'When we go back, I'll give you more. *Quinientos pesos más*,' said Max.

'I way for you 'ere.'

30

The apartment block was part of a long stretch of seemingly identical low-rises making up the rest of Calle Ethelberg, as far as Max could see; a slim dark cube with seven pairs of windows and a recessed doorway for a façade. Only its number and the small pale satellite dish fixed to the roof like a defiant boutonnière identified it from its neighbours.

The main door was locked, as expected. He'd brought his tools: an electronic pick gun and a torque wrench. An old snitch of his called Drake Henderson had given him lessons in lock-picking as a twenty-fifth birthday present. Back then they'd used manual tools – wrenches, hammers and metal picks – and the average American lock had taken eight minutes to open. They were the best and the worst of locks, depending on whether you were the picker or the picked. Now the skill was mostly electric, just one principal tool – a battery-powered pick gun – combined with brute force and timing.

It had been a while since he'd broken into a building, but it was a classic pin-tumbler Yale and he knew exactly what to do.

It was pitch dark. He turned on his small flashlight.

He was standing at the edge of a long and narrow lobby, leading to a staircase with small potted palms either side, the tiled floor in between depicting a map of Cuba. No reception desk, no chairs, no cameras.

There was an elevator to his right and, on the opposite wall, a dozen wooden mail slots, in three rows, labels on each pigeonhole. He found the name 'Vanetta Brown' at the start of the second row, in typewriter capitals, a number '5' in brackets after it. The slot was empty, as were the others, which meant that technically everyone was home.

He took the stairs up.

On the first floor were two doors on opposite sides of a marble landing, a red Roman numeral stencilled on each, with a peephole right above them. Apartment I was quiet. From II came the sound of canned monologue – a TV playing.

A small party was winding down behind door III on the next landing: cigar smoke, overlapping conversations and faint music. Nothing from IV.

He tiptoed up the next flight of stairs.

Complete silence on the landing.

He knocked gently on the door of Apartment V and listened. When he didn't hear anything he knocked again, slightly louder.

She was either fast asleep or she was out.

He went to work on the lock.

He couldn't see much of the room because the light was faint, barely making it through the window, which was encrusted with dirt and dried rain residue. The apartment was hot and the air smelled stale and slightly chemical, as if the place hadn't been aired for a while.

There was no one here. He'd known that almost as soon as he shut the door behind him. The apartment felt familiar, so much like his own did whenever he walked in – the same sense of inter-rupted vacuum, of being in a void with a black hole at its centre.

He torch-panned the room. A bookshelf dominated it, cover-ing the entire left wall, floor to ceiling, even incorporating the space above the side door, where two shelves overlapped the top of the frame. Nearly every title was Spanish. There were histo-ries, biographies, travel books, atlases, encyclopedias, plenty of politics, bound volumes of Castro's speeches; in between a smattering of fiction, all pulpy romantic novels, which surprised

206

him, but then he guessed even great minds needed diversions. He followed the library to the window. On the bottom shelf, stacked loose, were a dozen copies of *Black Power in the Sunshine State*. He noticed a piece of paper sticking out of one.

It was a compliments slip from the publisher.

'To Vanetta – With best wishes on this great day! – Antoine'.

Antoine Pinel, he guessed, publisher and owner of Cuban X-Press.

The address was on the paper: Centro de Negocios, Miramar, Habana.

He put the slip in his pocket and carried on looking, the torch beam landing on a small TV and an old VCR on a white stand. Until recently, all video equipment had been banned in Cuba, although that hadn't stopped people from acquiring it on the black market or from visiting relatives. Raoul Castro had reversed the law and there were now DVD players and video cameras on sale in electronics stores – though with prices starting at a year's salary, it was just another kind of prohibition. He checked the VCR for an Abakuá marking, but found none.

He looked through the stack of tapes – Cuban soaps, documentaries and cookery programmes mixed in with *The Cosby Show*, episodes of *Oprah* going back fifteen years, some Spike Lee and Denzel Washington films, and virtually everything Will Smith had appeared in, including *Wild Wild West*, which made her a diehard fan. He compared the handwriting on the Cuban and American television tapes. They were completely different: the former was cursive and semi-legible, the latter printed and mostly capitalised – distinctly male writing. Someone had made the American tapes for her and they'd been doing it for a long time, because the print on the older recordings had faded.

When he left the room he found himself in a corridor linking four rooms.

He worked them left to right.

A small, cramped kitchen with barely room for one: refrigerator and cupboards bare, the cooker smelling of cold fat and cleaning products.

The bathroom was completely empty. No toiletries anywhere, no paper in the holder. He checked in and behind the cistern. Nothing hidden there.

The third door led to a study. It was a simple set-up: a desk with a manual typewriter and an unplugged lamp, a wooden chair with a cushion tied to the lower back; above the desk hung a corkboard, its surface sun-bleached with outlines of whatever had been pinned there.

Last of all was the bedroom. The curtains were closed, so he turned on the light. It was small and congested. The four pieces of furniture – a single bed and nightstand, an antique oak closet with double doors and a matching chest of drawers – took up most of the available space.

The chest of drawers was empty, as was the closet, which had a mirror inside the door. No clothes or hangers, no food, no toiletries, no suitcase.

He checked behind and under them. Nothing.

When he opened the nightstand drawer, something white rolled towards his hand: a small plastic pill tub with a childproof cap.

He read the label: Zofran – made by GlaxoSmithKline.

He recognised the name, but couldn't place it. The tub was empty. He slipped it into his pocket.

She'd moved out. Why? And where to?

As he went to leave the room he paused at the door, looking it over one more time.

Had he missed anything?

Yes, he had. The study: he'd forgotten to check behind the desk.

He went next door, put the typewriter on the floor and moved the desk. On the ground, standing with its face to the wall, was a photograph. He supposed it had fallen off the board.

He picked it up and turned it around.

At first it didn't make sense, what he was looking at. A blankness came over him. A complete absence of thought or feeling, a numbness of mind.

He sat down at the desk, torch in hand, the image in the spotlight. The photograph was of two people, a man and a woman. They were standing in a street, both smiling, their arms around each other's shoulders. The woman was Vanetta Brown – much older than the proud, defiant woman whose face he'd memorised, but time had spared her its worst. She was dressed in a denim skirt and black blouse, her grey-streaked hair worn in cornrows. The man at her side was taller and darker than her, and also twelve years younger. Max knew their age difference, because he knew when they were both born – and because he also knew who the man was. He'd known him well, or so he'd thought.

Joe Liston.

He closed his eyes, took a deep breath and looked again, the light he held quaking like nudged jelly.

The photograph had been taken over a decade before: Joe was younger and far slimmer, his hair styled in the sharp fade cut he'd sported when he still had enough on top to flirt with baldness.

Now nothing made sense.

Joe had come here, to Cuba, to visit Vanetta Brown.

Why? Had they been friends? *Lovers*?

Max went back to their final conversation. He remembered the look on Joe's face when he asked him if he'd been to Cuba, the way he'd changed the subject abruptly.

He spotted a small pinhole in the photograph's border. He turned the picture over, looking for an inscription or a date, but there was nothing.

His mouth had gone dry. He couldn't swallow. He wanted to search the apartment over again, pull all the books out of the library, but he knew he couldn't. He didn't have the time.

*

He switched off the light and opened the front door a crack to check that the landing was empty.

It wasn't.

An old woman in a dark-blue dressing gown was standing in front of the door, looking right at him. They both got a shock. She gasped and took a step back.

'*Quien son usted?*' she whispered. The door of the opposite apartment was ajar and light was spilling on to the landing. He thought he'd been quiet.

She was short; her dressing gown completely covered her feet and the back hem trailed her by a few inches. Her curly hair was grey going into white and framed tiny, skewed features set in chalky, lined skin that sagged about her cheeks.

'*Quien son usted?*' she asked again, louder. Her voice was clear and strong and seemed to belong to someone much taller and bolder.

Max stepped out and closed the door behind him. She retreated two steps.

'*Soy un amigo,*' he said, as quietly and as gently as he could.

'*Americano?*'

'*Si.*'

'*Policiá Americana?*'

'*No, no señora. Soy un amigo.*' Max edged towards her, making her back away towards her own apartment. She was standing between him and the stairs.

'*No.*' She shook her head. '*Usted no es su amigo. No le conozco.*' Her voice rang around the landing, the echoes sharp and metallic.

'*Hablas Inglés?*'

She nodded, clasping the edges of her gown together tightly.

'I'm a friend of Vanetta's.'

She cleared her throat.

''Ow you fine dis place?'

'She gave me the address.'

'No' true,' she said, wagging a finger at him. 'She *no*' do that. She *no*' have visit. She never *have* visit.'

210

'She gave me her address,' Max repeated, shrugging, palms out, pantomiming innocence while sneaking a look down the stairs. He knew he had to go, but he'd have to get past her. She was frail and easy to push past. She'd call the cops. Teofilo's bike couldn't outrun an elephant if the elephant was standing still. Best to try and salvage the situation, convince her that he was telling the truth.

'She *no'* give you dis a'ress,' she said. 'She no' tell no person. 'Ow you come here?'

'Car.'

'Is no car ou'side.'

'It's parked behind the building.'

'You *lie.*'

'No.' Max advanced a step, thinking she'd move back, but she didn't budge. She wasn't scared of him.

''Ow you get key?'

She'd doubled up on the volume and aggression. People were going to hear her, for sure. People were going to come.

'*No es importante,*' he said.

'*No, señor. Es muy importante!*' She took a step forward. Max held his ground. They were almost touching.

'Where's Vanetta? If you know, please tell me. I have to find her.' Max had raised his voice too.

''*Ow* you get key?'

'I have to find her. This is *very* important.'

''*Ow* . . . you . . . get . . . *key*?'

She said the last slow and loud. Her voice echoed around the stairwell.

Upstairs a door opened.

'Please—' Max began but stopped when he heard voices – male and female – downstairs. They were saying their goodbyes and there was laughter.

''*Ow* . . .?' the woman screamed. Max clamped his hand over her mouth, grabbed her in a headlock and started pulling her back to her apartment.

211

A voice below asked what the noise was, if everything was OK.

A man in a faded purple T-shirt and tartan boxer shorts appeared at the top of the stairs leading to the floor above. Stocky going to fat, clouds of dark fluffy hair on his upper arms, a thick moustache, no hair on top of his head, bar a few stray tendrils, the man looked like he'd just got out of bed and was trying to work out if he was dreaming.

Max saw the man and stopped. The old woman slapped at his arms and stamped on his feet, screaming under his hand, her throat making a sound like a drag car stuck in mud.

Max and the man on the stairs eyeballed each other, neither moving.

The old woman was now making wretched, caterwauling noises. She shook one fist at her neighbour and punched Max with the other.

The man on the stairs woke up in a snap. He took two steps down. Then he leaned over the banister and scooped a hand back and forth towards his shoulder: the universal come-up-here-fucking-*quick* sign.

The old bat bit Max's hand. She got her teeth into the flesh at the base of his thumb, dug in and clamped down unbelievably hard, breaking the skin, drawing blood.

Max cried out and yanked his hand away, spinning the woman around in a full circle. The woman tottered forward, then sideways, grabbing out at the wall for support, before falling flat on her back with a yelp.

Max bolted down the steps. Four people – two men, with two women behind – were rushing up. He bulldozed his way past, nearly knocking one over the banister. A woman screamed. The old woman splutter-yelled: '*Aaa-se-sino! Policiá! Policiá!*'

On the first floor, someone tried to get in his way. He pushed them over.

He sprinted across the lobby, outside and down the street, back to his last point of reference: Teofilo and that useless junk-heap bike. How the fuck was he going to get away on *that*?

But it was no longer an issue.

Teofilo was gone from the intersection.

In front of him in the dark was nothing but an empty road with a small twister of stray trash dancing in the middle.

In the breeze he caught a hint of perfume – a scent he recognised. He tried to place it: classy and expensive, old-fashioned. He remembered buying his wife perfume – a bottle of Ysatis by Givenchy.

Then something cool and hard was pressed up behind his right ear.

'*Manos arriba.*'

It was a woman's voice. Max did as he was told and put up his hands.

31

He didn't know how many people were behind him. The woman cuffed his wrists behind his back, clamped her hand on top of his head and forced him down like a plunger, before pitching him face-forward with a kick to the back, her every action under-scored with a whiff of perfume. He landed heavily on the sidewalk, his chin bouncing off cement.

She spread his legs and frisked him, tossing out the contents of his pockets – the lock-picking tools, torch, wallet, the photo-graph, Zofran tub and the publisher's note. He saw her in glimpses: feet shoed in flat polished loafers with rubber soles, black-stockinged calves, a hint of skirt, dark hands patting down his shirt, manicured nails, a flash of pinkie ring, a thin silver ID bracelet, the shade of her pale-blue blouse coordinating with that of her nail polish.

'Stand,' she ordered. He dragged himself to his knees, but couldn't make it to his feet. She grabbed him by the arm and lifted him upright. She was slightly taller than him and almost as broad about the shoulders. He couldn't see her face.

She'd come alone. He thought about how far he'd get, how fast he could go with his hands chained behind his back and his balance off. Not far or fast enough. Plus she had a gun. So he thought instead about what would come next, and how he'd explain breaking into someone's apartment. Maybe trying to run wasn't such a bad idea.

She shove-walked him down to the bottom of the road to where a white Suzuki was parked. It had tinted windows and no markings of any kind. She opened the back door. He dipped down and clambered inside. She got in behind in the wheel.

The interior was a standard prowl-car rig – hard cushioning, no handles on the doors, a thick grille between him and the front seats, shatterproof glass, a radio on the dash – but it was infused with her scent, lilac and a strong hint of rosewood.

They drove off down Calle Ethelberg, where more lights had come on in the apartments. A small crowd had gathered outside number eighty-seven.

'The penalty for housebreaking here is twenty years, minimum. We don't have parole or time off for good behaviour. In Cuba, a sentence is a sentence: the time you get is the time you serve,' the woman said, once they'd got on to the main road to down-town Havana. In conversation her voice was softer and warmer than Max had expected, and she spoke perfect but studied English, her pronunciation and accent fighting to a tight draw. It made what she was saying sound far worse. 'The penalty for spying is more severe.'

'I wasn't *spying*.'

'You entered a restricted area and broke into the home of a government-protected citizen. And you're American. So that makes you a potential spy,' she said.

'Bullshit,' Max snapped. 'I didn't even know it was restricted.'

'It is.'

'Well, if that's your idea of restricted . . . I got there on the back of a *bicycle*. Anyone can walk in.'

'Nobody does – usually,' she said.

'What do you mean by "government-protected citizen"?'

'Señora Brown is a close personal friend of Fidel Castro. They have a long history.'

'Fuck,' Max whispered. Just how much shit had he stepped in and how deep did it go? Vanetta Brown would have known Fidel through her former in-laws, the Dascals. They'd been Castro's fundraisers in Miami. Vanetta had met Ezequiel, her future

215

husband at a talk Castro had given on Flagler Street in the late 1950s. She might even have been introduced to Fidel then. Vanetta's coming to Cuba wasn't a simple case of fleeing to a country with no US extradition agreement. She'd had a personal connection here – and a powerful one.

'What were you doing in Señora Brown's house?'

'I was looking for her.'

'Why?'

'I need to talk to her,' he said. 'That photograph you took off me? The man there is – was – my friend, Joe Liston. He's dead. He was murdered in Miami a couple of weeks ago.'

'What's that got to do with Señora Brown?'

'She's a suspect. Miami Police think she had him killed.'

'*Had* him killed?'

'They think she hired a hitman.'

'Did they send you?'

'No one sent me.'

Three police Ladas sped along the opposite lane, blue lights flashing. Max thought he saw her shoulders tense a little as the cars approached and relax once they'd passed.

'What proof do they have?'

'Her fingerprints were found on bullet casings at the scene,' he said, mentally parcelling out the information, calculating how much to tell her and how much to keep back. Things didn't feel right. They hadn't from the moment they'd left. The trappings of law enforcement were all in place – gun, cuffs, frisking – but there was a notable absence of procedure, of rules: no back-up, no ID shown, no on-the-spot questioning, no talking to witnesses. It was as if she'd been waiting for him, expecting him. And what had happened to Teofilo?

'You sound doubtful,' she said.

'I am,' he continued. 'It doesn't make sense.'

'Is that why you've come – to make sense of it?'

'Yeah. That was the plan, till you showed up.'

She glanced at him briefly in the rearview mirror. She had

216

pretty, hazel eyes. Max felt a smile instinctively coming to his lips but quashed it. What was he thinking?

'Do you know Vanetta Brown?' he asked.

'Let's keep this simple,' she said. 'I ask, you tell. OK?'

'Sure.' He nodded. 'You speak great English, by the way.'

'Don't patronise me.'

'It was a compliment.'

'Don't compliment me either.' She knew what he was trying to do – build enough of a rapport to get her to lower her guard – and she was heading him off at the first pass.

'Fine.' He shrugged.

They were in the suburbs, bumping along pitted cobblestone streets whose sidewalks sported smart whitewashed edges, and whose grand post-colonial houses hid dilapidated façades behind trees and wild bushes.

'You're not exactly the first person who's come here to meet with Black Panthers,' she said. 'It's a regular little pilgrimage: reporters, groupies, naive idealists, families of the people they killed.

'Earl Gwenver preys on them. He'll set up a meeting with the Panther of choice – for a fee, of course. Half upfront, half on delivery. He takes them out to a deserted spot, threatens, sometimes beats them, and then brings them back to their hotel rooms and takes everything – except passports and plane tickets. Sometimes, if there's a national shortage, he helps himself to the toilet paper. They never go to the police. They're American. They're not supposed to be here. They just leave, as quickly as possible. This was supposed to have happened to you. Why didn't it?'

'Gwenver and I never got round to talking money,' said Max. 'Did you hurt him?'

'He'll live.'

'That's a shame.' She glanced back at him.

'Who are you?' he asked.

They were close to central Havana. The traffic got a little

heavier, the streets brighter and more built-up. People everywhere. He heard music and singing. They passed half a dozen couples dancing the mambo with frozen smiles and focused eyes, while a group of tourists filmed and photographed them, moving uncoordinated hips and flat feet in imitation, snake-charmed by the beat, oblivious to the three young boys threading through them, dipping quick little hands into bags and back pockets.

'You were put under surveillance as soon as you arrived,' she said. 'All Americans are, for obvious reasons. On your first day you bought a phonebook from a prostitute. You made calls to former Black Panthers, posing as a writer. Then you entered Gwenver's orbit. Now you're in my mine.'

'What do you want?' he said.

'Before you went to prison, you specialised in finding missing persons. How good were you?'

That completely blindsided him. He suddenly felt himself shrinking as the environment he was in began to reveal its claws. He hadn't just been watched, he'd been *researched*. How far back had they gone? And how deep? It couldn't have been too hard a dig. He was on the internet. His 1989 trial had made the news and there were clips of it on YouTube. But what else did they know?

'It paid the bills,' he said, keeping his tone on ice.

'Well, Señora Brown is a missing person,' she said. 'I want you to find her.'

'What do you mean by "missing"?'

'She's vanished. On the fourth of April, she was supposed to attend a function – a ballet about the life of Martin Luther King at the Grand Theatre. She didn't show. We went to her apartment the next day and found it empty – just like you did. Most of her personal effects were gone. No note, no phone call. This is a surveillance state. People don't just disappear here. Even the ones who escape – they always turn up somewhere, somehow.

'Out of the blue, we heard about the policemen murdered in Miami. And then you arrived.'

Max looked at her with surprise. She knew about Eldon and Joe. And she knew about him. So she'd already made the connection.

'We don't just have eyes and ears here. Miami watches us and we watch Miami.'

'So who do you work for? The state?' he asked.

'Everyone works for the state.'

They drove past the Habana Libre and then to La Coppelia. She found a spot close to a blue trash bin and parked.

'If you haven't been able to find her, what chance do you think I've got?' Max said.

'If things were that simple, you'd be under arrest now.' She turned and looked at him, the light picking out her profile. She had long black hair, tied back in a ponytail, and appeared to be wearing make-up. 'You're to stay here until you either find her or you find out *exactly* what happened to her.'

Max leaned over to the grille. 'Are you saying I can't leave?'

'Not until your job's done.'

'Fuck you. You are not allowed to do this to me.'

'Why?'

'I'm an American. I'm not one of your fucken' people.'

She didn't thaw. She kept every sub-zero ounce of cool.

'Then you can go to jail with our "fucking people". And if you think surviving seven years in one of your prisons was hard, you really don't know what hard is. Here, it's six to a small cell, if you're lucky. And you won't be. The inmates despise foreign criminals, because compared to them, every foreigner has a better life – especially Americans. But the lowest of the low in our jails are the thieves. People don't have a lot to begin with. Possessions come a very close second to family.'

'I'm no thief,' he said.

'No? Those are thieves' tools.'

'I was a spy a moment ago.'

'What are spies if not thieves?'

Max looked out of the window at the bin. He focused on a pair of roaches scuttling up the middle, heading for a small gap where the lid was warped open.

'You can either spend a little longer doing what you came here to do in the first place. Or I can drive you to headquarters,' she said.

God, she reminded him of Wendy Peck. Same shit, different day, different country.

Max thought about it. Again, he had little choice. Maybe even less than in Miami. Whichever way he looked at it, he was already halfway to prison.

'If I go along with this, will I get access to files, reports, witness statements?'

'No,' she said. 'You're to proceed as you would have done.'

'But I'll be covering the same ground you did, chasing up leads you already know go nowhere.'

'Weren't you following? We had no leads. No one saw anything. No one knows anything.'

'What happens if I don't find her? Or don't find out what happened?'

'You keep looking.'

'What happens if I still don't find her?'

'You keep looking.'

'Anything you can tell me, a little nugget to get me started – anything at all?'

'Señora Brown formed some complicated alliances.'

'The Abakuás? She was in with them. Is that it?'

She didn't reply. She gathered up everything she'd put on the front passenger seat and got out of the car. He heard her putting things on the roof. Then she opened the passenger door.

'Step out.'

Max came out and finally saw her face: dark skin, high cheekbones and a strong, almost mannish jaw contrasting with those stunning hazel eyes, which were both piercing and fiery. He

would have considered her beautiful, if not for the severe, pro-
hibitive demeanour, and, of course, the circumstances.

'Turn around,' she said.

She unlocked the cuffs and slipped them in her pocket.

'Get your stuff.' She nodded to the roof where his things were
lined up – plus an additional item: a cellphone.

'My number's programmed in,' she said. 'Call me every night
at 8 p.m. exactly. Do not use any other phone to call the
number – especially not a landline.'

'Who are you?' Max asked again.

She got back in the car.

'Don't you have a name at least? If I'm going to talk to you
every day, I'm going to have to call you something.'

She looked at him through the window, her features lost to the
darkness again.

'Rosa Cruz,' she said.

'Is that your real name?'

He wasn't sure, but he thought he heard her laugh as she
started the engine and drove away.

32

Max sat at his room's desk at the Hotel Naçional and stared at the photograph of Joe and Vanetta Brown, desperately wanting it to be fake, a piece of digi-optic trickery, familiar heads imposed on convenient bodies – but there was no chance of that. No way. The photograph was genuine, the bond the two shared writ large in their easy, comfortable smiles, the way their bodies leaned slightly one into the other, as if mildly magnetised, Joe's hand cupping her shoulder protectively, her arm disappearing behind his back. The Joe he was looking at here was slim and muscular, which meant he would have been a street cop when the picture was taken. Before he turned full-time desk-jockey, he'd been a fitness freak. Well, maybe not a freak, but certainly a devotee: two-hour work-outs and one-hour runs, five times a week without fail. Being 'job-ready', he called it. And then there was his diet. That had always made Max laugh – Joe Liston, scourge of suspects and hold-out witnesses, the man who could scare a confession or a rollover with a level stare and a twitch of his biceps, only ate salads or white meat for lunch and drank herbal tea instead of dosing himself alert with the coffee pot. He'd been totally dedicated to his job – in mind and in body.

Max tried to remember ever seeing Joe in the polo shirt he was wearing – a dark-blue Lacoste – but couldn't. He'd never paid more than cursory attention to Joe's clothes anyway.

The hairstyle definitely dated the picture, the fade cut Joe'd started sporting to disguise his greying temples. The photograph had to have been taken sometime between 1989 and 1996.

Max homed in on the background detail in the image. They were standing in a street of pastel-coloured buildings with tiled terracotta roofs and blue, white and red-striped awnings, all hung with wooden signs, a bright-green parrot the only one he could clearly make out. Vertical Cuban flags were threaded through the lattice of telegraph wires above the road and a black 1950s Pontiac was parked close by. It didn't look like Havana: the buildings were understated and modest in size, indicating a smaller town.

He focused back on the two of them, considered them as an item. How long had Joe been in contact with her? How many times had he visited her? It was more than just this one time. He'd been visiting her regularly. When was the first time – and when was the last?

Joe and Lena had married in 1982. Max couldn't remember Joe so much as looking at another woman after that. Had he and Vanetta Brown been lovers or just really close friends?

He tried to make some sense of it. Joe had been working for the Feds, working against Vanetta Brown, working for the very system she was challenging. The Joe Liston he'd known – now *thought* he'd known – would never have broken the law and travelled to Cuba to meet with a cop-killer, unless it was to extradite them. He never would have associated with criminals, let alone befriended them, and put his career and his family's livelihood on the line in the process. Joe had always done what he believed in, and he'd had a strong moral sense. He'd never compromised on that. Vanetta Brown had always maintained her innocence. And Quinones had told him that Joe found no evidence of wrongdoing by the Black Jacobins before the raid happened. Maybe she'd been telling the truth, and only Joe, Quinones and a couple of other Feds knew it. Maybe Joe had been working with her to clear her name.

That was some kind of explanation – *if* she hadn't had him

killed. Although he was leaning towards her being framed for the Miami murders – and leaningly strongly – he couldn't be sure. The photograph showed them as friends – possibly lovers – yet it was an old picture and things often changed between people. There was no worse an enemy than an old friend, and a former lover could be a curse. Had Joe let her down in some way – deliberately or otherwise? Had he broken her heart?

Max was looking for a connecting motive between the murders, but maybe there wasn't one. Maybe this was a settling of separate scores, Vanetta taking out two people who lived in the same city.

And what exactly was Vanetta Brown into here, in Cuba? Just how complicated were her 'alliances'?

He'd find out, somehow. He had to. He was stuck here and couldn't return home empty-handed.

He thought of Wendy Peck and Rosa Cruz, both after the same person. Neither even entertained the possibility that he wouldn't find her. Maybe they both knew she was in Cuba. They just didn't know where.

He had Wendy Peck's angle, but not Cruz's. He guessed she was secret police, but he didn't think what she was asking of him was state-sanctioned; otherwise, why tell him not to call her number on a landline, and give him a phone? Cellphones had been banned in Cuba until recently. They were expensive. She was going to a lot of trouble to make sure this stayed between them.

Outside, he heard music – tribal drums, squalling sax and vigorously strummed acoustic guitar – followed by whooping and applause and much splashing in the pool. He got up, stretched, rolled his neck and looked out the window. There was some kind of synchronised swimming event going on. A dozen stick-thin women in white costumes and rubber caps studded with rose-head moulds were swimming with their right legs up in the air. They formed a perfect circle, swam a few turns and divided into two, then three, then four smaller circles, all spinning in time.

Max turned back to the room and looked it over – the faded grey paint on the walls, the narrow twin beds with scratchy sheets, the antique furniture and the odour of stale gravy trapped in the grain, the chairs and their stained cushions, the amateurish painting of a sunflower in a vase. Like the hotel, it was clinging to its grandeur with broken, grubby fingers.

He remembered what Rosa Cruz had told him about American tourists being watched and he wondered where they'd put the listening device. He'd fitted a few when he was a cop, bulky, palm-sized radio transmitters with tiny aerials, adhesive pads and the on-off thumbnail switches that had been at the forefront of seventies snooper-tech. Now the equipment had become much smaller and way more sophisticated, but he was sure the core principle of covert miking was unchanged: fit the device to something so familiar it goes unnoticed. He thought of searching the room, but he couldn't be bothered. He didn't care if they were listening to him. What would they hear? Him breathing, yawning, belching, sniffing, pissing, coughing, farting? Tameka had told him he not only snored, but he talked in his sleep too. 'You'd make a lousy adulterer,' she'd said over breakfast one morning. Which was funny – in an unfunny kind of way, now that he thought about it.

He took his wallet and lock-picking tools over to the safe. He keyed in the code – the date of his birthday in reverse – and opened the little metal door. He immediately noticed that something was missing. Not his passport. That was still there. Not his money either. That hadn't been taken. The people who'd entered the room when he was away weren't thieves and they really didn't need money. They'd only come for what was theirs: Gwenver's red and black notebooks.

He stood looking dumbly at the safe, his mind blank, shock and fear scattering his thoughts. He wondered if the Abakuás would come back for him next.

He put the things in the safe and locked it anyway. Then he brushed his teeth and took a hot shower.

Afterwards he lay down on the bed and stared at his reflection in the cold TV screen. He wasn't tired. He knew he wouldn't sleep much. Worrying, thinking. He reached for the remote on the bedside cabinet, but knocked it off. It landed on the floor with a light crack.

As he leaned down to pick it up, he saw that the back had come off, the batteries had rolled out and a coiled wire was poking out. A small white-and-silver transmitter was attached to the exposed end of the wire, seemingly directed straight at him, as if expecting him to say something, make a statement.

He stood, grabbed the remote as if it were a microphone and began to sing loudly, way off-key, a cracked and tuneless voice, aiming for sarcasm, but settling for a kind of snarling, spitting, yet winded rage:

'While the storm clouds gather far across the sea,

'Let us swear allegiance to a land that's *free*!

'Let us be grateful for a land so *fair*!

'As we raise our voices in solemn prayer.'

He cleared his throat and roared:

'*God Bless America!*

'Land that I *love*!

'Stand beside her, and guide her

'Through the night with a light from above.

'From the mountains, to the prairies,

'To the oceans, white with foam,

'*God bless America!* –

'*My home . . . sweet home.*'

When he was done, he signed off:

'That was the voice of the free world wishing you terrible nightmares and bidding you a really bad fucken' evening.'

He ripped out the bug and threw it across the room. He didn't hear it land.

33

The next morning Max took a cab to the offices of Cuban X-Press in Miramar. He had his passport and all his money on him, secreted in the thigh pockets of his cargo pants. He hadn't wanted to chance the Abakuás coming back to his room and making off with it. In any other big city it would have been the dumbest thing to do, but Havana's streets felt safe, swaddled in an authoritarian net, the cops and secret police waiting to pounce if it stirred.

Miramar was a whole world removed from downtown Havana. Before the revolution, it had been an upscale suburb, the capital's very own millionaires row, where gangsters, diplomats and the social elite had lived together but apart in magnificent, sprawling mansions. A sheen of exclusivity still clung to the area. The same mansions now housed foreign embassies, government agencies and think tanks, foreign corporations and hotels. There wasn't a clothes line or camouflaging flower basket in sight, no cracked and paint-stripped façades, no families living eight to a room, no sense of teetering ruin. The streets were wide, clean, well-maintained and almost entirely free of traffic or people. The sidewalks were lined with massive jaguey trees, seemingly supported by aerial roots cascading like dirty water, their branches and leaves so thick they created cool pools of shadow around the trunks. There were pretty, empty parks whose benches were as decorative as their dainty flowerbeds and carefully pruned trees. The only thing wrong with the place was the Russian embassy building, a grim concrete monstrosity with the presence of a cooling tower and the design of a spacecraft that had crashed nose-first to Earth; a jarring and desperate exclamation mark in the babble of history.

When Max reached the Centro de Negocios – a white modern office complex – he walked into the lobby and asked the male receptionist for Cuban X-Press. He was told the company had closed down four years before and that Antoine Pinel had retired. He asked for Pinel's home address, claiming to be a bookseller from Canada with some outstanding business to conclude.

The receptionist made a few calls and asked him to take a seat. Half an hour later he handed Max the address and directions on how to get there. Pinel lived ten blocks away, off 5th Avenue.

With its rusted bars on the windows and thick, weather-blackened walls, Antoine Pinel's home had a crude penal aspect to it reminiscent of an old frontier town lock-up, the last stop of a condemned man. The house's lower-right corner was smothered in dense green ivy, the plant tentatively invading the rest of the building, exploratory fingers reaching up along the wall and under the tiled roof, disappearing into the house itself.

The man who answered the door had probably once been tall, but age had stooped him, made his head hang down, almost unnaturally, as if his brain were too heavy for his neck. He wore a loose and floppy light-blue cardigan, shapeless grey slacks and a yellowed white shirt with maroon rabbits on it. His long white hair covered his ears. His features were those of a St Bernard – droopy and downcast, hanging in tiered folds, dominated by a long, thick nose and dark eyes that seemed to be the tip of a profound and powerful melancholia.

'Mr Pinel?' The man nodded. 'I'm sorry to disturb you at home. I got this address from your former office building.'

Pinel considered him from the quarter-opened door, a little bewildered but mostly curious.

'Do you speak English?' asked Max.

'French, Spanish, Russian and German too. How many languages do you speak?' Pinel's voice was smoke-cured, deep and throaty, but he was smiling, already sure of the answer. His teeth made Max think of a strip of cheap leopard-skin print – yellow, black, with the odd dash of brown.

'Just this one,' he said.

'What can I do for you?'

'I'm looking for someone called Vanetta Brown.'

'*Vanetta?* Well, she's not here.' Pinel shrugged. There was no hostility or suspicion about him and he opened the door wider, suggesting he welcomed the company, even in the form of a complete stranger. Despite the aura of tragedy about the old man, Max had him down as one of life's kidders, the sort who could be relied on to raise a laugh at a funeral.

'I didn't think she was.' He showed Pinel the picture of Joe and Vanetta. Pinel took a pair of glasses out of his shirt pocket and scrutinised the photograph for a moment, his eyes scanning slowly left to right, and then left again, where they lingered. Max watched his face for a reaction but detected nothing.

'Come in, Mr ...?'

'Mingus.'

'Interesting name.' Pinel looked at him anew.

'My dad was a big jazz fan.'

Pinel stepped aside and let him in.

The interior was surprisingly cool and clean. It had a rustic theme, with wooden panelling on the ceiling and walls, grey flagstone flooring, a fireplace and thick oak doors leading to three rooms. The furniture was all antique – a matching couch and two easy chairs, glass-panelled bookcases with locks on the doors – and a tall brass floor lamp in each corner.

'I'm making coffee. Can I offer you some?'

'Is it Cuban coffee?' asked Max.

'No. French. I get it from Martinique. I go there sometimes. I have a French passport,' he said. 'You don't like Cuban coffee?'

229

'I find it weak. But then my idea of coffee's something that'd cure a coma.'

'Coffee in the Caribbean is generally not strong. Caffeine and hot climates don't mix.' Pinel led him to the kitchen, which was spotless and had a view of the street through its barred windows. On one wall was a large map of Cuba. The island resembled a bent nail, stood on its head. On another wall hung seven framed photographs in a single straight line. They were all the same, yet different – Pinel in a light-grey suit, white shirt and black tie, standing against a leafy backdrop, with a woman on his arm. The woman changed in each picture. They were all in bridal dresses. They got darker and younger as Pinel got older.

'Where are you from, Mr Mingus?'

'Miami.'

The old man motioned for Max to sit at the table by the window, a sturdy wooden thing draped in a blue vinyl covering.

'*La Ciudad de gusanos*. City of worms. That's what Castro calls it.'

'We don't like him much either.'

'An understatement. When he fell ill, your people celebrated in the streets. And I read that they've got a huge party planned in the city stadium to celebrate his death. I find that disgusting.'

'Feelings run high,' said Max, looking at the map pinned to the wall in front of him.

'Everyone has a hard-luck story.' Pinel smiled and went to tend to the espresso pot rattling on the stove, the space between them gradually filling with the rich aroma of fresh coffee.

According to the morsels of information Max had gathered from the hotel internet earlier that morning, Antoine Pinel was the third of five children born to a wealthy Parisian industrialist, the sort of self-made man who'd expected his progeny to follow in his footsteps like wind-up replicas. Antoine had rebelled at an early age. At thirteen, he'd been expelled from a Jesuit-run school, for having sex with a cleaner; at fifteen, he joined the French Communist Party. Six years later, in 1957, he went to

Cuba to fight for Castro. He was caught in Santa Clara with a suitcase full of pistols and ammunition and hand grenades. He was imprisoned, but freed several months later when the town was captured by rebel troops led by Che Guevara. He fought alongside Guevara and was among those who rolled into Havana on January 8, 1959. Pinel returned to Paris two years later and became involved in the movement for Algerian independence. He participated in the infamous riots of October 1961 – 'The Paris Massacre' – where two hundred people died at the hands of the police. Pinel was arrested and spent another eighteen months in prison. After his release, he returned to Cuba, where he'd lived on and off ever since, working as a translator for Castro and other regime bigwigs, as well as running a variety of publishing companies, which produced everything from official histories of the Cuban revolution to chick-lit.

'How are you finding it so far, Cuba?'

'It's as I imagined it would be – but also ... not really that way at all,' said Max.

He nodded. 'You're confused. That's how it always starts. Cuba changes the hardest heart.'

'Is that what happened to you?'

'*My* heart was never hard. I've lived here forty years. I tried going back to France a few times, to see if I could live there again. But every time, I found something about my country had changed in a way that I didn't like, that I could not understand. Here, nothing really changes. It just stops working. And then eventually, maybe, sometimes, it gets fixed and things go back to the way they were. I like that.' Pinel took the gurgling coffee pot off the fire and brought it over to the table.

'Cuba was America's whore and then Russia's mistress,' Pinel said as he poured the coffee. 'America fucked her, pimped her out to gangsters, took all she had to offer and paid her pennies. Russia kept her, in a certain style. But it couldn't really afford her, and it was an old and largely impotent master. Then it died and left her with nothing. Now Cuba's alone. She has some suitors, the ones who are in love with what she was, but not as she is now. Venezuela is passionate but its pockets aren't as deep. China is interested, but it's a long-distance affair, only occasionally consummated. And then there's Canada and Spain, but they don't want to annoy the original pimp, America, which still keeps its boots under her bed, in Guantánamo, waiting to start the whole cycle again.'

Pinel lit an all-white Cohiba cigarette, which smelled just like a cigar. 'Forgive me for rambling. I don't get a lot of visitors. May I ask what you want with Vanetta Brown?'

'The man in the picture—' Max began.

'I forget his name . . .'

'You knew him?'

'I would not say that I knew him,' Pinel said. 'We met only three times.'

'You met Joe? Joe Liston? This man?' Max tapped the picture.

'Yes. What is this about, Mr Mingus?'

'I'm a friend of Joe's.'

'I remember he was a cop. Are you a cop, like him?'

'I was. Thirty years ago. Joe was my partner back then. Now he's dead. He died recently.'

'That's terrible.' Pinel's naturally downcast mien sagged a little more. 'Was he ill?'

Max decided not to tell him the truth. 'It was sudden.'

'No suffering.' Pinel nodded. 'That is the best way. One minute here, next minute gone. I hope to die in my sleep, so I can't tell the difference.'

'When did you meet Joe?'

'The first time was around eighty-seven, eighty-eight. The Russians were still here.'

A year before Max had gone to prison.

'Are you sure?'

'Yes. I met him again in 1994 or 1995, after I published her book.'

'Which book?'

'The one she wrote. *Black Power in the Sunshine State.*'

'*She* wrote that?' Max frowned.

'Under a pseudonym.'

'Kimora Harrison?'

'You have read it?'

'Yes,' said Max. 'But it's not an autobiography. It's written in the third person.'

'That was deliberate. She did not want to draw attention to herself. She had many enemies.'

'You mean Dennis Peck's family?'

Pinel nodded.

Max thought back to the book. It had been more about the Black Jacobins as an organisation – what they'd stood for and all the good they'd done in their short lifespan – than it had been about Vanetta Brown and the murder of Dennis Peck. That had only taken up a small part of a narrative more concerned with ideology and philanthropy than with clearing her name and rebutting the case against her.

'Did she ever mention someone called Eldon Burns?'

'Yes, yes, of course.' He nodded. 'She hated him. She wished him dead. He led the raid on the Jacobin House, and she held him personally responsible for the death of her daughter and husband.'

'Did she elaborate on that?'

'No.' Pinel stubbed his cigarette out in a glass ashtray. 'But she often said that although it was wrong to wish ill on people, she hoped to live long enough to look into Eldon Burns's dying eyes.'

'His dying eyes? Those were her exact words?'

'Yes.' Pinel nodded.

'So she talked about killing him?'

'No, no. She is not a violent person. Or even a hateful one,' said the old man. 'She simply wanted to be the last person he saw before he died.'

Max thought about that for a moment, and filed it away.

'What about Joe? What was he doing here?'

233

'Didn't he tell you?' Pinel looked at him suspiciously.

'He was a Miami cop,' Max said. 'He came here illegally. It would have been the end of his career if anyone found out. So, no, he didn't tell me. He didn't tell anyone. Not even his family. But he left instructions in the event of his death. I have a letter for Vanetta from him, to be delivered personally.'

'What does it say?'

'I don't know. It's sealed.'

'You did not open it?'

'Joe Liston will always be my friend.'

Pinel drank his coffee and met Max's gaze, digesting the lie, assimilating it, buying it. Then he smiled and bared that wet leopard-skin sliver again. 'Did you know he was a Black Jacobin?'

'Yes.'

'I think he was helping her with her book.'

'How?'

'Research. That's what she told me. But I never asked the details. I was just interested in the finished work,' said Pinel.

'What about their relationship?'

Pinel frowned.

'Were they friends or lovers?' Max prompted.

'I never had the impression they were lovers.' Pinel smiled. 'Veteran's intuition.'

'When was the last time you saw Joe?'

'Before your nine-eleven, so ... in 2000.'

'What did you talk about, generally?'

Pinel took out another cigarette and tapped the end on the table. 'Your friend was fascinated by this country, especially the relationship between Fidel Castro and the blacks here.

'Castro made racial discrimination illegal when he came to power. One of the first things he did. Cuba was an equal opportunities country long before yours. Before Castro, blacks were second-class citizens. There was a saying then – "*Si tu ves un doctor negro, ese es el mejor doctor de Cuba*" – which means: "If you see a black doctor, that's the best doctor in Cuba." In other words, a black person had to work five times as hard as his white counterpart. Being only very good wasn't an option. A black Cuban had to be the very best.

'Three-quarters of Castro's support for blacks was down to politics and ideology, the rest was personal. When he started the revolution in the mountains, most of his supporters were poor blacks. They sheltered the guerrillas, fed them and joined them. They formed a strong bond. They were against the same thing. Blacks were – and still are – Castro's foundation. His base.'

'Was that why he gave asylum to so many Black Panthers?'

'In part, yes,' said Pinel. 'He knew they were criminals, of course. He is neither stupid nor naive. But at the time the Cold War was at its peak and granting left-wing black American fugitives sanctuary gave the imperialists across the water the finger.'

'What about you and the Panthers? You published their autobiographies.'

'Yes, regrettably,' sighed Pinel.

'Why "regrettably"?'

'I had big ambitions. I thought I would find another George Jackson or Malcolm X. But, alas, no. Their stories were identical. Bad blaxploitation. The hero is the poor downtrodden black man, or woman. The villain is always 'The Man': white, racist and powerful. The hero is innocent of murdering the cop, the bank teller, the shopkeeper, yet he has to flee because he will never get a fair trial because The Man runs the justice system. And it always ends the same way – here, in Cuba. The hero becomes bitter and twisted. At first he is grateful just to be free, but then he has to live in this strange country with its secret police, its enforced poverty, its rationed food, its constant shortages, its lack of ghettos and freedom of speech. The hero gets confused. He is no longer a victim. He is in a country of victims.' Pinel chuckled and blew smoke out through the window bars.

'You sound contemptuous,' said Max.

'Ah, that I am. Working with those people broke me, forced me to retire. They thought their books were selling thousands, that I was ripping them off. In reality they barely sold. But what did they know or care? They didn't believe me. I went from being "Frog Brother Number One" to "That Thieving White Devil".'

He finished his coffee. Max sipped his. It was the best cup of coffee he'd had in Cuba and he didn't expect to drink any better, so he was savouring it.

'Vanetta was very different, of course.' Pinel smiled. 'She never mixed with her so-called brothers and sisters. In private, she despised them, considered them little more than common criminals who'd given the cause a bad name. She shunned their functions, their get-togethers. The feeling was mutual. As far as they were concerned, she was a killer, like all of them, and no better. They had a name for her: "Miss Shitdontstink".'

'Do you think she's innocent – of killing Dennis Peck?'

'We're all capable of making terrible mistakes under pressure, but I believed her when she told me she was innocent.'

'Even though you'd heard it all before?'

'Not the way she told it.'

'Oh? How was that?'

'The other Panthers claimed they were acting in self-defence or were framed by "whitey". Vanetta never said that. She told me she was several miles away during that raid.' Pinel lit a cigarette. Max noticed how the tips of Pinel's index and middle fingers were stained dark brown.

'Everyone lies sometime.'

'Not her.' Pinel was defensive in his insistence. Max wondered if he hadn't been sweet on her.

'When was the last time you saw Vanetta?'

'In 2002, when I was still working. She wanted to publish a brand-new edition of her book,' Pinel said. 'It was going to tell an amazing story, the complete truth about what happened to her in Miami.'

'And?'

'I was enthusiastic. But I never heard from her again.'

'Didn't you try to contact her?'

'Yes, a few times. Then I gave up. And a few years ago, I closed my business,' Pinel said. 'Maybe she's with her family.'

'She remarried?'

'No. I mean her late husband's family. The Dascals. She is close to them. Camilo and Lidia – Ezequiel's parents – left America in 1962, on the eve of the embargo. They settled in Santiago de Cuba, Cuba's second city,' Pinel said. 'The Dascals are friends of Castro. So was Vanetta – until they fell out.'

'They fell out? When?'

'It had to do with the Haitian boat-lifts,' Pinel said. 'Cuba has a large Haitian population, close to a million. They live on the eastern part of the island, along the Caribbean coast. It's very different from here. The people speak Haitian Kreyol as well as Spanish. Castro has always been pro-Haitian, always given the refugees a home, because he and his brother were briefly fostered by a Haitian family. It was probably why he was friends with Vanetta. She set up two centres for newly arrived Haitians. The main one was in Santiago, the other in Trinidad. She called the places "Caille Jacobinne" – Kreyol for "the Jacobin House" – same as the one in Miami.'

'When was this?'

'Twenty years ago.'

'Are the centres still there?' Max pulled out a map from the side pocket of his cargo pants and opened it on the table. Santiago de Cuba was down at the bottom, near Guantánamo. Trinidad was closer, on the south coast, not far from the Bay of Pigs. He circled both places.

'I don't know,' said Pinel.

'What about these boat-lifts?'

'That was around 1994, when Haiti was going through its big political upheaval. The president, Aristide, had been overthrown by a CIA-backed coup three years before and the military junta was slaughtering his supporters. Many Haitians fled to Miami by boat.'

'That I remember,' said Max. He'd seen it on TV in prison, bloated Haitian corpses washing up daily on Florida's golden shores, the tourists who found them threatening to sue the state for ruined holidays and associated psychological traumas.

'Those who made it to Florida were not given the welcome Cubans are. They didn't get the "dry foot-wet foot" option. It was "wet foot-wet foot" for them. They were put in detention camps until your government had invaded Haiti, the idea being that they'd all be shipped back once the Marines had restored order, installed a convenient puppet as president and had "free and democratic" elections.

'Vanetta – through her connections here – offered these Haitian refugees an alternative. They could come to Cuba instead of going home. A secret deal was struck with the Clinton administration and over the next few months, boats made the round trip from Mariel Harbour to Miami, bringing back anyone who wanted to come. A hundred or so people arrived every month.'

'What was in it for Castro? If it was secret, surely he couldn't use it as propaganda,' said Max.

'That was the agreement he made with Clinton, yes. Of course, he was eventually going to tell the world how he'd treated Haitian refugees humanely, taken them in when America refused them. You know how it goes.' Pinel smiled. 'But it backfired. You remember the original Mariel boat-lift?'

'Sure.' Max nodded. Yes, he remembered that too – and how. Between 1977 and 1980, when relations with the US had thawed, Castro allowed 125,000 Cubans to leave and join their families in Miami. They sailed from Mariel in a flotilla of over-filled, leaky boats. But this act of goodwill had a hidden catch: Castro took the opportunity to offload the dregs of the country's prisons and psychiatric hospitals along with the exiles. Some twenty thousand criminals and psychos were processed by US immigration services and set loose on an unsuspecting population and an unprepared police force. Already a cocaine war

238

zone, Miami came close to falling apart. It had been a nightmare, the worst.

'The Clinton administration decided to get a little revenge on Castro for that,' said Pinel. 'They'd already been quietly purging American prisons of Haitian criminals and sending them back to their homeland by plane. They diverted some of them to the Cuban boats. They sent us some real monsters.'

'Jesus.' Max immediately thought of Solomon Boukman. 'How many?'

'I don't know. We had a brief but memorable crimewave here in the mid-nineties. Murders, robberies and rapes. Tourists attacked. It was hushed up, of course. The boat-lifts were stopped and most of the perpetrators were tracked down and killed on the spot. But not all. A few disappeared into the Cuban underworld.'

'The Abakuás?'

'That's right. They recruited the cream of that bad crop.'

'Is that why Castro fell out with Vanetta, because he blamed her?'

'No. They fell out because Vanetta reportedly helped some of these criminals escape the Cuban police.'

'Why?'

'No idea. She never told me any of this herself. I heard a rumour. It may not be true.'

'Did she have links with the Abakuás?'

'Everyone has links with them. One way or another, whether they want to or not,' said Pinel. 'Again, another rumour – but this one possibly more credible – is that they funded the Caille Jacobinne centres.'

'Really?'

'*Nothing* was running in the country during the Special Period. Except for Caille Jacobinne. Haitian refugees still came and settled here. I suspect Castro found out where the money to do this was coming from and that was the end of his friendship with Vanetta.'

239

Max remembered what Rosa Cruz had told him about the complicated alliances Brown had forged.

'Did it surprise you, when you heard any of this?'

'Not really.' Pinel shook his head. 'This is Cuba, Mr Mingus. Nothing is as it seems and no one is who they say they are. That's part of its charm. You'll get used to it.'

34

He left Pinel's house shortly before sunset, under a reddening sky, with the sound of crickets in his ears. The old man encouraged him to walk the length of 5th Avenue, get a boat across the Almendares river to Vedado and then pick up the Malecón and follow it all the way around back to the hotel. A good eight-mile trek, Pinel said, but it would be good exercise and a great experience all wrapped into one – 'aerobic tourism', he'd called it.

Max had set off, using the Russian embassy as a bearing. He'd decided to catch a cab or a bus downtown as soon as he got on to the main drag.

Yet there were no taxis to be had. The few that passed were already taken. He walked for an hour until he came to a bus stop, crowded with people, all office workers heading home. It was hard to tell management from menial because their clothes looked like they'd come from the same first-jobber catalogue. Pressed slacks, long-sleeved shirts and cheap leather shoes polished to their last sparkle for the men; knee-length skirts, blouses and high-heeled pumps for the women.

Max joined them, standing to one side, sweating, catching his breath, stretching his slightly aching legs. Curious sideways glances swept and assessed him. He studiously avoided all eye contact and stared either up at the sky and the stars that were starting to show or to the far end of the road, from where, he hoped, a bus would soon appear. He heard a distinct volume drop in the previously lively conversations, voices doused to whispers and the word-count dwindling from paragraphs to one-liners, and then monosyllables, before hitting a solid zero. The group lost its previous cohesion as bodies moved away from one another and became remote islands, facing every direction but his. He realised his presence at this hour was unusual, a foreigner slumming it on state-sponsored transport. They probably thought he was a spy or someone they couldn't risk being themselves around. He felt suddenly bad about being there, intruding on their lives, fucking up their quality time, filling them with needless dread.

The bus turned up just as he thought of leaving. It was a *camello*, or camel, a vintage Special Period innovation meant to cut fuel costs, so named because the vehicle was little more than a recycled bus hull welded and bolted on to the bed of a massive articulated lorry, the middle section dipping between the wheelpoints, giving the front and back distinctive humps. The commuters on the bus, pressed so tightly against the windows that their faces were crushed, reminded him of hostages. He didn't think anyone was going to be able to board, but the office crowd, numbering more than a dozen, made their way to the doors, which opened slowly and with difficulty on to a wall of tightly packed bodies, not a sliver of space between them. Somehow, one by one, the people disappeared inside, a little at a time, first a foot, then a leg, a hand, arm and shoulder, before their whole bodies were slowly sucked into that condensed mass of humanity – with a little help from the driver, who had got out of the cabin to ease them in with small pushes. There wasn't a single complaint from the bus, not even a moan of discomfort or show of inconvenience. When the last person had been swallowed up, the driver turned to Max and asked if he wanted to get on, but Max shook his head. The driver pushed the doors shut, then climbed back into his cabin and the bus took off down the road, belching thick fumes.

Max resumed his trek, hoping for a cab but resigned to the long haul. It was now dark and the warm air smelled both sweet and briny, the sea breeze mingling with the scent of sap and flowers. Off in the distance he could see downtown Havana, the whole tourist seafront area a bright orange spill of electric lava heading for the water's edge.

At the end of 5th Avenue, Max paid a man with a small motor boat twenty pesos to take him across the river so he could start on the long home stretch.

He heard the bar before he saw it, on the corner of a side road feeding into the Malecón, the loud music drowning out the sound of the passing traffic and the waves; not salsa or jazz, but a tune he recognised from years before – Duran Duran's 'Skin Trade', a song he'd liked a lot before he found out who was singing. He'd mistaken it for late-period Chic or peak-period Prince.

He couldn't have missed the bar anyway. It had two lit-up Christmas trees either side of the door, and strings of twinkling fairy lights in the windows, whose panes were bordered with snow spray. He stopped and gawped.

A small group of men and women stood opposite, close to a parked Super 88, the dim light obscuring all but their outlines and the metallic twinkle of the women's short sequinned dresses. He smelled their perfume and cigarettes, then sewage and a hint of jasmine coming off the street.

The place was called La Urraca – whatever that meant. Thirsty, sweaty and desperately needing a piss, he decided to go in.

It was practically deserted, the only customers, a man and a woman standing close together talking in a corner at the end of the bar. The bartender – decked out in red trousers, braces and a white T-shirt – eyed Max as he came in.

The décor was Christmas-on-steroids: gold wrapping paper and red velveteen bows for wallpaper, bands of gold and silver tinsel forming half-smiles on the ceiling, two strings of dusty cards along a wall; opposite a popped advent calendar, a paint- ing of Santa riding a reindeer chariot through the night sky, and

243

another fully decorated tree, with a mound of presents, in the corner. The loud music made all the decorations tremble.

It was one strange fucken' sight.

'*Agua mineral per favor*,' Max said to the bartender.

'*No agua*.' The man shook his head and raised his eyes to a row of plain brown bottles lining the shelves above him, no indication as to the contents. He had thinning sandy hair, almost translucent eyelashes, indigo eyes and the flushed face of a dawn-to-dark drinker.

'*Usted tiene una soda?*'

'*Qué?*'

'*Soda*: Coca-Cola, Sprite?'

The bartender looked at him without expression.

'*Hablas Inglés?*'

'*No.*'

Max glanced over at the couple. The woman had her back to him. She was over six foot tall, slender and had long, lustrous black hair cascading almost to the small of her back. She was wearing a short gold dress, high heels and black-seamed stockings with a gold butterfly at each ankle. The man was shorter and broader. He had on a denim shirt and jeans. His hands moved animatedly as he spoke. Max could hear his voice cutting through the music, the tone angry. The woman stood absolutely still.

'Toilet?' Max asked the bartender, who nodded to a door to his right.

The festive motif didn't carry over to the john, a narrow cubicle with a filthy, clogged toilet bowl and a broken chain dangling from a rusty cistern. It stank so bad he held his breath and didn't look down, targeting his jet by ear and taking in the graffiti instead: addresses, phone numbers, male and female names, drawings of doggy-styling and cocksucking.

When he went back out, the music was playing louder, the sound distorted, Duran Duran singing something about doctors of the reva-loootion baybee.

244

There was a glass of something clear and fizzy waiting for him on the bar.

Max didn't want it, whatever it was. He reached into his pocket, pulled out a ten-peso note and pushed it over the counter. The bartender palmed the cash and pointed to the glass.

Max was about to say something apologetic and valedictory when he heard the dry crack, followed by a short, piercing scream. He turned and saw the woman staggering towards the door, holding her face, the man yelling, about to follow her. He saw Max looking at him and stopped where he was.

They eyeballed each other. The man looked fit and very strong. And he was angry – so angry his big hands were shaking.

The barman turned the music up another notch.

The woman was gone. She'd dropped her purse – black leather with a gold clasp. As Max looked at it, the man kicked it over to him, saying something inaudible, his lips curling. Max guessed he'd insulted his manhood. He didn't care.

The man reached into a pocket and produced a straight razor. He opened out the blade, the longest Max had ever seen, fit for shaving a horse. Max tensed and took a couple of steps away from the counter, his heart pumping.

The man spoke again, his mouth moving as the chorus of 'Skin Trade' played, making him look comical, standing there, cut-throat razor in hand, seemingly lip-synching to a song by three Brits in heavy make-up.

The song faded to a finish and started again. The man shrugged and walked out of the bar, stopping outside the doorway to look up and down the street. Then he headed left, fast.

Max didn't even think about what to do next.

He went after the man.

In the street, the group was still standing by the car, talking as if nothing had happened. No sign of the man or woman.

245

Max ran up the road.

It was deserted. There were narrow alleys, branching off left and right. He checked each one.

He heard nothing.

He carried on.

The road got a little steeper.

More alleys.

Suddenly a piercing cry came from behind, to his right.

Then another, almost immediately: shrill, anguished and pained.

He span around and headed towards the screams.

Another cry – worse – louder, closer.

And continuous.

A man's voice, shouting.

The sound of running feet.

Then he saw her, coming towards him. She had blood down the front of her dress. Blood on her legs and hands, blood all over her face.

Right behind her, chasing her, came the man in denim. He had blood on him too – on his hands and shirt, on the razor.

'*Venido aquí!*' he yelled.

As the woman reached Max, she rushed behind him, cowering.

Now he was facing her assailant.

'*Qué te den por culo!*' snapped the man, out of breath, sweat-sheened. '*Comprende, cabrón?*' He clicked his fingers, signalling to Max to move.

The woman was whimpering.

'*Por favor . . . El quiere matarme,*' she pleaded. '*Por favor, señor.*'

Max eyefucked the man.

The man eyefucked him back.

Max's body language said: *I'm not moving.*

The man's expression said: *Like hell you're not.*

The Cuban struck out. A deep, arcing swipe at Max's neck, the blade slicing the air with a thin whistle. Max leaned back

246

abruptly, knocking the woman over. The blade missed his face by a whisker.

The man was off balance. Max reacted fast. He threw a wild right hook at the Cuban's jaw. He connected. Bone cracked and teeth splintered.

The man went down with a thud.

Max kicked the blade away and checked him. He wasn't quite out. He was halfway in, but not deep enough to sink into unconsciousness. That would usually have been OK, the guy he'd slugged waking up to a world of harsh but not irreversible pain. But this scumbag hadn't just beaten on a woman, he'd cut her up, disfigured her. He deserved more damage.

Max turned back to the woman. She was on her feet, pushing past him. She started kicking at her prone assailant.

Max grabbed her, pulled her away, her long thin legs flailing at air, shoes flying off.

She got loose and turned to him, but couldn't see him because her hair was covering her face. She reached up, moved her hands around the middle of her scalp, worrying her fingers deep into her hair. Then she gripped it and pulled it all off, dropping her arms to her sides, the long locks hanging down like a nest of tarred snakes.

Underneath, her head was close-cropped, short back and sides and a strip of hair on top, military-style. And there was something completely wrong with her features, he noticed – not just the extended bloody grimace the razor had opened up from her lip to the end of her cheek, but the whole way she looked now that he was seeing her up close, in the light.

'She' was a man.

Max couldn't help himself.

'The ... *fuck* ...?'

'What you mean "the *fock*"?' the transvestite snapped. 'You disappoint? Yes?'

'No. No! Just ... just ... surprised,' he said.

'You think you big *heroe Americano*? You save the damsel in distress, yes? But you see me, you think, *What* the *fock* I do? Yes? That what you think now, yes?' The transvestite's voice had spiralled down octaves.

'No. It's not like that. I mean, I . . . I've got nothing against you . . . you people.'

'*You people?*' The transvestite was indignant, and stepped in to glare down at Max. He was a tall man, even without the heels. 'Is no' my lucky night, yes? I get rescue by a focking American bigot.'

'I didn't mean it like that. I . . . I . . . Look, it . . . it came out wrong. I'm sorry, all right.'

The transvestite kissed his teeth, then winced and gasped as the display of contempt made his wound smart.

'That shit? He live?' He pointed to the man on the ground.

'Yeah,' said Max.

The transvestite stepped over to kick his head.

'Hey!' Max grabbed him by the arm.

'He try kill me! You see what he do to my face?'

'Calm down, OK? Cool it. *Tranquilo, si?* You . . . you've got to get to a hospital.'

'Hospital? I can no' go.'

'Your face is bleeding bad.'

'You have car?'

'No. Why don't you get a cab? A taxi.'

'Taxi? Taxi see me, they no' take. You with me, they take me.'

Max wanted to walk away, go back to his hotel, forget it. He'd done his good deed. He'd saved the guy's life. Wasn't that enough? Why the fuck had he gone into that damn bar in the first place? Why hadn't he just pissed in the street? He really didn't want to do this. He really didn't want to be here at all. But he couldn't just leave the guy here, bleeding.

He looked down the road, where cars were criss-crossing the Malecón.

'OK, yeah,' he said.

'*Vamos.*'

248

35

In the hospital ward, Max watched as a female doctor sewed up the transvestite's face.

The man's real name was Benedicto Pacifico Juan Maria Ramirez – 'Benny', for short. In the taxi, he'd insisted he was called Salma, as in Salma Hayek, the Mexican actress.

Benny yelled and cried as the doctor, wearing thick blue kitchen gloves, slowly repaired the rip in his cheek, piercing, threading, piercing again and then pulling the sundered flesh tightly together. No anaesthetic, no painkillers; just iodine tincture for disinfectant, overproof rum through a straw to take the edge off, a flame to sterilise the needle and a bowl of hot water for the clean-up. Frontier medicine at its finest. The doctor tried soothing Benny with comforting words and a bedside tone, but you can't talk down that kind of pain, so she resorted to yelling at him to be still when his protests threatened to undo her work. Max felt for him a little. He knew the agony Benny was going through. He'd been there, many years before.

The hospital, like the ward, was in an abominable state. Max half-knew what to expect when they pulled up outside. The building was modern but three-quarters finished, the walls unpainted, some of the windows lacking glass, laundry hanging from every floor. The entrance had been partially blocked by a big dump-truck scoop piled high with bags of fetid trash and surrounded, like a moat, by a wide stagnant puddle. As they went inside, they'd fallen in behind a woman pushing a wheel-barrow with a man stuffed inside it, his arm drooping over the side, his fingertips brushing the ground. The woman told the nurse at reception that he was her father; he'd broken both legs in a fall and the ambulance hadn't turned up. The nurse explained the ambulances were either busy or busted.

They'd all taken the elevator. Only one of four was working. Its doors were meant to be glass-fronted, but the panes had either been broken or never put in, so plywood covered the gaps to stop people falling out.

Despite this overture, the conditions in the ward still shocked him.

Every remaining bed was taken, the mattresses and pillows bare and filthy. Old men and women lay naked and alone, hooked up to drying IV sacs and withered blood bags that had the appearance of large rotting grapes. There were roaches crawling all over the baseboards, piss and shit and vomit on the tiled floor, squadrons of flies convening on the walls, which had possibly once been white, but were indeterminate shades of grey and yellow. The ubiquitous Che Guevara portrait hung on one of the walls; his slightly upturned, averted gaze and faintly thunderous expression taking on a whole new meaning, as if looking away in anger at what had become of his ideals, the people he'd fought to free dying squalid, undignified deaths in the bowels of a system that had promised them better lives.

Nurses and doctors tended to the patients as best they could. Their bleached and starched white coats and uniforms were practically luminous. They may have been working in a huge, overspilling petri dish, but they looked good doing it. The lighting was temperamental, bulbs going on and off at random or suddenly burning too brightly and fading close to total blackout. Every electrical socket he could see was potentially fatal, missing covers, dangling wires, spitting sparks. The air was thick and hot and practically visible. None of the several big fans on the ceiling were working. In fact, there was no air conditioning whatsoever, just a few wobbling floor fans, all positioned around a single bed in the corner, close to an open window. The bed was ringed by four wire shopping carts, a block of ice in each, dripping into buckets beneath. The fans were blowing chilled air on a dead body.

When the doctor cut the thread at the thirty-first and final stitch, a long black suture ran from the edge of Benny's right cheek to his lips, making it look like he had all but the last leg of a tarantula in his mouth. Benny inspected himself in a small mirror the doctor handed him. He started sobbing. The doctor sat with her arm around him, patting him on the shoulder, saying nothing. When he'd quietened she told him they'd run out of gauze bandages, so he had to keep the wound dry and clean, and not to scratch or pick at it. She gathered up her things and left. Max followed her.

'Excuse me,' he said. 'Can you help me with something?'

'It depends,' said the doctor. She was slender going on thin, with age-scored olive skin, shadows under tired blue eyes. Her straight brown hair was tied in a bun and streaked with bands of grey.

'Can you tell me what Zofran is? What it's for.'

'Zofran? I've never heard of it.'

'It's made by GlaxoSmithKline.'

'Then we won't have it here because of the embargo.'

'I just need to know what it is.'

'I can look it up. But I have to see to some patients, and I'll be some time,' she said. 'Can you wait here?'

Max looked around the ward, at the busy roaches and the shit on the floor, the cooling corpse in the corner, the filthy walls.

'I'll be outside,' he said.

In the hospital forecourt, he checked his cellphone. He'd missed three calls from Rosa Cruz. It was now after midnight. He wanted to call her, if only to leave a record that he'd checked in, but there was no signal.

Benny stood holding his shoes and wig, pulling sequins off the front of his blood-soaked dress and flicking them on the ground.

251

'I thought Cuba prided itself on its health care?' said Max. 'That place'll kill you soon as cure you.'

'There is nice hospital here. But is for show. For journalist and tourist. This place is for Cuban.'

After an hour the doctor came out.

'Have you had chemotherapy?' she asked Max.

'No.' He patted his shaved head. 'This is just vanity. Why?'

'Zofran is an anti-emetic, commonly prescribed for nausea and vomiting after chemotherapy. It's also prescribed for morning sickness.'

'How can I get hold of some?'

'Here? You can't. I can give you the name of our equivalent.'

'It has to be Zofran.'

'Then I'm sorry.'

Max lowered his voice. 'Can I get it on the black market?'

'What black market?' She smiled. 'There's no black market in Cuba.'

'My mistake,' he said. 'Thanks for your help.'

'*De nada.*' The doctor turned and went back inside.

Max looked over at Benny.

'You gonna be OK?'

'No,' growled the transvestite in his natural voice, which was deep and raw. 'With my face?'

'You take care of yourself.' Max started walking away.

'Where you go?'

'Back to my hotel.'

'Where you stay?'

'What's it to you?'

'You hotel is far and is no taxi. My home is close. Five minute. You can stay to the morning.'

'I'll be OK,' said Max.

'You know where you are?'

'I'll find my way back.'

'Is dangerous, this place.'

Max looked around. There wasn't a single light on beyond the hospital perimeter. He didn't have the first clue where he was. Trying to get back to the Malecón from here at this time of night with his passport and money on him wasn't the best idea.

'You no' have to worry,' said Ramirez. 'I no' interest in you. You too old. No offend.'

'None taken – trust me.'

'I live with two girl.'

'Real ones?'

'You make the fun with me? The girl in my house, they dancer from the Tropicana. You know Tropicana?'

'No. What is that? A stripclub?'

Benny looked at him indignantly.

'No, Mister *gringo ignorante*. Tropicana is most famous night-club in Cuba. It exist long time. Before Castro.'

'So it's a respectable place?'

'*The* most respectable place in Cuba. You know Meyer Lansky, Sam Giancana – the gringo gangster? They always go Tropicana.'

'Sounds like a real respectable joint.'

'You come with me?'

He'd been here before – a crossroads moment, with a right way and a wrong way, the paths impossible to tell apart. He wouldn't know which he'd taken until things either turned out fine or it was too late to turn back.

He didn't trust Benny. Nothing to do with him being a trans-vestite, but everything to do with his wearing a disguise. Benny was good at being two people. But hadn't Gwenver and Pinel told him that this was the way of the country, that seeing was not believing? Miami rules didn't apply here.

'After you,' said Max.

36

Benny Ramirez lived on the second floor of a high-rise called the Erich Mielke Tower, designed and built by East German architects in the late sixties to house visiting factory technicians and planners, as well as high-ranking members of the Stasi, who had schooled their Cuban counterparts in the finer points of surveillance, interrogation and torture. Everything in the building was labelled in German, from the ground plan to the fire escapes.

The apartment itself was a surprise. Max had been expecting utilitarian grimness, but walked into quarters that must have once been assigned to someone of high rank. The place had the whiff of privilege about it, with parquet flooring, high ceilings, decorative cornices and panelled doors.

Benny showed him his room. A lifesize cardboard cutout of Salma Hayek wearing a bikini, a headdress and an albino boa constrictor caught the eye and drew it deep into a budget boudoir with glossy dark-blue woodchip walls and a small bed-side lamp in each corner, red muslin cloths draped over the shades. When Benny turned on the lights, hazy red bounced off the blue and gave the space a thick mauve tinge. Salma was propped up next to a dresser complete with a theatre mirror, an abundance of make-up, creams and perfume, a hairdryer and four wig stands, one bare. Half a dozen short sequinned dresses of different colours, each covered in clear plastic, hung from a clothes rail on wheels.

Max went to the bathroom and washed the dried blood off his hands and arms, neck and face. The water was tepid going on cold. He noted the Che Guevara portrait on the wall, hanging upside down by the toilet.

When he was done, Benny sat him down at a table in the living room. He offered Max a choice of Jack Daniels, rum, coffee or orange juice. Max chose the juice. Benny disappeared into the kitchen and came back with a glass of liquid that had the colour and consistency of cartoon egg yolk, before locking himself in the bathroom, where he took a shower.

He emerged half an hour later, wrapped in a yellow towel. He had the body of a prematurely tall but underdeveloped teenager: hairless, bony, lacking any kind of muscle tone and very pale, a creature of the night, the colour of a ghost. His face, however, was that of someone who'd known more rainy days than sunny ones, and those rainy days had brought deluges rather than passing showers. Max guessed he was in his early thirties. Age had already drawn a thin crease around his slender neck and scratched at the corners of his slightly slanted, sharp green eyes. Like the best-looking Cuban women Max had seen, Benny was prettiness personified in flint.

They made small talk at first. Max told him he was a tourist from Miami. Benny asked him a few cursory questions about Miami, whether it was anything like *Scarface*, which he owned on pirate DVD. In fact all the films stacked neatly near the TV in the corner had a Miami connection, from thrillers to romantic comedies, to most episodes of *Miami Vice* and something called *Dexter*.

'Who was the man who attacked you?' asked Max, when the conversation had edged beyond the casual and cursory.

'I no' know.' Benny shrugged.

'You were talking to him long enough.'

'I no' know him. He come to me, drunk, start talk. Then he

255

realise I no' lady, he hit me. Then he try kill me. Then you come and stop him.'

That didn't sound right. The man hadn't looked drunk at all, just pissed off.

'He was arguing with you,' said Max.

'He was argue with himself.'

'What do you mean?'

'He know I no' woman. He know.' Benny tapped his head. 'But he still want me. And that drive him crazy.'

'OK,' said Max. Best to let it go. What did he care? It wasn't his business and he was out of this slice of life in a few hours.

'What about you?' he asked. 'Are you like a – a woman trapped in a man's body or something?'

'I no' *transsexual*.' Benny shook his head. 'That *no*' me. I no' want cut off my *pinga* to make *papaya*. And I no' *travestido*.'

'You're *not* a transvestite?' Max frowned.

'I dress like woman for job. Is all. I do this for job. For money. *Travestido*, they do it for fun. Job is no' for fun, yes? Job is for money. Dress, wig, the shoes is my uniform. Cop or soldier wear uniform – *I* wear uniform.'

'But why dress as a woman?'

'When I start, I dress like man. I no' make much money, because homosexual is minority. Only homosexual man go with me. If I look like woman, then *hetero*sexual man go with me. Some time they make mistake – they drunk, they no' see very well. Some time for them is experiment. They want to try sex with man, but they no' want man to look like man.' He glared at Max, daring him to debate this rationale. Benny's serious expression was undone by the furry half-smile snaking up towards his ear.

'You make a lot of money?'

'Is more than the doctor do my face.'

Max chuckled at that.

'Is good place for homosexual, Meeyami?'

256

'It's open-minded, sure. Anything goes and no one cares, as long as you're not bothering them. What's it like, being gay in Cuba?'

'Is no' easy, is no' fun. You know Fidel?' Benny mimed spitting on the floor. 'He no' like homosexual. The Cuban people, many, they no' accept. Cuba is small country, with small idea. They think we have medical problem. They think we disgusting. They think we pervert.'

'Many parts of America are like that too,' said Max.

'You have homosexual friend?'

'No.' Max thought back. He'd never come close to having a gay friend. He'd been a regular homophobe in his youth. Not that it was called that then, pre-political correctness. Faggot this, faggot that. Castro was the name of the gay area in San Francisco. He hadn't had an active dislike of gays. He'd never insulted them to their faces or beaten them up, and the sight of two men holding hands or kissing had never repulsed him, but he'd always laughed at gay jokes and told plenty himself. Locker-room talk. None of his friends had been any different. It was only when he started going to discos and getting into the music in the mid-seventies that his attitude changed from passive intolerance to vague, inactive acceptance. Forget the bullshit sixties and the hippies talking peace and love because they were too stoned to stand up and put their clothes on, the disco era was the only time when racial and sexual boundaries broke down: black, white, gay and straight had danced to the same music, side by side. It hadn't lasted.

'You know, when I was fifteen, I was – how you say? – *afeminado*?'

'Effeminate? A man that's like a woman?'

'*Exactamente*. You know what they do to me? The government? They send me to place in the Sierra Maestra. The mountain. It was concentration camp for homosexual. They think they can change homosexual into macho heterosexual man. *Pendejo estupido!* You know what they do to me, to make me *hetero*sexual? First: they talk-talk-talk-talk-talk-talk. *La homosexualidad es una perversión burguesa. La homosexualidad está contra La Revolución. La homosexualidad es una invención Imperialista.* Then they give me electronic shock in my head, like what they do for the crazy people. For two month, electronic shock in the brain and the talk-talk-talk in my ear.'

Max wasn't surprised. That had happened in America too – and still did. 'How many were there?'

'Many peoples, men, womens, boys, girls. Fifty, sixty peoples,' said Benny. 'They make me cut tree with axe and carry rock. All the time, every day. *Heterosexual* man with fifteen children can no' carry the rock they make me carry! But *I* carry the rock. Because I *hate* them. Hate make me *strong*. But I stay *homosexual*. Fidel, he no' understand. He think he can change nature. He think him God. He think him can make sea go back. He focking idiot.'

'How did they know you were "cured"?'

Benny tried to laugh, but winced in pain. 'You know, they so stupid. They make the homosexual man and the lesbian woman fock each other. And they film this. Fidel make porno. And the man in charge of the camp say, "You are both heterosexual! Congratulation! *Viva Fidel!*"'

'After I get out, I lead "normal life". I get job. I was cook in hotel. And I get marry.'

'*Married?*'

'*Sí.* Normal life, you know. Like you life. My wife, she name Pilar. She was lesbian I fock in camp. We have arrangement. She do her thing in secret, I do my thing in secret. Lot of secret sex. Is OK, in secret.'

'What happened to her?'

'She leave Cuba in 2000. Pilar was dance instructor. They travel to Nicaragua for show. She leave Nicaragua, go to Unite State. She live now in England. In England homosexual can be marry. Is legal. *País civilizado.*'

'When did you become a prostitute?'

'I do this long long time. When I work in hotel, I fock the guest. Lot of homosexual tourist come to Cuba. They no' pay me cash, they buy me present, you know. But, when Pilar go, the government say no more job for me, no more house. They say I know she want to leave. I help her. Sure I know, but I no' "help" her. Boolshit. So what I can do? I become sex for professional. I have no choice. I—'

He was interrupted when the front door opened and two statuesque black women walked in, carrying on an animated conversation for a few beats, until they saw Max sitting at the table. Their voices frizzled out abruptly, making a sound like mangled tape. Their faces creased with confusion and their bodies stiffened. And then they saw Benny and immediately loosened up, all beaming bright smiles as they came towards him, calling his name, throwing out their arms, as if they hadn't seen him in years. Then they got a look at his cheek, and they both stopped and screeched at the same time. That was when Max noticed something he hadn't fully processed when they walked in: the girls were identical twins. Their faces were exact reproductions of each other – thin, sharp looks, piercing dark eyes, wide, pouting mouths with the same mid-lip parting, showing a glimmer of front tooth. They had the same short afro hairstyle, wore the same baggy grey sweatpants with pink bands on the side of the leg, white Ellesse T-shirts, and a thin gold bracelet apiece on their left wrists. They smelled of cocoa butter and perfume, and had traces of glitter on their faces and arms.

Benny introduced them as Luana and Jia. Max wondered how he could tell them apart.

They chatted with Benny, fussing over him. Max couldn't understand a word. Not that it mattered, as they ignored him completely, not even throwing him a glance when Benny demonstrated how Max had saved his life – standing up, punching at the air, shouting '*Pow!*' – and then cupping his stitched-up cheek in agony when the reenactment provoked the wound.

Max felt himself getting tired. His eyelids kept shutting and he blacked out for a few seconds.

Eventually, he laced his fingers together and used his hands as a cushion on the table. He tried to think of what he'd do in a few hours' time, back at the hotel: shower, shave and go rent a car. He thought of a comfortable bed in an air-conditioned room. He thought of Sandra. He thought of their old home, of conversations with her in the kitchen. He thought of a parallel life where he hadn't killed people.

And then, quietly and quickly, sleep stole him out of this place.

Max was shaken awake.

Roughly.

Benny stood over him, pale and goggle-eyed, sweat on his upper lip. He was wearing jeans and a T-shirt. The TV was on, the volume loud.

Max sat up and blinked and rubbed his eyes. It was morning, broad bright daylight streaming through the window. The twins had gone. He checked his watch. It was after eleven. How long had he been out?

'Look, look at this,' said Benny, pointing at the TV screen.

Cuban station. Cuban news. Mild snow on the picture, the sound a tad distorted. A street with two parked police Ladas, an ambulance, cops keeping a crowd at bay. A reporter babbling over the image. Max couldn't understand a word of it, but he could hear the excitement in the voice.

The camera panned to take in the whole view: fenced-off buildings, palm trees, trash in the gutters, the ocean in the background, cars passing on the Malecón. Then it stopped at a building.

Initially, Max didn't recognise the place, because it looked so dingy and ordinary in the daylight, and so different on the screen. Then he noticed the Christmas trees either side of the entrance.

It was La Urraca.

The reporter was interviewing the barman, whose face looked redder and sourer and older and puffier on TV, as if an evil spirit had mistakenly taken possession of a rotting tomato.

'That man who attack me?' started Benny, and then paused to take a deep breath through his nose. He swallowed. Breathed out. 'They ... they find him in the street. He dead, Max. He *dead*.'

Max stared at the screen, at the barman talking, not recognising the voice at all from the night before, not catching a damn word.

'It wasn't me,' he said to the TV.

'What you mean, it no' you? You hit him.'

'He was alive when *we* left him.'

'The reporter say he dead.'

'You saw it. I hit him. I knocked him out. Yes. But I didn't kill him.'

'Is no' what they say. They say you kill him.' Benny was shaking.

'What?' Max was confused, somewhere still asleep, still dreaming, his thoughts sluggish, groping for sense.

Benny's bottom lip trembled.

'You understand the Spanish?'

'No,' said Max. 'What's he saying?'

'He say description – of me and you.'

Now the reporter appeared on screen – a young man in a crisp white shirt and black tie, standing at the end of an alley where, behind him, in the distance, police were working. The camera zoomed in on someone sweeping the contents of the gutter with a dustpan and brush. Nearby lay a lumpy form covered in a white sheet.

'The cop look for us now, Max. They say they look for – for ...' Benny listened. 'For white man, tourist, tall, no hair, big body and – oh no! Oh fock!'

261

A face filled the screen. A black-and-white mugshot – full face and profile. It was Benny, younger – maybe by ten years – smiling slightly at the camera.

'Is me,' he said.

'No shit.'

'I was arrest when Pilar go.'

'They know where you live?'

'No. I no' live here official. But they know soon.'

Max took out his phone to call Rosa Cruz. He pressed the on button. Nothing happened. He stared at a plain black screen. The phone was dead. He took out the battery, put it back in and tried again. It was still dead.

Despite the noise from the TV, he heard people on the stairs outside, doors opening and slamming, children's voices. He heard conversations through the walls and ceiling, coming up from the floor. From the street came the sound of cockcrows, traffic and horses' hooves and laughter.

The man had been alive when they left him. When had he died? Max tried to remember hearing him crack his head. He hadn't, but small details were lost in the heat of the moment. He tried to recall the man's face. He got stuck after the colour of the Cuban's eyes and his moustache.

'There's a reasonable explanation to all this,' said Max. 'The man attacked you, cut you up with a razor. He was trying to kill you. You can go to the police. Explain. They'll see your face. They'll understand.'

'Max,' said Benny. 'This is no' America. I am homosexual prostitute dress as woman. They maybe know we tell truth, but it no' matter. I guilty. You – *Americano*, the enemy – you kill *Cubano*. You guilty. We – you and me – we guilty.'

Max thought about just walking out of this nightmare there and then. But Benny knew his name and nationality. The Cuban cops would catch him in no time.

He had to get in touch with Cruz. Explain things to her. Convince her that this was all an accident. He hadn't meant to

262

kill the guy. It was self-defence. And, besides, how the hell could he find Vanetta Brown locked up in jail?

'What we do now?'

'What do you mean "*we*"? I'm getting the fuck outta here.'

'You go?'

'Yes, I go. I'm sorry, but I can't get involved.'

'What? You *is* involve. Is *you* kill this man! Is you fault!'

'I was saving your fucken' life. You're welcome!'

The TV news was showing an aerial view of the Malecón. A long traffic jam of stationary cars backed up along the seafront lane, baking in the sun. Then it switched to a ground-level shot of a cop standing in the middle of the road directing traffic. Cars were moving slowly around the source of the blockage – a parked ambulance, flanked by four cop cars. A big crowd had gathered on the Malecón wall.

The live pictures cut to a static shot.

Another face appeared on the screen, another still photo-graph – and *another* face he knew; again, in younger days, when the eyebrows had been black instead of white.

Earl Gwenver.

'What's this?' Max nodded to the TV.

Benny didn't answer. He didn't need to. The camera zoomed in on a body being stretchered towards the ambulance, leaving a trail of water on the sidewalk. A different reporter – a woman this time – was doing the running commentary. Her tone was more measured, but her words were no easier for Max to under-stand.

'What are they saying?' he asked.

'This man. Him dead.'

'When?'

'Yesterday.' Benny looked worried.

'*Yesterday*?' Max heard the reporter say the word '*Americano*'. 'How?'

'You know him?' asked Benny.

'How did he die?'

Max thought of what he'd told Rosa Cruz about hurting Gwenver.

'They no' say.' Benny took a few steps away from him. 'Max? You kill him . . . as well?'

'No.' Max shook his head. 'But . . . I . . . I . . . Fuck!'

As Benny listened to the TV, his eyes grew wider.

'My God!'

'What is it?'

'You no' understand what she say?' he asked, gesturing at the screen. Max shook his head again.

'They say they look for – for *Americano* – big, white, no hair. Same. They look for you. They say you kill two peoples.'

Max stared at the TV, trying to think logically, rationally.

'We can no' stay here,' said Benny.

If you run you're guilty, thought Max. Even if he turned himself in and submitted to the mercies of the Cuban legal process, it could mean months in jail while he cleared his name. And then – *if* they believed him – he'd be deported, his chance of finding Vanetta Brown for ever gone. Once he was on American soil, Wendy Peck's threat would become a reality. And that was the best-case scenario, based on the assumption that Cuban justice worked like American justice – which, of course, it didn't.

'We must leave. Leave Habana. I have friend. He help.'

'A friend?' said Max, dazed, half there.

'Yes. Outside Habana. In Trinidad.'

Max thought of the map in his pocket. '*Trinidad?*'

'Yes.'

Max stared at Benny. He'd been intending to go there. Had Benny looked through his pockets? Maybe it was just coincidence.

'Is he a good friend?'

'Yes,' said Benny.

'How good?'

'The best. He no' call police. He can get us out of country.'

Max thought about it. He didn't want to leave Cuba. He

couldn't go home without Vanetta Brown. But he wasn't going to tell Benny that right now.

'How are we gonna get to Trinidad?'

'Car,' said Benny.

'You got one?'

'I get one.'

37

The car was a dusty brown four-door 1957 Chevy Bel Air convertible: long and low, with silver-anodised trim pieces on the fenders, hood and front grille. The interior was mahogany-panelled on the doors and dash, the seats wide black leather, but the wood's gloss had long gone and the seats were sweat-circle worn and showing stuffing and springbox through split seams.

Benny had stolen it three blocks from the apartment. It was the only parked car around. He simply pulled hard at the door and the lock gave up with a squeal and a pop. After he'd hotwired the car, they took off, Benny at the wheel. Despite their hurry and panic, he'd found time to pack a suitcase and remember his make-up kit.

Max sat in the passenger seat wearing one of Benny's wigs, most of the hair tucked under his shirt collar. The thing was stiff to near fossilised with hairspray and itched like hell, its synthetic locks mixing with his sweat and tickling his back to irritation.

He felt faintly fucken' stupid.

But, most of all, he was a compacted mess. His guts were in his mouth, his nerves wound tightrope taught and tripwire sensitive. Every cop he saw made him fraught; and there were plenty around, standing out bold and starched blue against the salt-eroded dirty grey Malecón, eyes roving, looking through every windshield, earpieces crackling, hands brushing hip holsters. His bearings were all messed up. The poles had been inverted, the co-ordinates reset, the trajectories redefined: the cops were after *him*.

And he was worried about the car.

The car was a serious goner. The top was up and the windows closed. Inside it was oven hot and raining condensation. There was a small hole in the floor right under Max's feet, letting in air and fumes. The transmission and suspension were screwed in tandem. Whenever Benny switched gear it took a few long seconds for the car to respond. It would buck violently like an over-oiled coinslot bronco, emitting a stream of sputtering noises that built to a long, loud grunt before the gear changed with a loud clank, making the car shudder so hard that the windows rattled open.

They left the Malecón, passed the lighthouse and took a roundabout. Traffic was slow but fluid. They overtook belching trucks and lumbering horsecarts, and then followed a pink *camello* through a tunnel, which brought them out into the suburbs.

Max turned on the radio and roved the dial. Five: salsa. Seven: Cuban jazz. Nine: a vintage Fidel speech. Eleven: a Cuban soap with canned laughter. Fourteen: a Cuban children's choir singing revolutionary songs. Sixteen: Cuban rap.

No news.

Benny said absolutely nothing. He was looking straight ahead, his lips clamped tightly shut, his face rigid. He was plain terrified. This was it. The moment he'd feared all his life. The magisterial knock on the door, the dictator state bearing down on him with all its might.

Of course, Max was scared too – like a motherfucker – but he'd been here before and he'd had it worse. For now he still had options, room to manoeuvre, space to think, holes to wriggle through and a wide open road.

He broke down his predicament: he had his passport, his money and his credit cards. He could get out of the country, except he couldn't go back to America without Vanetta Brown or proof of her death.

Right now, he was no closer to finding Brown than he was

267

yesterday. And he had the Cuban police after him, wanted for one, possibly two murders.

'How many people in your block have a TV?' he asked Benny.

'I no' know,' said Ramirez without taking his eyes from the road. He was a different person in men's clothes. The stitches and stubble around his jaw gave him a dangerous, feral look, and tiredness had robbed his eyes of their previous sparkle. He could have been a former boy-band star who'd fallen on hard times and had to resort to petty crime to make ends meet. 'No' many. Television in Cuba is big luxury.'

'They all got jobs?'

'Everyone in Cuba have job. Why you ask this question?'

'Do you talk to your neighbours?'

'No.'

'Did any of them know you dressed as Salma?'

'No. I go out at night. I sleep day.'

'How long have you been living there?'

'Why you ask me question like you a cop, Max?'

'Just answer.'

'No' long. Eight, nine week.'

'That whole time, no one saw you?'

'No. Building dark. Stair dark. If they see me, they see woman. No man.'

'OK.' Max nodded.

The TV reporter at the Gwenver crime scene had said they were looking for a man matching Max's description, but she hadn't mentioned his name. The barman at La Urraca had also described him. Then there was the doctor at the hospital. The police would put it together very quickly, if they hadn't already.

Benny wasn't officially listed at his address. The car they'd stolen would be reported, but the police wouldn't connect them to it until they found out where Benny lived.

Which gave them a day's head start at the most, two if they were lucky and the police slow. He doubted they were.

He told Benny his thoughts. Benny didn't react. He overtook the *camello*, which had pulled into a stop and was disgorging its battered, wilted passengers. They were heading into country now, wide open fields stretching to the horizon, some ploughed, some planted, some fallow.

Max switched his thoughts to Vanetta Brown. She'd had chemotherapy when she was still living in Havana. Her cancer must have gone into remission because if it hadn't, Rosa Cruz wouldn't have sent him after her. Cruz knew she was alive. Brown had fallen out of favour with Castro, fallen in with the Abakuás, and with Haitian criminals.

He had two theories, parallel, but going in opposite directions, one that held up, one that didn't.

Vanetta, dying of cancer, decided to settle scores. She sent an Abakuá hitman to kill Eldon and Joe. The killer had dug up Abe Watson's grave and used his gun for the murders. Why? Revenge. Eldon and Abe led the raid that had left her daughter and husband dead. The hitman had then taken Joe out. Why? If Vanetta's prints hadn't been on the casings, he could have reasoned that it was to take out the one person who could have linked her to the murders. But that just raised more questions.

So what if Vanetta had nothing to do with the murders, apart from knowing the victims? She'd been set up. The hitman had come from Cuba. Joe Liston had been to Cuba. Joe had known Vanetta. Vanetta had had links with the Abakuás. Maybe Joe had found out something. Maybe he'd seen something. The person or people behind the murders had framed Vanetta as a diversion. They knew her story, and maybe they'd killed Eldon to create an even thicker smokescreen.

Yet his gut didn't buy it. His gut was telling him she was innocent.

But that was all he really had to go on. Instinct.

There were pieces missing from both theories. If Vanetta was guilty of ordering the hits, what was her motive for killing Joe? If she was being framed, then who by and why her?

269

The traffic had thinned to single cars and plenty of empty space between. No surprise. Cuba had sixty thousand vehicles for eleven million people, spread over a land mass of more than forty thousand square miles. Cuba didn't run on oil. It ran on its wits and resourcefulness. And it threw nothing away.

The road ahead was an even black streak cutting through a landscape of lush green grass, orangey-brown soil and tall thin palms. The smooth surface was roadkill-splattered. Turkey vultures – big black beasts with small egg-shaped red heads and sharp white beaks – swooped down low, almost clipping the heads of passers-by with their claws, pausing long enough to tear off a chunk of rotting meat, and then split for the skies before an oncoming vehicle meted out the same fate.

They rolled under bridges. They passed a farmer driving a herd of goats. They passed bus stops with small crowds waiting in the baking heat. They drove through sugar cane fields, tobacco fields, coffee fields. Max saw signs for Playa Girón – the Bay of Pigs – 110 miles, Cienfuegos 115 miles, Trinidad 132 miles. He saw more state billboards hailing the revolution and pumping propaganda in red, blue and white capitals:

Socialismo o muerte! Patria o muerte!

Max carried on punching a finger at the radio. He got frequent bursts of static, music fading in and out, in between, crystal-clear speeches and peals of laughter.

Benny looked over and managed a meagre smile.

'You look ugly as woman.'

'Fuck you. It's your damn wig.'

Benny laughed a little.

'You sorry you help me?'

'We're way past that,' said Max.

'OK. I say again. You *regret* you help me?'

'Maybe we'll both regret it.'

Max worked the radio, getting nothing.

'What you look for?'

'News.'

'What is time?'

Max showed him his watch: 1.10 p.m.

'You miss. Go back.'

He went back along the dial. Chatter. Jazz. Samba. More chat. Then a snatch of a very familiar tune – the Mellotron intro to 'Strawberry Fields Forever'.

'Stop!' said Benny. 'Is news now.'

'That's the Beatles,' said Max.

'Is news. Listen please.'

Max heard a woman's voice speaking fast. He heard 'Habana' and 'Malecón' – or something close to it. He may even have caught 'Urraca'. But he wasn't sure because the words were circling his ears in a dissonant buzz, all starting or stopping in sharp 'eh' and 'ay' and 'ah' sounds. He listened for his name and Gwenver's. He didn't hear either.

Five minutes later, Benny switched off the radio.

'You understand this?'

'No,' said Max. 'I thought I had some Spanish. I was wrong.'

'Is like on TV. They find two dead peoples in Habana in one day,' said Benny. 'They look for me and *Americano*. They say to Cuban peoples to contact police if they see us.'

'I didn't hear our names.'

'They give my name. No' you.'

'Have they said anything about the car?'

'No,' said Benny. 'Who is the dead black man? They say him *exilio Americano. Pantera Negra*. Wanted for crime in Unite State.'

'That's right.'

'You no' tourist, no, Max?'

'That was last night. This is a different day.'

'Is the same day. Who you are? What you do here, in Cuba?'

'Tell me about your friend – the one in Trinidad.'

'What you want to know?'

'Who he is, what he does, that kind of thing.'

'Why?'

271

'Just tell me,' said Max.

'I want to know what you do here.'

'Don't argue. I don't owe you an explanation.' Max gave him a sharp look. Benny tried to stare him down but couldn't.

'OK . . . Him name Nacho Savon. I know him long time.'

'He a transvestite too?'

'You no' funny, Max. Him work for government, for Minister of Interior.'

'*The Ministry of the Interior?* Isn't that the secret police?'

'Relax, is no' what you think,' said Benny. 'Him work with computer. Him expert with internet and mobile telephone. Do all technology for listen in telephone. But that not all he do. He also sell telephone and computer *por la izquierda*. Is illegal, you know. Is how I get my DVD – from him.'

'His colleagues at the Ministry know this?'

'Sure, but they no' care. He sell to them also. And he *expert* at job,' said Benny. 'He give you new telephone.'

'I see,' said Max. 'Where does he get the contraband?'

Benny frowned. 'Is like *contrabando*? Is same, yes?'

Max nodded.

'He have contact.'

'You mean the Abakuás? He buys from them?'

'Everyone buy from Abakuá. Is like the mafia here.'

'I know.'

'Now *you* tell me about youself, Max.'

'You know everything you need to know. Just drive.'

Benny muttered something under his breath. Max caught a mild whiff of rot, day-old bad meat. He guessed the heat and the stress had derailed the healing of the unbandaged wound. He rolled down the window.

No one was following them. Cars were overtaking them regularly. They were barely doing fifty. He doubted the car could do more. If it was a race between the Chevy and another vehicle, the Chevy would finish fourth.

Max searched the sky for helicopters. All he saw were vultures

272

circling and scenting, small ragged t-shapes floating among the clouds, looking for death.

Up ahead, two small crowds had gathered on either side of the road, shepherded by men in yellow shirts, khakis and caps, holding clipboards. One of the men stepped out into the road in front of the car. He started waving.

He was flagging them down, getting them to stop.

'That a *cop*?' said Max. 'What's happening?'

'Is hitch-hike official.'

'A *what*?'

'Here is law to pick up hitch-hiker,' said Benny. 'If man with yellow shirt tell you stop, you must stop.'

They were getting closer, the people all looking expectantly at the car.

Benny suddenly lost whatever defiant confidence he'd had. His shoulders slumped, his arms drooped, his hands slackened around the wheel. He was on state-controlled auto-pilot, doing what he was told without thinking.

The car got down to a crawl. Max felt his heart racing. He scoped the crowd: ageing to old men and women, and beautiful young girls, in tight jeans and tighter crop tops, heavily made-up, crowding the official, flirting with him, competing for his attention.

The official – with a blossoming paunch and a thin moustache – had big eyes for a pair of shapely *mulattas* carrying rucksacks. The adults hung back, looking at the girls and especially the official with silent disgust.

Benny turned to Max. 'Let me do this, OK?' he said. He was calm and resolved, a doctor quietening a patient against the inevitable.

The official came towards them, writing something on his clipboard. Benny wound down the window. Max lowered his head and pretended to doze.

The man greeted Benny and then retreated a step when he saw his face.

'*Accidente*,' said Benny.

The official asked his name and where they were coming from. José Yero, Benny replied to the first question, Havana to the second.

The official wrote it down. He asked where they were going. He was brusque, but non-aggressive, trying to move things along. Benny said Sancti Spiritus.

Could they take two people to Cabaiguán?

Yes, sure, said Benny. It was on the way. No problem.

The official thanked him for doing his duty for the country and the revolution. *De nada*, said Benny. The man called out two names. The *mulattas* came forward. Some of the waiting women gave the girls the finger and mouthed obscenities.

Max tensed in his seat.

Benny glanced at him, panicked.

One of the girls leaned in the window and said, '*Hola.*' Her open expression and friendly smile froze into a frightened grimace as her eyes went from Benny's face to Max, scowling under his wig.

He had a flash of inspiration. He locked eyes with the girl, licked his lips and blew her a kiss.

The girl stepped away from the car in disgust. She said something to her friend. From the sound of things, and her body language, she didn't like the look of either her prospective driver or his passenger.

As the official came back towards them, suddenly there was a loud cheer from the crowd. They were all looking past the car up the road, from where a *camello* was coming. The bus indicated and pulled in. People started moving towards it.

The official waved Benny on. They could go, he said.

As Benny started up the car, Max saw people still standing at the stop: two young uniformed cops talking to a pair of older men in white *guayabera* shirts, aviator shades and shoulder holsters. The men were leaning against a black Mercedes with tinted windows. They weren't looking at the cops.

They were looking straight at the Chevy.

Benny pulled the car out on to the road, letting out a sigh of relief.

'How much further to Trinidad?' asked Max.

'Thirty miles.'

'Any more hitch-hiking stops?'

'Maybe,' said Benny. 'The law start in the Special Period, when we have fuel shortage and the Russian stop sending new bus. Private transport become public transport.'

'Couldn't work in America,' said Max. 'Too many sick fucks out there.'

He tore off the wig and threw it out the window. It disappeared under the wheels of the oncoming bus.

38

They reached Trinidad in the late afternoon. The town was timewarp-jammed somewhere south of 1890, a living, lived-in monument to Cuba's Spanish colonial past. Cobblestone streets, the colour and texture of filthy ice, ran between bright, colourful, terracotta-roofed houses, whose every doorway and window was encased in white metal grilles. There were barely any cars around. The town was too small and its inhabitants way too poor to afford to run them. They got to where they were going on foot, on rickety bicycles, on the backs of donkeys or crammed into horsedrawn carts. There was no state propaganda to be seen anywhere, no hectoring reminders of the present to wreck allusions to the past.

Benny drove through town and parked the car at the end of an empty road. Max stretched and shook the cramp from his legs, relieved and grateful to be out of that clanking, asphyxiating sweatbox on wheels, his curiosity about Cuba's legendary mode of transport bludgeoned right out of him.

They started walking. It was hotter and drier here, on the Caribbean coast; the sun brighter and rawer than in Havana, zeroing in on them like they were ants caught in the crossbeams of a sadistic child's magnifying glass. The breeze, blowing down from the surrounding Escambray Mountains, stirred sandy dust loose from in between the cobblestones and carried with it a rank taint of old damp shoes – in reality, the fumes wafting from the local tobacco-processing plants and cigar factories.

The dismal stores were poorly stocked and sparsely lit, selling basic necessities to townsfolk and state tourist tat to foreign visitors. Of whom there were plenty: busloads of three-hour itinerants mass-doddering behind a tour guide in a bright-red polo shirt, poking around the churches, taking pictures of the pretty town centre and glancing around the museums, before being corralled into one of the local taverns. Here the patrons drank out of earthenware goblets, and the only drink on sale was canchánchara – a local brew of water, honey, lime and Santero rum. According to Benny, it tasted like cold tea spiked with flu remedy. It went down mild and harmless but had a hard rebound. It didn't make the tourists too drunk to walk back to their transport, but it did induce an almost beatific sense of well-being and benevolence in even the most jaded box-ticking globetrotter.

As the visitors were ushered out to their parked buses, they'd be surrounded by some of the town's hard-faced children – dirty, bony-torsoed, camera-ready charity beacons begging for convertible pesos. If they received their alms in standard currency, they'd throw it on the ground, spit on it and curse their benefactor. Then they'd ask for *real* money. After the tourists had gone, the kids would pool their takings and divvy up among themselves, while they waited for the next bus.

Max and Benny passed a circle of them sharing out a pile of coins in the street. One for you, one for me. Everyone equal. No squabbles. No complaints. State socialism made simple. State socialism without the politics. What would become of them, Max wondered, when the regime died or changed or fell? Would they still hold on to those egalitarian principles or would they learn to trample on each other in the lifelong race for the runaway buck? He knew the answer. It was the same everywhere.

Nacho Savon didn't look too pleased to see Benny. He body-blocked the entrance and glowered at his friend, while moving the door back and forth, the hinges squeaking and grinding lightly – in time, it seemed, with his indecision. He was a stout-legged,

277

square-torsoed little man with an explosion of wild, thick, unkempt greying hair that stood completely upright, as if he'd shoved his finger in an electric socket to get the dirty-mop-caught-in-a-wind-tunnel look just right.

The two faced each other silently, gawking at one another, waiting for the other to make some kind of first move. Benny smiled as much as his stitches allowed. Savon's expression wavered somewhere between hostility and sadness. Max speculated on what had happened between them. Benny's body language said he was the good-for-nothing lover who never called or showed when he said he would, disappeared for months on end, and only returned when he was in serious trouble, tail between his legs and repentance on his breath, swearing it was the last transgression. All he was missing was a handful of cheap flowers wrapped in plastic and he'd get the part. Savon was the idiot who always took him back, vowing it was the last time . . . until the next time.

Savon finally broke the face-off to look at Max, noticing him for the first time. His eyes were small, bulging and almost completely black. He had a ruddy complexion. Max thought he bore a passing resemblance to an irate cooked shrimp casting one final pissed-off look at the top of the food chain from the end of a fork. He was wearing a brown cotton shirt, calf-length khaki shorts, white socks and black Reeboks whose thick, air-cushioned soles made his feet look like small hovercrafts. His shorts rode halfway down his groin and his shoelaces were undone. Max was usually contemptuous of men who dressed half their age, suspecting them of being immature narcissists or narcissistic chickenhawks.

'*Quién es el?*' Savon asked Benny.

'*Le llaman "Max".*'

'*Extranjero?*'

'*Si. Americano. El no es mi novio.*'

'*Su chulo?*'

'*Vete a singar!*' said Benny.

278

Savon opened the door wide and beckoned them in with a scoop of the hand and a defeated grumble.

They followed him into a lobby that was as cold and clean as a new refrigerator. The walls were spotless white and completely bare, except for the ubiquitous Guevara picture, slightly bigger than any Max had seen elsewhere. The aircon was jacked all the way up. Icy, odourless air immediately enveloped them, chilling their sweat so quickly it gave them goosepimples and made them shudder.

Savon started talking. Max pretended to be interested in Guevara's photo-portrait, those humourless features and cruel eyes, gazing off into bloody destiny. He listened in to what was being said behind him. The words were the usual mystery to him, but he could hear the emotions burdening them, the sorrowful anger that shaped them.

Savon was delivering a monologue that sounded prepared, worked on and rehearsed over and over in his mind, so much so that he could have been talking to himself. He was trying to keep his tone civil and reasonable, but beneath it a volcano's worth of pent-up grievance was coming to the boil and his voice would occasionally rise to a snarl and snap, before he'd rein himself in. Benny was silent. Max imagined him hanging his head and taking the punishment – or at least pretending to.

But when he did finally start talking, a few beats after Savon had finished what he was saying, Benny sounded perfectly normal, neither chastened nor apologetic. Savon was initially quiet as he heard him out. And then, suddenly, he exploded into laughter, the first roisterous peals sounding more like yells.

Max turned around and saw Savon bent over double, clutching his belly, heaving out hilarity.

Benny looked at Max and winked.

Later that evening they ate dinner on the second floor, in another chilly bare room, where the furniture consisted of a single wooden table, four chairs and a large plasma TV on the wall.

279

Savon had prepared a pork and black bean stew, with white rice and a side of fried plantain. The food was delicious, but the vibe was bad. They ate in complete silence. Both Benny and Savon kept their eyes fixed on the hillocks of food in front of them, cutlery moving furiously from plate to mouth, as though racing each other to the finish. Max took his time.

The TV news showed a rerun of the report about the two murders in Havana. Benny's only comment – apart from a sonorous belch that echoed around the room and provoked a short but murderous look from Savon – was to tell Max that it was identical to what they'd heard that morning.

After Benny had formally introduced them, Max discovered that Savon spoke perfect English, albeit with a mild Germanic clip to his accent. Max asked him to charge his phone, and he obliged, taking it away with him.

When it was done, Max had tried to call Rosa Cruz, but there was no signal. She hadn't called him either.

Savon and Benny finished dinner almost simultaneously. Benny said he was going to bed and left. Savon then relaxed. He made small talk of sorts while Max polished off his food. Then he cleared the table and returned with a bottle of rum and two glasses.

'Benny says you saved his life,' Savon said, pulling up a chair.

'He was in a jam.'

'He's always in a jam.'

Savon took what Max at first thought was a deck of playing cards from his breast pocket, but it was really a pack of Romeo y Julieta cigarettes – beige and maroon, with a centred cameo of the lovers at the balcony. He offered one to Max, who declined with a shake of the head.

'None of you Americans smoke, do you? You lead such healthy, dull, uneventful lives.'

'We have quicker ways of killing ourselves,' said Max.

Savon uncorked the bottle and the sweet heady smell of vintage rum hit Max between the eyes. When Max passed on the booze too, Savon smiled pityingly. He poured himself two fingers of orangey-brown alcohol, liqueur-like in consistency. He took a sip and lit his cigarette.

'I don't care who you are or what you've done. But you're in a lot of trouble – and you're in my house,' said Savon.

'I didn't kill Earl Gwenver, and the man who attacked Benny—' began Max, but Savon cut him off.

'It's not my business or my concern.'

'Benny said you could help.'

'I can get you out of the country – for a price.'

'How much?'

Savon looked out of the window, feigning thought, his eyes already decided. He had a view of the Iglesia y Convento de San Francisco, which appeared on the back of the twenty-five-cent coin. By day the church's belltower was pale green and yellow, but now, at night, it was illuminated by spotlights and became a gaudy glowing cactus floating in the dark.

'You will need to get to the east coast, to a place near Guantánamo. That's a two-day drive – at least – depending on your car,' said Savon. 'You can't use the car you came in. It's been reported stolen by now. And as I'm sure you've seen, there are not many cars in Cuba. Plus yours has Havana plates. Once the search for you spreads out of the capital, you'll get caught in no time. I can provide you with a car. Part of the package.'

'How much?' Max repeated.

'Five thousand pesos – tourist pesos.'

'Five *thousand*?' Max had slightly over six in his pockets. 'What does that buy? A one-way trip on a leaky boat?'

'No.' Savon shook his head with a smile. 'That gets you on the Wetback Express, an American military supply ship bound straight to Miami.'

'How the fuck are you gonna swing that?'

'I "swing" it all the time.' Savon blew a plume of smoke at a mosquito flying in his vicinity. The insect plunged to the table. 'Do you know how most of the stuff I sell comes into the

281

country – the laptops, phones, satellite dishes, the video and DVD players? Via your people. The occupying force.'

Max shrugged. He wasn't surprised.

'They've been doing it for years. Decades. And recently, with Fidel being sick, they've stepped up operations. They're flooding Cuba with cheap computers and phones. The idea is, the price will come down, so more people can afford them. You've heard the term "black ops", yes?'

'Sure.'

'They call this – what they do here – "brown ops", because they're spreading shit. Looking to destabilise the regime by stealth. An online counter-revolution, if you like. Get as many young people on cellphones and computers as possible. Give them access to a technology the state cannot possibly control, and – theoretically – they'll organise protests that will bring down the government.'

'So you play both sides?'

'I play *my* side,' said Savon, draining his glass. 'The whole Cuban-American interface is handled by a group of Spanish-speaking soldiers based in Santiago de Cuba. I do business with them all the time. They call themselves the "Texas Playboys". They've got these nicknames, after their hometowns. The ringleader calls himself "Señor Dallas". There are also Señors Austin, Houston, Galveston, El Paso and Fort Worth. They have other scams going on, besides the CIA one. They sell food, drink, cigarettes, clothes – anything and everything American. And they also run the Wetback Express.'

'You never been tempted?'

'To leave Cuba? No.' Savon lit another cigarette and smiled. 'What would I do in Miami? Wait tables? The American Dream isn't for anyone over forty.'

Max laughed. There was something honourable, even admirable about Savon. He may have had the heart of a mercenary and the threadbare soul of the intrinsically corrupt, but he was upfront about it. Max knew they could do business, that he wouldn't get ripped off. Savon was a player, no more dishonest than the two warring systems he was exploiting.

'This five thousand pesos, is it negotiable?'

'The price is usually ten thousand,' said Savon. 'I'm giving you a discount because you'll be carrying cargo.'

'Like what?'

'Benny. He goes with you.'

'*Benny?*'

'All the way to Miami.'

'You're fucken' kidding, right?'

'That's the deal. You go to the pick-up point with Benny. If he's not with you, you don't get on board. Take it or leave it.'

Max didn't need any baggage, especially not in the shape of Benny, whom he didn't trust. But that wasn't all.

'What if I don't want to leave Cuba right now?' he said.

'If I don't hear from you in the next four days, the boat's gone,' said Savon. 'Take my advice – whatever it is you're doing here, forget it. Leave. Go home. You're a marked man. At this moment, the police in Havana are checking all the hotels, looking for missing guests. If they don't know your identity yet, sooner or later they will. Once they circulate it, you'll have to find a cave to hide in because everyone in this country is a potential informant. It's not that they want to be, but they're scared not to be.'

Max looked out of the window. The lights on the church tower had been turned off and it was completely dark and quiet. Savon yawned and drained the last of his rum.

Max reached for the money in his side pocket. 'Four days, right?'

'Starting at midnight.'

Max counted out five thousand pesos in fifties, twenties and tens. Savon took the money and asked for Max's phone. He programmed a number into it and instructed him to head for a small town on the south coast called Cajobabo. He was to call the day before he wanted to leave.

'Why are you helping Benny?' Max asked, when Savon had pocketed the cash.

'I'm not helping him. I want him out of my life – well out, well away – but somewhere safe, somewhere he can start again. Although I have a feeling that wherever he goes, he'll find trouble. Some people are just pre-programmed to fuck up.'

'Love's a weird thing, isn't it?'

'Who said anything about love?' Savon smiled sadly.

39

In Trinidad people rose early for work, at the hotels on nearby Playa Ancon or the tobacco farms and factories at the edge of the mountains. Max and Benny drove past them at the crack of dawn, workers walking through the cobbled streets in formation, a double line of men and women of all ages, growing steadily in length as it ambled out of town. They were singing, post-revolutionary labourer songs originally intended to bolster spirits and reinforce beliefs, but in voices so low and a delivery so mournful, these spirited hymns to proletarian solidarity and patriotic duty were recast as dirges, laments for a bygone ideal. The marching workforce sounded like a defeated yet proud and noble army heading homeward.

Max was driving the bottle-green 1953 DeSoto Firedome that Savon had left outside his house, with keys in the ignition and a full tank of gas. Benny was in full drag, wearing a sunflower-print dress with white frill trim that on a woman his age would have looked prim and outmoded, but he carried off in a style all his own. He'd darkened his face with foundation and hidden his stitches under the fringe of a straight black wig, around which he'd tied a headscarf that matched the thick brown leather belt cinched about his skinny waist.

Max could usually spot even the most convincing transvestites by looking at their hands and wrists – always too wide and too thick – but Benny would have fooled him in broad daylight: his hairless hands were small and slender, with an almost complete absence of knuckle, and fine, reedy fingers topped off by fake

285

pointed red nails, those of a woman of leisure. Benny looked better than good: he was almost perfect.

'What's the deal with you and Nacho?' asked Max.

'Is private.' Benny had been downcast and silent since they'd left. 'No' talk to me about him, OK?'

'Happily,' said Max. He switched on the radio and surfed the channels, getting nothing but multiple varieties of Cuban music and no news. He turned it off.

The sky was black fading to blue, sunbeams slashing it pink and red, the horizon fringed with hot gold. Stars were glittering their last and the half-moon was fading to a wraith-like outline. The landscape ahead remained swaddled in a dense, silken early-morning mist, which teemed with rainbows and kaleidoscopic forms as it trapped the first soft rays of light. They passed rows of royal palms, whose pale grey trunks towered fifty feet above them, gangling and ridged, topped with green tips and drooping leaves, laden with birds singing down at them.

Max opened the window. The air was clear and cool and mint-tinged. He took a deep breath and held it in.

'What a beautiful country,' he whispered to himself. 'What a pity.'

Caille Jacobinne was easy to find because it was impossible to miss – just as Savon had told him it would be when Max asked about it. Not only was it the sole building around for miles, it was the size of an aircraft hangar. The walls had been painted with the image of the Haitian flag: solid horizontal blocks of blue on red and a white square in the middle bearing the nation's crest and motto, '*L'Union Fait la Force*'.

They made a left off the main road and followed a dirt path down across a grassy field. The path widened the closer they got to the centre, mushrooming into a wide, circular clearing of hard-baked orange earth that lapped around the property.

'Where we go?' asked Benny.

'I'm a tourist, remember? I'm going to do some sight-seeing.'

Benny snorted derisively and folded his arms as Max got out.

In the forecourt were the remains of a children's playground – a semi-dismantled climbing frame, swings, a slide missing its platform and half the steps of its ladder. Further on was an empty wood-and-wire chicken coop, the timber blackened, the wire rusted the colour of the soil. A grey mule was standing by a post. It turned its head to watch as Max approached, its ears perking up as he drew closer.

The front of the centre bore the name 'Caille Jacobinne', painted in large, black italics. Either side of the door was a giant mural of Toussaint L'Ouverture's silhouette, on pale blue. Within the silhouette were smaller paintings of Che Guevara, José Martí and the Castro brothers, illustrating the ideological links between the two revolutions.

Max walked around the building, which backed on to a small stagnant lake. The water's surface was a murky green gloss, part-matted with leaves and droning with flying insects. The prow of a capsized, half-submerged rowing boat stuck out of the middle, held there by the head of an uprooted palm tree.

He returned to the front entrance and tried the door. It was unlocked.

The inside was cavernous, dark and quiet; a place where day never broke, a place that felt completely abandoned. He wedged the door open with a rock while he searched the walls for a light switch. He couldn't find one.

'Hello?' Max called out. He was answered by echoes.

He stepped in and let his eyes adjust. Gradually, the darkness yielded to him, parting around sequinned voodoo flags hanging from the rafters and separate clusters of lit candles placed close to the walls, four on either side, two at the very end.

The candles were on a pair of altars, wooden blocks painted black, each laden with an icon in the middle – a plaster Black Madonna cradling a small, pink-skinned Jesus. The statue was surrounded by foot-long crucifixes, bowls of drying fruit, bottles of rum, human skulls, coins, machetes, postcards of Miami and

American flags in small glass jars. The wall to his right was painted with vast murals of voodoo deities, the gods and their goddess wives. He recognised some of them: there was Baron Samedi – the god of the dead and dweller of graveyards – in his top hat, tails and cane, his face pancaked white and his eyes red and staring right at Max. He thought immediately of Solomon Boukman, who'd worshipped Baron Samedi and offered enemies to him in sacrifice. Here Samedi was depicted alongside his foul-mouthed spouse, Maman Brigitte, dressed like a cheap hooker in a short tight black dress with half-open zippers on the thigh. She was brandishing a champagne glass full of red chilli peppers in one hand, and a black rooster in the other. Close to them, dressed in green, was the beautiful Ayida-Weddo, goddess of fertility, rainbows and snakes, holding a small baby in her arms, as her husband, Damballa, dressed in a white suit and a cravat with an egg-shaped pin, watched over her shoulder. Further on was the religion's only white god, Mademoiselle Charlotte, shown here as a sexy but sinister Californian surfer babe, long blonde hair and piercing blue eyes, coming out of a pool of boiling water, naked and dripping wet, her fists clenched. And then there was Ogun Feraille, god of fire and war, sitting cross-legged on skull-shaped hot coals, holding crossed machetes with white-hot tips. All of the giant figures were painted against a background Max initially mistook for smoke or clouds or some kind of fog, but on closer inspection he saw that it was actually images of people fucking, fighting, dancing, eating, working, sleeping: life's crude tapestry realised as a nebulous pagent of end-results. The candlelight intensified the colours of the mural, and as Max walked by the flames, the gods seemed to move, to turn a fraction in his direction, to follow him. He crossed to the other side of the room and found that the wall was identical in design, as were the twin altars, which bore the same objects as their opposite counterparts.

He moved to the end of the building, where a huge group portrait filled the back wall. His eyes were quickly snared by the painting's focal point – Vanetta Brown, staring right at him, her earthy supermodel looks intact, her expression part welcoming, part quizzical, the glint in her eyes matched by that of her hoop earrings. She sat in the middle of a small gathering of men and women stood behind her in a tight semi-circle. Vanetta's hand was resting on the head of a small black animal, which appeared to be some kind of cat. It had its tail hooked around her lower leg.

As Max came closer, the painting yielded more details. He recognised the backdrop – Caille Jacobinne itself, and the fore-court he'd crossed. He also noted the incongruous design running along the bottom of the portrait: two skylines, silhouet-ted in white. Havana and Miami.

His gaze travelled back to the phalanx around Vanetta Brown. Men and women, all but one dark-skinned. He took in their clothes – shabby, patched, too short, too big, too long. They con-trasted with Vanetta's blue denim jeans and long-sleeved blouse with white buttons. He followed her left arm to the hand she'd rested on the animal's head.

He scrutinised the black shape by her feet. It had no features, no face of any kind.

And that's when he realised he wasn't looking at a cat, nor any kind of animal, but at the silhouette of a person. A child.

Max shuddered. He looked around quickly.

Someone had been here to light the candles, but the place felt empty.

He followed the painted Miami skyline. It wasn't the modern one, but the cityscape he remembered from his youth, before the drug money added the fangs and the economic boom the inci-sors.

He noticed a building he didn't quite recognise, close to the Freedom Tower. He'd thought it was the old courthouse, but it was too broad, unless the artist had made a mistake.

And then it moved.

Someone was sitting there, facing the wall, painting.

'Excuse me?' said Max, walking over slowly. The painter was working on the tip of the Freedom Tower. '*Per favor?*'

The painter stopped what he or she was doing, frozen in mid-motion – arm extended towards the wall, the tip of the brush an inch away from it – as if their power switch had been tripped and their body had immediately shut down.

Max looked the painter over: dressed all in black, a broad-brimmed hat and leather gloves, a shapeless garment like an overcoat or a cassock, shoes with thick, bulbous, upturned caps poking out from under the hem.

'Do you speak English? *Hablas Inglés?*'

No reply. No motion. It was as if he were talking to a mannequin. Max stepped closer and his foot kicked something metallic. He looked down and saw a ring of paint pots, all different sizes and colours, four deep around the figure by the wall.

'You been to Haiti.' It was a statement rather than a question, and the person who'd made it was male and spoke in a rasping voice with an accent that had made the round trip from Haiti to New York: Afro-Franco-Brooklyn.

'How do you know?' asked Max.

'The smell.'

'What smell?'

'Of the country.'

'What about it?'

'You still carry it.'

Max stopped just short of acting on an impulse to sniff himself. He glanced around to see if they were alone. The gods on the walls made him feel crowded and observed, and Vanetta Brown's gaze was suddenly intimidating.

The painter still hadn't moved, the tip of his brush poised close to the drying spire.

Max tilted his head to get a better look at the man. He was wearing an opaque black veil that fell from the brim of his hat down to his shoulders.

'I'm looking for Vanetta Brown,' said Max. 'Have you seen her?'

'I ain't seen anyone in years.'

'Do you know where she is?'

'No.'

The painter remained as rigid as before. Absolutely no movement, not even when he spoke. Max was amazed at how steadily he could hold his arm, without the merest hint of a tremor.

'What about the child at her feet?'

'Osso?'

'Osso – is that its name?'

'What about him?'

'Why did you paint him that way – all black?'

'Black was what he was.'

Max looked at the silhouette. The child couldn't have been older than four or five.

'What happened to him?'

'Left here long ago. Went Santiago way, I heard. Fell in with a bad crowd.'

'What kind of "bad crowd"?' asked Max.

'A crowd that's bad instead of good.'

Max studied the mural again, scrutinising each of the dozen or so faces around Vanetta. The man immediately behind her, almost in the middle of the group, was light-skinned. He stood out not only because of his complexion, but because his clothes were different from the others' – grey mechanic's overalls instead of tatty hand-me-downs. And he had been painted slightly larger than the rest of the group. When Max moved a few steps further back, he saw that the man was actually standing a little in front of the gathering, closer to Vanetta.

He returned to the child's silhouette. Pale traces glistened through the black matt paint, hints of features, a head and eyes and fingers.

'You painted *over* him,' said Max.

The painter rested the brush on the nearest paint pot and

291

turned towards Max. He took the hem of the veil between his fingers and slowly lifted it, uncovering his mouth and nose, then the rest of his face.

Max took a step back, surprised and confused.

The painter was old, his dark skin floppy and lined, his beard pure white. His eyes swam about in their sockets, their gaze forever swivelling in random directions, like a pair of ball compasses trying to catch a bearing off fluid poles.

The man was blind.

'I'm sorry. I didn't know,' said Max. 'How long . . . ? How do you manage? How do you *paint*?'

'From memory.'

Max looked around the walls again, coming back to the spire the man had been working on, its delicacy and detail, guilt piggybacking his amazement and wonder.

'What happened?' he asked.

'The night I finished this, Osso poured battery acid on my eyes while I was sleeping,' said the painter.

'Why?'

'Guess he didn't like my work.'

'What didn't he like about it?'

The painter didn't answer. Max looked at the silhouette, at the head, stared into the black, focused on the faint hints beneath, trying to draw out the child's features, but couldn't.

'What happened to him?'

'He ran away. No one knows where. He vanished.'

'Was there something wrong with his face?' Max asked.

'His face was just the start of it. There wasn't nothin' right to that kid.'

'I'm sorry,' said Max.

'I'm not,' replied the painter. 'You can't stop what's coming to you.'

40

Benny still wasn't talking as they drove away. He was locked in turmoil, nibbling the inside of his bottom lip, scraping lipstick on to his teeth. Max checked the cellphone: still no reception.

He considered what he'd found out at Caille Jacobinne.

What were the chances that the child on the mural and the man who'd killed Eldon and Joe were the same person – Osso? Vanetta had known him. The way they'd been painted, it appeared that the kid had been attached to her and she to him. She'd protected him, maybe even loved him, when everyone else had shunned him. Osso was damaged goods then, already psychotic and prone to sadistic violence: he'd attacked the painter's eyes, the artist's vital organ. And then disappeared. Had Vanetta taken him away?

The triggerman had a pronounced harelip. Perhaps he'd been born with a more severe deformity – a cleft palate – that subsequently had been fixed. Maybe Vanetta herself had paid for the operation. He'd been grateful to her for his new face, his new lease of life, and their bond had tightened and strengthened.

When Vanetta fell ill, she'd sent Osso to Miami to settle her scores. What better way of repaying the love she'd shown him than by killing those who'd broken her heart?

But that was all supposition, tenuous at best. And it didn't feel right. Not right at all.

For the first few hours they were alone on the road, nothing in front of them, nothing behind. The mist cleared and the sun began slow-cooking the earth. By midday heatwaves were shimmering above the ground and every part of the car was too hot to touch. Max poured sweat and fidgeted while Benny stayed cool and quiet. The windows were open, but the smell of fresh herbs was long gone and the air was manure heavy, with a little wood and stubble smoke pouring in for diversion.

The DeSoto ran better than the Chevy. It was faster, quieter and far smoother, yet it was nothing but charmed scrap, souped-up junk rolling on mismatched, rimless wheels, powered by a too-small engine. The interior was uncomfortable. The front seats, uniform as opposed to individual, had been re-upholstered with a mixture of thin foam and what felt and sounded like stacks of old newspaper. All the backseat lining had been replaced with a flapping patchwork of towels, curtains and faded bedsheets. Still, it looked good from the outside at least, a car with road presence, taking up the bulk of the lane; its body long and flourished with art deco touches, and a grille reminiscent of bared teeth.

They passed farmers tilling the soil with hump-backed oxen and ploughs. The farmers would stop and stand and gawp at the car, as if it were something they'd heard about but never seen. Some took off their straw hats or caps and waved and yelled out greetings. Benny scowled and muttered insults.

Max tried the radio. Static and white noise came through the speaker, with snatches of music and talk fading in and out. He turned it off.

The road got worse the further into the country they ventured, the blacktop cracking and breaking up, and then gradually vanishing altogether until the way ahead was nothing but a strip of rutted and potholed dirt. They rolled through villages and small towns untouched by the tourist peso and UN handouts, desolate outposts of small, low-level buildings and high-heaped rubble where there were hardly any people. Max had to stop and brake and swerve to avoid hitting stray farm animals – goats, pigs, chickens, donkeys and, once, a huge packhorse that had blocked the road and wouldn't move until it had taken a stupendous dump.

It was after they'd passed the horse and were heading for the next drive-through town that Max noticed the Mercedes.

He immediately recalled the pair of plainclothes cops at the hitch-hiker stop on the way to Trinidad. The car was the same model – a four-door 190 Turbo with tinted windows. It wasn't anywhere close, but hanging back a good quarter-mile, classic tail procedure: keep your target in sight but stay out of sight, even though it was impossible on an open country road with barely any other vehicle between them.

Max spotted a small roadside fruit market coming up and stopped.

He got out and pretended to inspect the stall – one foldaway table for coconuts, one for bananas, one for mangoes and one for bottled water, everything reeking and fly-infested. The seller was an almost toothless old man in denim overalls. Max bought coconuts and water. The seller hacked crude holes into the coconuts and made eyes at Benny, who was sitting behind the dusty windshield, reapplying his lipstick in the mirror.

Max looked up the road and saw the Mercedes had stopped, its chrome and glass glinting in the sun.

He took out his phone. He had a signal. He called Rosa Cruz. Her phone rang over a dozen times before going to voicemail. He killed the call without leaving a message.

He went back to the car with his purchases, flies following him.

'I no' hungry,' said Benny.

'Suit yourself.'

They set off again, Max watching the rearview. The Mercedes was on the move, trailing a cloud of dust.

'Who you telephone?' asked Benny.

'Ghostbusters.'

'What?'

'Never mind.'

Max drained both coconuts and lobbed the shells out of the window as soon as they were back in open country. The Mercedes was a long way behind, but it was following.

Max tried the radio again. Static on every channel.

'Is country here. Radio no good. Wait when we get close to big town. Ciego de Ávila, Camagüey – place like that,' said Benny.

They rolled on. They passed a Soviet-era watchtower, a kind of pillbox mounted on a single stilt, poking out of the earth like a fossilised periscope. Vultures were gliding low around it.

'You got family in America?' Max asked Benny.

'No.'

'Friends?'

'No.'

'You got family here?'

'A sister and two brother. We no' speak.'

'What about parents?'

'My mother, she die. She was kind person. My father, we no' speak. He shame with me, for be homosexual. He say, I no' his son.'

'Sorry to hear that.'

'Why you sorry? Is no' *you* family,' said Benny.

'Figure of speech.'

'And youself? You have family?'

'No. My parents are dead. No brothers or sisters,' said Max.

He assumed his father was dead. He'd split when Max was ten. There'd been a few birthday postcards – from California the first year, Michigan the next, then Buffalo. Then nothing. Max thought of tracking his father down a few times, always after he'd been drinking on his own and listening to mournful jazz – a Chet Baker vocal usually got him to that place. His dad had been a bass player in a jazz band. He'd had regular gigs in hotels, done some radio and spent a year in a TV-studio house band. Max used to wonder if his old man hadn't turned out like Baker, a decrepit junkie with false teeth and a retinue of hateful ex-wives. The last time Max thought of looking his father up he'd been sober. It was on his thirty-fourth birthday. Sandra told him how ironic it was that he searched for missing persons, when he couldn't even look for the biggest missing person in his life. So he'd made a few calls and got as far as finding out that Mingus Snr had lived in Portland, Oregon, with a black woman called Janet. He could have gone further, all the way up to his father's front door or grave marker, whichever it was, but he didn't know what he'd say to him if he were alive, and he didn't want to know how he'd died. He'd left it there, hanging, a mystery. He told his wife he preferred it that way, that anything else would be an unnecessary disruption of lives long gone in opposing directions. It wasn't like Max had really missed his father. He hadn't hated him for leaving, or even really blamed him. He'd accepted his mother's side of the story, that his father had had a thing for women, especially black ones, and that he'd been something of a total asshole. They hadn't even been close: his old man had spent a lot of time on the road, and when he was home he'd been self-absorbed and distant, always locking himself away to practise bass, the deep humming notes shaking the walls of their row house, the only sound Max could remember him making. When he'd gone for good, it hadn't made any difference, hadn't changed too much of a damn thing. Now Max couldn't even remember what his old man's voice had sounded like, the kind of accent he'd had, whether he'd smoked or drank, how he was built, the colour of his eyes; neither could he recall any particular acts of kindness or cruelty, which, he supposed, wasn't such a bad thing. He'd grown up with nothing to hate and nothing to miss. Some people never got over their parents. Not him. His father had passed through his life almost unnoticed, leaving a space that Eldon Burns had filled. Eldon Burns had been all the father he'd needed.

'You have child?' asked Benny.

'No.'

'Why no'?'

'Never happened.'

'So after you is no one? When you dead, you *extinto* – *dinosaurio.*'

Max laughed. 'That's me.'

'Is no problem for you?'

'No problem at all.'

Max looked in the rearview mirror. The Mercedes was still there, hanging back, not closing the distance.

'What you do?'

'There's a car behind us.'

'Of course. Is road, Max. Is for car.'

'It's been following us for more than an hour.'

Benny checked in the mirror.

'That Mercedes. Is no' cop.'

'Secret police then?'

'Is no' possible. We change car. They no' know we here.'

Max called Rosa Cruz again. Voicemail. He put the phone back in his breastpocket.

He tried the radio. Same static.

The road ahead turned smooth as they approached a stretch of asphalt cutting through a swathe of pale reeds. It was lined on both sides with white headstone-shaped monuments inlaid with black-and-white photographs. Underneath these, painted in blue, were names and lifespan dates, and at the bottom, in red, the name of countries: Angola, Bolivia, Nicaragua, El Salvador, Panama, Grenada, Jamaica. They were memorials to the revolution's fallen heroes, back when Cuba was exporting guerrillas instead of doctors.

Suddenly they heard thick scrunching and popping sounds coming from under the car, like they were driving over broken glass, and a foul stench of putrefying fish overcame them.

'What is *that*?' Max pulled his shirt hem over his nostrils and Benny held his nose.

One of the back tyres blew out. The car skidded. Max hit the brakes and turned the wheel sharply. The car came to a sliding stop.

'Look.' Benny pointed at the empty road. Max saw nothing but a stretch of blacktop, melting and buckling in the sun, the edges oozing into the shallow trenches skirting the road.

Yet when he looked closer he saw that the road surface was actually alive, and on the move. Little round lumps were crawling out from one trench, scuttling along and dropping into the other. It wasn't asphalt – melting or freshly laid or otherwise disintegrating. The path ahead was completely covered in thousands of small crabs, dark-brown shells and bright red-tipped pincers, doing their sideways-across walk. Further on he noticed gaps in the swarming surface – orangey-white grooves steaming up in the heat – where a prior car had crushed its way through and which the crabs were respectfully circumventing.

Max got out of the car to check the damage. The back-left tyre was flat, pieces of busted-up, broken-off crab sticking out of the rubber like jagged spikes. A thick double-yellow lightning bolt smeared the road immediately behind them where the car had skidded and crushed dozens of ambulating crustaceans into a thick goo, adding to the ammoniac stench.

The crabs were absolutely everywhere, a slow swarm of brown shells inching across the blacktop with sharp, tiny clicks, bright beady little pinpoints for eyes, every last one looking right at him, pincers snapping. They were moving under the car, circling the wheels. They were close to his feet.

Max kicked a bunch of the things out of the way to clear a space for him to change the tyre. In the trunk he found a spare and a toolbox.

The wheel nuts were grime-sealed and it was tough work getting them off. The heat and the smell were killing him. Some of the crabs had stopped moving. They were looking at him through their little orbs of fire as he toiled and sweated and gasped and grunted and cursed. The longer he took, the more crabs stopped and gathered around in a loose circle, leaving only about twenty inches of space, a no-go zone, every one of them clapping their pincers together, until it was the only sound he could hear, a million arid clicks.

When he got the wheel off, one of the crabs began inching towards him. It was slightly larger than the others and had darker pincers, purple instead of red.

As he fitted the replacement, he tracked the crustacean's slow but deliberate progress. He tightened the first nut, then slotted in the second. The crab was almost at his ankles, its pincers splayed and curving downwards. He stopped what he was doing and stood up.

The crab stopped and looked at him, its eyes shielded by the overhanging shell.

Max recognised the absurdity of his predicament. He'd faced off with killers who'd pointed both barrels of a shotgun at him; he'd been threatened with bottles of acid, petrol bombs and spinning saw blades; one time someone had tried to syringe-spray syphilitic pus in his eye – and that was all *before* he'd been to prison. But here he was now, in Cuba, squaring up to a fucken' *crab*.

Then he noticed the Mercedes. It had reappeared at the edge of the crab flow, stationary, the engine idling. He didn't know how long it had been there.

He looked down at the crab, which hadn't moved. Then he took in the hundreds of crabs around him, poised in the intense heat, their shells like the shields of a medieval army protecting itself from a hail of arrows.

He bent and continued working on the wheel, threading on the bolts and tightening them. He'd got to the last one when the main crab advanced. The others followed, a slow-motion forward-ripple passing through the mass of dull, dark-brown shells, propelling those in the front row towards him.

The lead crab snapped its pincers at his ankles. Max struck at it with the spanner, sending it flying off into the reeds.

Then the Mercedes rolled forward. He heard the wheels and

the full weight of the car crushing crabs. He heard the pop and crunch of shells bursting. He heard what he thought were tiny high-pitched screams.

The car passed him by very, very slowly, grinding the crustacean carpet down to a foul mustardy sludge. The windows were almost as black as the bodywork, but he could sense someone looking right at him, and, in the back, he discerned the outline of a head.

After the Mercedes had passed, he looked down at his feet, expecting to be besieged by crabs, but the creatures had mostly disappeared, the stragglers shuffling off the edges of the road.

41

They drove solidly for the rest of the day, covering a hundred and fifty miles by sundown.

At nightfall they stopped for food at Camagüey. Max bought them sandwiches and water, and in a souvenir store he got a pair of cheap sunglasses and a green military cap with a star-shaped patch of the ubiquitous Che Guevara physiognomy sewn on the front. It was a size too big and he looked like a tourist gone drunk native, but it did the trick.

The 'Strawberry Fields Forever' intro came on the radio as they were pulling out of town. Benny translated.

The news wasn't good. The police had expanded their search outside Havana and were setting up roadblocks. They were using tracker dogs and doing helicopter sweeps. They'd found where Benny lived and linked him to the stolen Chevy. They'd interviewed the car's owner, who was heartbroken because the vehicle had been in his family for five decades. The newscaster then went into a rambling rant about how the Chevy was more than just a car, that it was a symbol of Cuba's proud, dogged resourcefulness in the face of the inhumane imperialist embargo. The newscaster promised that the thief would be severely punished for stealing this national emblem that had been handed down through generations with love and socialism – and for stabbing the spirit of the revolution in the heart.

No mention of Max's name, only Benny's. And Benny didn't look in the least bit worried. He giggled at the propaganda inserts, and stretched and yawned as he translated the rest, wafting the carrion taint of his infected wound about the car.

Max opened the window. He remembered how they'd run manhunts when he'd been a cop, backdating the details they released to the public by a day or more, so their target wouldn't know how close they really were. He guessed things were done the same way here, maybe with even less information.

How much did the police know and how close were they? They'd hardly seen any cops on the road or in the towns they'd left behind. Not in uniform anyway. But heads always turned their way and when eyes stuck to them a few beats too long, Max would tense up and expect to find the worst waiting for them at the next turn. It never was.

The Mercedes never reappeared. Who'd been driving it? The secret police? They would have pulled them over. The Abakuás? Maybe. Osso and his accomplice? Whoever it was had followed them after they'd changed cars in Trinidad. Which meant they'd tracked them to Savon's house. The men in the *guayabera*s had been talking to uniformed cops, which told him they were connected to the state in one capacity or another. Someone had been keeping tabs on them – on him. He tried to think if he'd seen the car in Havana. He hadn't noticed it, but it didn't mean it hadn't been there, all along.

Max called Rosa Cruz again. He'd lost count of the amount of times he'd tried to get through to her. He was so used to her voicemail message he practically knew it by heart. He never said anything, just listened in to dead air as he weighed up the pros and cons of letting her know where he was now and where he was heading tomorrow. Sometimes he almost told her, sometimes he didn't come close. Was his finding Vanetta Brown more important to her than catching a supposed double murderer? He hadn't spent enough time with her to make an educated guess, so he always killed the call. Then he started thinking about it all over again. It was a good way of taking his mind off the deep shit he was sinking in.

*

303

After Camagüey the road faded into an arid imprint of a throughway, barely signposted and completely unlit. Max felt himself unwinding involuntarily. His eyelids got heavier and his head kept drooping forward over the wheel. He had hot wiry pains in his legs and back from all the driving and tension. The sticky, warm breeze blowing through the window made him even drowsier. He turned to ask Benny to do some driving, but Benny was asleep, his head bouncing gently in time with the scalloped road.

Max decided to stop. In a wooded area, he turned off at a byway and parked near a grove.

The sky had clouded over, the air was weighted with the smell of brewing rain, and on the western horizon lightning streaks were flailing at the earth, as if softening it up for the downpour. Swirls of fireflies clustered in the dark, tracing thick figure-eights in green and yellow embers, before disappearing in a sharp buzz. Tentative drops of rain landed on the roof.

Benny woke up and yawned, and then gasped as he accidentally pulled at the stitches.

Max closed his eyes, looking for sleep, but he couldn't find it. He was too wired and too beat to relax.

'Can I ask you question?' Benny said.

'Go ahead.'

'Have you ever be in love?'

'Kind of question's that?'

'I'm curious. You so angry people, so fill with hate. I can no imagine you happy.'

'I was happy with my wife. I loved her. A lot,' said Max grudgingly, wishing he hadn't. Exhaustion had lowered his defences.

'She leave you?'

'Funny,' said Max. 'No. She died.'

'You still wear marry ring.'

'Reminds me of her.' He looked at his hand. The ring was a little looser on his finger. He could turn it around freely. He'd lost weight.

'You no' remarry?'

Max saw Tameka again, her dark skin and the sexy severity of her face, the rose tattoos on her breast, ankle and hand. He'd been close to popping the question – *real* close. 'No.'

'You have girlfriend in Meeyami?'

'No.'

'Is no surprise.'

'Go fuck yourself.'

Benny chuckled.

'What about you?' Max yawned. 'You been in love?'

'One time, yes. Big, *big* passion,' said Benny. 'It was Russian man. Wladimir.'

'When was this?'

'Long, long time. He was big, beautiful man. Outside and inside. Kind, generous. The *best*!' said Benny. 'It was good when the Russian in Cuba. Everyone have the food, the clothe, the soap. Everything function. But the Russian peoples, they no' nice. They *snob*. They *racista*. They no' mix with the Cuban peoples. They no' learn *Espanol*. They have they own school for the children, speak just the Russian. They have they restaurant, they club, they gym. All is separate. All is just for they. The writing in all they building is Russian. Wladimir was no' like they. Him different. So intelligent. He love the Cuba culture.'

'So what happened?'

'We together for one year. Then – like that – him go. I no' know where. He no' say nothing to me. He just go,' said Benny, his voice clotting. 'At the beginning, I no' understand. I have confusion. Then a friend tell me, the Russia government is like we government. They no' like homosexual. So I suppose, they find out about him and me. And him get transfer. Maybe they kill him. I no' know.'

'Sad story,' said Max, but he didn't find it sad at all, because he only half-believed it – if that. Benny was mid-thirties at the most, so he would have been a teenager when the Russians left Cuba. He claimed he'd been married and worked as a cook, but

305

now Max was thinking that was bullshit, that he'd been a hustler all his life. Maybe the story about the camp had been a crock too. But what did he care? Tomorrow, with any luck, he'd be rid of Benny. After the town of Las Tunas, they'd come to a fork in the road. One way went towards Guantánamo and the Wetback Express, the other to Santiago de Cuba, the Dascals and – maybe – Vanetta Brown. Max was going to put Benny on a bus in Las Tunas.

'My heart it break. But is OK now. Is fix,' said Benny. 'I think peoples have three love – first love, then love for life and then the last love. Wladimir was my first love. So I think, in Meeyami, maybe I find the love of my life.'

'There's no love in Miami,' said Max. 'Just people using people, and people getting used by people.'

'I no' believe you. I think you heart break when you wife dead. I think you see the world through you tears. You no' stop cry for her.'

Max thought about what he'd said and how almost right he was. 'You're not just a pretty face, are you, Benny?'

'You think I *pretty*?'

'Figure of speech. It means you're not as fucken' dumb as you look.'

Max slept, but it was shallow, broken sleep. He kept ducking in and out of consciousness, snapping into wakefulness at the slightest sound, his hand grabbing for a gun that wasn't there before he'd even opened his eyes.

306

42

At daybreak they set off again, Benny at the wheel.

He'd changed into a plain chocolate-brown dress and a curly black wig. He'd also applied an ultra-heavy layer of make-up to hide the stubble thickening around his jaw.

They drove uphill for the first hour and crossed a plateau where the road banked on to a pocked and craggy rockface to the right, a view of endless green fields and woodland to the left.

Max reached over to turn on the radio when a flash across the rearview dazzled him. A car was hurtling up the road behind them, a bright looming ball of chrome and glass.

It was the Mercedes. And it was no longer feigning innocence, but in full-on pursuit mode.

Benny had seen it too. Now they could hear the roar of its powerful engine drowning out the tinny sound of the DeSoto.

'How fast can this go?' asked Max.

'No' *that* fast.'

Then they heard a siren – coming not from the Mercedes, but from a white police Lada on its tail. Benny changed up a gear and pushed harder on the gas.

The Mercedes reached them in seconds and came bumper-close, hovering behind the Firedome like a wasp about to strike. Max put on his seatbelt and braced for impact, but the car swerved into the other lane and drew up alongside them. Benny went faster. The Mercedes kept up with no effort. Now the Lada was drawing closer, its blue light flashing, the siren lacerating their ears. Max looked across at the front window of the Mercedes, trying to see inside, but all he met was his own panicked, confused face in the tinted glass.

Then the car left their side in a 1400-horsepower whoosh, disappearing around a bend in the road with a puff of exhaust.

The Lada drew nearer, but the Firedome was almost as powerful. Max was about to tell Benny to step on the gas some more, when the police car suddenly slowed down.

As they took the bend they saw the Mercedes again, parked sideways-on in the middle of the road, blocking all but a sliver of each lane.

Benny hit the brakes and the Firedome came to a sharp screeching halt, about ten feet from the Mercedes.

The Lada careered to a stop behind them, the siren growling to silence as two uniformed cops jumped out, machine guns in hand.

The driver and passenger doors of the Mercedes opened simultaneously. The same two men from the hitch-hiker stop got out. They hadn't changed their clothes – loose white *guayabera* shirts, black slacks, aviator shades and heavy brown shoulder holsters. One had on a gold necklace.

The uniforms flanked the Firedome doors and jammed their gun barrels through the windows.

Max and Benny put their hands up.

The cop on Benny's side reached in, snatched the keys out of the ignition and pocketed them.

'*Salga!*' he snapped.

Max and Benny didn't move, didn't look at them.

'*Salga!*' the cop shouted, jabbing his gun barrel into Benny's temple.

'*SALGA!*'

Benny got out, then Max.

The cops pulled them away from the Firedome and made them put their hands on their heads. The uniforms shouted at them some more. As usual Max didn't understand. Right opposite

where he was standing, a hunk of fresh roadkill – species indeterminate – lay at the side of the road. The blood was glistening.
Max wondered if the Mercedes hadn't hit it. He wondered also
if Cubans ate roadkill when times got tough. They did that in
Florida.

The cops were a pair of sweaty kids. The one covering Max
had a cluster of unripened zits on his chin. Benny's had freckles
and ginger hair. The pair were nervous as hell, like this was the
first time they'd done an auto-stop outside of class. Their guns
were quivering, their eyes popping and edgy: nervous energy
feeding off adrenaline. They had an audience to impress: the
guayaberas, who were leaning against the Mercedes, their thick
arms folded across broad chests, watching.

The cops took turns frisking them. Freckles covered them
both while Zits patted Max down with light slaps and pushes.
Then he did the covering as Freckles went to work on Benny,
asking his name as he worked his hands over Benny's body from
the top down. Benny was about to answer when Freckles
reached his crotch. Max saw the confusion on the uniform's
face, and the hint of laughter – or was it pleasure? – on Benny's
as the young cop found his dick and balls. First Freckles pressed
down, then palpated, then squeezed, then sprang back, shaking,
looking up at Benny, horrified.

'*Tu es – tu es – un – un . . . hombre?*' gasped the cop and then
blushed.

'*Si señor*,' said Benny in a deeper voice than usual.

Max almost smiled. It wasn't just him: even in broad daylight,
with that ugly tramline stitch up his cheek and the stubble on his
chin, Benny passed. He was a hell of a woman.

The *guayaberas* laughed loudly and said something to the
freckled cop, who was wiping his hands manically on his shirt.
He laughed with them – forced and shallow – and flashed an
ingratiating grin, but his eyes were enraged blisters. Nothing
worse than wounded pride in a jittery kid holding an HK MP5,
which fired 650 rounds per minute.

Benny asked why they were being stopped.

'*No hable maricón!*' yelled Freckles, jamming the barrel into his chest. '*Cuál es su nombre?*'

Benny gave his real name.

The *guayaberas* did sissified whoops and blew kisses.

The zitty cop asked Max for his name. Max flicked a look at the *guayaberas*, who were staring at him.

'*El tiene quizá un pozo!*' shouted the *guayabera* with the gold necklace, humping the air. Zits laughed. Max got the gist of it.

'*Cuál es su nombre?*' repeated Zits.

'You speak English?' Max asked him calmly.

'*Qué?*'

'*Inglés?*'

The cop was confused. '*No. Es usted un turista?*'

Zits was Max's height and half his weight. Brown-eyed and pale, coffee on his breath. He had his gun pointed at Max's head, his finger on the trigger and the safety off. In America, cops kept their fingers on the trigger guard until ready to fire. They didn't do that here.

'*Si,*' said Max.

'*Pasaporte?*' The cop held out a hand. As he did so, he lowered his gun so the barrel was pointing to the ground.

That was a mistake.

Max had one chance.

He pretended to reach for his pocket, but switched moves and made a grab for the cop's arm.

He never reached it.

At the instant he was about to make contact, Benny screamed.

Max and the cop turned together as a vulture tore the wig from Benny's head, its claws caught in the hair. The big bird twisted sharply, hitting Freckles full in the face with the hairpiece, before arcing over him and slamming beak-first into his back. The vulture flapped in panic and squawked in agony as it tried to get away and free itself from the wig while upside down. The cop staggered back and forth, and started pirouetting on the spot, screaming in terror and crying for help, as he tried to smack the bird off with his gun.

The *guayaberas* were roaring with laughter. Zits stood immobile, mouth open, not knowing what to do. Suddenly Freckles's HK erupted in a loud blast. Bullets sprayed the Mercedes and both *guayaberas* went down. Max dived on Benny, knocked him over and shielded him as bullets flew over them. The shooting continued. Glass shattered, metal punctured, casings tinkled down on the road. All around them birds flew out of trees and bushes and off telegraph poles.

And then it stopped.

It was absolutely still.

Max looked up. The roadside was dense with bluey, acrid gunsmoke and there was no one standing. The two uniformed cops were lying close by, their bodies riddled with bullets, weapons on the ground, smoke coming out of the barrels. Freckles lay on his side with a finger curled around the trigger of the MP5. Zits lay on his back, his guts bubbling over his belt. He was still alive, just about, but not for much longer.

Max worked out what had happened. Freckles had shot the *guayaberas* and spun around, trying to get rid of the vulture, his finger still on the trigger. He'd sprayed Zits, who'd returned fire – instinctively or accidentally – killing Freckles and the vulture, which was now a headless lump of mincemeat and feathers.

Max tossed the HKs into the bushes.

The Lada had been shot to pieces, the windshield gone, two tyres ripped open, the light half smashed, the tank leaking.

He went over to the Mercedes, where the *guayaberas* lay side by side. The one with the necklace was still twitching. His shirt had turned red. He was inhaling air and exhaling blood, moaning very faintly, his foot slapping back and forth on the ground, like a half-busted wiper. The man next to him was motionless and missing his face. Somehow his shades had stayed on.

Benny stumbled over, pale, shaking as if from a deep chill, wiping the dirt off his dress.

'What happen?'

'They shot each other. You OK?'

'*Si* . . . *No*. I no' know.'

'You're not wounded?'

'No.'

'Have you checked our car?'

'What?'

'Did our car get hit?'

'What you say?'

'The car, Benny. Go make sure it's OK.'

'This man still live, and you . . . you ask about *car*?'

'He's as good as dead,' said Max. 'And we have to get out of here.'

'They take key.'

'Get it,' said Max, pointing at the uniforms.

'You want me to look in . . . in *body*?'

Benny was borderline hysterical. Shock, adrenaline, fear, confusion: nothing to do but scream.

'Benny,' said Max calmly. 'We have to go. Now. Before anyone sees us here. Otherwise we will be accused of their murders. You understand? These are not just people. They're *cops*. I really need your help to move the bodies and the cars. And I also really need you to get the keys out of that man's pocket. OK?'

'No,' said Benny. 'I no' do that. I no' go in dead people.'

'Why?'

'Is bad luck.'

'*Bad luck?*' Max was incredulous, but he kept his cool. There was no time to argue. 'OK. Just get in the car.'

Max tossed Freckles's pockets and found the keys.

He went over to the Lada and opened the doors. The radio was crackling, a female dispatcher's voice. She was laughing. A small Cuban flag hung from the mirror.

He dragged Freckles off the road by his shoulders and dumped him in the back with his gun. He went over to Zits, who was not quite dead.

312

Zits was trying to talk, but his words were getting lost in his last gasps.

'Sorry kid,' said Max.

He got behind the cop and lifted him half-up by the shoulders. The cop let out something like a scream, but it came over as a giggle. Max dragged him to the Lada and laid him across the front seats, head resting on the passenger side. By the time Max had finished adjusting him in the car, he was dead.

Max put the car in gear and rolled it off the side of the road. The Lada crushed its way through the bushes, but then stopped, its way blocked by two stunted trunks. A quarter of the tail-end stuck out.

Two turkey buzzards had landed on the road. One was already pecking at its dead brother or sister or cousin, trying to get at the meat through the feathers and fake hair. The other vulture was strutting towards the original bit of roadkill.

Max walked towards the Mercedes, ignored by the birds.

He stopped.

Something wasn't right.

The *guayaberas* were still lying there.

The car hadn't moved.

But its engine was on.

It was humming, low.

He hadn't heard it start.

Someone was inside.

It wasn't Benny. Benny was in the Firedome.

Max ran towards the Mercedes.

The car span its wheels and sprayed gravel. It reversed and turned sharply and stopped again, slanted diagonally, facing him.

Max stepped back towards the edge of the road. If whoever was inside was dumb enough to try and run him down, they'd go right over the edge.

They'd worked that out too.

The Mercedes rolled back and righted itself. And then it shot

313

forward and tore up the road, back the way it came, disappearing around the bend.

Max ran over to the *guayaberas*. The survivor hadn't made it.

He took their guns – chrome .357 Magnums. He found speedloaders in their pockets and took those as well. He pulled the bodies off the road and rolled them down the slope.

Back in the Firedome, Benny was sitting in the passenger seat, his head down, crying.

Max started the car.

As they drove away, he saw vultures above them, moving towards the roadside.

43

Max floored the gas. The needle tipped between sixty and seventy, but the car didn't seem to be going fast enough to outrun what had been invoked.

The landscape blended into a blue-green-ochre-grey blur. Up far ahead, the outline of the Sierra Maestra mountains marked out the horizon, running across the junction between sky and earth like a crude rip. Beyond the mountains lay Santiago de Cuba and the ocean.

They screeched through one village after another.

They didn't talk and didn't look at each other. Max focused on the road. Benny had stopped crying but his eyes were shut tight and he sat bunched up in the seat, hands clasped together, fingers overlapping in a bloodless weave, gnawing away at his inner lip, looking like he was praying that this was all a nightmare, that he'd wake up back in Havana.

Max slowed the car as they approached a road sign: Las Tunas 28 miles, Bayamo 35 miles, Guantánamo 59 miles, Santiago de Cuba 73 miles.

The Mercedes hadn't reappeared. Not that he'd expected it to. But he *had* expected police Ladas, and maybe a helicopter. A regular chase. Yet nothing came. The rearview stayed clear of everything except the dwindling road and the growing distance between them and the bodies they'd left behind.

Had the *guayaberas* been police? No. Cuban cops didn't carry American guns – especially not brand-new Smith & Wesson Magnums. He inspected the bullets in the speedloader: full metal jackets. They'd always made him think of model rockets with filed-down points. He popped one out and scanned the brass casing for markings. He barely had to look. The disembodied wings were stamped clearly on the side.

Why go through that elaborate stop-and-search charade? Why not just pull them over and take them away at gunpoint? Had those dead rookies been cops or Abakuás – or both? If that was the case, they were double-fucked.

How long before the bodies were found? He hoped the vultures were plentiful, damn ravenous and fast.

They had to do something about the car. He thought of ditching it but walking was impossible. Plus they'd be exposed, vulnerable and easy to catch. They could steal another, he supposed, but traffic here was becoming a rarity and all the vehicles he'd seen so far were trucks, mopeds and horsedrawn carts.

'You'll have to change,' he said to Benny. 'Dump the dresses.'

'*All* the dress?'

'Yeah.'

He couldn't look at Benny too much right now, because he reminded him of the young men he'd seen in prison, the first-timers. Benny had their expression – terrified, confused, realising that things were going to start off bad and then get a hell of a lot worse.

'We in big troubles. We should leave country now. Call Nacho.'

'I can't do that.'

Benny said nothing. Gnawed his bottom lip. Ruminated.

'Is because you have to finish you mission, yes?'

'The fuck are you talking about?'

'I know why you come here, Max. Is to find someone. *Americana* criminal. Black Panther. The Haiti woman,' said Benny.

Max hit the brakes and Benny jerked forward so violently that his head almost hit the dash.

316

'How the fuck do you know that?'

'*No soy estúpido*, Max. I am next to you always. I see what you do. That man who die – Gwen-e-verre – the one you kill? He was Black Panther. He run from police in Unite State. Yesterday, you stop at the Haiti place. I know who you look for now. Is simple for me to calculate. Like mathematic.' Benny shrugged.

Max knew he hadn't exactly been discreet, and a natural-born schemer like Benny, always working out an angle, could easily have figured out what he was doing here.

'So you know her?'

'She famous for help the Haiti peoples in Cuba. Is right, yes? Is her you look for?'

Max nodded. 'What else do you know about her?'

'That's all,' said Benny.

They drove on.

'Why you look for her? Is for money?'

'No.'

'I know America government pay lot of money for her.'

'How do you know that?'

'Everybody know.'

'It's not about money,' said Max.

Benny lowered his voice. 'You work for you government?'

'No.'

'Then why you do this?'

'It's complicated. When we get to Las Tunas, I'm going to give you some money. You're going to get on a bus to Guantánamo. Call Nacho when you get there to sort out the boat.'

'You no' come?' Benny was surprised.

'No.'

'Why?'

'I have to find Vanetta Brown.'

'Max, is no' possible.'

'What's not possible?'

317

'I can no' leave Cuba on that boat if you no' there with me.'

Max hit the brakes again.

'That's bullshit!' he shouted. 'Nacho wanted to get rid of *you*, not me.'

'No.' Benny shook his head. 'He want you to leave as well. He know if the police catch you, they make you talk. And you will say who help you. Then Nacho is focked. Before we leave him house, he tell me I can only get on boat if I with you.'

Max looked at him.

'We should go to Cajobabo now, Max. Forget this Van-etta. Save youself.'

The left side of Benny's face had by now swelled up around the suture in a dull ball, stretching out one half of his features, so that the healthy part seemed squeezed together. Benny's left eye was bloodshot and glassy, and the smell coming off him was foul.

'I can't,' said Max. 'I'll call Nacho in Las Tunas and straighten this out.'

'You can try. But you have deal with him now. He take you money, you shake hand. With Nacho, when you shake hand is final. No more negotiation.'

'Are you fucken' with me?'

'No.' Benny held up his hands. 'I swear is true. I no' want to be here with you, Max. Is for me too dangerous. But I have no choice. What happen to you, happen to me.'

'*Christ,*' whispered Max, again coming close to feeling sorry for Benny but too mired in mistrust to exchange doubt for pity.

Benny tried the radio. Static. He switched it off.

'Is no' too late. We can go to Guantánamo now, leave Cuba tomorrow,' he said, close to pleading.

'I'm not leaving. That's final.'

'Fock you!' Benny folded his arms and slumped in the seat, pouting, arms folded, in a defeated, infantile sulk.

'I'd say I'm sorry you got caught up in this, Benny, but if

you'd been straight with me from the start, this wouldn't have happened. You could have stayed in Havana.'

'*Gringo joputa!*'

'Stay in that zone,' said Max and started up the car.

Max realised what to do about the car as they drove through Las Tunas.

In the town, teams of two were adding slogans to several wide-wall murals depicting a quartet of men in Moses beards and olive fatigues looking across a Cuban landscape populated by men and women toiling in a field. In between the images ran three-dimensional block capitals in red, white and blue proclaiming the glory of socialism and the revolution.

Max noticed that one of the walls was only half-finished. *Hasta La Vic*...it read, in the same Cuban national colours. The official graffitists were nowhere to be seen and they'd left two state-issued half-gallon paint pots and brushes in the middle of the sidewalk.

Max took the red and blue paint pots and a brush and drove off with them.

They stopped at a riverbank a few miles away.

Benny changed back into the jeans and T-shirt he'd been wearing when they left Havana. He dumped the contents of his case – his best dresses, his shoes and wigs – into the flowing water, watching them float away in the current as if they were lovers on a leaving train.

Max painted the front of the car red and the back blue. He was crude and clumsy in the way he slapped on the paint, and there wasn't enough to do the sides, but it made the Firedome look like a different car.

When he was done he tossed the paintpots into the reeds and reached into his pocket for the phone. He couldn't find it. He searched his other pockets and then he looked inside the car. Nothing. The phone was gone. It must have fallen out of his pocket during or after the shoot-out. His immediate thoughts were for Rosa Cruz and what would happen when the cops found it – either on the roadside or in the Lada he'd driven off the road, right next to the body of a dead cop. It was already beyond bad for him, but how much did she have to lose? More or less than he did or just about the same?

44

The further east they ventured, the more Max was reminded of Haiti. The villages were a lot like the ones he'd seen there, mud huts that seemed to have sprouted out of the ground whole, their roofs thatched with wind-blown detritus, the entrances and windows cut by natural erosion. The exteriors and doors were painted in deliberately clashing bright colours – yellows and blues, oranges and greens, pinks and browns. Any state propaganda on the buildings was incorporated into lavish and detailed voodoo paintings, religion dwarfing rhetoric; deities loomed large and smiling from the heavens, releasing the doves that landed on Fidel's shoulder as he made his Havana victory speech in 1959; deities fought Batista's troops alongside the revolutionaries; deities helped repel the Bay of Pigs invasion; and deities watched over Cuba as sharks with Star-Spangled fins circled. The message on the walls was as obvious as it was tacit: 'We're with you, Fidel, but you *owe* us.'

He'd never shaken off the horrors he saw in Haiti: people eating dirt and cornmeal for breakfast, lunch and dinner; the Cité Soleil slum on the edge of the capital, home to half a million people living in clapboard shacks literally propped up on shit – human and animal – for a whole square mile; and all those children, eyes the colour of skull sockets, faces tragic and confused, wondering why in the hell they'd been so stupid as to leave the womb. He'd returned to Miami with a sense of low-watt outrage that this barely breathing calamity of a place was fewer than two hundred miles away, that the richest nation on earth could have allowed things to get so bad in its own backyard.

But he'd also returned to Miami with $20 million dollars.

He tried to do what he could to make things right, in his own way. He set up the agency with Yolande Pétion, half-believing and half-deluding himself that he was giving something back, that he was helping Haitians, that he cared. Some days he even believed his bullshit, but most of the time he believed it was sincere and well-intentioned enough to eventually wash out as truth.

When Yolande was murdered he saw his actions for what they were. The old twisted moral code that had wrecked his life was still setting the pace, guiding the way he did things.

Joe once said that Yolande's death had been the moment when it went bad for him, the start of his slide. Joe was wrong. Joe hadn't known about the Haitian money. Joe had believed the crap Max told him about Sandra's insurance policy paying out, about Sandra's mother leaving him some property he'd sold for a profit. The truth was he slipped up when he decided to keep the money instead of turning it in. The slide kicked in moments later and lasted all of the twelve years it had taken to get here. Even when he thought he'd gained purchase, that the downward trajectory had levelled out, all he was doing was taking longer to get to the next lowest point. He could have stopped all of it from happening if he'd done the right thing, but he'd never done the right thing his whole life – just the wrong thing with the best intentions, over and over again.

But the slide would end, here, and soon.

He could feel it.

45

They reached Santiago de Cuba in mid-afternoon, yet the city was in near darkness. The sky was layered solid with undifferentiated volumes of grey, sunlight straining weakly through them, its essence diluted in shadow. Those street lamps that worked had come on, a bulb burned in every house and office block, and all the cars that had them were driving with headlights on full beam. Those that didn't made do with flashlights taped to the hoods.

They passed the Antonio Maceo monument, its statue depicting one of the heroes of the Cuban War of Independence sat atop a rearing horse, looking back over his shoulder at the highway, arm extended, fingers beckoning, as if inviting all newcomers into the city. Before it, twenty-three gigantic bronze machete blades stuck out of the ground at acute angles, suggesting offence or defence depending on the opinion and position of the viewer. Tourists were being hurried down the steps of the monument by guides glancing fearfully up at the sky – a look and gesture replicated on the face of every pedestrian on the road, speed-walking along their way, as if expecting more than mere rain to fall.

They drove through the outskirts, navigating streets that twisted between shabby stone shacks with cracked and blistered walls, warped tin roofs and shutters and doors both locked and held upright with twine and wire. A little further on, they navigated through a slightly more upscale area of elegant but decaying Spanish colonial-era houses, the missing segments of the terracotta roof tiles replaced with wood and strips of corrugated iron painted rusty orange.

Cuba's second city was different from its first. Every single building was low-lying and hurricane humble. People here lived side by side, not one on top of the other. There were no ugly modernistic obelisks to spoil the illusion of a place trapped in perfect amber.

Max tried the radio. It had been dead all the way through the mountains, and it was still silent. Not even static or squeaks came through the speakers.

The first thunderclap sounded like an explosion, the second like the gates of heaven being battered and the third like they'd been breached. The car vibrated with each eruption.

Two fat raindrops pancaked on the windscreen and clung to the glass, thick and globulous, like egg whites, before being shaken apart and splitting into jagged appendages, which shimmied slowly down towards the wipers.

After another eruption of thunder, the rain fell hard and heavy, slashing at the streets with a sound of chains whipping over piles of coins, stomping on the car like a million little lead feet. The streets turned grey to black and began to ooze and then flow.

Lightning came in bunches as they reached the town centre, flash-framing the world about them in dazzling, silvery bursts of colour: grandiose churches and museums and government buildings appeared and disappeared in split seconds, all speared with long white rods of rain.

The downpour intensified. They inched past a cemetery and then a park where leaves were being torn from branches, branches wrenched from trees and bark stripped from trunks. The ground swelled and liquefied; grass and flowerbeds were flooded out of their roots and swept into the street.

They moved deeper into the city, the Firedome filling with the smell of unchecked damp and worn rock. The darkness thickened along with the rain and visibility was cut to inches. They could barely see where they were.

Max pulled over.

They sat there, the storm attacking the car, punching and pushing it, trying to wash it away.

Benny started humming a tune that sounded familiar, a little like a hymn or Christmas carol, his voice high-pitched and tinged with delirium. He needed a doctor, antibiotics and rest. Max didn't know what he was going to do about him. They had two days to make the boat and the sickness was gaining on him fast. Max could see it, smell it, feel it working its way through his unwanted companion.

He had to find the Dascal family.

He had to find Vanetta Brown.

And somehow he had to avoid getting caught by the Cuban police and the Abakuás along the way.

Why hadn't he told Wendy Peck to go fuck herself and taken his chances with the US legal system?

If he could have had that moment in Little Havana again, would he have chosen differently?

Of course not.

One look at her and he'd known she would have made good on her threat. She'd have pulled out all the stops, called in favours to make damn sure he went to jail. Once back inside, he wouldn't have gotten out. The justice he'd evaded before would have caught up with him. He'd have been doing time for more than just money laundering and tax evasion.

Yet it wasn't only Peck who'd brought him here.

If he was honest with himself, if he squared up to the person he really was, he'd have to admit he would have come here anyway. He couldn't ever have let this go. If he'd been younger, he'd have been prepared to kill Vanetta Brown for what she'd done. But now what he really wanted to do was talk to her. He wanted to look her in the eye and hear her explain and justify herself and her actions. He didn't care if she was wrong or right, if he'd feel empathy or hatred after she'd said her piece. His memory of his best friend was already stained with spilled secrets. He just wanted to hear the rest. How he'd react, what he'd do to her, he didn't know. And that was *if* she was guilty.

A short while later the wind changed direction, coming in from behind them, causing a break in the rain, so they saw exactly where they were for the first time.

It was a wide street. Opposite stood pastel-coloured buildings with recessed doorways and windows, and the same Mediterranean-style terracotta roofs that were all the rage in Coral Gables. The rain began again, cascading off the tiles and crashing loudly on to the sidewalk, slopping out into the road in great dirty washes. They had parked next to a long row of small stores with entrances sheltered and kept dry by red-and-white-striped plastic awnings, the wooden signs, lashed freely by the elements, swinging back and forth in their brackets. A pair of street lights flashed on and then off again at random intervals, as if gauging the storm's resolve and tenacity. The stores themselves were lit up and Max could see faces in the windows, looking at the downpour.

The street felt faintly familiar. Like everything in Cuba, there was always something here to remind him of home, and this place recalled Key West a little. He was thinking of Captain Tony's on Greene Street and the old-timer with a parrot on his shoulder who'd told him a story about its most famous patron, Ernest Hemingway. Poppa H used to bring complete strangers – literary groupies and wannabe writers on pilgrimage – to the bar and get them paralytic-drunk. At closing time, when they staggered out, Hemingway would cold cock them with a right hook in full view of passers-by. Max couldn't recall what the old-timer looked like, but he did remember his parrot and how it could say 'cocksucker' in three languages.

The parrot . . .

He pulled out the photograph of Joe and Vanetta. There it all was, in the background: the colourful buildings, the stores and their candy-striped awnings, the hanging wooden signs, the most prominent and striking of which was the one he could see before

326

him, swinging and twisting under a street lamp. It was green and red and shaped like a parrot.

They'd come to the very same street.

The store was called Discos del Loro, and there were three people inside – a young Asian couple and the manager, who was sat behind the counter, reading a book and smoking a cigarette.

He looked up when Max and Benny walked in, acknowledging them with a nod and a welcoming-enough smile, before going back to his book and smoke. He was a slim black man with grey hair and a wispy moustache. The couple stood soaked through and dripping on the light-green linoleum floor, making a show of searching through the racks, the man appearing interested in a CD he was holding while the woman looked around at the decor.

The store wasn't large by any means, but the available space was diminished further by a huge inflatable parrot hanging from the ceiling, its back and head, beak and wings coated in thick dust. Triple-tiered wire racks ran along the walls, well stocked with CDs, the genres delineated by handwritten Day-Glo-pink cardboard stars stuck to the ends of the rows: salsa, jazz, merengue, rap, reggae, rock. The plain green walls were hung with black-and-white photographs of Cuban musicians. Most were relics, seated old men and women in three-piece suits or ballgowns, wrinkled hands clasped around battered acoustic guitars. Above the din of the rain, Max could just about hear Miles Davis's muted trumpet coming through the speakers – or something that sounded very close to it. He couldn't quite make out the song.

Max and Benny wandered around the store, Max trying to figure out the best way to approach the manager for information – was he a cash or charm person? – while pretending to browse through the CD cases. Cuban rappers struck the same posse poses as their American counterparts, but they didn't

327

brandish guns and pit bulls; the reggae artists did that blissed-out, blurry, stoned-in-search-of-spirituality look they'd copied from Bob Marley; the rockers were squeezed into tight jeans and leathers and threw devil signs and scowls, while the salsa musicians all dressed like cruise-liner bands.

While the Asian couple checked out the centre rack, given over to '*Ritmos del Santería*', Max and Benny moved to the right of the store, by the window. The manager's eyes didn't leave his book.

The standard Korda photograph of Che took centre place in the right-hand rack, except this one was mounted on white card and had a quotation written at the bottom.

Toda la música del 'rock-and-roll' es decadencia imperialista. Toda la música del rock-and-roll es degenerada. Es el enemigo de la Revolución.

Max chuckled. How many Western popstar radicals had worn Guevara T-shirts? The real Che would have burned them on a pyre of their own records. The real Che would have been right at home with the Bible-belt reactionaries who proclaimed rock and roll 'the Devil's music'.

The manager put down the book, hoisted his legs over the counter and slid across it, cigarette in one hand, ashtray in the other.

'Sorry, officer, we're all out of Bon Jovi,' he said when he reached Max. His accent was distinctly Haitian, with Cuban flavourings.

'Did you just call me "officer"?'

'It's a little game I play, to keep myself from falling asleep.' The manager smiled and showed a set of sandy teeth, complete and crooked, but for the left canine, which was missing. 'You're American. You're military. You're in my store. And a man of your age, I'm thinking, is either a country man or an eighties rock man. Am I right?'

'What makes you suppose I'm military?'

'Your build, your bearing, your ... disposition,' said the

manager, making a show of looking him up and down, miming a deductive process.

'What kind of "disposition"?'

'A man used to being in charge.' The man puffed on his cigarette. Benny stood by the counter, legs apart, in a defensive posture. 'How am I doing so far?'

'You get third prize,' said Max. 'I am American but I hate Bon Jovi. Country too. All that drinking and whining and inbreeding. Not for me. As for military, that's not me either. Besides, how many American soldiers have you ever met?'

'A lot. They come here all the time. For their rap and their rock music. "R and R" for their "R and R". What does that mean, when they say "R and R"?'

'Rest and rehabilitation.'

The man laughed. 'That's funny. Your people don't get much of either here. They've got their own bar, you know?'

'In Santiago?'

'Yes. By the bay. A place called The Lone Star. That's where they all hang out. You might want to too, if you're homesick for a burger and a "Bud". Is that short for "Budweiser" or "buddy"?'

'One and the same,' said Max. The Lone Star: he thought of the group of rogue soldiers Nacho had talked about, the ones who ran the black market with the Abakuás – the Texas Playboys.

'You can't miss the place. Just go to the marina and follow the pretty girls. Sooner or later you'll get there,' said the manager.

'How is that allowed, an American bar operating here, on Cuban soil?'

'I don't know how it all works.' The man shrugged. 'I don't make the rules. I just follow them – most of them – the important ones.'

He glanced back at Benny, who was looking out the window, and then turned to Max. 'Are you here for something or are you just keeping out of the rain?'

'Just passing through,' said Max. 'You worked here long?'

'Ten years. Why?'

'You know these people?' Max showed him the photograph of Joe and Vanetta.

The man smiled immediately. 'Of course. That's Sister Vanetta and her friend Joe. They both look younger. A lot younger.'

'Didn't we all. Did you know Joe?'

'As well as you know people you see once every two years. He comes in here with Vanetta whenever he's in town. He loves Bruce Springsteen. He made me a tape a while ago. Remember those things – cassettes?'

'I even remember eight-track,' said Max.

'Well, we got talking music one day. He was curious about Cuban sounds. This was way before that *Buena Vista Social Club* movie. I made him a tape of my favourites. Salsa, soul, jazz, heavy rock, rap, punk. We've got all kinds of music in Cuba. He was fascinated. And he made me a tape of his favourites. Except it was nothing but Bruce Springsteen for ninety minutes.'

'You too, huh?' Max laughed. He'd had the Joe Liston-made Springsteen tape experience long before, maybe in 1978 or 1979 – a mixture of studio and live stuff. Joe designed the cover – an outtake from the *Born to Run* cover shoot, with Clarence and Bruce standing side by side – and he typed the inlay, annotating the songs with source albums where they were studio, dates and venues for the live material. Joe's blind missionary zeal made Max feel guilty enough to listen to the tape the whole way through in his car, but he absolutely hated it. Nothing stuck. In fact, he felt so drained of patience at the end of the compilation that he tossed the cassette out of the window, along with the case. Now he wished like hell he'd kept it.

'You still got his tape?' Max asked.

'Somewhere. I never told him what I really thought, because I like him too much, but Springsteen wasn't my thing. Too *gringo*. No offence. And the man can't sing, if you ask me.'

'None taken. I think he's kinda crappy too.'

The manager laughed. 'What sort of music do you like?'

'These days, not a lot. I used to live for music. Now it's something I can do without. Whatever's new, I've heard it all before.'

'Did Joe send you here?'

'Yes and no.'

'How is he? It's been a while since I've seen him.'

Max looked outside at the rain pelting the window, buffeting the parrot sign, rivulets running off the beak and claws. 'Joe's dead. He died recently.'

'Ah, I'm sorry to hear that. He was a really nice guy,' said the manager, and seemed to mean it.

'Yes, he was. That's kind of why I'm here. How well do you know Vanetta?'

'Personally? Not well. First-name terms, though no more than a hello and a how-are-you,' he said. 'But she gave my family our start in this country. Twenty-three years ago, I came over from Haiti with my parents. When we arrived, we lived in Caille Jacobinne, the centre she built for us. She helped us find jobs and homes. We got an education. We owe her our lives. She did a lot of good for us – for all of us here. Not many people are like her. Do a lot for you, for absolutely nothing in return. You know we don't even have to stay in Cuba, if we don't want to? We can go back any time we want. Not that anybody does.' The manager was tearing up a little.

'Joe left me something to give her in person. Do you know where I can find her?' asked Max.

'No. But you can try her family.'

'The Dascals?'

'Yes. They live on Avenida Moncada. Near the barracks.'

Castro loved bullet holes. Where they were still standing, the façades of every building his guerrillas had shot at in 1958 were left in their post-firefight state – pocked and cracked and full of fifty-year-old shrapnel. They were the revolution's Stations of the Cross.

331

The fortress-like Moncada Barracks, with its battlements and pillboxes, was the most sacred building of all, the revolution's very own manger, the place where the armed struggle against Batista officially started, on July 28, 1953, when Castro led his first raid. The attack failed because of poor planning and inadequate weaponry and manpower. Castro was quickly captured, show-tried and imprisoned. The barracks' perimeter walls had been badly riddled with gunfire, so the government of the time repaired them. In the 1960s, the walls were personally demolished by Castro, who drove the inaugural bulldozer, and the remaining building was converted to a school. Then, in 1978, Castro had the walls reconstructed exactly as they had been and a portion of the barracks was turned into a museum commemorating the revolution's baptism. For the sake of ambience and authenticity, the new walls were also shot to hell, until they looked roughly like the originals had after the failed raid. The fortress was then painted mustard yellow and the bullet holes filled in with black and brown paint, so that they would be for ever visible. Cosmetic stigmata: the government now shooting at its memories.

The houses opposite the barracks were Spanish-style bungalows in various stages of shored-up ruin. They'd once belonged to officers and their families but now were the property of the state and inhabited by the regime's upper tier. The designs were interchangeable, as was the vegetation around them, a stock palm tree and a thicket of colourful, untended bushes affording a degree of privacy. The exception was the house on the corner, a wooden, two-storey, red, white and blue gingerbread, lavish in design, with slate roof and ornate balconies shaped like curled vine branches. It was the Dascal family home.

Max parked close by, and he and Benny dashed through the still pelting rain up to the porch. He knocked on the door. They waited. Raindrops pinged off the windows. Plants had been tipped out of their baskets, and the soil was being washed clean off the roots. A child's toy horse on wheels was rolling back and forth with the wind.

The door was opened by a tall, black-haired woman with a dishrag in her hands. She had the beginnings of a smile on her face, like she'd been expecting someone else. She lost it when she saw Max and Benny standing there, dripping wet and getting wetter.

Max was about to introduce himself, but she spoke first.

'He said you'd come.'

'Who?'

'You're Max, aren't you?'

'Yes.'

'Max *Mingus*?'

'That's right.'

She grabbed on to the door frame, her head leaning towards it, her whole body subsiding. 'Joe is dead, isn't he?'

'Yes. He is.'

'What did he die of?'

'In Miami it passes for natural causes.'

'He was . . . murdered?'

Max nodded. She closed her eyes for a second and breathed heavily through her nose.

'Is Vanetta here?'

'Come in,' she said.

46

She closed the door behind them and introduced herself as Sarah Dascal – daughter of Camilo and Lidia. She was Vanetta Brown's sister-in-law.

Before Max could say anything, she started quizzing Benny. Max hadn't wanted to bring him to the house, any more than he'd wanted to leave him in the car, in case the police found him. He'd chosen the lesser of two bad options.

Benny reeled off a fake name without missing a beat. What was he doing with Max? Again Benny didn't falter, plucking a fast yarn out of the air, saying he'd been hitch-hiking outside Ciego de Ávila. What did he do for a living? Waiter. Where was he heading? To Guantánamo to visit his sick father. As he spoke, her smirk deepened, her mouth forming a gradient, half her lips pointing up, the other down.

Pivoting very slightly back and forth on her heels, she looked Benny over, moving from his eyes to his wound, which had now turned borderline purple, checking out his clothes, the T-shirt sticking to his chest in dark patches, the damp jeans and sodden sneakers, before returning to his eyes. She asked what had happened, how he'd got cut. Benny unconsciously took a step back towards the door, as if trying to edge out of a sudden spotlight. He stammered something about an accident. What kind? He didn't answer. His mouth moved, but his voice was hiding. She snorted derisively. Benny lowered his head like a chastened child, drenched in a bucket of shame.

She turned to Max. She was a couple of inches taller than

him, slender going on skinny, whatever curves she had were hidden in baggy brown corduroy slacks and a plaid shirt a few sizes too big. He guessed her to be in her late forties or slightly older. Her face was evenly tanned, but tired and lined, the distress played up by her curly, too-black-to-be-natural hair, which she wore too short to hide her ears. They jutted out like the chipped handles of an old soup cup.

'Follow me,' she said.

They walked down the hallway to a large sitting room with two interconnecting doors and wallpaper patterned in thick pale-grey and white stripes, making the place seem cage-like. She showed them to a pair of parallel black leather couches with a long coffee table in between and asked if they wanted tea. Max said yes and she disappeared.

Max guessed the power had gone, because the light was coming from half a dozen oil lanterns placed on the floor, the flames dancing in the room's natural darkness, the shadows gathering close about them. The place smelled of stale cigars and fresh paraffin. Behind him he heard the ticking of a clock, and in a corner, every few seconds, a drop of water fell into a metal container. He noticed how some of the furniture and all the bookcases were covered in clear, thick plastic sheeting. It reminded him of a murder scene.

She came back with the tea in a large aluminium pot, set on a tray with some cups, and poured them each a cup, dropping in a slice of lemon.

Then she sat opposite Max, took a sip of tea and began talking in perfect English, her accent showing British and Australian roots. She spoke in short bursts, contained monologues, delivering concise bits of information and then pausing for another hit of tea, before going on. The brief silences that followed would be undercut by the clock and the leak dripping into the metal bowl.

Both her parents were dead. Her father had died of pneumonia in the late eighties and cancer had taken her mother in 2001.

Her sister, Kara, had gone to work in Honduras, where she'd met a man and followed him to America, she said distastefully. She thought Kara might be living in California, but she wasn't sure. So it was now just her, her husband Patrick and their three children, two girls and a boy, aged thirteen, eleven and nine. She'd been expecting them all back when Max knocked on the door. She said she worked for the Department of Reforestation, and spoke a little about how Castro was way ahead of the curve when it had come to protecting Cuba's environment.

Max understood what she was doing. She was testing the waters, warming up for what she really had to talk about. And she was checking him out, that was obvious in the disconnect between her eyes and speech. The eyes took in his every mannerism, from his sympathetic smile to his air of concentration as he listened to her and the way he held his cup – not by the handle, but with his paw clamped around it, as he would a glass. There was a classic trick to putting people at ease: you picked up on their gestures and mimicked them, turned yourself into a mirror. He knew she was sharp enough to see through that. He let her talk, asked nothing, betrayed no signs of impatience and expressed shallow condolences for her losses and smiled politely when she talked about her children. She wasn't easy to like or even empathise with. She had that natural Cuban hardness, but in her it went deeper still.

She put her cup down, glanced briefly at Benny and then back at Max.

'What happened with Joe?' she asked, finally.

He told her the broad strokes, how they'd been having dinner, how Joe had mentioned Vanetta's name, how he'd been shot seconds later. He didn't mention the background and he didn't talk about the killer.

'Did they catch anyone?'

'No.'

'Do they have any suspects?'

'Plenty,' he said. 'Joe was a cop. Put a lot of people away.'

'Was that the first time he'd mentioned Vanetta to you?' she asked.

'Yeah. Everything I know about her, I found out after his murder.'

'Who told you to come here?'

Max handed her the photograph and told her where he'd found it.

Sarah stared at it for a moment and then put it on the table. 'I took that with the camera Joe bought me,' she said, and then frowned. 'How did you find Vanetta's address in Havana?'

'It's what I do,' he said.

'You must be as good as he said you were. Her address is a state secret.'

'Don't I know it.'

'Did you get into trouble?'

'No,' Max lied. He felt the sofa dip as Benny repositioned himself. He was sitting perilously close to the edge and leaning forward, nervous as hell, looking like he wanted to bolt.

'Where's Vanetta?' asked Max.

'She left, two months ago, in September.'

'Left?'

'She used to live here too, in this house. Now she's gone.'

'Where?'

'She's not really in the country any more.'

'She's either in Cuba or she isn't. Unless you're trying to tell me she's dead,' he said. 'I know she's got cancer.'

'She's not dead. At least I don't think so. I'd have been notified.'

'So where is she?'

'You don't understand.'

'No shit.'

Sarah frowned again. 'This is my house. The house of my family. The house where I'm raising my children. I invited you in. You're a guest here. Please don't be disrespectful.'

They looked at each other, neither yielding. The clock timed

337

the silence. A dozen seconds went by and another drop of water splashed in the bowl.

Max broke the stand-off. 'How well did you know Joe?'

'He came here regularly.'

'Did you like him?'

'Yes. Very much. His visits were always memorable. He had a way of filling a room with his presence. He always made us laugh. And he was very fond of Cuba, admired much of the way we did things,' she said, with an inward smile.

'I liked Joe too,' said Max. 'I liked him a lot. He was my best friend, the kind you only get once in a lifetime.'

'You wouldn't be here if he'd meant any less to you,' she said.

'No, I wouldn't. I don't know what Joe told you about me – it can't have been all good – but know this: I haven't come here for revenge, I only want answers.'

'Answers?' she said. 'It would've been better if you'd come for blood. That's easy. You pull a trigger and walk away. If you leave it at that and don't think about it, things have a way of making sense. Answers are complicated. They usually create more questions. How much truth can you handle, Max?'

'All of it.'

'So be it.' Sarah smiled slightly.

'When did you last talk to Joe?'

'Right after Vanetta left. Maybe a day or two. He was calling from Canada.'

Max remembered Joe telling him he was going to Vancouver on the department's dime, some convention on terrorism.

'Why did he call?'

'Two reasons: to talk about you and to get a message to Vanetta.'

'What was the message?'

'He said he was being followed in Miami.'

'Did he say who by?'

'No,' she said. 'But it could only have been related to Vanetta. Although he'd made every effort to be discreet when he came

338

here, he thought that man – Eldon Burns – had him under surveillance.'

'Eldon was retired,' said Max. 'He was powerless.'

'People like him are never powerless.'

'Did he *see* anyone tailing him?'

'He didn't give any details.'

Joe hadn't been the paranoid sort. If he'd thought he was
being followed, then he was. Max wondered if it hadn't been
Wendy Peck.

'Did you pass on the message?' he asked.

'I couldn't. And I told him. I have no way of reaching
Vanetta, even in an emergency. She's in a secret location. The
sort you can't just . . . phone.' She glanced at Benny, drawn to
the bulge in his face, her nose wrinkling at the smell of virulent
decay.

'Joe asked me to tell you two things. The first was where to
find Vanetta – in case anything happened to him. He didn't think
his life was in danger, but he suspected something. He said it
would be best if you heard everything directly from her, so you'd
understand why he'd done what he had. Unfortunately, I can
only point you in a vague direction.'

Benny finished his tea and put the cup on the table. Max had
barely touched his. As an inveterate coffee drinker he'd never
understood the point of tea. To him it was like non-alcoholic
beer and ultra-light cigarettes. Why bother?

'Vanetta is being treated in a hospital on a small island in the
Windward Passage – that's the stretch of ocean between Cuba
and Haiti. I take it you know what I mean by *camino muerto*?'

'Yeah,' said Max. 'A road that doesn't appear on any official
map.'

'The term applies to more than just roads. It refers to any sensitive location, any place our government doesn't want the
general public to know about. Towns, prisons, storage facilities,
military bases, bunkers and even some . . . islands. Vanetta is on
one of them. The hospital doesn't use names. Patients have

numbers – barcodes. It's very discreet. Fidel is rumoured to have been treated there after he fell ill.'

'So this is a government place?'

'Yes and no,' she said. 'Our government leased the island to the Russians in 1964. They built the hospital. It was exclusive, meant for the Eastern Bloc elite and their allies. Fidel and his inner circle also used the facilities.'

Sarah looked at the photograph on the table for a moment.

'I thought Vanetta and Castro fell out a while ago,' said Max.

'That's right.'

'So why's she there?'

'When the Russians left, the government was desperate for money, so the island – and other assets – were leased again, on condition that the new buyer kept the hospital open, including paying all the running costs. In exchange, whoever bought it was allowed to build a house and have the full protection of the Cuban army and navy. The identity of the buyer or buyers was never revealed. The sale was arranged at the highest levels. The place has changed hands on at least two occasions,' Sarah explained.

'So Vanetta knows the owner?'

She nodded.

'Who is it?'

'She never told me his name. Although we're as good as family, she has her secrets.'

Max looked briefly at Benny, who'd been following every word.

'I heard she fell out with Castro because of her associations with the Abakuás,' said Max. 'Do they own the island?'

'I don't think so,' said Sarah. 'What would they want with it? Not their style. And they don't deal directly with the government.'

'Tell me about Vanetta and this owner.'

'In the 1970s, Vanetta set up Haitian refugee centres in Cuba, similar to the original Jacobin House in Miami. They were fully funded and supported by the government. Haitians came to settle in Cuba. Not a lot, but a steady stream. They were generally welcome because they could work the land, and the Russians always needed labour for their various projects. Vanetta had problems with the arrangement because she felt the Haitians were being exploited. Yet she saw the greater good. The benefits outweighed her doubts.

'In the Special Period the money wasn't there for the centres. The government could barely feed the country, let alone a bunch of newly arrived immigrants. Vanetta suddenly had the fate of six hundred people on her hands, people she'd promised a better life to. It was either send them back or find a solution.'

'The Abakuás?'

She nodded.

'So she was willing to work with Castro's sworn enemy, after everything he'd done for her?'

'Desperate people do desperate things,' said Sarah. 'She was truly desperate. And their need was greater than hers.'

'So what happened?'

'The Abakuás provided the centres with food, clothes and basic medicine. But at a high price,' she said. 'They had always had a problem selling goods. They couldn't exactly do it in the open.'

'So they used the centres?'

'That was the deal Vanetta made. People used to come from all over to buy. The Abakuás used the Haitians as salesmen. But it ended as soon as the government opened the country up to tourism in the early nineties. The Abakuás didn't need the centres any longer. They had the hotels.

'Fidel knew what she'd done. He turned his back on her. She still retained some privileges – like her Havana home – but she no longer had his ear, nor access to the inner circle. She managed to keep Caille Jacobinne running by going to some of Cuba's friends – the Canadians, Spanish and Brazilians all helped a little here and there. But it was never enough,' said

Sarah. 'Then in 1997 she was diagnosed with colon cancer. She handed over to her deputy, Elias Grimaud. She was operated on in Havana and made a full recovery. Then she met her new benefactor.'

'The man on the island?'

'Yes. Elias had been dealing with him in Vanetta's absence. He'd got him to agree to fund Caille Jacobinne for a period of time. Maybe ten years.'

'Why?'

'The man admired Vanetta,' said Sarah. 'When they met, she told me how impressed she was with him. He knew everything about her, what she'd been through, the good she'd done in Miami and in Cuba.'

'What did he get out of helping her?'

'Vanetta didn't say. In fact, she didn't really say much else about him.'

Sarah glanced again at Benny, who was now sitting back on the couch with his arms crossed.

'How do I find the island?'

'Unless you know someone in the government's inner circle, or you can bribe one of the coastguard to take you there – which is highly unlikely – then I don't know,' she said. 'And for what it's worth, I'd strongly advise you against going there. The area is heavily patrolled. They'll either sink your boat with you inside it or they'll arrest you.'

Max said nothing. His head was spinning too fast to settle. He heard Benny clear his throat.

'You said there were two things Joe asked you to tell me. What was the second?' asked Max.

'He wanted you to see what he'd been doing here. It's up-stairs.'

47

Sarah unlocked the door to Vanetta Brown's bedroom and switched on the light.

'Has the power come back?' asked Max.

'It was never off,' she said, frowning. And then she understood. 'Because the lamps are out downstairs? No. I just like it that way there, when I'm alone. It's comforting.'

They stood in a wide and spacious room of pale-blue walls and varnished dark wooden floorboards. A pair of framed maps of Cuba and Haiti hung side by side over the bed to the right, and original Haitian paintings took up the adjacent walls, both depicting lush jungle scenes. He'd bought similar pictures for his and Yolande's office in Little Haiti. Yolande had dubbed that particular style 'bullshit naif', the artists depicting their homeland as a tropical paradise populated by every species of wild animal, when in reality the country was deforested and so barren people had to steal soil from the neighbouring Dominican Republic to grow anything.

After the initial view, he caught the smell of the place. Stale sweat, heavy medication, rubbing alcohol. It reminded him of old people's homes; life curling up in failing bodies.

Max went over to the French windows and opened them wide. Warm rain hit his face, and then the wind carrying it cooled his skin. He breathed in deeply. The street lights had come on and their sodium-orange glow made the pelting rain look like flaming matchsticks and the Moncada Barracks like a gigantic hunk of processed cheese, plastic and faintly rancid.

He turned back to the room, considered it again. It served three purposes – work, rest and play – and was divided and ordered accordingly; the office in the middle, the bed, wardrobe and chest of drawers to the right, and then the space he was standing in, her library.

A tall brass floor lamp with a tasselled shade stood in the corner near an easy chair with a coordinating footstool and a small table on wheels. Behind it was a wide bookcase with knick-knacks on every shelf: snowdomes – Miami, Port-au-Prince, Santo Domingo, Caracas, the Key West buoy with its '90 Miles to Cuba' inscription – and small square mahogany boxes with the names of countries carved on the sides – USA, Haiti, Russia, China, Angola.

Max opened the USA box and found it filled with sand.

'From Miami Beach,' said Sarah. 'Vanetta called it "travelling by proxy". She was allowed to leave the country, but never did, until recently. For obvious reasons.'

Near the window was a hi-fi stack – a record player, cassette deck and radio, one on top of the other, and a glass-fronted cabinet beneath with about fifty LPs inside, taking up most of the free space. He glanced over the album spines: James Brown, Sam Cooke, Billie Holliday, Sarah Vaughan, Paul Robeson, Aretha Franklin, Marvin Gaye, Stevie Wonder, Ella Fitzgerald, Sly and The Family Stone's *Stand* and Bob Marley's *Legend*. They liked the same music.

He went to the desk, on which sat a chunky keyboard dwarfed by a computer monitor. Three black-and-white photographs of differing sizes, spaced unevenly apart, were fitted to the wall a few inches above the monitor. He guessed she'd placed them that way so they'd be the first thing she saw when she looked up from the screen.

The last photograph was the largest: a young girl, no older than six or seven, standing in a garden holding a plastic windmill on a stick. Round cheeks, corkscrew curls, a big smile and dark, sparkling eyes.

'That's Melody, Vanetta's daughter,' sighed Sarah. 'She'd have been thirty-eight now. She was bilingual in English and Spanish. She laughed in both languages. A bright, happy little girl.'

'Vanetta have anyone in her life?' Max asked, looking along to the next picture. It was of Vanetta, Ezequiel Dascal and Melody again. Ezequiel was holding his daughter up to the camera and the little girl was looking straight at it, pointing to the photographer with her toy. Ezequiel was tall and bespectacled, a thin, sharp goatee elongating a round face. He looked something like Sarah, only kinder, gentler.

'Like a lover, you mean? *Vanetta?*' Sarah laughed. 'To love someone you need to find a kind of inner peace. Vanetta's not at peace. She's at war. Even now. She'll die fighting. She always said she hoped to live to see Eldon Burns on his knees before her, begging for his life. Just like Ezequiel was, before him.'

'Didn't Ezequiel and Melody die in the Jacobin House, when it burned down?'

She looked at him. 'Like I said – how much truth can you handle?'

'What do you mean?' Max grabbed her arm. She winced and stared down at his hand until he let go.

'*Don't* do that to me again,' she said.

'I'm sorry,' he said, embarrassed.

She rubbed her arm. Her stare flexed into a glare. Then it softened and she looked past him at the wall.

She touched the bottom of the first picture – a group shot of Vanetta, outdoors, seated in front of a gathering of men and women standing around her smiling.

It took him a few moments to place the photograph.

But he did. It had been taken outside the centre he'd visited in Trinidad. In fact, the photograph was as good as identical to the mural.

But there was one major difference.

The child hadn't been blacked out.

He sat at Vanetta's feet, one arm curled around her lower leg, either for support or comfort. She was resting her hand on top of his head, as if stroking or patting it. Although the photograph was too small to highlight more than the most perfunctory facial features, the deformity to the child's mouth was obvious. He seemed to be munching on a large flowerhead, chomping at it from the stem up, his teeth just reaching the petals. The boy had a cleft palate.

'Who's that?' Max pointed to him.

'I don't know,' said Sarah.

'Did Vanetta ever mention someone called Osso?'

She thought about it, thought hard, but shook her head.

Out of the corner of his eye, he noticed Benny slouching in the armchair, his arms folded over his stomach, his feet up on the rest.

Max studied the rest of the group. He saw the light-skinned man in the middle, dressed in overalls, standing directly behind Vanetta. He remembered how he'd been depicted on the mural, slightly bigger than the others – taller, broader, more promi-nent. His complexion and clothes aside, the man was almost unremarkable. A little over average height and of medium build. He had soft curly hair, midway between Caucasian and Afro.

'Who's this?'

'That's Elias.'

'Can you put me in touch with him?'

Sarah shook her head. 'I haven't seen him since he collected Vanetta.'

'Collected her?'

'He came to take her to the island.'

'In September?'

'Yes,' she said. 'Maybe he's on the island with her. Maybe not. He has family in the Dominican Republic. And the centres have been closed for over a year.'

'You said he collected her. What was he driving?'

She laughed. 'Funny you should ask. It was a Mercedes. One of the grand old models. When Vanetta saw it, she said, "*Mi coche fúnebre ha llegado temprano*." "My hearse came early." She's funny like that.'

Had Elias been the one following him?

The triggerman's accomplice – his driver – was described as 'white'.

Elias was light-skinned enough to pass.

If that was the case, then the man on the island – Vanetta's benefactor and saviour of Caille Jacobinne – was behind the murders in Miami. But who was he? Someone rich, scared and connected enough to buy himself a hideaway protected by the Cuban military. Was he one of the hundreds of people Eldon had fucked over?

Vanetta had been on the island since September. The murders had happened in October. Plenty of time to get her prints on the bullet casings, especially if she was sedated. But why frame her?

Unless Vanetta had ordered the hit herself. The man on the island had admired her enough to fund her refugee centres. Maybe that extended to settling her scores. She'd run out of time to strike back at Eldon legally, so she'd resorted to violence. Feasible, but lifelong pacifists didn't turn into murderers in their final moments. Of course, she could have changed over time. That was possible. But then it was back to the same old question: why have Joe killed? Joe was her friend, her helper, her confidant.

Eldon and Joe had both been shot through the eyes and the casings had borne the black wings – the Abakuá MO. Sarah said they wouldn't have leased the island. What if she was wrong? The most successful criminal organisations always adapt and evolve with the times, he thought. The Abakuás had outlived countless regimes in Cuba. And they'd outlive many more. Wendy Peck had told him they had infiltrated the regime from the bottom up. Sarah was underestimating them.

'What was it Joe wanted me to see?' he asked.

'Vanetta was planning to return to America to clear her name. She was building a case, a defence. Joe was helping her. Not just with information. He was negotiating on her behalf with the FBI. She met with an agent on a few occasions.'

'In Cuba?'

'Yes.'

'Was his name Jack Quinones?'

'Yes,' she said. 'You know him?'

'Vaguely. What was his involvement?'

'He was helping Joe with information. Getting it to him, so he could bring it to her. It took a long time, putting it all together, cross-checking, finding more. Joe brought her everything. It's here somewhere . . . on CD. I don't know where, exactly.'

'Sure she didn't take it with her?'

'I packed for her. One small bag with her pyjamas, a dressing gown and some toiletries. That was all.'

Max turned on the computer. While it was booting up, he checked the desk drawers. Pens, pencils, plain paper, headed paper, notebooks – everything blank and new – but no CDs or computer discs.

He panned the room.

'There a safe in here?'

'No.'

Then, from below, he heard voices – children – and a man calling Sarah's name.

'That's my family,' she said. 'I've got to go. If you need anything, come ask. Stay as long as you need. And,' she looked across at Benny, who was fast asleep, 'we're having *sopa de frijoles* for dinner. You're welcome to join us. Both of you.'

'Thanks,' he said. 'Tell me something. You know exactly what I'm going to find, don't you?'

'Pretty much, yes.'

'But it's something I need to see for myself, right?'

'Joe told me Eldon Burns was your mentor. Taught you everything you know.'

'Everything I *knew*,' he said. 'I know differently now.'

'I hope so,' she said and left the room.

He looked on the computer, which was running Windows 98.

There was a single folder on the desktop, marked 'Miami'.

It contained one document: a mess of tiny circles and arrows, which turned out to be a flow chart. He magnified it to 300 per cent. The circles had names in them. He zoomed in some more.

Eldon's name leaped out at him. It was at the very centre of the chart, bold black letters in Arial script, with black, red, blue and green arrows pointing away from it in every direction to other encircled names. Some of the arrows were solid, others dotted.

Right below Eldon's name, in brackets, were letters and numbers: CD 1–5.

There were many more familiar names linking back to Eldon.

Abe Watson: CD 8.

'Halloween' Dan Styles: CD 10–12.

Victor Marko – the political fixer whose bidding Eldon did: CD 13–17.

Melody Dascal Brown: CD 23.

Ezequiel Dascal: CD 23.

Special Agent Jack Quinones: CD 24–26.

Detective Dennis Peck: CD 25–26 + CD 29–30.

These were linked to over twenty other names he didn't know.

Max hit print.

He shook Benny awake.

'I need you to go through the books on the shelf. Take every one of them down. Ruffle the pages, shake them.'

Benny blinked and stretched and yawned. 'What I look for?'

'CDs.'

'*Eh?* In *book?*'

'*Si. Vamos!*'

While Benny started taking books off the shelves, Max went

back through the desk and filing cabinets. He looked behind and under both.

He searched the chest of drawers. He dumped everything on the floor. Clothes, jewellery, a couple of photograph albums, a gun case with a Tokarev pistol and two full clips. He pulled out the drawers. He flicked through the photo albums and shook them. Sheafs of loose snapshots fell on the floor. He ignored them.

He went through the wardrobe, through all her jacket and coat pockets.

He threw everything out.

He stripped the sheets and cases off the bed and pillows. He pressed into the mattress with his fists.

He pushed the mess he'd made to one side and tapped at the walls, then the floorboards, looking for hollows.

He opened the first of the three filing cabinet drawers and groaned. It was crammed tight with hanging folders, themselves bursting with paper. He prised out the first.

Then he heard music. Familiar music. *Loud* familiar music. Choppy funky guitar, that four-to-the-floor beat, piano, brass, a whistle. 'Chug-chug! Beep-beep!'

Donna Summer's 'Bad Girls'.

Benny was dancing around with an album sleeve in his hands, singing along about how you can't score if your pocket's tight.

'The fuck you doing?' Max shouted.

'Work is better with music!' shouted Benny, crotch-humping the air in perfect time.

'Turn it off!'

'You no like Donna?'

'Turn. It. Off!'

'*Momento*. I like this movement now!' Benny went into serious-rhythmic-hump-convulsion mode as Donna wailed about bad girls, sad girls, such dirty bad girls, beep-beep!

Max had loved Donna Summer back in the day. He'd even had the album Benny was holding. Also called *Bad Girls*.

But right now he fucken' hated it.

Then he noticed something on the floor, something Benny was strutting his funky stuff all over.

Half a dozen CDs.

'Benny! *Stop!*'

'OK, OK!'

Then Benny noticed the discs lying there too, his foot on two of them.

'Oh! Shit! Is you CD, Max.'

Max picked them up – blue TDK CDs numbered in red. He found the rest in the album covers, slipped in with the vinyl.

48

He fed the first disc into the computer. It span intensely for several seconds and then an icon appeared on the screen. He clicked on it and a light-blue folder appeared: 'Eldon Burns'.

He opened it up. It was divided into subcategories, more light-blue folders with headings: 'Reports', 'Photographs', 'Associates', 'Witness Statements'.

He started with the photographs. Eldon as he was before he'd died: stooped, frail, white-haired, vulnerable, harmless. An old man in a tailored sports jacket and open-necked shirt, leaving his big house and getting into a taxi; getting out of the taxi and walking up the steps to the 7th Avenue gym; leaving the gym in the late afternoon and going back into his house. Always alone. No one waiting for him.

The pictures were all digitally time-stamped.

Vanetta had known his routine and where he lived.

Eldon had been a soft target, an easy kill.

Who was the photographer?

Max propped the flow chart up against the monitor and reached for the next CD.

Slowly, all through the night that followed, he pieced together what had happened to Vanetta Brown.

The discs were filled with confidential FBI documents, reams of eyes-only material that could only have come from Quinones: witness testimonies, transcribed wiretaps, over a hundred photographs, forensics reports and autopsy results. It was enough to bury Eldon and everyone he'd ever done business with several times over.

And then there was the work Joe had done. From 1985 to March 2008, he'd been conducting a personal, private and completely secret investigation. He'd interviewed more than two hundred people in North America, their every last word recorded and preserved as a sound file and a transcription.

Max read. Max listened. Max saw.

The deeper he delved, the more his certainties collapsed.

He couldn't believe it, but he knew it was all true.

He took two breaks. The first was for dinner. Him, Benny and the Dascal family sat around a table and ate chickpea and bacon soup and chewed on freshly baked bread.

When he got back to the computer, he realised he couldn't recall much about the dinner. He couldn't remember what the soup had tasted like or whether or not he'd even liked it, let alone very much about Sarah's family, except that they'd all spoken English and the talk had been small and polite. Towards the end of the meal, Sarah had told him they were welcome to spend the night. He'd thanked her, he supposed. He'd been far away, thinking about what he'd just read, about what was still to come. Thinking about Joe and all the secrets he'd kept, the ones he'd uncovered, the lonely risks he'd run.

More CDs. More chart arrows flowing upwards and sideways and downwards; all leading back to Eldon, pointing at him, incriminating him, puncturing him.

Max's eyes and head ached, and the monitor became harder to look at. His hands shook. He felt angry. Angry at a memory. Angry at a ghost. Tension squeezed the top of his neck, then clamped the base of his skull, pressing, tightening, not letting go.

He went out on the balcony for air, but it was still raining hard and he got drenched in seconds. He didn't mind. He took the soaking with his eyes closed and his mouth open. Back inside he dried his face and hands on the curtains.

Somewhere in between, Benny had turned on the radio, which was now receiving. He'd gingerly interrupted Max to tell him the news was coming on. The intro floated into the room weak and archaic, as if from a séance, and then it was incomprehensible Spanish babble.

Benny translated: they'd found the bodies of the cops by the roadside, the newscaster said. The police were sure it was the work of the duo wanted for the murders in Havana. He gave no explanation as to how they had come to this conclusion, but extolled instead the two uniforms, saying that they were heroes of the revolution, young martyrs who'd given their lives to keep all Cubans safe. Then there was something about finding the stolen Chevy Bel Air in Trinidad. The suspects, the newscaster went on, were now believed to be heading for the Santiago de Cuba area. Then the newsreader went off into a rant about the inhumane US embargo and how the imperialist neighbour had forbidden its citizens from travelling to Cuba because it didn't want its people to know that everything they'd been told about the country was a tissue of lies and misinformation used to justify the barbaric and pathetic embargo. But, he continued, the imperialist bully had failed because many of its courageous and intellectual citizens still came to Cuba regardless. You can recognise them quite easily, he went on: they say they are from Canada.

Max should have been shocked.

But he wasn't.

He wasn't even worried. Not for now. Compared with what he was reading and discovering, his current problems seemed far away, a trifle concerning some random stranger.

Benny though, was plain terrified. He was shaking. The bad-meat stink was coming off him strong and his wound was pumping a thick seep of clear fluid. He was in dire need of a doctor.

Max looked at the maps on the wall. He saw the Windward Passage, clearly marked on both, but no sign of an island between the two countries.

His eyes fell on Guantánamo, first the town, then the province. Nothing there about the American base, although the whole world knew where it was.

And that's when he had an idea how to find the island.

Sometime later, Sarah came in with a pair of towels. She told them there was soap in the bathroom, but to use it sparingly because it was running low and had to last the family another ten days.

She took in the mess in the room. She asked how he was doing. When she saw the look on his face, she nodded and left quietly.

He finished close to dawn. It had stopped raining and cocks were crowing.

He looked back over the notes he'd made and retold himself Vanetta Brown's sad, shocking, violent and, above all, heart-breaking story.

49

Later that morning Max and Sarah said their goodbyes over coffee in the living room. The house was empty. Her husband had taken the children to school and then gone off to work. Benny was sitting with the CDs, the flow chart and all of Max's notes in the car, waiting, ready to go.

Max thanked Sarah for her hospitality and for the things he'd found out, even though that new knowledge had destroyed him.

He was glad Eldon was dead, that Vanetta Brown had had her revenge. Eldon had deserved it, even that late in the day, when it barely counted or made much difference. But he still didn't know why she'd killed Joe, her friend and ally, her helper. That was a question he'd be asking her soon, in person, face to face. He hoped she had as good a reason. Anything less just wouldn't do.

They drove down to the bay.

The rain held off, but the sky seemed undecided and volatile, the clouds blackening in dark knotted frowns one moment, thinning away to a blue-patched graphite the next. Sunlight came through weak and grainy, its heat carried on a cold undertow.

Santiago de Cuba had had its lustre washed clean away. It was waterlogged. Trapped rain shook loose from every branch and leaf, droplets hung from telegraph poles like empty chrysalises, rooftops dribbled at the corners, windows and doors teared and sweated, brick walls were soaked right through. The Emilio Bacardi museum – in every postcard and brochure, a chalk-white

356

grandiosity with Roman Imperial overtones, from its striated colonnades to the Latin spelling of its name across the façade – stood humbled and drab, the colour of cold cigarette ash. The huge angel perched above the entrance to the Asunción Cathedral, head peering over the ledge as if counting in the worshippers, seemed ready to topple over into the square below. Flags drip-dried on their poles, too soused to flap. Craters had flooded in every road and formed broad lakes, which would re-form no matter how many cars drove through them, making great dirty wet swan wings as they passed. The waters would break apart but a little, only to flow back into one another, ready for the next disturbance. The streets slipped and slid with beached detritus and overflowed sewage, the mess sprinkled prettily here and there with bright, desiccated blossoms. People picked their way gingerly along the sidewalks, covering or holding their noses, looking where they trod.

Benny had taken a turn for the worse overnight. He sat huddled in his seat, shivering and sweating like a junkie at peak withdrawal. Max could hear his teeth chattering in between parched, overheated gasps. His wound had wilted like a malignant soufflé, the skin sucked inwards, the area from mouth to ear now a shade of blackened purple that completely camouflaged the stitches. Max rolled down the window to chase out the stink, but Benny begged him to close it, complaining first that he was freezing, then that the breeze was so hot it was making him boil.

'*Go to the marina and follow the pretty girls.*' That was how the manager of Discos del Loro had told Max he'd find the Lone Star. So that's where he went, looking for girls.

He stopped the Firedome opposite a row of shuttered stores at the end of a sloping road. Despite his condition, Benny insisted on coming with him, preferring to be on the move instead of staying in the car. Better to be caught on his feet than on his ass, he said.

The marina was skirted by a long, wide boardwalk, the

wooden planks browned and softened by the storm. Sailboats were moored alongside the half-dozen jetties that projected out into the sea. Deckhands were slopping out the hulls and wringing the sails. A few small kiosks sold coastal tours, scuba-diving lessons and fishing expeditions – all prices the same, state-capped and the profits state-flowing, competition extinct. There was no custom. Vendors sat bored in the booths, staring up at the sky, reading newspapers, gazing out across the bay at two boats approaching in the distance. The cleaners kicked or swept dead gulls and fish back into the sea, and brushed trash into soggy mounds, which they sifted for bottles and cans, depositing them into carrier bags. Rival variations of 'Guantanamera' played from speakers, the song's air of crushed melancholia and resignation for once a wholly appropriate flavouring to the surroundings.

Benny coughed and swayed and walked with his arms locked around him in a tight embrace, as if holding his body together. Max had to wait for him to catch up. There were a few uniformed cops around, arms behind their backs, legs apart and stiff, a click away from snapping to attention, as if expecting a visiting dignitary. They weren't looking at Max or Benny. Their eyes were focused on the sea.

Max looked across the bay. What he'd thought were two boats were really four: speedboats, close together, as if racing. He followed their intended course to an empty jetty further up the boardwalk, where there were no boats or kiosks or cops. A small group of women had gathered there.

They were in their early twenties – possibly younger – one prettier than the next, dressed and made up like they were going out partying, even though it wasn't even midday. High heels, spray-on jeans, miniskirts, tight midriff-baring tops, navel piercings. They stood chatting and smoking and fanning themselves with magazines.

The boats pulled up either side of the jetty and the passengers disembarked. All men. Seven white guys, two blacks, one Asian. Ass-half-out jeans, khaki shorts, chinos, back-to-front caps or bandanas, sunglasses, tattoos, sneakers, crew cuts or shaved heads. They high-fived and fist-bumped. They laughed and joked as they swaggered down towards the girls. Their voices were loud, the accents unmistakable: Americans. And no matter how loose and fun-bound they seemed, they all had the chiming, measured gait that said military.

Max heard stuttering attempts at Spanish met with fluent Spanish-tilted English. Then some names – Rusty, Evander, Bill, Travis. Hands were shaken or kissed. *Mucho gusto,* said the girls, one curtseying, a few giggling, all swooning.

Formalities over, they headed up the boardwalk.

Max and Benny followed at a distance.

The boardwalk gradually petered out. First the guardrail stopped quite suddenly, then the walkway ceded, strip by strip, to sludgy sand, until all that remained of the original structure were two parallel wooden planks placed across the sloping earth and loose rocks that made up the shore. The ocean here was oil-rainbowed and churning with mud, the lapping surf a cara-melised ochre.

Up ahead they saw a long concrete pier, built up with ware-houses, gasworks, mountains of stacked containers, and sta-tionary cranes.

The group had by now splintered, the men and women paired off and separated. One of the black men had instigated it, moving to the side with a woman in a pleated blue skirt that barely covered her ass and a long ponytail that bounced up and down the length of her back. The others followed suit, one for all and all for one. When Max turned to look behind him, he saw another group of women starting to form at the jetty.

Their group climbed a short flight of steps, ambled along the pier and then turned and disappeared between two warehouses. It was the last Max and Benny saw of them.

The path was boxed in by the backs of adjacent warehouses and ended at a high sandstone wall topped with spikes and razor wire. In the middle of the wall was a thick brushed-metal door that opened from the inside.

Max walked up to it and knocked.

A metal shutter went back almost instantly. A pair of brown eyes set in frowning dusky skin appeared in the open rectangle.

'Yeah?' The voice was gruff and Latino-American.

'Can I come in?' asked Max.

'Unit?'

'Civilian.'

'How you know 'bout this place?'

'Bar talk.'

'What bar?'

'In town. Can't remember the name. They all look and sound the damn same,' quipped Max.

The man chuckled. The shutter closed with a slam. Max and Benny exchanged glances.

The shutter reopened.

'Got ID?' asked the man.

Max took out his passport, opened it and held it up.

The man studied the picture a moment and then eyed Benny.

'Who's that?'

'He's with me,' said Max.

'He looks sick.'

'He's getting better.'

Three bolts went back in quick succession.

Max was shocked and confused by what lay behind the door. Everything he saw was very familiar, yet completely out of place. Benny was awestruck. His fevered eyes blinked rapidly, his mouth hung open in a dazed smile, drool forming at both corners. They were both speechless, each processing their bewilderment. And for a moment, neither could move, because the place they'd just come to was unlike any they'd ever expected to find here.

At first glance it was a typical Cuban city street: opposing rows of one- or two-floor Spanish colonial buildings, with drab, unimaginative slabs of Soviet-inspired geometry breaking the flow. The cobbled road had been pedestrianised and was bustling with human traffic wandering up and down the main throughway and white-bordered sidewalks.

But suddenly the image cracked and fell apart. Halfway up the street, set on a tall grey pillar, were the glowing golden arches of McDonald's. A single red pulsing neon arrow beneath them pointed right. A little further up, to the left, the cheery avuncular face of Colonel Sanders beamed out from an elevated red-and-white KFC sign.

Every single store, restaurant and coffee shop in the road was American. A Walmart occupied what might once have been the home of an upwardly mobile – now exiled – family. It was so well stocked that goods lay piled on the floor. A CVS pharmacy was doing brisk business out of a Cold War-vintage building with faded Russian lettering on the wall. There was a Starbucks, a Subway, a Johnny Rockets, a Chuck E. Cheese, a Domino's Pizza and a Taco Bell.

They made their way down the street, threading through a loose, ambling crowd of off-duty American military, mostly young and male. Apart from Benny, the only Cubans were young women: walking hand in hand with soldiers, sitting on their laps outside bars, dancing on tables inside, leading them into houses that advertised hourly rates in the windows.

Every few feet of sidewalk stood a statue of a cartoon Castro – green fatigues and cap, black boots, a leering triangle of teeth clamping the end of a cigar, flashing a peace sign. Each one had been defaced in some way. Insults scrawled on the face or spray-canned on the body, and many festooned with Bush-Cheney or McCain-Palin election stickers.

The only cars were some of the same vintage bangers the Cubans drove, but in far better condition. The bodies sparkled with fresh coats of paint and wax, the chrome gleaming and the windows as good as mirrors.

They passed a busy casino whose greeters were Cuban babes in tailcoats, bow ties and black basques. A Sinatra soundalike drowned out the noise of the slot machines and roulette wheels with a note-perfect rendition of 'Pennies From Heaven'. Next came a seven-lane bowling alley, a toy shop and an air-rifle range with tin Castros, Guevaras and Bin Ladens as targets. First prize was a 'genuine Cuban flag'.

Towards the end of the road they came across a store called Gitmo Gear selling souvenirs from Guantánamo Bay Naval Base. The store peddled live iguanas – the base's unofficial mascot – in cages, and two varieties of dead ones – stuffed whole or pickled in big glass bottles of formaldehyde. You could also buy iguana keyrings, pens and mugs, and his 'n' hers fridge magnets, where the iguanas came dressed in Bermuda shorts or paisley bikinis. T-shirts were also on sale: 'Welcome to the Taliban Towers – The Caribbean's Newest Five Star Resort', read one, the words printed over a silhouette of the base's entrance, a manned watchtower overlooking a stretch of razor-wire-capped wall. Other designs included an orange Camp X-Ray number depicting a skeleton in a hijab and a grey muscle shirt with a cross-armed iguana set against Stars and Stripes – 'Joint Task Force: Defenders of Freedom'. The T-shirts came in all shapes and sizes, from the XXXXXL elephantine to baby-wear.

As he was looking through the window, Max noticed something reflecting against the glass – a neon sign in the shape of a large five-pointed star, flashing red, white then blue.

He turned. It was coming from the largest house in this bizarre, hermetically sealed road: three floors high with balconies, shuttered windows and a Texan flag planted on a pole by the entrance.

The Lone Star.

50

A gloomy reddish light and a deep hit of pungent second-hand cigar smoke greeted them as they walked in. Then loud music, a rock-rap hybrid that must have been real popular back home because men were frugging away like saplings in a cross-wind – air-guitaring, devil-signing, headbanging, hip-thrusting – while the women around them were grooving along in states of arrested grace, their motion, like their good-time smiles, diplomatic, their eyes saying, *esta música es gringo caca.*

The place was crowded but not packed. Along the sides and in corners sat large gatherings of soldiers and women talking and laughing, the women mere accoutrements, like the ashtrays, pitchers, shotglasses and sodden coasters covering the long tables.

On the floor men stood around in tight quintets, drinking their first beers, eyeing the clusters of women invariably positioned opposite, silent and available, a gap of open, navigable space between them. The bar was off to the right. It was well staffed and seemed to stretch to infinity, guaranteeing that every customer was served quick. It sold nothing but American beer, liquor and soda – plus the big fat Cuban cigars practically everyone seemed to be chugging on.

Waitresses carried drinks from bar to table and returned empties from tables to bar. They were tough-faced pretty and hard-bodied sexy in uniforms of bright-pink, green or orange PVC stetsons with flashing neon strips for bands, matching bras, thongs, boots, tasselled PVC chaps and a spray of gold glitter. Customers shoved tips down their G-strings and bras. If hands tried to go further they'd be discouraged by a glare from one of several bouncers prowling the joint – big guys in tight T-shirts and steel-capped boots, pepper spray and brass knuckles clipped to belts.

Max and Benny wound their way across the floor. Women tried to catch Max's eye. Some tapped him and asked for the time or a light or simply said, *hola*. They all avoided Benny. A few held their noses as he passed.

Max stopped a waitress and asked where he could find Señor Dallas. He'd taken a wild guess. Dallas was the alias of one of the Texas Playboys. The waitress shrugged and pointed her finger upwards. When she saw he didn't understand, she led him and Benny to a recess behind two tables and pointed to a staircase at the end. Max thanked her and offered a twenty-peso tip. She looked at the money contemptuously and walked off.

Upstairs it was a whole different scene. The theme from *Rocky* was playing, accompanied note for note by the large crowd gathered in the middle of the room, where a boxing ring stood lit up by three harsh white spotlights.

Two topless women were squaring off, in thongs instead of shorts and bright-red comedy boxing gloves, several sizes too big and soft like down pillows. They were both on rollerskates, punching and parrying while trying to remain upright, monitored by a female referee in a sheer black catsuit. She broke them apart when they clinched, urged them to get more aggressive when they moved too far apart. It was stupid instead of sexy, but the three of them were taking it seriously, the fighters unsmiling, throwing jabs, the ref screwing up her face in concentration.

Neither fighter landed a clean blow. They circled, out of each other's way, then rolled forward, feinting. Max admired their skill in staying upright and swinging without falling over. He assumed from their perfect hand-to-eye coordination and poise, the way they used the skates to add more power to their shots, that they'd possibly trained as dancers or gymnasts. The all-male audience didn't care about any of that. The men cheered whenever breasts jiggled and buttocks wiggled. They showered the stage with beer and bills.

Max guessed he wouldn't find who he was looking for here.

He and Benny went up to the next floor.

They pushed through two sets of heavy doors, which served to muffle the noise from below to a faint din.

They found themselves in a surprisingly elegant, even tasteful space of crimson carpets, plants, wooden tables and chairs, two lit chandeliers, and almost no people. A couple sat at the back, holding hands, deep in quiet conversation. Three bouncers hung by the bar at the far end of the room, talking to the bartender.

Max went up to them.

'What can I do you for?' asked the bartender. He was stocky and shaven-headed. A moustache sprouted around his mouth in a thick black horseshoe and a name was tattooed on his neck in curly script.

'Is Señor Dallas here?'

'Nope.'

'What about Señor Houston?'

'Nope.'

'Señor Austin?'

'He don't come out in the day. Arlington, Crawford and Plano are here right now.'

'Crawford?' Max smiled. That was where President Bush had his ranch. 'I'd like to talk to him.'

'What about?'

'Business.'

'Kind of business?'

'Kind you get paid for.'

The barman looked him in the eye an instant, glanced over at the bouncers, then back to Max. 'Take a seat over there.' He nodded to a table in a corner.

Max and Benny sat while the barman spoke to one of the bouncers, who walked away.

Then the barman came to the table and sat down in front of Max.

'I don't know you,' he said. He had on a white snap-button shirt with the sleeves rolled up past his elbows. Max could see more tattoos – 'USMC' on his forearm, bald eagles on each hairy hand, something covering his chest.

'I asked for Crawford,' said Max.

'I don't know you,' the man repeated. Hispanic accent. 'How you know me?'

'I don't. I asked for Crawford.'

'Well, that's me.'

'Why didn't you say so at the bar?'

'I'm telling you now. You a cop?'

'No.'

'You look like a cop.'

'I get that a lot,' Max said.

'Who are you?'

'Someone who needs something.'

'What?'

'A map of Cuba.'

'Tourist board'll give you one of those for free.'

'Got one of those. I need one of yours. Military.'

Crawford rubbed his chin, then stroked his moustache, flattening the ends with the tips of his index and thumb.

'Why?'

'I'm lost,' said Max.

'Ain't we all?' Crawford smiled. He took a pack of Marlboro Lights out of his breastpocket and lit one. 'You sure you ain't no cop? Cause if you are and don't tell me, that's some entrapment shit, *ese*.'

'I'm not a cop.'

'Press?'

'No.'

'Terrorist?'

'Please!'

'Are you?'

'Like I'd tell you,' Max sighed. 'What about that map?'

'What about it?'

They eyeballed each other. Max didn't give him the cop stare, didn't hold his gaze for long. Crawford knew cops all too well. He had a bump in the middle of his nose and lines of scar tissue through his brows. Max guessed he'd been a fighter at some point before he'd joined the army. Maybe the sex show downstairs had been his idea.

'Look,' said Max. 'If I don't get what I want from you, I'll just drive down to Guantánamo, find me another place like this and ask nicely.'

'Ain't no other place like this in Cuba, *ese*.'

'You want to do business with me, let's do business. You don't, just say the n-word – as in "No" – and I'm gone.'

'Long way to Gitmo, homes.' Crawford blew smoke over his head.

'Then I guess I'll have to be leaving about now.' Max tapped Benny and motioned for them to leave.

Crawford smiled, shook his head. 'OK. Sit down. I can get you that map. No problem.'

'How much?'

Crawford pretended to think, but he was really evaluating Max, working out how much he could get out of him. He took in the crumpled clothes, tired face, the white stubble growing on Max's head and jaw. Then he looked at Benny sitting next to him, woozy, shaking, leaking and stinking with infection.

'Two Gs,' he said.

'Tourist pesos, I suppose?' Max had but seven hundred pesos in his wallet.

'*Pesos?* Where you think you're at, *ese?*' Crawford laughed. 'US dollars.'

'I don't have any on me,' said Max. 'And two grand is way too much.'

'How bad you want the map?'

'Five hundred bucks bad.'

'Not bad enough, homes.'

'Easiest five bills you'll ever make.'

'Why you say that?'

'I'm sure you've got one just lying around here someplace.'

Crawford looked at him again. Recalculated.

'A grand and it's yours.'

'Five or I walk.'

'What you want it for?'

'I'm looking for buried treasure,' Max said. 'Or maybe I just collect the things. What do you care?'

'It's US Army property.'

'Five hundred. Or I really will have to go. And maybe not even all the way to Guantánamo. I'll just ask one of those fine, upstanding defenders of freedom downstairs to give me one for free.'

Crawford grimaced. 'You got a credit card? There's an ATM down there.' He pointed to the other end of the room. 'By the phonebooths.'

'Mastercard won't work here. Cuba doesn't like American companies, and American companies don't like Cuba,' said Max.

Crawford chuckled out a mouthful of smoke and crushed his cigarette. 'You ain't *in* Cuba now, *ese*. In case you ain't noticed. This, right here, is America. *American* territory. Same as Gitmo. Same as any US embassy. Sovereign-nation shit. A home away from home 'n' all that.'

'I don't get it.'

'The Beard sold us this street, years ago. It's ours.'

'Bullshit.'

'God's truth. Everything's for sale up in this motherfucker. The Commies are cashing in before they crash out.' Crawford shrugged.

'When did this happen?'

'I dunno. Before my time. Fuck does it matter anyhow? You want that map or what?'

Max got up and crossed the room, past the door, past the couple. To his left he saw two phonebooths, soundproofed wooden boxes with glass windows and a padded chair for comfort. In between them was a Bank of America ATM.

When Max returned, Crawford had fixed himself a drink and was draining the glass.

'Took your time, homes.'

'I was calling my mother.' He showed Crawford the money. Crawford held out his hand. Max shook his head. 'C-O-D.'

Crawford chuckled. 'OK. Back in ten.' He stood, hitched his jeans and straightened his shirt. 'Say, your friend there?' he pointed at Benny. 'He looks pretty fucked up. Stinks some too. I can get him antibiotics for another five bills.'

'You wanna scoot over to the CVS outside and pick up some medicine out of the goodness of your heart, I'll give you a tip,' said Max.

'All they sellin' in CVS is condoms and lube, bro. I can get him some righteous army shit, kind we use in conflict.'

'*No.*' Benny shook his head, glowering at Crawford.

'Feisty little fucker, ain't ya?'

'Leave him be,' said Max.

'What happened to his face?'

'Cut himself shaving.'

'Yeah . . . *right.*' Crawford turned and left.

Max watched him walk out the door.

'I no' like him,' said Benny.

'Me neither.'

'I no' like this place.'

369

'Me neither.'

'Is like this, Unite State, Meeyami?'

'I haven't seen topless boxing before, but then I don't get out much,' said Max. 'This, here, isn't America, Benny. This is where assholes come to die.'

Benny laughed, then winced.

'I have something to tell you . . .' Max began. 'I called Nacho. Just now. When I got the money. I've made the arrangements. You're leaving Cuba tomorrow.'

Benny sat up, blinked. His eyes didn't clear. They were pink and glassy, the irises like copper coins sunk in shallow pools of rosewater. 'I no' understand.'

'After we're done here, we're going to Cajobabo. It's two, three hours' drive away. That's where you get the boat from. Forty-eight hours from now you'll be in America.'

'You no' come with me?'

'No.'

Benny looked confused.

'But Max . . . you must come with.'

'I've told Nacho I'll make sure you sail off into the sunset.' It wasn't the way the conversation had gone at all, but the last thing he owed Benny was the truth.

Benny was trembling, clutching the T-shirt about him for warmth. The back of his chair was slick with sweat. He began to cry. At first Max mistook the sobs for more shakes, but the tears ran down his face and splashed on the table.

'What's the matter?'

Benny grabbed Max's arm, hard, his fingers an ice-cold clamp.

'I thank you, Max, for what you do for me. Ever since I meet you, my life is good. Everything work out OK. You bring me good luck.'

'You must have had a seriously shit life if I'm your idea of good luck,' said Max. He pulled his arm free. 'Besides, I didn't do anything for you, Benny. You just tagged along for the ride. And your stop's next.'

370

Max searched for his handkerchief but couldn't find it. He looked around the tables for napkins, then at the bar, but saw none.

'What will you do?' Benny asked. 'How you get on this place, this secret island?'

'I'll think of something.'

'How you get off?'

'I'll think of something. I'm the least of your worries.'

Benny dabbed at his face with his shirt and sniffled.

'You two sweethearts breakin' up?' said Crawford, above them. Max had neither seen nor heard him come back. He was fanning himself with a map.

Max took it from him and opened it on the table. Then he opened the smaller official, state-issued map. He compared the Windward Passage on both. One map showed blue sea, the other a small but distinct island in the shape of an imperfect octagon, in between the easternmost tip of Cuba and the northern coast of Haiti.

'You satisfied?' said Crawford.

Max paid him.

Crawford counted the money, folded it and slipped it into his breastpocket.

'Hope you find what you're looking for – whatever it is,' he said as he stood up. *'Adios amigo.'*

They walked back to the car.

It was mid-afternoon, the sun had come out and the city was baking. The boardwalk had dried off and filled with tourists. More American soldiers were coming into town via the sea and women were waiting for them. The puddles had shrunk and the city's rich bronze and yellow tones had returned.

A small tailback had formed on the road where they'd parked the DeSoto. The stores were all open, their shelves so empty that it was impossible to tell what they sold or their specialities.

The rain had washed off much of the Firedome's makeshift

paintjob. The car was almost green again, the red and blue reduced to the faintest stains, the plates cleansed of mud.

Benny went to the passenger side, and as Max took out the keys to open the door he saw Benny look up, puzzled, confused, his gaze moving to just above Max's left shoulder.

For an instant Max thought Benny was going to faint, but then he smelled a hint of perfume behind him, something expensive and old-fashioned. And he saw his wife's face again, clearly.

He made the connection, placing fragrance and owner at the very moment the cold, hollowed point of a gun barrel was pressed hard behind his ear.

Again.

He raised his hands.

'I tried to call you,' he said to Rosa Cruz.

'You didn't leave a message,' she replied, yanking his arm down and cuffing his wrist.

51

To the innocent or uninitiated, the dried bloodstains on the wall and floor could have been mistaken for splashed coffee. They shared the same coppery black tone. Max passed the time waiting for Cruz to start questioning him by identifying the source wounds. It beat worrying about his future. That was well and truly gone.

A Morse code of brutality and coercion, truths beaten out of bodies: the big tentacular splash on the yellowy tiles right by his bare feet had almost certainly come from a busted nose. It reminded him of the stain on the 7th Avenue ring, almost in the middle. No matter how hard Abe had scrubbed at the canvas, it never came out, just got blacker and blacker over time, as if in wilful opposition to all that soap and water and elbow grease. When Eldon changed the canvas he found the blood had soaked into the wood below.

To Max's left were smaller drops, in the shape of toppled capital 'B's or figure '9's, with the centres filled in: split lips had made those. The bigger puddles by the drain that ran perpendicular to the right wall were from cracked mouths and broken jaws. Finally, he guessed the droplets and fine spray pocking the glossy off-white walls was splashback from flailing fists.

He recognised some kind of karmic justice at play, the judgement going against him, the penalty a dose of his own medicine, and then some. In Miami, in his time on the force, they'd routinely beaten the crap out of suspects. The practice had stopped shortly after he'd left. Now interrogation rooms in Miami were air-conditioned, camera-surveilled and miked up – everything on the record for the record. An interrogation was little different in tone and theme to a hard job interview.

No such luck here.

This was old-school prehistoric, beat the truth out of you, get you to confess through broken teeth and sign on the line in blood. Then lock you up and throw away the key. *Adios motherfucker.*

He was cuffed and chained by the right wrist to a square cast-iron table, and again by the left ankle to a ring in the floor. The chair was cast iron too. He could hardly move without the cuffs pinching and cutting his skin, edging for the bone. They'd taken his shoes and socks. His feet stank, but what the fuck? It smelled bad enough in here already. It was windowless and the walls were thick. The air was rancid with old blood, piss and sweat, and it was so hot he could almost smell his flesh baking a little. His mouth felt dry, his bladder was bursting and sweat was slithering from the top of his head all the way down his back. He wriggled at the sensation.

He was being watched by a young guard sat in the corner by the solid metal door. Thick hairy arms folded across his chest, legs wide apart, chewing, dark half-moons spreading out from his armpits. Whenever Max looked his way, he'd be staring at him, detached and one-dimensional. All Max could hear were the inner rumblings of the man's stomach, his shallow breathing, the scraping of his shoes on the floor, his gun clanking against the chair frame as he took a deeper breath.

Max wondered how Benny was doing.

While Rosa Cruz was cuffing Max, Benny tried to run, but he was so weak, he fell flat on his face and couldn't get up. Cruz grabbed him by the collar and dragged him to her car, pushing Max forward with her gun. She'd been parked right across the road, waiting for them to come back. How had she tied them to the Firedome? He hadn't asked. She put both of them in the back, a wire grille separating them from her.

374

She'd called it in on the radio and driven off at speed. The city centre flashed by. Then they were in the crumbling, flat suburbs and pulling up to a row of anonymous concrete office blocks. No signs anywhere, just metal numbers power-drilled to the walls and immaculate squares of grass in front of every building.

People were exiting the block as they marched in. Men in shirtsleeves and side holsters. They stopped and stared at her and her haul, especially Benny, who stumbled the whole way, tripping over his feet.

In an air-conditioned office, with desks and plants and men and women at computers and on phones, every one of them wearing a gun, Cruz talked to a man, then a woman.

Then they went down five flights of stairs, the temperature going up as they descended. Their destination was a corridor with cells to one side, interrogation rooms to the other. She pushed them past the cells, alternating male and female cages crammed with miserable, half-naked, grimy bodies, their terrified eyes staring out of the gloom, everyone absolutely quiet, almost all bruised and bloodied; communal buckets for toilets, no light, no beds.

She'd shoved Benny into one room, Max in the next.

His door stayed open while she cuffed Benny to the metal furniture. Outside, he saw a man clinging to the bars of a cage, looking at him. A guard came by and smashed the man's fingers away with a nightstick. The man screamed. The guard flashed a ratchet. Sadistic fucker.

It was the same guard who was watching him now.

Rosa Cruz came in.

She held the door open and nodded to the guard, who got up and left. She sat down and opened the US military map on the table.

She looked different in the light: severe, no nonsense, all business, practically forbidding. She was wearing a plain dark-blue blouse, slacks and a gun on her hip. No jewellery. No make-up.

375

Her forearms were roped with large, prominent veins. He guessed she worked out daily. It told in the tautness of her skin and the glow of her face, with its delicate balance of African and European features – dark-brown skin and deep-brown eyes with clear bright whites, a small nose and wide, full mouth. Like a lot of black women who kept themselves in shape and possibly dyed their hair, it was impossible to tell how old she was, but she'd definitely left her twenties behind and didn't seem the sort who'd miss them. Her face showed every indication of baggage carried up a hard road.

'Have you found Vanetta Brown?' she asked.

'I need a piss,' he said. 'And I wouldn't mind some water.'

'Have you found Vanetta Brown?' she repeated, staring at him, expressionless, tone level and slow, reminding Max of a language tape for beginners.

'Not yet. Guess I never will now.'

She tapped at the map. 'What's this?'

'What it looks like. A standard-issue US military map of your fair country, showing places that even you might not know about: little towns with no name, an offshore island or three – also with no name – and those funny roads that start in the middle of nowhere, keep on going awhile and stop right where they started – nowhere. You can't miss them. They're all marked in red.'

'Where did you get it?'

'From someone on that *camino muerto* Castro sold to the US army.'

'*Leased*, not sold.'

'Like Guantánamo?'

'Exactly. Only the terms are fairer. We can kick them out whenever we want and the rent is inflation-indexed.'

Max laughed. 'I thought you people were commies.'

'Socialists. There is a difference. The Americans call that road "Freedom Row". We call it "*La Alcantarilla*" – "The Sewer".'

'For once I agree with your side.'

376

'You've gone a little native.'

'That would be pushing it,' he said.

'Cuba leaves its fingerprints on all who pass through.'

'I really need that piss.'

She tutted under her breath, stood and went outside, returning a few moments later with the guard. He was carrying a black plastic bucket and a bottle of water. He handed the water to Cruz and pushed the bucket under the table with a foot.

'Aren't you going to uncuff my hand?' Max asked her.

'Don't flatter yourself.'

Max unzipped himself with his free hand and pissed into the bucket as Cruz and the guard watched.

After the guard took away the bucket, she sat back down, uncapped the water and handed it to him. It was cold. Max glugged the bottle half empty.

'Tell me about Señora Brown,' she said.

'She doesn't have long to live. She has terminal cancer. But I guess you know that already.'

'No, I did not.'

'The Dascal family didn't tell you?'

'They're senior government people, friends of our leaders. I don't have the authority to interview them.'

'Didn't your superiors talk to them?'

She didn't answer.

'I thought the Cuban secret police was supposed to be state of the art? I mean, how many times did the CIA try to kill Castro? About a million, right? They failed every time,' he said. 'And now you're telling me a member of Castro's *inner circle* – someone he knew *before* he came to power, someone he's looked after and protected all this time – goes missing and you people don't even think to question their family? Because that's what the Dascals are to Vanetta Brown – family.'

'The situation is more complicated than you realise.'

'Care to tell me how and why?'

'No,' she said. 'When did her cancer come back?'

'That you should know.'

'Why?'

'Remember the night we "met"?' he said. 'You found the stuff I took from her apartment – a compliment slip, a photograph of Vanetta and my friend Joe, taken here, in this city, and an empty bottle of Zofran: medicine commonly prescribed to treat the side-effects of chemotherapy.'

She frowned, her brow forming a swirl of tight creases. 'I thought you only stole the compliment slip. The medicine and the photograph were yours.'

'I found them in the apartment,' he said.

'Impossible. After she disappeared, we went through her apartment inch by inch, item by item. We catalogued each object. We're experts in this kind of procedure. Even the dust gets put back the way it was. That medicine bottle and the photograph were not there. I guarantee you. Where did you find them?'

'The pill bottle in a bedside cabinet drawer. The photograph, on the floor, behind the desk in her study.'

'Obvious places we'd look, don't you think?'

'Sure. So either your people got sloppy, or—'

'We do *not* get sloppy.'

They could have missed the pills and photograph – if they were first-timers, *and* dumb. Which they weren't. So the objects may have been planted after the search. If that was the case, then who by and why?

Cruz cleared her throat. 'I'm guessing the reason you obtained this map is because you've found out that Vanetta Brown is presently in another secret location – the old Russian hospital. It specialises in cancer treatment. And it's very discreet.'

'If it's good enough for Fidel . . .'

She ignored him.

'Where is the hospital?'

'You know about it, but you don't know where it is?' he said.

'Everyone knows about it.'

378

'But you don't have the *authority* to know where it is, right?'

She scowled at him, saying nothing.

'What kind of investigation are you *running*?' Max snapped.

'The exact location of that hospital is more than just a state secret,' she said calmly. 'Only Fidel, Raoul and their very closest associates know where it is. My boss doesn't. And her boss doesn't either. But *you* do. So tell me.'

Max had a little leverage, a bargaining chip. His only one.

'I've been doing all the talking,' he said. 'Now it's your turn.'

She gave him a quizzical look.

'What's going to happen to me?'

'Depends on what you tell me,' she said. 'You don't have any choice here, and you know it.'

'I guess innocent until proven guilty doesn't apply?'

'No one who's sitting where you are is innocent.'

'Thought as much.'

He was fucked either way. Might as well give her what she wanted. What the hell, it was over.

He pointed to the spot in the Windward Passage.

She stared at it, then scrutinised the map.

'How were you going to get there?' she asked.

'Isn't that hypothetical now? By the by? Fantasy? A waste of breath?'

'Tell me.'

'I really don't know,' he said. 'Hadn't thought that far ahead. I like to improvise. Play a situation like jazz. You like jazz?'

She answered with a stony stare. He guessed she didn't.

'Your only chance of getting on that island from here is to swim,' she said. 'You won't find anyone stupid or desperate enough to take you there by boat. No matter what you offer them – a million pesos or a bullet in the head. They'd take the bullet sooner than help you. The waters are heavily patrolled.'

'Oh well . . .' He shrugged. 'You know the island's privately owned, right?'

'Everyone knows that.'

'Who owns it?'

'I don't know.'

'He bailed out Vanetta Brown's centres. Kept them going for ten years.'

'I don't know who he is.'

'Vanetta's deputy – Elias Grimaud – knows him. You know Elias?'

'No.'

'You never met him?'

'No.'

'What about a guy with a hare lip? Possibly called Osso?'

She shook her head.

'He killed Joe Liston and Eldon Burns in Miami. And I think he's on that island too.'

'So you're saying Señora Brown was behind the murders?'

'The pieces fit,' he said. 'On forensic evidence alone, it's a lock. Her prints were on the casings. As far as Eldon Burns's murder goes, she had a strong motive. She also had connections with the two people I suspect carried out the hit – Osso and Elias. They were Caille Jacobinne alumni.'

He told her about the CDs, and what he'd found out.

'You're right,' she said, when he'd finished. 'The pieces do fit. Except for Joe Liston.'

'I agree. That doesn't make any sense. Never has. Which is where my other theory kicks in,' he said. 'Vanetta was set up. Maybe someone wanted Eldon and Joe dead for unrelated reasons. Or maybe they wanted one of them dead and killed the other as a diversion to throw the investigation off course. I don't know. Either way, they put Vanetta's prints on the casings to create a smokescreen. But it has nothing to do with Vanetta and never did. That's my gut talking.'

'Do you always trust your gut?'

'Yeah,' he said. 'But I don't always listen to it.'

'Why do you think your friends were killed?'

'Take Vanetta out of the equation and I have absolutely no

idea. Could be a million reasons. But one thing's for sure. The answer's on that island.'

She brushed a lock of stray curls away and inspected the map again. Max drank the rest of the water.

'You ever kill anyone?' he asked her.

She didn't answer. She didn't have to. He knew anyway. How many times had she even drawn her gun with the intention of using it?

'This guy with the harelip – he's *very* dangerous,' said Max. 'I saw him put a bullet through Joe's eye with an automatic. An old school Colt forty-five. Never known for their accuracy. Now, I used to be a pretty good shot back in my day. I won a couple of pistol championships, but even then I couldn't have done that with a revolver, let alone an auto.'

'I'll be armed.'

'Take my advice. You see Mr Harelip first, shoot him on the spot. Doesn't matter if he's sleeping under a tree or stark naked in the shower. Kill him where you find him.'

She nodded, but a filament of fear lit up behind her eyes. He knew she didn't have it in her. Despite the circumstances, he felt sympathy for her.

But it wasn't his problem any more. Her welfare was none of his business. There were other things to talk about, like just how fucked he was right now.

'Those four people shot on the road between Camagüey and Las Tunas? Two of the men, the ones in the white shirts—'

She interrupted him. 'Which four people are you talking about?'

'What do you mean?'

'You said *four* people were killed?'

Max was confused. 'Don't tell me you don't know about *that* either?'

'I don't.'

Yeah, *right*, he thought. She was going to get him to incriminate himself, talk and talk and talk his way into an ever-deepening hole.

381

'You listen to the news?' he asked her.

'The news?'

'Yeah, lady, the news. Your national news. On the radio.' He hummed the intro to 'Strawberry Fields Forever'.

She looked at him like he'd lost his mind.

'Why don't you start again? Slowly, step by step. From the beginning. Tell me about these four dead men.'

'Come on! Stop fucken' me around!' Max snarled. 'You want a *confession*? Is that it? Well, you're not going to get it because I didn't do it. Ballistics will show that those four men shot each other.'

'Ah . . . *those* four men?'

'Yeah, *those* four men – two uniformed cops and two other guys.'

She stayed calm. 'The men in uniform were not police. They were all Abakuá.'

That didn't surprise him. 'So you do know about it?'

'Yes, of course. But how do you know about it? Were you *there*?'

He slammed his free fist on the table. 'For *fuck's sake* lady. Of course I was fucken' *there*. That's me they're talking about on the *national . . . fucken' . . . news*!'

She sat back puzzled, shaking her head.

'That song you just sang – sing it again. Please.'

'*What?*'

'Please.'

He tried, but he was too pissed off to get anything out. He took a few deep breaths, let his anger simmer down, and then hummed the song again, all croaky and out of tune. She joined in towards the end. She didn't have a bad voice.

'*Milagros en la cocina*,' she said, when they'd finished. 'Miracles in the kitchen. That is from a popular cooking show.'

He was silent.

'I listen to it when I'm home. It's on five times a day. It started during the Special Period, when we had food shortages. It gave us recipes, new ways of using our rations.'

'Are you sure?'

'Yes.'

'A *cooking* show?'

'You thought it was the news?'

'Yeah.'

'Who told you that?'

Max nodded at the wall, to his right.

She laughed. '*He* told you that? And you *believed* him?'

'My Spanish isn't too good. In fact, I can't understand a fucken' word out here.'

'So what do you think has been happening? What did he tell you?'

Max was too stunned to talk. His head had gone light and he felt nauseous, like he was going to faint.

'Those four dead guys in the road ...' he started, but couldn't continue.

'Take your time,' she said gently. 'When you're ready. Tell me what happened?'

Max glared at the wall, as if he could penetrate it somehow and see Benny. A faded bloody handprint loomed out of the lumpy cream gloss, waving at him.

He cleared his throat and told her what Benny had been saying on the road, how he'd 'translated' the 'radio news'.

Rosa Cruz started laughing. A chuckle here, a chuckle there. Then a short burst of laughter. Followed by a torrent. Laughter crashed out of her, in loud and deep and thunderous bellyaching guffaws, sounding like logs rolling down a long steep hill. Max shot her an angry look to quiet her, but her eyes were closed. When they opened and she saw his expression, she just laughed louder and harder, making farmyard sounds – neighing and snorting and grunting.

He felt like a fucken' idiot. Why hadn't he even *suspected*? It wasn't like he didn't know Benny was a lying, manipulative sack of shit. Why had he done it? Probably to scare Max into leaving Cuba as fast as possible. What other reason was there?

Cruz eventually laughed herself out. She gasped for air and composed herself before talking again.

'We know those men shot each other and that one car got away. There were tyre marks,' she said, her eyes still hotwired with mirth. 'We removed the bodies and cleaned up the scene. You see, when local crimes are committed, we don't announce it on the news. We find the guilty and deal with them. The general public is none the wiser.'

'What about Gwenver? That was on *TV*.'

'Earl Gwenver? He was found floating in Havana Bay. Shot in the mouth seven times – an Abakuá execution. The television news only reported it because some American tourists were videotaping the body in the sea – otherwise we wouldn't have mentioned it. Americans like to put their lives on the internet. We said he drowned. Did your friend tell you the police were after you for his murder, as well?'

Max nodded. She didn't laugh this time.

'What about the other body that was found in Havana, around the same time as Gwenver – on one of the roads off the Malecón?' he asked.

'The old woman? The one hit by her drunk son's car?'

'*That fucker.*'

Max told Rosa practically everything that had happened after he met Benny, although he omitted all mention of Nacho Savon and Trinidad.

She listened without comment. The humour gradually left her face and the severity crept back in, like a teacher sneaking back into a riotous classroom and making it fall back into line without uttering a word.

'Did he tell you about the cow?' she said, when he was done.

'The *cow*?'

'The cow. Benny Ramirez killed one near Santa Clara. That's a serious crime here. The penalty is ten years in prison.'

'Is Castro a closet Hindu?'

She rolled her eyes. 'There is a shortage in Cuba. Has been

384

since the Special Period. It's illegal to kill a cow without permission. Our constitution guarantees children under the age of sixteen a glass of milk a day. Children are our future,' she explained. 'Benny killed a farmer's only cow. He sold the carcass to a hotel in Havana. Only tourists eat beef. The farmer's son tracked him down to a bar in the capital. He was going to cut Benny up, just like Benny cut up his father's cow. Luckily for them both, you intervened.'

'I wish I hadn't.'

They fell quiet. Outside, someone was running a stick back and forth along the cell bars. Inside, it remained still, the air stifling, Max's anger turning over. Benny wanted to leave the country not for any ideological reason, or because he wanted a better life, but because he was facing jail ... for killing a cow. Max – with his American passport and his money – had been the best way out. He'd almost made it too. In all fairness, Max didn't blame him. What would he have done in Benny's position? The same damn thing. What did it matter anyway? Only his pride was hurt. That would pass – and quickly.

'So let me get this straight,' he said. 'I'm not wanted for any serious crime here?'

'Outside of theft, breaking into and entering a restricted government building?'

'Not that shit *still*?' Max groaned. 'What are you going to do?'

'Tomorrow, we go to the island together,' she said. 'I know someone in the coastguard. He owes me a favour. He can get us there.'

'That simple?'

'Yes. But what happens once we're there is out of my hands.'

'You'll have back-up, right?'

'I'm going with you.'

'I said *back-up*.'

'It's just us.'

'How come?'

'As I keep telling you, it's complicated.'

'It's also fucken' dangerous. You don't know how many people are on that island. I'm guessing the owner might have himself a little army.'

'He doesn't need one,' she said. 'He has us.'

'Are you sure?'

She shook her head. 'I'm just guessing.'

'Right . . .' Max looked at the handprint on the wall. The fourth finger was missing.

'Where were you heading to, when I arrested you?' she asked.

'Cajobabo.'

'Were you going to put Benny Ramirez on the Wetback Express?'

'You know about that too?'

She smiled.

'The person who'll take us to the island is in a town called Imías. It's near Cajobabo,' she said. 'We'll drop Ramirez off on our way.'

'You're gonna let him *go*?'

'I don't want the likes of him here. He's a blight on our society. He belongs in Miami – with the rest of them. As for you, you're spending the night here, in a cell. It's for appearance's sake.'

'Whose appearance?'

She didn't answer.

52

'You hate me now, yes, Max?' said Benny from the back of the car, his face close to the wire divider.

It was early afternoon and they'd been in Rosa Cruz's Suzuki a good hour, speeding along the road linking the provinces of Santiago and Guantánamo. The scenery was blipping past, and Max was trying to catch some of it, but he was having trouble keeping his eyes open.

He hadn't slept at all. It had been impossible. After she'd finished with him in the interrogation room, he'd been marched up to the next floor and shoved into a single cell. No bed, a bright light permanently on, mosquitoes and moths for company, the floor and walls slick with damp and fungus, a hole in the ground for a toilet. He couldn't lie or sit down, so he stood still or paced about. They'd taken his watch away – along with his belt and shoes and everything else they found on him – so he couldn't tell if it was day or night. It had been so quiet there, he'd thought he was alone. Then one of Castro's speeches had been piped into the block at full volume, an endless harangue delivered in a cadence ranging from angry to explosive. Max couldn't believe people willingly stood through those epic diatribes in the blazing heat, let alone the enthusiastic applause and full-chested chants that followed their conclusion. The silence that filled the corridor afterwards was almost blissful. But just as he'd gotten used to it, another speech came on, louder and longer than the first one. He'd stuffed his fingers in his ears, but it was no use. It went on all night, a cycle of ever-decreasing moments of stillness broken by El Jefe's ever-lengthening discourses played at ever-increasing volumes. Cruz was wearing earplugs when she finally came to get him out that morning.

They went back to the Firedome for his possessions. He took the CDs, flow chart and the notes he'd made, and she put them in a rucksack, along with the two Magnums and spare ammo from the glove compartment.

Then she took him to breakfast. He paid.

'Why you no' want talk to me, Max?' Benny slammed his open hand at the wire.

Rosa told Benny to shut up and sit back.

Max stared out the window.

They passed the perimeter of Guantánamo. The base was very clearly marked out, its name spelled in block white capitals, each individually mounted on a pedestal and set apart, like it was an exclusive tourist resort or golf club. A high barbed-wire fence stretched for miles around the area. Equally tall rectangular state billboards stood in front of the fences, denouncing imperialist aggression, imperialist greed, imperialist imperialism and the imperialists generally. Every one carried a different picture of Fidel Castro – the bushy-bearded young revolutionary in khakis and kepi, frozen in mid-oratory, wagging a declamatory index at a midpoint between sky and audience, a dove perched on one of his broad shoulders; the elder statesman, staring pensively at the camera, index to temple; the old tyrant, reigning over his broke and broken-down nation, his beard thinned and wiry, his octogenarian face raisin-textured. It was as if the state was using the billboards to trial a definitive image of its leader, something it could plaster everywhere and market to Western trendies and postcard-socialists like it had the Korda photograph of Che. Fidel Castro was gradually being transmogrified into myth.

Max turned on the radio. He punched through the channels, looking for music. He found some – the intro to 'Strawberry

388

Fields Forever' – and quickly turned it off. Rosa Cruz suppressed a laugh.

They parked, as per Nacho Savon's instructions, at the top of a hill, near the disused Russian watchtower overlooking Cajobabo Beach. The area was overgrown with waist-high grass and a wild explosion of thick plants bending gently in the breeze. A path had been cut through the vegetation and led to a rocky beach bordered with hillocks of dried seaweed.

They waited in silence, watching the sun slide towards the sea, a splattered lozenge staining the sky every shade, from auburn to crimson, as daylight bowed before a spread of emerging stars.

Right before nightfall, a container ship came into view a few miles out and stopped roughly in the middle of their line of vision. A few moments later they noticed a small boat cutting across the water, headed in their direction.

Max turned to Benny. 'Your ride's here.'

Two men were waiting for them down by the beach, one dark-haired, one bald, both armed with M-16s. They'd come in a rigid inflatable boat, which they'd pulled ashore.

'Mingus? Ramirez?' the dark-haired man called out.

Max told Benny to wait and went over to the vessel.

'You're taking him, not me,' he said to the man.

'Order's for two.'

'Change of plans,' said Max, nodding to Benny. 'It's just him. Ramirez.'

The man gave his assent with an indifferent shrug.

Max rejoined Benny.

'You're all set,' he said.

'Thank you, for what you do for me.'

'You know you don't deserve it.'

'Why you want we finish like this?'

'Because you're a piece of shit.'

'You no' mean that, in you heart.'

'I mean it every place.'

The dark-haired man was looking their way, tapping at his watch.

'I no' so bad peoples,' said Benny. 'Is this country make peoples do this thing.'

'Bullshit,' said Max.

Benny tutted and sighed and took a couple of steps away from him, his back to the sea.

'Is nothing I can say to you? Make you think good of me?'

'No.'

'OK. Is how you want, is how you want.' He shrugged. 'But I *no'* forget what you do for me.'

'Don't come looking for me in Miami.' *If I make it back*, he thought.

Benny held out a hand, fingers trembling. His mouth was downturned and his eyes had misted up. Whether it was sickness or remorse or plain acting, Max couldn't tell. Benny certainly looked the part – vulnerable and full of regret, sincere enough to swing the benefit of doubt in his favour. And something almost moved in Max at that moment, but pride caught it and held it back. He didn't take the hand. He tightened his jaw and looked past Benny at the men by their boat, at the ship in the distance, waiting to sail to Miami.

Benny sighed again, the air modulating as it crossed his throat.

Then he walked away, crunching over the rocks, head down, shoulders sagging.

'Hey,' Max called out.

Benny stopped and turned.

'Mend your ways, all right?' After he said it he wondered why he'd bothered. He'd had better opportunities in life than Benny, and he'd had a chance and a very good reason to change, yet he hadn't taken it and his wife had died on her way to visiting him in prison. People didn't change; they just got better or worse at being who they were.

'*Vaya con Dios, Max.*'

'*Adios Benny.*'

Max headed back towards the hill. Behind him he heard Benny's footsteps fading away and then the boat's motor grumbling to life.

At the top of the hill, he found Cruz standing there with a smirk on her face, the wind brushing back her hair.

'That was touching – seeing your man off to sea,' she said. 'Sure there wasn't a little something going on between you?'

'Fuck off,' he said.

They both laughed and went to the car.

53

They pulled up at a concreted parking spot overlooking the Cajobabo river. They were an hour early. Around midnight a man called Marco was coming to take them to the island. All they had to do was wait. She suggested Max get some sleep, but his tiredness had gone, chased away by mounting anticipation. He opened the rucksack. As well as the Magnums and CDs, there were two pocket torches and a leather video-camera case. He took out one of the guns and checked it, dumping the shells, spinning the cylinder and inspecting the barrel. It had been well maintained. It still smelled of oil.

Spotlights lit the riverbank. A group of teenagers was holding a high-diving contest, watched by some people around a camp-fire. One after the other, the kids – boys and girls – scaled the dark cliff that flanked the water to a jut close to the top. From there they plunged into the river, landing in between two tethered wooden floats laden with lanterns. The divers were superb – highly skilled, executing all manner of moves, the like of which Max had only seen on TV.

'I think you like it here, in Cuba,' said Cruz. 'I saw the way you were looking out of the window when we were driving. To you this country is a beautiful woman you don't have the guts to talk to.'

'I've been to worse places,' he said.

'You could always stay.'

Max laughed. 'And ask for asylum? On what grounds? They wouldn't want me here.'

'You can't be sure.'

'*I* wouldn't want me here. Besides, your coffee's shit.'

She wound down the window. A scent of jasmine wafted into the car on the edges of a fresh sea breeze. They could hear the children shouting and clapping, and then a solitary splash as a diver hit the water.

'This is some favour you're pulling in,' said Max. 'This guy Marco must owe you big.'

'He does,' she said. 'He's my ex-husband.'

Max wasn't surprised to hear that. 'You stayed friends?'

'We have two girls.'

'How old?'

'Nine and seven.'

'That's nice.'

A black girl in a yellow bathing suit executed a perfect forward somersault pike, slicing into the water with a meagre splash and almost no noise. Her friends gasped and applauded enthusiastically when she surfaced.

Rosa Cruz cleared her throat.

'There's something I have to tell you,' she said, a quaver in her voice.

'Go on.'

'I've been a bodyguard for about twenty years. I started by protecting foreign ambassadors' wives, then their children, then the ambassadors themselves. I was good at my job. Vigilant, efficient, effective. I saw everything, anticipated everything, left nothing to chance.

'I rose up the ranks. I was promoted to government officials for a while. Then it was foreign assignments. I went to Bolivia, Mexico, and I even went to America twice, to the United Nations. That was both a job and also a kind of test. Some Cubans who go abroad don't come back. They defect. I did not. I did my tour and returned.'

'Because of your kids?'

'They hadn't been born,' she said. 'You may not understand

this, coming from the land of free enterprise and capitalism, but I *like* it here. I like the system, the way it eradicates a lot of competition between people. I like that the state looks after you. You're guaranteed a job for life, if you want one. It may not be a good job, but it's a living. You come and leave at exactly the same time. You know roughly where you'll be next year. No one can buy your livelihood out from under your feet, break it up and sell the pieces for profit. That suits me. I think, when you reach a certain age, you want things to stay the way they are. And in Cuba they tend to.

'When the government was sure of my loyalty, I got promoted again. This time protecting Castro's inner circle. Not all the way in, but close. Call it his *outer* inner circle. The job came with benefits. I had a better car, a better house, better rations. I liked that. And I liked the person I was guarding too.'

'Vanetta Brown?'

'That's right,' she said. 'I'd never met someone more courageous and honest than her. We used to talk a lot. About America, racial politics, race in general. And other things too. She loved soap operas and liked to read terrible romantic novels.'

'Did you ever meet Joe?'

'Twice.'

'What did you make of him?'

'I could see why Vanetta trusted him. He was a lot like her – and completely unlike you,' she said.

'That he was.'

She took a deep breath. And then another.

'When Vanetta disappeared, I was demoted,' she said. 'I don't blame them. I deserved it. She was my responsibility, and she vanished.

'I lost my privileges. The house, the car, the extra rations. But I still had a job. Now I take the Libyan ambassador's children to school. They're nice.'

He heard the bitterness and resentment in her voice, despite its even, acceptant tone. He heard how she'd hidden her crushed emotions away under the sharp creases of professionalism, letting them build, twisted and warped, yet undetected, out of sight.

'A while ago, I decided to find Vanetta myself – or at least what had happened to her. I thought, If I do that, they'll give me my position back.'

Max looked at her. She was nominally watching the divers.

'So ... what you're saying is, this isn't official and never has been? You're doing this independently, without the state's knowledge?' he said. 'That's why there's no back-up?'

'Yes.'

Max sighed. 'Are you all full of shit in this country or is it just me?'

'I'm sorry.'

He thought of Wendy Peck again and how she'd done exactly the same thing. Cuba was nothing but Miami in a grubby rearview.

'Technically, this means I'm free to go, right? I could hitchhike back to Havana, enjoy the rest of my stay and fuck off home?'

'Yes. If you want. I won't stop you,' she said.

And he sensed that she meant it. That she wanted him gone, out of the way; he'd fulfilled his purpose and was now surplus to requirements, baggage.

That got him thinking.

'Surely the all-seeing, all-powerful state knows Vanetta is on that island. Sarah Dascal would have told them what she told me.'

'As I said before, it's complicated,' Rosa said.

'I think you can tell me all about the complications now, don't you?'

Another heavy breath, filling her lungs to their capacity, then a slow exhalation. She was both steeling and calming herself.

'OK ... As you know, Vanetta had fallen out of favour with Castro because of her connections with the Abakuás. The state had her under surveillance.'

'Were you watching her?'

'I wasn't *spying* on her. That's a different division,' she said indignantly. 'A few months before she disappeared, she was seen meeting a man in Santiago de Cuba. She met him several times. They were photographed together. The man was followed back to the base in Guantánamo. Our sources there told us he was an FBI agent. His name was Jack Quinones. You know him?'

'Not very well. Continue.'

'We assumed she was negotiating her return to the US. We thought she'd maybe cut a deal to reveal what she knew about the workings of our government in exchange for immunity.'

'How much did she know?'

'She was *close friends* with Fidel.'

'So why didn't you arrest her?'

'We were going to. But then she disappeared.'

'When you say "we", you mean the state – not you person-ally?' said Max.

'Yes, sorry. It's a habit,' she said.

'And when she vanished, you – the state – assumed she'd gone back to America.'

'That's right.'

'What about the Dascals? They know exactly where she is.'

'The Dascals were mentioned in one of the reports I read. Not in much detail. Just a few lines. They'd said that Vanetta was terminally ill,' she said.

'Was that all?'

'Yes.'

She watched a young boy climb up the rocks and ready him-self, puffing out his chest, shaking his arms. He dived, like a starling off a branch, freezing briefly in mid-air, his skinny body flat and T-shaped, before twisting, somersaulting and straightening into a smooth line that disappeared into the water.

'Don't you understand how this goes?' she said.

Max thought about it for a second. More time than he

needed. Of course he understood how it went. He'd been there before.

'Make it fit, make it stick?'

'I'm sorry – what?'

'Here's how it goes,' he said. 'The official theory – that Vanetta sold Castro out, betrayed him to the Americans – is the one the state is running with because it suits them. Or rather, it suits the people who are putting it about.

'Vanetta is out of favour with Castro. She was dealing with criminals behind his back. She betrayed his trust. So as far as he's concerned, she's already no good. She's on the FBI's Most Wanted list with a big price tag on her head. That she was meeting an FBI agent could have been for only one reason: she wanted out. But she wouldn't leave Cuba to go to jail in America. Therefore, she must have been cutting a deal.

'When she disappeared, there's only one place she could have gone – back to the imperialists. It fits. Vanetta's not around to deny it, so it sticks. It makes sense. It's a solid story. It holds up. The truth is irrelevant. In fact, the truth is an inconvenience. If it ever came out, it might seriously embarrass a few people. They'd lose their houses, their cars, their extra rations. Isn't that about right, Rosa?'

'Yes.' She fidgeted in her seat.

'So what are you doing contradicting the official account? It's a risky play for you. If it goes wrong, you disappear. Only, I'm guessing someone as smart as you has found a way around that problem. You've been vigilant, efficient, effective. You've seen everything, anticipated everything. You've left nothing to chance. Right, Rosa?'

She didn't answer.

'Mind if I ask a question?'

'What?'

'Why have you packed a video camera for this trip?'

Again, no response. Just another *deeeep* breath.

'I can tell you why. You're not going to bring Vanetta Brown back to Havana at all. You never were. You're going to that island to get evidence of where she really is,' he said. 'You're going to film her giving some kind of statement from her deathbed. Something that completely contradicts the official version, the one Castro believes. And then you're going to go back to Havana – alone – and blackmail your way back to your precious position? That's it, isn't it? That's what this was all about? A bigger house, a nicer car, some extra rice?'

Silence. No one was diving in the river.

'I checked every hospital in the country to see if they were treating her,' she said. 'When I came up with nothing, I knew she had to be in one of the secret facilities.'

'And you used me to find out which one – for your own gain,' he said.

'You sound disappointed.'

'I expected better of you.'

'Why? You trusted a transvestite prostitute.'

'Who you just freed because he was a *witness*, right? Fuck that spiel you gave yesterday about him being a blight on your society. You wanted him gone.'

'I'm sorry, Max,' she said. 'But what did you expect when I arrested you – the truth?'

Now it was his turn to be quiet. He should have been furious about now, brimming with rage at being used for petty ends, but instead he felt a weird sense of calm, akin to the impregnable deflation that follows relief; as close to inner peace as he'd ever come. For the first time in his life he understood the world he lived in. Everyone had an angle, a play. Every smile came with a sneer, every kiss had a bite, every caress hardened into a slap, and every helping hand curdled to a fist. All the truth in the world added up to one big lie.

'You're right,' he said after a while.

'You're not angry?'

'What's the point?' he said. 'It's too late for that. And anyway . . . you know what? I don't care. I really don't. I've come too far, gone too deep and gotten too close for any of this to matter any more. Whatever's out there on that island is all I've got left.'

A light splashed over them from behind, exposing the car's dusty brown interior. A car was approaching.

'And I believe it's time to go,' he said.

54

The waters of the Windward Passage were calm and glassy, and the boat sailed across like a disembodied ice skate, smooth and straight, its engine making a gentle purring rasp as it powered along at an even speed. There was no moon, but the sky was suffocated by a billion stars, and a bluey nimbus played along the edges of the southern horizon, as if something big and radioactive were about to emerge from the sea.

Below deck, through the storeroom porthole, Max watched Cuba disappear. The outline of the land and the handful of yellow and white lights along its underpopulated coast were swallowed up by the night, until there was nothing to mark the place he'd come from but the vessel's wake, rippling out over the ocean.

The boat was an ageing Russian patrol vessel – one hundred feet of chipped and patchy grey paint and dents, a bridge with two boarded-up windows and a third cracked down the middle by what could have been a bullet. At the prow was a stubby barrelled artillery gun, so rusted and archaic, it resembled a rejected museum artifact bolted on for show.

Rosa sat with him checking her gun. She racked back the slide, caught the ejected round, then popped out the clip. The spare round went back in the clip, the clip went back in the gun, the slide snapped back in place with the round in the chamber, and she depressed the hammer, flicked on the safety and reholstered the piece. She paused for a few moments, breathed, and then began again. It got irritating after the third time, but he said nothing. Although her face was mask-like in its calm, she was avoiding all eye-contact, occupying her mind to stop from thinking, keeping her hands busy to stop them from shaking. In times like these he'd chain-smoked. Joe had used wrist presses.

Marco was up on the bridge, the only crew.

He was a regular piece of work, a good foot taller than his ex-wife, with short greying black hair, heavily freckled features and lucent blue-green eyes – the kind commonly referred to as 'Irish eyes'. Sandra used to say Max had them – especially when he got mad or drunk or both.

Not that he and Marco had bonded over shared ancestry. The man greeted Max with a blunt territorial suspicion that bordered on hostility, mentally sniffing him out and sizing him up, trying to ascertain what he was doing with and to Rosa, and if he could handle himself in a fight, should it occur. Max offered a handshake all the same, just to keep things civil. Of course, Marco ignored him, looking at the hand like it was a shit-covered mop. Rosa intervened. She and Marco got talking. He spoke his native tongue in a way that stripped the language of its every musical nuance, packing his words into wads so tight that the sentences came out in extended grunts. Oafish as he sounded, it was obvious he still tended an out-of-control bonfire for Rosa. It was in his eyes, going all puppy sweet, and in the hopeful smile he couldn't keep off his mouth as she spoke to him; he was a fool in love, knowingly jumping for tactically withheld bait, thinking the effort alone might be enough to melt the heart. But Rosa was cold, all business. Max guessed it had been a young love on her part, one she should have outgrown before they'd had kids and tied each other down.

That was the Marco who collected them in his fucked-up Lada jeep. Once on the boat, he'd changed. He became a nervous wreck, stammering a little and sweating a lot. It was obviously his first time breaking the law. And he wasn't getting any kind of induction in the shallows. He was going off at the deep end. Rosa snapped at him, determined where he was indecisive and doubtful. She was using him too. Maybe she'd even hinted at reconciliation. Whatever she said worked. Marco grew back his balls and started the boat.

They went down to the storeroom, four grey walls veined with rust, blue jackets and caps hanging on pegs. They each put on a cap and jacket. Max noticed the insignia on the round badge sewn on to both sleeves – a mariposa over the sea with a flying fish in its beak. He understood the meaning – and the bleak irony.

'If we get company, say nothing and look busy,' Rosa had said as they sat down. These were her only words to him.

Company came within the first ten minutes at sea. A helicopter flew over and shone a spotlight on the boat. Max kept away from the porthole. Upstairs, the radio crackled on the bridge and Marco answered in grunts. The chopper hovered over them a moment, then took off, swerving westwards.

Next they sailed close to a moored frigate and stopped, the engine turning. Another powerful light landed on the boat and reached into the storeroom. Neither Max nor Rosa moved. The radio spilled static and a voice. Marco grunted. Then they were on their way again, but at reduced speed, inching over the water.

Max stared up at the starry sky, which seemed a little closer than it had been moments before. He knew they were getting closer to Haiti. That was the thing that had struck him about that country, the way the distance between heaven and earth appeared halved – but not in some glorious, beatific way. Haiti had a feeling of celestial oppression about it, like God's kingdom was close to caving in on its very head.

They passed between a pair of cone-shaped buoys topped with blinking bright-red lights. Sirens suddenly sounded and a pair of speedboats roared out of the darkness, full-beam headlights on, hurtling towards them, a voice yelling over a loudspeaker.

Marco stopped the boat and killed the engine. There was clambering on both sides of the boat and then heavy feet moving above them, wandering up and down. Someone was asking Marco questions. He stammered answers.

Rosa went into panic mode. Her eyes darted around the store-room looking for an exit or a hiding place. Max crept up to the porthole. He couldn't see the boats.

The feet paced the deck. The questions kept coming and Marco kept stammering, every word faltering.

Then they heard feet clanking down the stairs. Two pairs. Rosa drew her gun, but Max shook his head. She holstered the weapon.

Someone tried the door.

Marco had locked them in. A harsh voice called up the stairs.

Marco stammered.

'*Rápido!*'

Marco tried to say '*Si*', but sounded like he was imitating a cartoon snake.

They heard another set of feet on the stairs, the sound of keys jangling.

They were fucked.

Rosa knew it. She was saying nothing, but looked panicked.

The radio crackled. It was answered by the voice that had been questioning Marco. As Rosa listened, tension eased off her face a little.

The feet went back up the stairs.

The two people outside the door followed suit.

There was sudden activity above, as bodies moved left and right across the deck and climbed down the side. Someone somewhere laughed.

Then it became quiet. Nothing but the waves slapping the side of the boat. Max and Rosa exchanged glances, Max look-ing at her for an explanation or a theory as to what had just happened. She offered neither.

But her panic was gone.

The engine started up, the water churning under the boat, and they resumed their journey.

The speedboats followed. Max peeked through the porthole.

He saw four people in each launch, one manning a mounted machine gun.

They passed more buoys – green lights, blue lights. He remembered the same order of lights on the route to Vanetta Brown's place in Calle Ethelberg. They were on another kind of *camino muerto*. The island was very close.

After a short while the boat slowed and they came to a stop. The escort turned and headed away.

They could hear Marco moving around above, walking first to the prow and then the stern. The radio stayed silent.

Then he came downstairs and opened the door.

'*Hemos llegado,*' he said to Rosa.

55

The island was no one's idea of paradise: two miles of back-to-back trees, its extremities fringed by sharp, square boulders which served as both coastline and barricade.

No sign of the hospital or the house.

The only lights came from the place where they'd stopped, a jetty lit by parallel lines of bulbs strung around poles, all joggling in the breeze.

A large hut with a corrugated-iron roof overlooked the harbour. Two men came out and walked down to Marco's boat. One was in shirtsleeves and wore his coastguard cap back to front, the other sported a vest and khaki shorts. They weren't armed. Their manner was relaxed and friendly, even welcoming, as if they were in dire need of company. Marco talked from the prow, speaking in his usual compressed grunts. He even managed a laugh.

After ten minutes of banter, the men left with a wave and returned to the hut.

Max and Rosa crouched low on the bridge, peeking through the window, watching everything, waiting.

Marco came back and mumbled something to Rosa.

Moments later, Max followed her over the side of the boat and on to the jetty. They tiptoed quickly across the wooden beams, keeping their heads down.

As they passed the hut, they saw through the half-open door: four men playing cards and smoking, another strumming a guitar.

Once out of the harbour, they found themselves on an asphalt road, which curved off around either side of the island. Rosa suggested heading right. Max said the hospital might be to the left, facing Cuba.

She agreed.

They took the left road and began walking quickly, sticking close to the side. They hadn't gone far before they spotted headlights coming their way.

They ducked into the woods.

A jeep rolled past, full beams on. It turned into the harbour with a blast of its horn and crunched to a stop. A man got out and went into the hut. He was greeted with a cheer.

Rosa led the way through the trees, flashlight in hand, rucksack on her back.

It was baking hot. The thick and clammy air reeked of compost and methane, nature cannibalising itself and belching heartily. They could hear the crush of their own feet over the sodden and steaming ground. Unseen creatures squirmed under layers of dead leaves and debris; and it was percussive too, with the landings of frogs and bewildered birds, the sudden dash of rodents, the tramplings of heavier animals.

Rosa navigated with purpose, not once stopping or even hesitating, at ease weaving through the thicket of towering palms and the twisted trunks of ficus trees. Max wasn't so adept. He tripped on exposed roots, slipped on fungi and got his face and arms lashed by air roots. He was soon out of breath and sweating, irritated and on edge, his heart pumping overtime, his legs aching.

The ground gradually began to dip and then gravity tugged them forward gently. They moved a little faster. The trees thinned and sharp sea air cut through the smell. And then they saw a row of small yellow lights.

The hospital made Max think of a steel-capped shoe with the leather ripped off the end and the metal exposed. Given the patients the place had originally catered for, he figured the design may have been wholly intentional on the part of the architect – an ironic comment on the system he or she was serving. But then again, for all he knew, the structure could simply have been another example of Soviet bad taste, like the embassy in Havana.

A trio of low-lying cubes connected one to another by short, covered glass walkways. Each building was four storeys high, but of a slightly differing shape. The first had a bulbous, brightly lit glass dome appended to its end, the middle structure was longer and sleeker, and the last stood taller and more compact than the others, more of a low-rise. Lights were burning on all the ground floors.

By contrast, the surroundings – a sprawling, sloping park dotted with benches, parasols, a sundial, a giant chessboard, pretty flowerbeds and a fountain – were as idyllic and serene as they were cosmetic.

'Not even a fence or a wall?' Max said from their vantage point at the edge of the woods. He'd guessed the dome was the entrance: a few vehicles were parked nearby, in the forecourt – two white ambulances and a pair of jeeps.

'It's not a prison,' replied Rosa.

'I was expecting more security.'

A guard sat outside the entrance, a rifle across his lap.

'More than you've seen already?' she said sarcastically.

It was quiet and eerie, and above all unnerving. He could hear the breeze stealing through the trees behind them and in the distance, waves breaking on the rocks. But in between, silence. There should have been some kind of noise coming from the hospital, a trace of the people and machines that kept the building operational.

'What did Marco tell that speedboat crew?'

'He said he's picking someone up.'

'Who?'

'He doesn't know. They don't know either. It's anonymous here, remember?'

'If this gets traced back to him, he could get into some serious fucken' trouble – which means you could too.'

'Sure,' she replied. 'If his name is Marco.'

'It isn't?'

'To you – and to them – it is.'

Max let it go. Marco had blagged his way in on a phoney ID – plus a surfeit of adrenaline, balls, terminal blind love and pure stupidity. Who were they fooling? The secret police would no doubt catch up with Marco real quick. And then they'd come for Rosa – unless she worked her scam in time. But none of that was his problem.

'Any ideas for getting inside?' he said.

'There's only one way in. Through the front.'

'That's crazy. We're going to ... just ... *walk in?*'

'Think,' she said. 'It's early morning. It's dark. No one is awake. We're in uniform – kind of. We can pass. And they are not expecting outsiders.'

Close up, the entrance turned out to be impressive – a perfectly round, very bright, latticed glass house, with all the light coming from three crystal chandeliers. Clouds of insects swam around the dome, their tiny massed bodies forming a misty, swaying halo.

Max and Rosa crouched behind one of the parked ambulances and checked on the guard sitting near the double doors. He wasn't moving.

They approached quietly.

The guard was slouched on a wooden chair, his legs stretched out and parted, feet pointing east and west. His head was propped up against the glass, and his cap pulled down over his face, brim overlapping his nose. He was fast asleep, breathing slowly and contentedly, the cap sucking in and puffing up in time with his lungs, like a bellows.

They'd planned for the challenge: they'd walk up to the door confidently, like they were meant to be there. If the guard asked them their business, Rosa would say they'd come to collect someone. If the guard let them pass without question, he'd be fine. If he didn't, they'd take care of him.

But he was asleep, so all that changed.

They edged closer. The guard was wearing the same kind of jacket they were, only he had on heavy black boots while they wore sneakers. His hands were folded across his stomach, inches from the automatic rifle.

Through the glass they could see there was no one inside the dome. In fact, there seemed to be nothing there at all but glass and a wall with a doorway cut into it.

They tiptoed past the guard, Rosa slightly ahead of Max.

She pulled at the door's grooved brass handle, but it didn't open. There were no locks. Then she saw the keypad.

Max took two steps back and looked the guard over. He had a photo-laminate clipped to his breastpocket and something tied to a black lanyard around his neck.

Max reached over and gently unclipped the photo ID from the pocket. He studied it. It was just the man's name and number.

He hooked his little finger around the lanyard and tugged softly. The guard hadn't shaved and the cord rasped as Max drew the slack across bristles.

Delicately, he edged the lanyard out from under the guard's uniform, mindful of upsetting the tilted cap, watching him carefully for signs of awakening. The edge of a thick black plastic card emerged from under the guard's collar. Max bent and carefully pinched a corner between his fingertips and lifted it out.

Rosa came across, stood between the guard's parted legs and pulled out a switchblade. Leaning over, she cut the card free with a quick side-to-side swipe of the blade.

The guard let rip an operatic fart – a loud, prolonged basso profundo eruption that sounded as if a Harley were going to come flying out of his ass.

Max and Rosa froze.

The man stirred. He moved his tongue around the inside of his lips. He yawned and groaned.

And then he opened his eyes wide.

Rosa was still bent over him, her cleavage hanging close to his face.

Max held his breath, Rosa hers.

The guard's pudgy young face cracked into a broad smile.

Then, slowly, he closed his eyes and went back to sleep.

The hospital's vestibule more than fulfilled its purpose. It was an uncomfortably bright, almost intense shade of white, suggesting an obsessive dedication to cleanliness and sanitation matched only by its committed anonymity. The floor didn't appear to have ever been walked on; the glass in the dome was so clear it was invisible; and even the air was strangely odourless – given the proximity of the sea – as if it had been thoroughly filtered and processed before being allowed to circulate.

The only touches of colour were on the concave back wall. Gold-leaf paint filled in the large, sunken capital letters spelling out the person the hospital was named after:

L E O N I D B R E Z H N E V

The letters were bookended by a pair of black-and-white photographs in borderless frames, showing the Soviet Union's erstwhile premier shaking hands with Fidel Castro outside the dome. They made an odd couple. Brezhnev, sweating through a white safari shirt, scowling in the sun, while Castro, standing a foot taller than his counterpart and ally, was chomping a cigar and smiling, as well he might: the hospital hadn't cost Cuba a thing.

Cold air enveloped them as they entered the main building. Rosa sneezed and then cussed at herself under her breath.

As they took in the environment they exchanged dumb-founded looks, their expressions mirroring the same two questions – where *exactly* were they and what had they just walked into?

To Max it resembled an exclusive private members' club, the kind you only get to know about once you reach a certain social echelon and strut a higher plane. It spelled bottomless money, connections on speed-dial, power on tap.

A plum-red carpet covered the floor, so plush and deep it swallowed the soles of their feet and every trace of sound. Light came from a pear-shaped chandelier both fragile and monstrous, like an ogre's tear. Spotlights in all four corners cast upward beams that splayed across the walls, bestowing an aura of intimacy and warmth. At the back was an impressive convex oak reception desk, the wood diffusing a rich, subdued glow. The wall behind it incorporated a great circular sculpture. From afar the sculpture appeared to be an abstract swirl of white marble, a pointless, sharp-petalled whorl. But closer inspection revealed the design to be a shattering cloud. Floating among the pieces were familiar faces – mini-busts of Communist superstars, the ideologues and the practitioners: Marx, Lenin, Trotsky, Stalin, Mao, Hoxha, Tito and, of course, Castro; man-made gods reigning in an atheist heaven.

In the space between desk and entrance were scattered small round tables and deep, overstuffed leather armchairs with wide wings and footrests. There was a large library, as well as an extensive newspaper rack with English, American, French, Spanish and Russian editions. Max half-expected a butler to appear, but there was absolutely no one around. It was utterly quiet. Only the mild smell of institutional antiseptic betrayed the fact that they were in a hospital. They had to be standing in the lobby of the patients' quarters, he realised: this would be the first thing new arrivals saw after the vestibule.

Close by, to the right, was a staircase – a high oak banister encasing broad stone steps, the carpet spilling down the middle, kept in place by brass runners. Beyond it was an elevator with wide brass doors. Six floors in all, four above, and a basement.

They took the stairs.

The walls were hung with black-and-white photographs of the island and the hospital in various stages of development. The first was an aerial shot of the island in its virgin state, fully forested, a dark torpedo in the pencil-grey ocean. Then the building work started. Trees were uprooted from the shoreline by trawlers with chains. Another bird's-eye shot showed about a dozen whole palm trees floating off the coast, some on their sides, others stuck upright in the shallows, as if trying to clamber back to land. Then came pictures of workmen, all Russian military – bulldozing, sawing, burning, mixing, digging – watched over by men in civilian clothes. The final photograph, near the top of the stairs, depicted the shell of the building, a seagull perched atop an incomplete wall.

On the landing, they faced a long corridor, with numbered doors either side, the light provided by wall-mounted electric candelabra between every other room. To the left they could see an empty office, its glass door painted with a Red Cross symbol.

'We should split up,' whispered Rosa. 'I'll check the rooms on this floor and the next. You take the others.'

Max went up to the top floor. A nurse in a white uniform sat behind a desk in the medical office, engrossed in a book, her bare feet up. Max guessed there were people staying here.

He headed quickly into the corridor, beyond the nurse's line of vision. The doors were numbered here too, odd to the left, even to the right. He tried the first door. Locked. He tried the one opposite. Locked as well.

So too were the next three pairs of doors.

Then the ninth opened.

He turned on the flashlight. An old man lay asleep on a bed, hooked up to a heart monitor and breathing through thin plastic tubes fitted to his nose. He was wearing Snoopy pyjamas.

Max heard someone stir in the room and moved the beam away from the bed. A younger man was curled up on a foldaway close by, and a few feet from him, another man was dozing in a chair.

Max left quietly.

The next few doors were locked. He was more than halfway down the corridor.

Door 13 opened, but the room didn't have anyone in it.

He continued.

Door 14: locked. Door 15: locked.

Door 16: open.

He crept in.

The curtains were half-parted on a view of the ocean: flat and calm, the colour of silvery soot, two speedboats circling in opposite directions, concentric rows of winking marker buoys bouncing lightly up and down in the water.

He turned on the torch. The beam met the bedside table: a swan-shaped vase filled with bright yellow and pink orchids, a bowl piled high with untouched fresh fruit, a glass of water, a white telephone, several bottles and capsules of pills, a box of Kleenex, and jutting over the edge, a book – *The Audacity of Hope* by Barack Obama.

He moved the beam across to the bed. Again, he'd come to the wrong room. The patient – another old man – was sleeping, almost upright, on a high bank of pillows. His head was so shrunken it seemed to be sinking into his yellow nightgown, the collar of which gaped around it like a toothless but expectant maw. His skin clung to his skull, as though it had been drizzled over the bone and left to set, waxen and opaque, the colour of cataracts reflecting a sandy shore. What hair he had clung stubbornly to the front and sides of his scalp in tight white florets. And there was a smell coming from his body, mingling with the sweet perfume of the orchids and fruit. It was an odour of medicated exhaustion, of slow death with the edges blunted and the countdown muddled, of a life close to the finish line.

Max switched off the torch and was about to leave when the patient called out to him.

413

'*Quién es usted?*'

The voice was groggy, withered and androgynous.

'Who are you?' it asked again, clearer this time, bolder.

And it was a woman's voice – an American woman's voice.

He flashed the torch back to the bed and found that she was looking right at him.

Vanetta Brown.

56

She turned on the bedside lamp and he wished she hadn't. She was hard to look at, hard to take in, hard to relate to the person whose face he'd memorised from the photographs. Cancer had all but erased her; reduced her to an outline, a faint tracing-paper sketch of someone she used to be, propped up by a stack of pillows and an adjustable bed. She was bone and cartilage dressed up in a loose and crumpled suit of flesh. Yet her eyes, though sunk back in their sockets, still had that defiant, penetrating glare, all haughty rectitude and fury; undimmed, unbeaten, unrepentant.

Max took off his cap and drew closer to her.

'You don't know me. My name is Max Mingus. I'm ... I've been looking for you,' he said. 'Sarah Dascal told me you were here.'

'How is she?'

'She's well.'

'And the children?'

'They're well.'

'I'm not going to see them again,' she said matter of factly. 'Do you know what that's like? Knowing you're never going to see someone you love again?'

'Can't say I do,' he said.

'It's like seeing the future. And that's never a good thing.' Her voice was an exhausted rasp scratching across a parched throat, sandpaper rubbing on hot stone. Her lips had thinned and become encrusted with dry, flaking skin.

She pointed to a chair near the bedside cabinet and motioned him to bring it over. The gesture was feeble, an approximate move, bereft of motility. The room was far bigger than he'd imagined it would be. There were places the light hadn't reached, corners screened off by darkness.

She pushed herself up a little, struggling those few inches. He wanted to help, because the effort she was making to accomplish something so simple was painful to watch, but he didn't.

'How did you get here?' she asked.

'It doesn't matter.'

'Where have you come from?'

'Miami.'

'That's a long way.'

'It's not that far.'

'You know what I mean,' she said looking at him, at his face, at the top of his head. 'What's the weather there like?'

'I don't know. I've been here a while. Looking for you,' he said.

He'd expected to know what to say. His time was limited and he only really wanted to know one thing. *Did you have Joe killed?* But looking at her, a spirit marking time in a withered, pain-racked body, he was no longer sure what to ask. The question seemed almost pointless.

'You know I'm dying?'

Max nodded.

'I don't have long. Days, maybe ... Not too many more, I hope,' she said. 'Every time I close my eyes, I expect it to be the last time. Every time I open them I'm ... disappointed. Another morning, getting woken up by pain. Pain everywhere. Breakfast is pills. The pain goes away and then I just spend time floating. And waiting. I can't do anything. I can barely read. I can barely think. What's the point?'

He didn't know what to say. He felt awkward, intrusive. He suddenly didn't want to be here, regretted he'd even come.

She smiled weakly. 'I'm sorry to be so morbid. Comes with the territory. I've been feeling a bit better, lately. It's strange. It

416

happened to my mother-in-law too . . . Just before she died. She started talking about going for walks, getting some air. A sudden optimism. She never did. You know what I really want now? I want to go home.'

'To Havana?'

'That's not home.'

'To America?'

She blinked twice and nodded slightly. 'I want to be with my family. With my daughter and my husband. When are you going back?'

'I don't know,' he said. 'Soon, I suppose.'

'Can you take me with you?'

'To Miami?'

'Yes.'

He almost said no, but caught himself. 'They'll arrest you,' he said.

'What's left of me.' She managed a chuckle. 'They're welcome to it.'

'You don't want to die in prison.'

'What difference does it make?' she said. 'Can I leave with you?'

'Why do you want to go back there?'

'To be buried with my daughter and my husband.'

'Won't you be flown home when you . . . When you go?' he asked.

'You know what happens when American fugitives die here, in Cuba? The American government refuses to allow their bodies into the country.' She smiled.

'I didn't know that.'

'Never underestimate our government's capacity for petty vindictiveness.'

He'd found a way into the question he wanted to ask. He'd take the long route, walk her back through her life and then forward, until they came to what he wanted to know.

'Vanetta,' he began. 'Can I call you Vanetta?'

417

She nodded.

'I'm a friend of Joe's . . . Joe Liston. There are some things I need to ask you. I know all about you – what you've been through. I've read all the files on those CDs Joe gave you. And I've put it together. I understand most of it, I really do.'

'What do you understand?' She leaned towards him a fraction, her bones creaking and popping, her body barely registering inside her nightdress.

'I know you didn't kill Dennis Peck,' he said.

'Everybody knows that. Especially the FBI. Yet they still put a price on my head and hung a label around my neck for something they *know* I didn't do. You know what they call me? A domestic terrorist,' she said bitterly. 'Dennis Peck's daughters grew up to hate me. And they don't even know the truth about their own father.'

She glared at him, the fire in her eyes momentarily overriding her weakness, cancelling out their frail body and its wasted, twig-like limbs.

'Dennis Peck was an undercover FBI agent,' said Max. 'He was in so deep that even now – dead – he's stayed in character. His family don't know a damn thing about him. They believe he was a detective in the Miami PD, who died a heroic death at your hands.'

She nodded. 'What else do you know?'

'Peck was part of a covert unit J. Edgar Hoover put together in the early sixties to infiltrate a network of mob-affiliated cops based in Florida. Those cops were headed up by Eldon Burns. He'd been doing business with the mob – the Trafficante crime family – for years. Drugs, prostitution, gambling, extortion, murder. The works.

'Burns did more than just look the other way in exchange for pay-offs and tip-offs. He was as good as a gangster himself. His cops helped organise the Trafficante's drug distribution network. And they carried out hits on those hard-to-get-to targets – witnesses in federal protection, top mobsters with armies of bodyguards.

'Now, mafia guys like to call themselves "connected", but Burns was the real deal, hooked up like the national grid. He worked closely with a political fixer, Victor Marko. Burns had politicians in his back pockets and businessmen in his front pockets. When something dirty needed to get done, he was the one they called.'

'Eldon Burns. Eldon ... Burns,' she whispered. 'He is an evil man.'

'*Is* ... ?' Max looked at her. The sharpness had gone from her eyes, which were fluttering. Max guessed it was the drugs, kicking at her head, disarranging her memory.

'. . . an evil man,' she repeated. 'Carry on.'

She was alert again.

'The Vietnam War was good for Burns. Troops were coming home strung out on smack. He saw an opportunity to get in on the game himself. To out-mob the mob,' said Max. 'One way or another, cops have always worked with criminals. It's the nature of the game. They use them as snitches. They let one carry on doing bad, so they can take down another doing far worse. It's all relative. When you're a cop, you either get in all the way or you don't get in at all.

'Burns and Abe Watson had worked with a drug dealer called Dan Styles. Halloween Dan. He used to sell reefer and pills in the ghetto, and then push heroin and coke to the upmarket crowd. Before 'Nam, heroin had been a rich man's drug. The only black people who could afford it were doctors or jazz musicians.

'Halloween Dan had a brother in the air force – Jerrod, a sergeant, stationed in Saigon. Him and Eldon came up with a scheme where Jerrod bought heroin in bulk from local suppliers and flew it into Hialeah airbase in Florida. Dan's people collected it. A third stayed in Miami, the rest went to the East Coast via Eldon's network of cops.'

'That's right,' she said. 'Heroin came into our neighbourhoods. It destroyed Overtown and Liberty City. Crime went way up. And all that good work we'd been doing – with education, job training, self-awareness – that was undone with a prick of a needle. Halloween Dan used to roll up on street corners in his Caddy and hand out free samples of that poison – getting brothers and sisters hooked, turning the recently emancipated back into slaves.'

She stopped to breathe. Her lungs made a swooning sound as the air pushed through crumbling passages.

'We tried reasoning with him,' she said. 'We even went to his headquarters, this bar he owned. Me and two others. I tried to appeal to his sense of community, his responsibility to his people, his decency. You know what he said? He said: "Bitch. Only colour I be interested in be orange 'n' green." And then he took me out into the street, in broad daylight, and made me kneel down. He stuck the barrel of his gun in my mouth and told me to suck it like I sucked my husband. Right there, in front of everyone. And I did it, because otherwise he would've blown my brains out. He said if he ever saw me in his bar again, he'd kill me and my family.'

She stopped and reached for her water, but the effort was beyond her strength. Max handed her the glass. She thanked him with a smile that radiated mostly from her eyes.

'If I lived by the law of the street, I would have killed Dan myself. Or sent people to do it,' she said. 'But if you follow the eye-for-an-eye, tooth-for-a-tooth dictum to its natural conclusion, everyone goes blind and nobody eats.'

'So you fought him another way?'

'Gandhi brought down the British in India by passive resistance. Dr King never preached violence,' she said. 'I organised the Black Jacobins to form picket lines outside Dan's drug houses, to stop people going in or out. I called sympathisers in the media and told them what was going on and what we were doing about it. Cameras and reporters turned up and filmed us. They filmed Dan as well, a few times. He tried to drive us out. He rolled up with a gang of armed men, trying to scare us off.

They always had dogs. But when he saw the cameras he left. This went on for two months. They killed Jacobins. They tried to firebomb the Jacobin House. We just intensified our efforts. If the white-controlled government couldn't beat us during civil rights, some two-bit punk couldn't either. Dan left Overtown and Liberty City. We turned the Jacobin House into a rehab facility and got everyone who walked in off smack. We thought we'd won.'

'And then came the raid?'

'Yes,' she said. 'Then came the raid. I knew who Eldon Burns was, locally. But I never met him personally. He ran that boxing gym. People had good things to say about him. Especially the kids he helped turn into fighters. They looked up to him. But people in Overtown and Liberty City were wary of Burns too, not because he was white or a cop, but because of his partner Abe Watson. Abe had a terrible, terrible reputation. He hated being black and he took it out on his own people.'

She paused, looked at Max a moment.

'Do you know Eldon Burns?' she asked. Her eyes were clear. Why was she referring to him in the present tense?

'Yes, I did,' said Max. 'I worked for him. Joe too. We were partners.'

'Joe hates him,' she said.

That present tense again.

'I know.'

'And you?'

'I was one of those kids who looked up to him. But then I grew up. Now I look down on him and everything he stood for.'

She scrutinised Max for a moment, looking at him in a way she hadn't, trying to see through him, trying to work out his play. She hadn't asked what he wanted from her, which he'd found strange. She'd accepted his presence in the room without question. It was almost as if she'd been expecting him. He'd put it

421

down to the drugs and the limited time she had left. Or maybe Joe had told her about him.

'I was in Miami Springs when the raid happened. I was visiting my aunt Cecile. She was sick. I'd spent the night with her,' she said. 'I heard the police gave no warning when they attacked the Jacobin House. They fired tear gas through the windows and came in shooting. Eldon Burns and Abe Watson led it. Watson shot my husband and daughter. And he killed Dennis Peck. I read about it years later, in the FBI's autopsy and ballistic reports.'

Max had read those reports twice. The FBI had secretly exhumed the bodies of Dennis Peck and Ezequiel and Melody Dascal to carry out autopsies. The remains were charred from the fire that had supposedly swept through the Jacobin House during the raid – but FBI tests and witness statements proved that the blaze was really started after the raid ended. Ezequiel had been shot twice in the back at point-blank range with a .45. The FBI coroner concluded that the bullets had gone through him and hit Melody, whom he had been shielding. Dennis Peck was also shot twice with a .45 – in the chest and in the head, at close range, execution/put-him-out-of-his-misery style. The FBI broke into the Miami PD's forensic-evidence lab and removed the bullets taken from the bodies. The ballistics showed they'd come from the same gun – Abe Watson's.

'How did you get out of the country?' asked Max.

'Joe,' she said. 'Joe knew where I was. He came to my aunt's house, while the raid was happening. I wanted to go back to Overtown, for my . . . my daughter,' Vanetta stopped. Her eyes filmed over with a wash of tears. She wiped at them and collected herself. 'My daughter was in the children's playroom with my husband . . . Do you know why we called her Melody?'

Max shook his head.

'When I was pregnant, Ezequiel would put his ear to my belly and swear he could hear her singing in there.' Vanetta's tears flowed. Max handed her some tissues from the box on the bedside table. She wiped her eyes and blew her nose and put the tissues up her sleeve. It was probably something she'd done out of habit over many years, but her arms were so skinny the ball of soft paper slipped out and fell on the floor by Max's feet. She didn't notice.

'Joe put me in the trunk of his car. He hid me in his apartment for a few days,' she said. 'I stayed at his place while the police looked for me. They looked everywhere. A real manhunt. But they didn't think to look in a cop's house. And then Joe brought an FBI agent round. I was moved to a safe house. I was there a week. The agent interviewed me about what had happened. You read my interview transcript?'

'Yes,' he said. 'How did you get to Cuba?'

'The FBI agent arranged the boat. Joe took me to the Keys. I sailed from there.' She nodded.

'Joe did that?'

'Yes. You look surprised.'

'How much did you know about Joe ... then?'

'That he was an FBI informant?' she asked. 'I guessed as much when he brought the agent to his house, from the way they interacted.'

'You hadn't suspected him before?'

'No.'

'And how did that make you feel – when you found out?'

'To be honest with you, I no longer cared. I mourned my daughter and my husband for a long, long time. It took ten years to – not "move on" exactly, but to accept that they were dead. Do you understand what I mean?'

'Yes,' he said. 'I do.'

'Joe – when he started coming here, he explained it all to me. Why he'd done it. And I understood. He was fair. He only reported what he saw,' she said. 'The Black Jacobins were never criminals. We never used violence. We never had guns. And we never sold drugs. We weren't separatists. We weren't racists. It was about empowering black people. Giving them a voice.

Uniting them as one. That way, I thought, we could be like the Cubans in Miami. Only nationally. A force to be reckoned with. It's because of the Cubans there that this stupid embargo exists today. Them and their money, buying politicians. I wanted us – black American people – to have that kind of power.'

'Why didn't the Feds move on Eldon?' asked Max.

'I don't know,' she said. 'Joe said Burns was very powerful. That he had dirt on everyone. Including Hoover. There were rumours about Hoover's sexuality, the kind that could have ruined him if they'd had substance. Joe reckoned Eldon might have had that substance, that smoking gun.'

'So why didn't they clear your name at least?'

'I wasn't exactly innocent,' she said. 'We were a left-wing organisation. I modelled the Black Jacobins on the socialism you see in Cuba. I had strong ties with Fidel Castro then. It would have been embarrassing for them to exonerate someone who was guilty of "working with the enemy". The Cold War was on. There'd been the missile crisis. There were reds under the bed. Even if I'd been cleared as a cop-killer, I'd still be guilty of being a commie, a red.

'Besides, the Miami PD had built a very strong case against me. Eye-witnesses in the raid – people I'd known all my life – swore they saw me shoot Dennis Peck. They supposedly found bullet casings with my prints on them at the scene. And I'd fled to Cuba. It was open and shut. The guilty don't run.

'And also ... of course, there's that other thing. That *main* thing. I'm black. And it was the South then. Why, not fifteen years before, Jim Crow had told Rosa Parks to move to the back of the bus. My innocence was largely academic.'

Max felt something close to admiration for her. And this confused him. He'd expected to talk to someone deranged by hatred – a hatred that, while justified and understandable, had long since become irrational, twisted by time and failing memory, and sharpened to a point by the bitterness of unacknowledged injustice. Yet he heard nothing of the kind. He understood why people had fallen under her spell. Even now she had the power to move and inspire. And this was making the question he was coming close to putting to her all that much harder to ask.

He looked out the window at the bluey-black ocean, the blinking buoys swaying on the gentle waves.

'The world changed. Communism collapsed. America got itself a new set of enemies,' she said. 'Joe visited me regularly. He was determined to clear my name. But then I got sick. And that changed things. I was on a clock now. I had a limited amount of time to get things done.'

She looked him straight in the eye.

'To get what done?' Max could feel his heart beating faster, that old familiar blood rush when he smelled a confession about to spill.

'People always die before they intend to. And they always leave a mess somewhere. I'm determined not to. I'm determined to put things in order.'

The words raced right out of Max's mouth before he realised. 'Eldon Burns is dead. They're saying you had him killed.'

She stared at him blankly. Her eyes dulled and dulled until he was staring at two pieces of felt.

Then she blinked. And frowned.

'What did you just say?'

'Eldon Burns. He was murdered in Miami last month.'

'What? When? Last month?' She shifted a little closer to him. 'Did you say *murdered*?'

'Yes. Shot. Twice. Through the eyes,' he said. 'And guess what? Two casings found at the scene had your prints on them.'

'Last – last *month* you say? But . . . *My prints?*'

She tried to laugh sarcastically, but coughed feebly instead.

'You're saying *I* killed him?'

'No, Vanetta, not me. They are. The Miami PD.'

'Is this why you're here? *To bring me in?*'

'No. Not at all.' Max shook his head. 'I don't blame you for wanting Eldon dead. He and Abe Watson killed your husband and daughter, and they killed Dennis Peck and framed you for it. All with the same gun. And that very gun – Abe Watson's .45 – was used to kill Eldon Burns. Your prints were on the casings they found at the scene.'

'That's *ridiculous*.' She was more astonished than angry. 'After everything we've just talked about – about how I was set up.'

'For what it's worth, I had my doubts from the start,' he said. 'It seemed implausible, to say the least. Unless you thought time was running out to do things the right way.'

'Do I sound that twisted to you?'

'No,' he admitted.

'You said, *they've* said, I "had" Eldon Burns killed? Who did I "have" do this?'

'A man with a hare lip – a Cuban.'

'You don't mean *Osso*?'

'You know him?'

'Of course I know him. I've known him since he was a child. I just saw him this morning.'

Max's heart skipped a beat.

'Where?'

'He lives here.'

'In the hospital?'

'No. In a house on the other side of the island. Why are you asking me this?'

'Osso killed Eldon,' said Max. 'And . . . he killed Joe too.'

Her mouth dropped. She put her hand over it. Closed her eyes. Breathed. Her lungs fought the air. Her chest wheezed. 'What did you just say? Joe's . . . Joe's *dead*? Is that what you just said?'

'Yes. That's why I'm here, Vanetta.'

'Joe was . . . was *murdered*?'

'Right in front of me. On Halloween. Same gun. Same killer. Same prints on the casings. Yours. Someone's framed you.'

Her eyes wandered. From Max. Around the room. To the table. Then back to Max.

'Joe is . . . Joe is my *friend.* Joe is . . . *dead?*'

'That's why I'm here, Vanetta.'

'I'd never hurt anyone . . . not even Eldon Burns. Or Abe Watson. God knows they deserve it. And I would never ever even think bad of Joe. He saved my life. He risked everything coming here to try and clear my name,' she said, crying. 'And you're saying . . . they think I . . . I had him *killed?*'

And Max knew for sure, without a doubt, that she was innocent. Someone had got her to handle the bullets, probably when she was asleep or whacked out in a painkiller daze. Someone had set her up as a cop-killer. Again. Someone who knew her history.

But why? Why her? And why them?

'You said Osso lives here. Is it with the man who owns the island? Who is this man? What's his name?'

She was sitting up, angry, trembling, feeble, her eyes bulging with anger.

She couldn't talk.

'Your deputy Elias Grimaud introduced you to this man. He funded your centres during the Special Period. Who is he? What's his name? Please tell me. Tell me and I'll leave.'

He reached out and took her arm. He cupped her wrist. Barely a pulse. He felt her eroded muscles reacting against his touch.

'Please, Vanetta. They killed Joe. Your friend . . . my friend. Our friend.'

Behind him, there came a sound. Two quiet taps. It sounded like a knock at the door.

But it wasn't that.

It wasn't that all.

Max turned, and a mighty pain exploded at the base of his neck, mushrooming into his head, rattling and blurring his vision.

He tried to stand. He tried to get his gun. But the room was tilting left and right, the floor was suddenly fluid, a rolling wave. And the pain in his head was intensifying.

The last thing he saw before he blacked out was Vanetta Brown looking at the person behind him. She was screaming, but he couldn't hear her.

And he realised that they hadn't been alone.

57

He opened his eyes to a bright blue-white blur.

First thoughts: it was daylight somewhere, morning – and he had a hangover, a great big fucken' hangover. Just *when* had he started drinking again? And how long had he been out?

His head was throbbing.

His mouth was dry and the light was frying his eyes. Typical post-binge syndrome. He shut them tight. He got a little relief, the pressure in his skull eased, the pain got turned down a few bars.

Then he remembered:

Vanetta Brown.

Who is this man? What's his name?

The blow to the back of his neck.

Then nothing.

Now this.

He breathed in deep. The air scorched his nostrils. The smell was powerful and familiar; commonplace, universal, vital – and nostalgic. It was a smell he used to love as a kid.

But it was overpowering.

And dangerous.

Gasoline.

His eyes flicked open in alarm, his vision suddenly crystal clear.

But what the fuck was he looking at?

*

A beach in broad daylight, viewed from high up.

He knew the view.

He knew it well.

It was his view, the one from his penthouse.

Miami Beach, south-west end of Collins Avenue.

He blinked.

It was a video, shot from his seafront balcony, playing on the biggest flatscreen TV he'd ever seen – a solid, hi-tech megalith of plastic and plasma beaming out an image so specious and vibrant he could practically smell the ocean through the fumes.

Somebody had gotten into his home and filmed this.

The video could have been shot any time it wasn't raining or cold – which was most of the year round in Miami. The beach was busy with sun-worshippers, little black dots doing their lazy to and fro across the cosmetic white sands.

He tried to move, to stand up, but the furthest he got was a slight upward lean of the torso and a minor shrug of the shoulders. He couldn't physically leave his seat or change much about his posture. His wrists were rope-bound to the legs of the chair he'd been placed on, the knots so tight his fingertips were cold from constricted circulation. Someone had similarly trussed up his legs at the ankles. He was barefoot, but he could hardly feel the ground on his soles. He couldn't even wiggle his toes. They were numb.

The metal chair had been bolted to the floor, the rivets shiny and new-looking, reflecting the glow from the TV.

The floor had been painted matt black, as had the walls and ceiling. He couldn't gauge the size of the room. It felt both small and vast, confined and huge, verging on the limitless.

Something on the floor caught his eye: crude white markings several feet wide and several feet long. He turned his head to make them out properly. Hieroglyphics, rendered in a glistening chalky paste with the texture and consistency of cake icing, only laid on thicker.

He was looking at the outline of a coffin with three crosses inside.

He recognised the style but his head was too scrambled and his senses too overloaded to place it.

He scanned the rest of the floor.

The coffin formed part of a bigger design, one that took up as much of the floor as he could see. Its core component – its very nucleus – was him. He'd been tied and bolted to the middle of a great inverted cross with beams that ended in sharp, stake-like points. Separate drawings floated around the spaces between the beams.

The paste sketch to his immediate right was a snake bursting from an egg positioned upright in a nest – *crown?* – of thorns. The serpent's body was formed of a mere three wavy lines, but its massive head had been carefully rendered: a semi-human face with diamond-shaped eyes, sharp, tapering brows, a thick-lipped mouth, two sabre tusks for front teeth, and a long forked tongue, which had lassoed a startled bird by the neck. The bird was a bald eagle.

Max was confused.

Then scared.

His heart began to pound, a desperate fist slamming at his chest, stodgy echoes rising from the well of his bones. His neck throbbed.

He knew exactly what he was looking at, exactly what he was sitting in, but he couldn't understand why. Nor could he begin to comprehend how he'd gotten from questioning Vanetta Brown to here. His head was still too fucked to shake sense out of his situation.

But his fear was mounting by the second.

He looked at the drawing behind him.

He could see a stickman on a boat. An unseen hand was pulling it, dragging at a rope attached to its prow. In a corner, in the distance, across the water, was an American flag, flying back to front.

431

The final drawing depicted a grinning skull sporting a top hat, tilted rakishly to the side. The skull had one eye, painted bright green.

Bullshit naif.

He knew where he was.

He'd been here before.

Not in this place of course, but in this situation: tied to a chair, in the middle of a voodoo *vévé*, the ceremonial markings drawn to honour a particular god or to summon a spirit.

He interpreted the *vévé*, reading the images in the intended sequence: anticlockwise, starting with the skull.

This represented Baron Samedi, dweller of cemeteries, stealer of souls, the voodoo god of death. Baron Samedi was habitually depicted as a skeletal Fred Astaire, tapdancing around grave-yards in a hat and tails, singing in the pain. Yet here he'd been given an additional feature and an uncommon one – that bright-green eye. Max studied it a moment, isolating it from the skull, removing the context. It was emanating a glow, a radiance. And it was very familiar.

Of course . . .

It was the Eye of Providence – the same all-seeing eye that topped the unfinished thirteen-step pyramid on the back of every dollar bill.

Baron Samedi had been *watching*.

Baron Samedi had unfinished business.

With him.

And it had something to do with money. Money was at the root of it.

'It' began to fall into place, quickly and terribly.

Joe and Eldon had been shot through the eyes.

Max was the stickman on the boat. He'd been lured here from America by a person he couldn't see. And America was inverted; it had turned against him.

Wendy Peck.

She'd found out about the money he'd brought back from Haiti.

432

She'd coerced him into coming here and looking for Vanetta Brown.

His mouth went dry.

His pulse was racing.

The room felt as small and tight as the trunk of a car.

He looked to the snake and the eagle. The approximation of the national emblem, the heart of the Presidential seal, was him again. He was American, he'd worked for the system. So this went back to something he'd done in his cop days, to something he'd done with Eldon and Joe.

And it was this:

He'd laid the egg the serpent sprang from. He'd created his own worst enemy; an enemy who'd always been with him, part of him – and so close he hadn't even noticed.

Lastly, the coffin and its three crosses. That was easy. That represented three deaths.

Eldon's, Joe's and his.

He was going to die here.

Soon.

Who is the man? What is his name?

Max knew now.

It was Boukman.

Solomon Boukman.

But he couldn't quite believe it.

Nor understand it.

He looked around the room.

'Show yourself!' he yelled.

His voice came back at him faintly. Which told him the place he was in was borderline cavernous.

'Show yourself!'

The room seemed empty, but he didn't feel alone. He sensed someone there, a presence – waiting, watching, taking its time to manifest itself. Boukman always did like his entrances.

The *vévé* was encircled by a wide ring of votive candles slowly melting on high silver sticks. The bodies of the thick purple, black and red candles were studded with animal teeth, broken glass, razor blades and run clean through with long nails. They'd been positioned well away from the *vévé*, because the paste was the source of the gasoline smell.

In between the candlesticks sat white porcelain bowls, some filled with water, others with red liquid, probably blood.

'*Show yourself!*' he yelled again.

He jerked his head around, side to side, back as far as he could twist, then forward.

The image on the screen suddenly changed.

Again, he knew the view.

He knew it well.

All too well.

Room 30 of the Zurich Hotel. Those bird-shaped mirrors on the walls.

Rudi Milk's porno flick was playing on the screen. 'Fabiana' and 'Will' were kissing and groping and stroking each other, their clothes coming off, as fingers popped buckles, unhooked clasps and straps, and lowered zips. Their exchanges returned to him from memory, the voices in sync with the action: Will mumbling, Fabiana laughing.

But no sound was coming from the TV.

No sound at all.

Then the screen twitched and the image cut out for a second, and that high-pitched, squealing static he remembered from the last and only time he'd watched the film came at him from every part of the room, stabbing at his head.

Yet he noticed a difference – not in the sound – but in the film itself. Something had just flashed up, something that had nothing to do with porn.

A solitary image he'd missed, both now and before.

As if the television was tuned to his thoughts, the film rewound to a few instants before the cut. It started playing forward again, only in slow – *slow* – motion, frame by frame, the action dealt out like gigantic poker cards.

There came the static burst, the sound slowed down, corresponding to the film's arrested pace.

What he'd taken for white noise was really a speeded-up voice speaking a single phrase.

A voice he recognised.

A voice altered with time and age, and . . . nature.

A voice saying something he'd last heard in 1982, in a Haitian accent – that melodious fusion of African and French, negotiating the hardness of English by stretching and softening its clipped vowels.

It was the voice of Solomon Boukman. His tongue had been forked. Eva Desamours – his lover and fortune-teller – had slit his tongue down the middle and he'd worn a brace to stop it rejoining. It was an image she'd cultivated for him, to make him appear like a voodoo spirit, a demon come to earth; something to scare people into believing he was more than human. The halves of his tongue rejoined when he was in prison, nature healing the breach. According to his medical records, his tongue had thickened in the process, grown heavier, and this affected his speech. When he spoke too loudly, he literally hissed. He'd become his image and his image became him.

'You give me reason to live.'

Or that's what Max thought he heard at first.

But no, it wasn't *quite* that.

That was his memory talking over what he'd actually heard. Which was:

'You *gave* me reason to live.'

Past tense.

Things had moved on.

Max felt cold sweat beading on his temples, a colder feeling in his stomach, pains and tremors in his legs. He was almost glad to be sitting down because the chair cushioned the shock.

Then it got worse.

The film had paused. 'Fabiana' and 'Will' weren't on the screen any more, and neither was he looking at a hotel room.

Something different was being shown to him.

And yes, he knew the view.

He knew it well.

How many times had he seen that picture? How many times had he looked it over? A million?

He'd defined and redefined its meaning, only to dismiss his conclusions and reappraise the image he was seeing again here. He'd looked at it in different ways, certainty following mystification.

La Coupole bar, Haiti, December 1996. Solomon Boukman stood right behind him, holding a gun to his head, smiling broadly. Max, oblivious, eyes lost in the distance. The gun was his own, a Beretta. Boukman had slipped it out of his holster without him noticing and turned it on him. As if to say: 'I could have killed you with your own gun.' Or: 'Look at me, standing right behind you and you can't even see me.' Or: 'You could die right now and be none the wiser.' Boukman had made sure he'd gotten the picture before he left Haiti. He'd written 'You give me reason to live' on the back of it. As in: I haven't forgotten about you, I'll *never* forget about you. The picture had been in one of the bags he carried his reward money home in.

The money . . .

Baron Samedi's *dollar-green* eye . . .

And then Max felt that old fear come back to him. In 1981, Boukman had tortured and almost killed him. Boukman had fucked him up good, fucked him up the way childhood traumas fuck up adults, left him scarred soul-deep.

He started shaking.

This was about to get *way* worse.

The film resumed. The couple were still frolicking. He watched, still unable to switch off the mental soundtrack.

The film slowed to a choppy crawl and then froze as another spliced-in image flashed up.

Max visiting Sandra's grave, taken from the side with a zoom lens. He'd put some fresh flowers by the headstone and was staring down at them.

The film resumed, but slowly, until it arrived at the next picture.

Someone – Boukman? – pissing on the gravestone and the flowers, the petals flying off the stems as if leaping out of the way in disgust.

And Max tried to jump out of his chair. He was angry. Mad. Mad enough to kill. He pulled and tugged and writhed and struggled. The ropes bit into the skin of his wrists and ankles, and tore. His arms and legs were so numb he didn't feel the pain.

'*You cowardly motherfucker!*'

The skinflick played on regardless. And the horrors kept interrupting.

Yolande Pétion, his former business partner, freshly dead on the floor of her house, shotgunned in the face.

Max and Tameka. Their first dinner date, at the sushi place on Lincoln Road. Tameka looking over his shoulder, right into the furtive camera, smiling.

She knew Boukman. She'd seen him.

Max's blood ran cold.

'*You gave me reason to live.*'

Tameka and him in the Bahamas, on the beach. Tameka lowering her sunglasses and looking at the camera again, smiling conspiratorially, while Max's back was turned to the ocean.

Vegas. Max asleep in hospital, face bruised, arm in a cast.

The fire that had burned down his marital home: his money, taken out of the safe and stuffed into a suitcase, flames close by.

Max lying in the street outside his house, unconscious. Boukman had burned it down, taken his money and saved him. Saved him for another day.

Baron Samedi's *dollar-green* eye . . .

Boukman had used the money to pay Milk to make the film. Boukman had turned his money against him.

His drug-money reward: the money of death.

Boukman had killed Milk and the people at his house, everyone associated with the film. He'd buried the bodies in the garden with the money he'd paid Milk. It was Max's money – and Max had dug it up, and turned it into the cops. *Just as he was supposed to have done in the first place.*

Tameka, lying in what looked like a desert, a hole in her head, blood soaking into the sand, a shadow falling over the body.

Fabiana and Will were done. She was complimenting him on his magic wand and stroking it with a forefinger. '*Call me Harry Focker, baby*,' mouthed Will. But Max didn't hear him. Instead he heard Boukman's voice on the soundtrack:

'*You gave me reason to live.*'

Abe Watson's .45, covered in dirt and worms.

Will lay naked on the bed and fanned his crotch with a menu, while Fabiana showered.

Eldon Burns coming out of the 7th Avenue gym. Had Eldon seen Boukman before he'd died? Of course he had.

Max and Joe eating together at the Mariposa.

Will left the hotel room in blue workmen's overalls and a beanie hat.

Every client Max had worked for in the previous five years, posed where he'd last met them. They were all smiling. He wondered if they weren't dead too. 'Clients' Boukman had sent him.

His whole life, from 1996 to the present, had just flashed by him.

'*You gave me reason to live.*'

And the film ended.

The screen went blank.

For a while he was sitting in near darkness, the glow of the candles sucked into the black surroundings, the light they emanated feeble.

The view of Miami Beach returned to the screen.

And Solomon Boukman spoke to him.

*

438

'Do you know what I meant when I told you, "You give me reason to live"?' Boukman's voice came from behind the TV, but seemed as close as a whisper in his ear. 'You saved my life then. I wish you hadn't.'

Up to that moment Max had been angry – and scared – and stunned. Boukman's presence tipped him into fury. He wanted to get at him and kill him. Kill him for what he'd done to Joe, kill him for pissing on his wife's grave – just plain fucken' kill him. He didn't care about his motives, his reasons. Fuck all that. He just wanted him dead.

He redoubled his efforts to break free. He thrashed and jerked and bucked against the restraints. He pulled and pushed. The flesh on his arms and legs ripped off in raw bloody gashes. The ropes yielded a fraction but no more than that and not nearly enough.

'I didn't want to live, but you *made* me live,' continued Boukman calmly. 'You gave me the kiss of life. You put your breath inside me. Part of you became me. My life became tied to yours. You gave me reason to live.'

His voice still possessed its erstwhile emotionless, monotonous quality, as well as a threatening sibilance. Yet it was also grainier, a few notes deeper and a little more strained than the one he'd remembered last hearing at his trial. Like him, Boukman had grown much older.

The TV was replaying the Zurich Hotel footage.

'For thirteen years I was in prison. When I got released, I had a lot of scores to settle.'

The TV began to move slowly left, pushed by someone tall and thin – too tall to be Boukman – an outline, slipping in and then out of the available light.

The TV stopped in a far corner.

Max peered into the dark void in front of him and saw a faint suggestion of a person, couched in the blackness. A pinkish light was coming from the ground. When Max looked closer, he saw the flaps of an open trapdoor and steps leading down.

'Why didn't you just . . . kill me?' he said.

'Revenge is never *enough*,' said Boukman. 'It was too easy to walk up behind you and put a bullet in your brain. I could have done that. I chose not to. How do you follow a murder? Imagine: you're dead and I'm looking down on your corpse, and I *still* hate you, I still want to hurt you. I want you to come back to life so I can kill you all over again until I'm satisfied. But I can't do that. Because you're already dead. So what do I do? How do I *keep on* killing you? How do I get *enough*?

'I do it little by little, piece by piece. I take *everything* away from you. Everything you love, everything you care about, everything you know, everything you're sure of. I kill your friends, I steal your money, I burn down your house with all your memories, I take away your livelihood. And I watch what it does to you. How the sadness cripples you. How the loneliness eats you up. How the poverty confines you, keeps you captive.

'And then I start *really* fucking with you,' Boukman said. His voice was detached from the words, as if he were reading out letters on an eye chart. 'I could have let you die in your house when I burned it down. But I made sure you got out alive. So you could start over, with next to nothing.

'I gave you a livelihood. You advertised yourself as a private detective, as I knew you would. What else could you do? I gave you clients. I invented them. I sent you actors playing cuckolds and adulterers. The work was beneath you, an insult to your talents, a humiliation. But you *had* to do it because you needed the money. I was paying them to pay you out of your own pocket. I was using *your* money to pay *your* salary. You thought you were watching them getting cheated on, when really it was you who was being cheated, you who was getting fucked.'

Max had stopped struggling. He felt tired and his wrists and ankles were burning and bloody. All the while, as he'd been watching the pictures flash up – Boukman's hand offstage, masquerading as bad luck or a cruel twist of fate, fucking up his life – he'd had a winded feeling in his gut, like he was stuck in

440

a downbound elevator, moving too fast. He knew he was beaten. But, really, when he thought about it, he'd lost a long time ago. Ever since he'd decided to keep that money he brought back from Haiti.

He considered Boukman's will, the will to do all those things – the planning, the choreography and, above all, the patience. Boukman hadn't acted out of anger. Anger had a definite end, a peak as sharp as its slope. Boukman had acted out of hatred. A hatred so long nurtured, it had become transparent and dispassionate: something he'd indulged, like a hobby.

Somewhere, a small part of him even admired the cruel genius of it, the clinical retribution – even if it had all been directed his way.

'And then there was Tameka. That whore. I paid her. And you ... you almost *married* her.' Max thought he heard Boukman chuckle. 'I could have paid her to become the second Mrs Mingus, if I'd wanted to. But that would have been too cruel.'

'Crueller than killing her?' asked Max, knowing that the question was as good as rhetorical.

'You didn't have to come here, Max. You had a clear choice. Prison or Cuba. But I knew you'd come. Just as I knew you wouldn't watch the film in time to save Joe Liston. You're too old, too slow, too blind. I know you well, Max Mingus. You look, but you can't see. You never could. Because you never wanted to.'

Boukman glanced over at the TV and the person stood next to it.

'You killed Joe because he was my *friend*?'

'That's right.'

'And Eldon? Why kill him? We'd fallen out.'

'We were almost colleagues once, you and me.'

Max immediately got what he meant. 'You were working with Eldon all those years ago?'

'How do you think I got away with what I did for so long?'

441

'Figures.' He'd as good as worked that out from the FBI files he'd read. Eldon had protected Halloween Dan, rendered him untouchable. The only problem was, Dan refused to keep a low profile; he just had to let the world and its mother know who he was. Boukman had been the very opposite – a man with a million faces, none of them his own.

'Eldon Burns turned on me,' said Boukman. 'When you and Liston were investigating me, he had a simple choice. Get rid of you or replace me. He chose you over me. No surprise. You were his heir apparent. He'd corrupted you your whole life, but you didn't realise it because you never really knew him like I did, saw him like I did. It was all right there in front of you, his evil, his corruption. All you had to do was *look*, Max. But like I said, you can't *see*.'

'That's why you had Eldon and Joe shot through the *eyes*, right? Some kind of message to me?'

'You're slow, but you always get there . . . in the end. Which is what this is . . . the end.'

'Did you tell Vanetta Brown who you really are?'

Boukman didn't answer.

There was a stillness in the room. On the TV the dead pornstars were fucking each other's brains out.

'Do you have anything to say, Max? Any last words?'

'Yeah. I do,' he said. 'You know, I thought *I* was fucked up, Solomon. But you . . . you take that cake and eat it. And you lick your fingers too.'

The dark space Max had been staring at shifted, grew a fraction lighter, as if a little of the night had been sucked from it.

'Say hello to Eldon from me,' said Boukman.

He walked away, slowly and soundlessly, down the lit steps.

58

Max realised he'd seen the tall, scrawny figure standing by the TV before. He recognised the pose, the way he carried himself. The glow of the screen and the nearby candlelight picked out the metallic printed patterns on his shirt – diagonal birds, either geese or pelicans, flying in formation, beak to ass, hem to shoulder. The birds were the same shape as the die-cut mirrors on the walls of the Zurich. He was looking at the very same man he'd spotted across the street from the hotel, the one who'd been staring at him when he got the call from Joe telling him Eldon was dead.

The man picked up a black plastic bucket by the handle and came over, carefully avoiding stepping on any of the *vévé*. He'd tucked his pants into gumboots, whose thick rubber soles made his every dainty, careful step squeal on the concrete.

When he was close, Max got a good look at the face Eldon and Joe had seen right before they died, the very same face he'd seen on Wendy Peck's surveillance photo – and whose even more deformed, embryonic version had hung on Vanetta Brown's wall.

There was still something of that child in him now. The upper half of his features was fragile, almost tender; the small, flat forehead, with its smooth and shiny brow, unmarked by worry or time; his eyes were wide and vacant lots, waiting on experience.

But the damaged mouth dominated. The thick bisection, making the right half of his lower face hang slightly askew from the left, as if waiting for a hand to slide it back into place. The middle lips, thin, ragged and scaly, like shards of broken glass threaded through razor wire; the ends overfilled dark brackets, a pair of fleshy screws keeping the rest in place.

'You're Osso, right?'

He didn't answer, but it was him all right.

He set the bucket down on a clear space, close to Max, who caught a full, intense hit of gasoline. His eyes burned and ran, his nose smarted at the fumes. He coughed and gagged and turned his head away.

Osso looked him over without expression, eyes reading him side to side, then up and down. He took a paintbrush out of his back pocket, crouched and dipped it into the bucket. He swirled the contents around a few turns, never once taking his eyes away from Max. When he'd finished, he tapped the brush to shake off the excess.

He squatted at Max's feet and painted on the paste. It was cold. When it touched the open wounds around his ankles they burned deep. Max gasped and groaned in agony.

Osso was the skinniest living, healthy person Max had ever seen. The knobs of his spinal bones protruded through the back of his shirt, making Max think of a giant lizard.

'You killing Eldon Burns, I can live with. I mean, if I'd known then what I do now, I'd've put two in him myself.'

Osso ignored him. He coated Max's feet all the way up the edge of his calves.

'But Joe ... *Joe Liston*? No. Not him. He was a fine upstand-ing man. His whole life, he only did good. And you .... you fucken' killed him anyway. You sack of shit. I know you'll say it wasn't personal, that you were only following that twisted fuck's orders. But you know what? I don't care. It doesn't matter. You pulled the trigger. You're just as bad. Just as guilty.'

Osso stopped painting to look at him. His mouth moved – only the middle, not the ends, and his lips parted, as if he were about to say something, but then they closed again. Max thought he saw anger flash across his eyes, clear and fast as lightning in an eclipse.

Osso stood up and walked behind Max.

Max felt the man's breath on the nape of his neck, passing over his scalp. Then Osso began brushing the paste on to his hands.

Max twisted his head around to look at him.

'That motherfucker adopted you, didn't he? You're his *boy*, ain'tcha? You call him *daddy*? You were born with a cleft palate. He had your face fixed and you were so grateful you became his bitch. That's the way it was, right? Say, can you even *talk* outta that fucken' thing?'

Osso continued what he was doing, but not in the same slow, careful way. When he got to the open sores on Max's wrists, he pressed the brush head down hard. Max screamed and jerked back and forth as the pain shot up his shoulders, frying and soldering his nerves.

'Hey?' Max gasped. 'How'd your *daddy* pay you for killing Joe? He promise you more *plastic surgery*? I bet he did. And you know what? He's right, 'cause you fucken' need it, you ugly motherfucker.'

Osso jabbed and twisted the brush into his wrist and held it there. Then he twisted it some more.

The pain doubled, then got even worse. It went all the way up the side of his head. Max screamed. His legs shook in the chair. He kicked out.

He . . . *kicked . . . out.*

Max'd felt his feet fly out and up. Free. No restraints.

He looked down. His feet had come out of the ropes.

When Osso had shoved the brush into his wrists, he'd bucked and pulled his legs so hard, his lubricated feet and calves had torn themselves loose.

And Osso hadn't noticed.

Max realigned his feet.

Osso painted halfway up his forearms, liberally slapping on the paste, caking his skin.

He gripped Max's chin with strong fingers and pulled his head back as far as it would go.

He bent to dip the brush in the bucket.

Max felt Osso's breath on his cheek and sensed the grip on his chin slacken a little.

Max glimpsed a chance.

And seized it.

The skull is the hardest part of the body, naturally designed and engineered to protect the brain, its most vital organ. At police academy they taught rookies the fine art of the head-butt. Max had been a good student.

He wrenched his head free with a sharp leftward twist and flicked it back at Osso's exposed chin.

He caught him right on the button, hard as any right hook.

Osso took it in a strange way.

Normally people went down for the count and beyond.

Not Osso.

The blow sent him shuffling sideways. Then he paused, staggered forward as if he'd been kicked in the ass, before veering off to one side, heading for the candles. For an instant Max feared he'd reach them and knock them over and incincrate them both. But Osso's self-preservation instincts just about outmuscled his urge to collapse and he stopped again, took a couple of halting backward steps and froze. He straightened himself and took a deep breath. He shook his head quickly once, then twice, confronting the twister that had taken his senses; realigning, rebooting.

He dropped the brush beside him. He turned to pick it up, but his rubber soles slid apart on the paste beneath his feet, smearing and blotching the *vévé*, as his long thin legs separated, painfully, in an impromptu split.

He caught himself with his palm. He took a knee. He breathed in deep. But he was inhaling heady, dizzying gasoline fumes and they were joining forces with the aftershocks of the blow he was trying to weather, and the two were fucking him up bad.

Somehow he managed to stand and face Max.

He looked at his captive through dull, glazed eyes.

He slapped at himself, but he missed and span all the way around.

Max stood up as far as he could – a semi-crouch – and tried to yank his arms free.

Osso went back down on one knee and put both palms on the ground, one right in the middle of the snake's head.

Again he managed to get back up, although his legs were rubber filled with cotton wool.

Max was pulling frantically, so hard the chair's bolts were starting to loosen.

Osso came towards him, tottering, his eyes rolling around the edges of his sockets like a sprung compass, more white than brown. His mouth was open, his tongue flopping out and sucking back in. He groped around his waist, hoisted up his shirt, exposing the pearl-handled grip of a pistol. He reached for it with his other hand. He didn't get to it. His hand closed around air. He looked down, perplexed. And then he fell to the floor, out cold, face down on the cross, inches away from Max.

Max yanked and heaved at his restraints. He used his legs as levers. He sat at the edge of the chair and tried to tear his hands free by brute force, but the knots were tight and fast.

Osso moaned. His leg twitched.

He'd be coming round soon.

Max intensified his efforts.

He put his right foot on the chair and leaned up with all his weight. His left wrist popped free. It was gashed and shredded open, blood dripping from his fingers.

Osso raised his head and grabbed at the ground. His hand slipped in the paste.

Max put his left foot on the chair and repeated the process.

Osso crawled to his knees.

Max prized and scraped his hand out.

Then he was free.

Max kicked Osso in the head, the flat of his foot connecting with Osso's chin. Osso's head twisted sharply round and he fell back with a bump.

Max snatched the gun out of Osso's waistband. Then he grabbed Osso by the hair, lifted his head up and smashed a fist into his already swollen jaw.

Osso was out cold.

The *vévé* was smeared all over the floor, the signs of their struggle marked out in blurred outlines and white footprints.

Max checked the gun – a full seven-round clip, plus one in the chamber.

He looked over at the basement steps, bathed in pink neon, and back at Osso.

He knew what to do.

Solomon Boukman emerged slowly from the basement.

He was in full sacrificial regalia – a white top hat with a red feather sticking out of its black-and-white-chequered band, a white tailcoat draped loose over his bare chest, white dress gloves, pressed black slacks and gleaming patent leather shoes. He'd painted his face in a two-tone layer of make-up, a black underlay with half a white skull over the right side.

He was chanting in Kreyol, invoking Baron Samedi, calling to him to rise from the depths, imploring to be made his vessel, to be vested with his power, to become his earthly hand – the taker of life, the giver of death, the stealer of souls. His voice was deep and sonorous, his enunciation clear and precise, unfettered by its lispy hiss.

Boukman entered the circle of candles. The flames fluttered and swayed on their wicks, a few going out as he passed, the thin smoke following him.

He advanced towards the figure in the chair, his steps slow and unhurried, his eyes catching and reflecting all the room's light, which danced over his entranced irises. He was completely oblivious to the mess that was the *vévé*.

*

448

Standing close to the man in the chair, Boukman crossed his arms and reached both hands into his coat.

He withdrew two short samurai swords, their shiny blades glowing green with the room's primary lights, the still-playing television and the ever-burning candles.

Boukman twirled the blades in the air, first in small arcs, his motions those of a conductor leading a large orchestra through a slow movement, building incrementally, note by note, instrument by instrument, to a dramatic crescendo.

Brutality undid his artistry, as the violence he was about to wreak took his arms. His poised curls turned to broad, heavy swings, the metal whistling crudely as it swiped and sliced through the air, itself becoming headier and thinner with petrol fumes.

Boukman's gesticulations got faster and wilder, the swords losing definition as metal and light fused and blended into a glowing, evanescent whole, leaving molten tracer loops hanging in space.

Boukman roared his final invocations in a fearsome, bestial growl, speaking Max's name, spitting at the man in the chair.

Then, suddenly, he stopped.

He raised the swords high above his head like horns.

He folded his arms one over the other and tightened his grip on the hilts.

He lowered the swords until he had the tip of the man's shoulders between the blades.

Osso had come to when Boukman was in mid-pirouette.

It had been a slow and arduous climb out of unconsciousness. He'd opened one eye, closed it, opened the other, closed it.

Then he'd come to, fully.

He breathed in and coughed and gagged and retched at the paste that covered his entire head and feet and hands.

He just had time to comprehend where he was and what was

449

about to happen, before the swords struck both sides of his neck at once, the razor-keen blades cutting clean through.

He carried a look of bewildered astonishment to the grave.

Boukman had the same look the instant he realised what he was about to do.

But his brain was a fraction too slow for his body. By the time he could have stopped himself, it was already too late.

Osso's blood geysered over his coat and chest and face.

Boukman stepped back, shocked, confused.

He looked around. Left, right, backwards, forwards.

And then he saw Max, who'd stepped out from the darkness.

Max underarmed the bucket of paste, splattering Boukman's front.

Boukman didn't move. He stood where he was, the bloody swords in his hands.

Max kicked two candlesticks over on to the *vévé*.

A gangway of flames opened up along the floor, fire whooshing up high into the air, almost kissing the ceiling, as it reached to all four points of the room within seconds.

Small flames pounced on Boukman's hat. Then they leaped down to his shoulders. One of his shoes caught fire. And then the tails of his coat.

No movement from Boukman. He stared at Max, seemingly oblivious to the blaze.

Max raised the gun and lined Boukman's head up in the sights.

He flicked off the safety.

Their eyes met.

And Max almost lowered the gun.

In the full light of the blaze, Max saw that it wasn't Boukman standing there.

It was Elias Grimaud. Vanetta's deputy, Osso's accomplice.

Boukman had always used doubles. This was no exception.

450

Had Boukman even *been* here?

'Where is he?' Max yelled.

Grimaud dropped the swords and started coming towards Max, walking through fire in a suit of burning clothes.

Max hesitated, couldn't take the shot, almost didn't want to. Grimaud was a goner. Let him burn.

But Max was covered in paste himself, a potential torch.

Grimaud reached out, his arms in flames, whether for help or to kill him, he didn't know.

Max fired twice. The first bullet hit Grimaud in the shoulder, the next in the chest.

Grimaud fell backwards, the incinerating *vévé* receiving his body whole and closing quickly around him.

Max watched the outline of his body burn a few moments more.

Then he ran for the basement.

It was empty.

No Boukman.

Nothing there but bare walls, a cement floor, three thick wooden beams holding up the ceiling, and pink neon tubes for lighting.

Boukman would have got out this way. And this was where Osso and Grimaud would have come through after they'd killed him.

Max looked for an exit.

Thick acrid smoke was rolling down the stairs and settling on the floor. The paint on the ceiling was bubbling and blistering. The striplights flickered. One of the tubes blew and spat sparks.

Max moved quickly to the centre of the basement, sweeping it with his eyes, turning in one direction, then another, checking behind the beams. The condensing smoke and failing lights made him see shadows and shapes all around, made him feel like he was encircled by ghosts.

He shifted to the left. The smoke thinned for an instant. He thought he saw a door in the far corner.

451

He started towards it.

Then he froze.

Someone was standing there.

Max aimed his gun.

'Boukman!'

The lights suddenly went out. A pair of neon tubes dropped out of their sockets and smashed on the ground. It was pitch black.

Max found it hard to breathe; the air was pure smoke and gasoline fumes. White spots were dancing before his eyes, his head was spinning, he wanted to heave.

He knew he was close to passing out.

Piece by piece the house began falling apart, as the fire raged through the floors above, burning out the supports. Masonry, metal, timber and slate broke off and came crashing down. The basement ceiling shook and screeched and fractured with every impact, leaking rivulets of fine dust, and the walls hummed with terrible vibrations.

Max felt something touch his face, swore it was a hand. He fired once, twice. He barely heard the shots above the crashing explosions. Muzzle flash lit up dense grey smoke and dust and darkness.

Then, behind him, near the steps, one of the wooden beams buckled and ruptured with a high-pitched braying sound. Part of the ceiling it was supporting gave way and a whole mass of concrete suddenly dropped into the basement, letting in a bonfire of rubble.

The area was lit up bright orange.

Max saw everything.

He'd inadvertently manoeuvred himself close to the door, so close that his leg was practically brushing the handle. And what he'd taken to be a person standing nearby was a tailor's dummy. The dummy was placed by a table and chair. A vintage theatre mirror, complete with a bulb frame, hung on the wall above it. All the glass was smashed. There were tubs of black and white

452

face paint on the table, tissues and make-up remover. A bundle of clothes was stacked on the chair.

Max turned the handle and pulled open the door.

He staggered outside.

The fresh air shocked his body. He went dizzy. He coughed and dry-heaved, tasting gasoline and smoke on his tongue, grit in his mouth. He blinked away dirt under his eyelids. His brows were singed and his skin raw and tender from the blaze. His body was made of pain. He wanted to lie down, or at least sit.

But he pushed himself forward a few more steps, away from the house.

Then he straightened up and started walking, and the walk became a jog, and the jog a run.

He tore over gravel. Next he was crossing cool wet grass. He slipped and fell on his face. He picked himself up almost immediately and kept going. He crashed through a boundary of trees, over dead leaves, broken branches and then more grass.

He only stopped running when he came to the end of the island. The ground fell away to the sea in a short sharp drop. To his right was a simple wooden jetty, where a speedboat was moored – an offshore catamaran with high-powered twin engines.

A short path led down to the ocean via a dozen steps cut into the rock face.

There was no one in the boat and no one on the pier. The catamaran was rocking side to side, the hull thumping against the wood, the moorings slapping at the water, which was disturbed and choppy, even though the rest of the ocean appeared calm.

Then he heard a sound.

A motor, still loud but becoming fainter by the second.

He panned the ocean.

He saw the multi-coloured marker buoys in the distance.

He saw the first hints of dawn on the horizon.

He saw a pair of gulls swooping low.

He saw clouds fringed bright orange, as if they too had fled the burning house.

And then he saw a boat.

It was speeding away – well away – heading out of Cuban waters, making for Haiti, almost airborne as it skimmed the tops of the waves, leaving behind a heavy wake, thick and pale and frothing.

Max looked back at the jetty. He saw a rope tethered to a post, its severed end in the water, the planks splashed and puddled with spray.

Boukman *had* been here . . .

Max didn't understand.

Why hadn't Boukman watched him die? Why did he bring him this far, only to leave before his helpers finished the job?

Max checked the gun. He still had four rounds left.

He started towards the jetty.

But he didn't make it.

He heard another sound, another engine.

A car, coming up fast behind him, headlights pinioning him.

A screech of brakes.

He dropped the gun and put his hands up.

59

It was Rosa Cruz, in one of the hospital jeeps.

She left the engine running and stepped out.

'Took your time,' Max said.

'Are you OK?' she asked.

'No.'

He looked out across the water. The boat was long gone, its wake blended with the waves, as if it had never been there.

Max turned and saw part of the house for the first time. A three-floor, red-brick building, more suited to New England than the Caribbean, partly hidden by a copse of palm trees. Flames were massing in the upper windows, and smoke was emptying from a hole where a section of the roof had collapsed.

'She told me what happened.' Rosa nodded to the jeep, where Vanetta Brown sat swaddled in a dressing gown, looking at them both. 'She wants to go home.'

'Me too,' he said.

He carried Vanetta down to the jetty and placed her very gently in the boat.

After he'd strapped her in, he stepped away and gave her a moment with Rosa.

Vanetta used all the strength she could muster to hug Rosa and kiss her on both cheeks. They exchanged a few words in Spanish, Rosa sniffing and wiping away tears the whole time.

Max stood awkwardly on the pier, out of earshot, to give them privacy, but he was desperate for them to hurry because they needed to get away before people came.

He looked at the horizon, towards Haiti, towards where Boukman had fled. He considered taking off after him instead of going to Miami, but he knew he'd never catch him. He'd had his chance to kill Boukman twenty-seven years ago. Joe had stopped him. He wished he hadn't now – for both their sakes, especially Joe's.

But were things really that straightforward, that simple, that brutal? Kill one person and live happily until you die of old age? Or had their lives always been on this course, locked in to a destiny they couldn't prevent, with Boukman one of a billion interchangeable axes wielded by fate?

And Max thought he understood now why Boukman had left when he had. Boukman had said that killing him outright was too easy, that it wouldn't have been enough. Boukman had wanted to watch him suffer. Boukman had wanted *satisfaction*. That's what all this had been about.

So maybe Boukman had decided that he didn't want to see him die at all, that he wanted to remember him alive – but alive on his own terms; as his prisoner, at his mercy. That way he'd have a sweet memory he could revisit over and over again for the rest of his days; a memory of Max Mingus in his final moments on earth, tied to a chair, watching the last twelve years of his life flash by. Only it wasn't the life Max thought he'd lived, but the one Boukman had given him.

That made some kind of sense. Even if it turned out to be completely wrong.

What would happen when Boukman realised Osso and Grimaud were dead? Would he think they'd accidentally perished in the fire? Or would he guess the truth?

Max didn't know.

Rosa came over to him. She took off the rucksack she'd been carrying on her back. Inside were the CDs, the flow chart and all the notes he'd made.

'Who was Solomon Boukman?' she asked.

'Unfinished business.'

'Is it finished now?'

Max glanced across at the ocean, then back at her. 'Did you get what you came for?'

She nodded.

'I hope it all works out the way you want,' he said.

'Same with you.' She held out a hand.

Max took it and held it for a moment. They pressed palms and disengaged.

Max got in the boat. The keys were in the ignition.

Rosa untied the moorings.

He checked on Vanetta. She had her eyes closed and her breaths were shallow.

He started the boat and turned to wave goodbye to Rosa, but she was already gone.

60

They reached the Florida coast at daybreak. The sun was beginning to crawl up from under the ocean and joggers were already on the beach, getting their regulation miles in before it turned too hot.

Max still had the gun, stuck in his waistband. He took it out and inspected it, felt its considerable heft. Abe Watson's pride and joy, his 1911 Colt – customised mother-of-pearl grips and its owner's initials, knife-carved on the trigger guard. 'A.J.W.' Abraham Jefferson Watson. The gun had killed Eldon and Joe, and put Grimaud out of his misery. It had also been used to murder Ezequiel and Melody Dascal, and Dennis Peck – and many more besides, some guilty, some innocent. He thought about all that for a moment, then tossed the gun into the sea.

Max sailed the boat up to the shore and carried Vanetta out.

She'd said nothing to him the whole way. She'd kept on nodding off, despite the noise of the engine and the bumpy ride. At one moment he even thought she was gone, but when he'd taken her pulse her eyes opened and she'd looked at him full of indignation, as if to ask, 'How dare you presume I'm dead?'

He laid her down in the sand, resting her head on a lifejacket.

She gazed up at the fast brightening sky, and then at him.

'Where am I?' Her faint voice was practically inaudible over the sound of the surf foaming on the shore and the tide's gentle boom.

He heard a chopper moving across the sky and, behind it, approaching sirens; coming their way, coming for them. He hoped the convoy included an ambulance.

'Home,' he said.

Vanetta put her fingers on the sand, sunk them in and gripped a fistful. Then she moved her fist to her chest and rested it there, close to her heart.

Max took her free hand and held it. It was warm, yet her pulse was weak and halting.

He gently stroked her face.

She looked into his eyes and managed the slightest, faintest of smiles that could have meant anything – relief, happiness, gratitude, or perhaps irony, because she'd heard the sirens too.

'Home?' she said.

He wanted to say hang on a little longer, that help was almost here, but she'd closed her eyes now and her face had a deep serenity about it, a contentment and peace he didn't want to breach in any way. So he watched over her, as the sirens grew louder and louder, mere seconds away.

Vanetta's smile broadened. Her fingers began to loosen in his palm and the sand she'd grasped leaked through the gaps in her fist, draining faster and faster on to her heart.

Although the sun was starting to shine and the breeze was warm and it was going to be a beautiful day in Florida, he felt like he'd come to the coldest place in the world.

INAUGURATION DAY

Miami Beach was unusually quiet, but then it was a highly unusual day; a first-of-its-kind, milestone moment. History was on the verge of being made in America and everybody wanted to play a part; everybody wanted their little piece of it, their 'I was doing this, when . . .' stake in the passage of time. It was the next best thing to being on reality TV.

The streets and beaches and stores were near-deserted. People were at home or in hotels and bars and restaurants, watching televisions or computer screens, waiting on President-elect Obama to take the oath of office and give his inaugural address; waiting to seal the deal with him.

Up in Washington, DC, it was freezing cold. But that hadn't deterred two million people from carpeting the length and breadth of the National Mall; a vast spread of humanity, all races and genders and ages, bearing witness, getting as close as they could and ever would to the paragon of possibility. It was the biggest-ever turnout for a Presidential inauguration.

Max watched the hushed and patient masses on one of the two plasma screens in the reception area of Sal Donoso's office. He'd arrived early for his appointment with the lawyer, who was going to hand over what Eldon had left him in his will.

The receptionist was ignoring him. She was transfixed by the same screen he was glancing at. Max couldn't help but read her the way he still automatically read people whose company he found himself in, no matter how temporarily. She was the wrong side of middle-aged to be working an entry-level job; glasses, short blue-rinsed hair, a brown suit and too much make-up. Her face bore unmistakable traces of an earlier life lived too hard, possibly to the brink. She gazed at the television admiringly, hands clasped together, no rings. He guessed she got lonely a lot.

After the police picked him up on the beach, they locked him up in a camp outside Hialeah for a week. He shared a dormitory with a boatload of Haitians waiting to be sent back, a few newly arrived Cubans waiting to be welcomed in, and people of other nationalities, mostly South Americans and Caribbean islanders, their fates undetermined.

He was interviewed four times. The police threatened to charge him with breaking the law for travelling to Cuba. He wanted to laugh at that and lecture them on the realities of the place, but he knew better; you can't beat a forty-something-year-old law in an argument, no matter how absurd and contradictory and hypocritical you find it. Then it was the FBI's turn. They took two passes at him. They asked about his dealings with Vanetta Brown and how he'd come to be in possession of classified government files. He told them a selective version of the truth, which omitted all names and most of what had really happened. It was a simple, solid story, and therefore easy to remember, so his interrogators didn't catch him out on contradictions, no matter how many different ways they asked the same question. They were good but he was better. The last person to interview him was some asshole from Homeland Security, who asked more of the same, only with a terrorism angle worked in. When he asked Max if he'd had contact with Muslim extremists, he almost told him, sure, when he drove past the Gitmo perimeter. Instead he dropped Wendy Peck's name. His interrogator left the room quickly, promising to return. He never did.

They let him go the next afternoon. No explanation. Just 'You're outta here' and approximate cab fare back home.

He opened his door to a few bills and a dusty void.

He made coffee in the kitchen and savoured the cup. He finished it too fast and made another, which he took out on his balcony. The view was exactly the same as the one Solomon Boukman had shown him, the one he'd filmed from the very spot where Max was standing. He saw it and tasted petrol.

Everything was familiar, as it had been. But then everything had changed too, and nothing would go back to the way it was.

A week later he was watching the news when it was announced that Wendy Peck had resigned her position with immediate effect – to spend more time with her family and pursue new opportunities, the statement said. Her superior commended her on a job well done and wished her the very best for the future.

Max logged on to his computer and looked up Justice4Dennis.com. The site had been taken down.

Vanetta Brown, however, still remained on the FBI's Most Wanted list: a domestic terrorist with a half-million-dollar bounty on her head, whose current whereabouts were believed to be Havana, Cuba. Like she'd said, her innocence was academic.

He wasn't surprised. Not at all. He knew how things worked. But it still made him sick.

In early December, he'd visited the Liston family. He told Lena and Jet what had happened in Cuba and everything that led up to it. He wasn't convinced that Lena hadn't known about Joe's secret activities, but he didn't push it. What did it matter anyway? And what good would the knowledge do him?

They both listened without much in the way of comment. They didn't ask if he'd killed Solomon Boukman. They assumed he had. When he left the house, Jet walked him to his car. He thanked Max and they shook hands and hugged, because they both knew it was his last visit, that he wouldn't be back, nor would he be asked back. Too much had happened on account of him. It was painful, but it was for the best.

465

He thought a lot about Rosa Cruz. Had she managed to blackmail her way back into her old job? He hoped so, but he had no way of knowing.

As for Benny Ramirez, Max was fairly sure it was him he saw in a small, empty café on the corner of Ocean and 6th one night: a tall thin man with longish brown hair, a handsome but hollow face, and a still-healing pink knife-scar extending the end of his mouth to the edge of his cheekbone. He was muttering to himself, or maybe singing, as he mopped the floor. Max considered taking a closer look, but he thought the better of it and moved on.

In mid-December he'd finalised the sale of his penthouse. A Uruguayan property developer offered him a million for it. It was almost twice what he'd originally paid and he was lucky to find a buyer. He took the deal.

He'd been packing up the little he was going to transfer to his new home, when there was a knock at the door. He found an urn outside with a note taped to it. The urn was moulded plastic sprayed in oak tones, the kind you could buy in any Walmart for about twenty bucks.

The note read: '*You'll know what to do. J.Q.*'

And he did.

He took Vanetta's remains to the City of Miami Cemetery, where the bodies of Ezequiel and Melody Dascal were buried side by side. He scattered the ashes over their graves. He stayed there a good while, trying to think of something to say, but no words came.

As he left, it started raining, first heavy drops, then a downpour.

A television was also on in the boardroom where Sal Donoso had led Max. The volume was muted as Obama took his oath on Lincoln's Bible, held by his wife. His two daughters and a couple of billion people around the world watched. The scrolling commentary explained the President had just fluffed his lines.

Donoso was immaculately groomed, his white goatee trimmed to a sharp point, his shoes shiny, his hands manicured.

The two men sat at the long conference table, on which were four box files and an envelope.

'Eldon bequeathed you these.' Donoso pushed his inheritance to him with his palm, as though closing a heavy door.

The files were labelled with Max and Joe's names and old badge numbers. Max had three files devoted to him, with yellowed-paper corners poking out from under the lids.

He opened up one of his boxes and dropped back into the dark end of memory lane. It was the late 1970s and he saw photographs and skim-read records of every bad thing he'd done as a cop, enough to land him in jail again, only this time for life without. No surprise there. Eldon had had dirt on everyone, even his most loyal footsoldiers.

'There are no copies,' said Donoso.

With a sense of dread, Max pulled Joe's box towards him. It slid across the table easily and felt light. When he opened it, he found it was empty.

'What's this?'

'Eldon could never get anything on him.' Donoso smiled. 'That's why he hated him so much.'

Max opened the envelope.

It contained the deeds to the 7th Avenue gym.

He managed a smile. Eldon had sent him back to the beginning, to where everything had started between them – and where it had finished. He didn't know what he was going to do with a crumbling old building in a neighbourhood no one wanted to live in, and with property prices already depressed to hell. He guessed he'd let it rot a little more until he thought of something better: decay or decision, whichever came first.

'What are you doing with yourself these days?' asked Donoso.

Max told him the truth. 'Going to bed early.'

He'd recently moved into his new home: a small house on

467

a quiet residential street in a small town with an active neighbourhood watch scheme and a very low crime rate. It was a three-hour plane ride from Miami.

Max had no way of knowing if Boukman would come for him again, if he wasn't already somewhere in this other life he'd started; embedded, watching, waiting, picking his moment. Maybe they were quits. Maybe they weren't. There was no statute of limitations on revenge, but the only thing Boukman could take from him now was whatever time he had left on the clock. He slept alone. He had no friends.

'I could use an investigator,' said Donoso. 'My main guy died of a heart attack the other week.'

'I'm done with all that.'

'If you change your mind . . .'

'I won't.'

He took MacArthur Causeway back to the airport. Miami Beach disappeared in his rearview and the city's busy, overcrowded, still-expanding skyline came stomping up to him like a phalanx of juiced-up bouncers in designer suits, all bulging geometry and mirrored glass.

His plane wasn't leaving for another five hours, so he had plenty of time to stop off someplace and burn the files.

He listened to the closing moments of President Obama's address, which promised no easy fixes and tough times ahead, appealing to Americans to come together and work through the myriad crises facing the nation. It was a sober, inclusive speech, free of sunny-side-up mantras and any suggestion of triumphalism. When he finished, two million people applauded and chanted his name syllable by syllable, the way they'd done up and down the country for a whole year.

Max thought of Joe, who would have been watching at home.

And his heart started sinking. He found he suddenly needed music – any music – to take his mind out of the sad thought-spiral he'd just caught. He switched radio stations but all he got

468

was post-address punditry. He roved the dial some more until he heard nothing. He thought he'd reached the dial's limit and was about to go back to the beginning when a song started – a drum-beat, a count-off in the background and then a jaunty violin.

He recognised the song.

Bruce Springsteen's 'Waitin' on a Sunny Day.'

Max was momentarily spooked. But once the shock had ebbed and the initial chills passed, he started smiling, hesitantly at first, and then quite broadly, as he welcomed in the song and started doing the unthinkable – singing along, singing along to *Bruce*, singing at the top of his voice, even though he didn't know any of the words and he wasn't sure how it went next.

LOS ENDOS